Kindness Stones

Kindness Stones

Stories for Melissa

Mark Allan Powell

CASCADE *Books* • Eugene, Oregon

KINDNESS STONES
Stories for Melissa

Cascade Books
An Imprint of Wipf and Stock Publishers
199 W. 8th Ave., Suite 3
Eugene, OR 97401

www.wipfandstock.com

PAPERBACK ISBN: 979-8-3852-4593-2
HARDCOVER ISBN: 979-8-3852-4594-9
EBOOK ISBN: 979-8-3852-4595-6

Cataloguing-in-Publication data:

Names: Powell, Mark Allan, author.

Title: Kindness stones : stories for Melissa / by Mark Allan Powell.

Description: Eugene, OR: Cascade Books, 2026.

Identifiers: ISBN 979-8-3852-4593-2 (paperback) | ISBN 979-8-3852-4594-9 (hardcover) | ISBN 979-8-3852-4595-6 (ebook)

Subjects: LCSH: Short stories, American | Fiction | Humorous fiction

Classification: PS370 .P69 2026 (paperback) | PS370 (ebook)

VERSION NUMBER 04/24/26

This book is a work of fiction and all characters except one are a product of the author's imagination—any similarity to real persons, living or dead, is purely coincidental.

for

Missy Baby

My gift is not for songs
But maybe, I hope, for writing stories.
So you can tell everyone
These are *your* stories.
I know it's not much,
But it's the best I can do.

Contents

Preface

I BEGAN WRITING STORIES as a teenager and have probably written a couple a month for more than fifty years. I call it "exercising the imagination" and it serves a purpose analogous to that for which others go to a gym.

I created a huge cast of characters in my head and developed profiles for each of them: back stories, distinguishing traits, values, beliefs, idiosyncrasies, and so forth. Then I would get a plot idea, pick a character, and write a story. And then one of my favorite things to do was to use the same plot idea, pick a different character and write another story—same events but inevitably different results or effects. Or sometimes I might tell a story in the first person four different times from the point of view of four different characters. At times I was acutely aware of how embarrassing my efforts would have been had anybody seen them: here I was trying to think "like a woman" or "like an African American," and no doubt failing in predictably, almost stereotypically dismal ways. But it was the *trying* that counted. The purpose was exercising my imagination.

In order for this to work I had to promise myself that no one would ever see or read any of my stories. If I thought it was even remotely possible that anyone would see them, I would avoid risks and think only in terms of what might please or displease possible lectors. So I would only save the stories for a few months and then delete them after reading over them one more time, sometimes with pleasure, often with chagrin.

My wife was vaguely aware of this hobby or discipline (at different times it felt like both—working out at a gym may be the same). I kept a file on my laptop called "Delete When I Die" and told her it wasn't porn, just stories I didn't want her or anyone else to read. This wife is the Melissa of the subtitle. I call her Missy Baby (short for Missy Baby

Sweetheart). I guess she accepted the notion that I couldn't exercise my imagination properly if she or anyone else was watching, but she also thought that maybe I could *also* write stories intended for more public consumption. So, a few years ago, when we were camping, she came up with the following proposal.

Each of us would create four characters. For me, they had to be four entirely new characters, not based on or even similar to any of the ones I already had.

Then, we would come up with ten "plot ideas," write them on scraps of paper, and put them in a jar.

When we had a free weekend or some other "set-aside" time, we would each pick one of our four characters, draw a "story prompt" out of the jar, and then go write stories for each other to read.

It was great fun and one end result was this collection: stories that potentially have appeal beyond a narcissistic engagement of my own imagination. I am a harsh critic of my own work, but I think that these are pretty good. They may not be for everyone, but I think a lot of people will find them engaging. There is definitely variety: sentimental, silly, sexy, inspirational, philosophical . . . if you don't like one, try another (but if you don't like two, you should probably give it up—life is short).

You might be interested in seeing the plot ideas that served as story prompts for these tales. Here they are in the order in which they were pulled out of the jar—with further indication of which character would be involved and which story in this book was the final result.

Story Prompt	**Character**	**Story in This Book**
There is a plane crash.	Angelica Blitch	Current Events
Someone gets a hobby.	Jasper Donovan	Jasper Gets a Hobby
Someone gets a new car.	Jasper Donovan	Jasper Gets a New Car
Someone's hair starts to turn gray.	Angelica Blitch	Slippery Slopes
Someone celebrates an anniversary.	Father John McCloskey	Tennis without a Net
Someone gets struck by lightning.	James Haizlet	Lightning Club
Someone moves.	James Haizlet	The Red Stapler
Someone hears noises in their closet.	Father John McCloskey	Noises at Night

Story Prompt	Character	Story in This Book
Someone gets $300,000 unexpectedly.	Jasper Donovan	Jasper Is Rich
Someone starts to look like someone else.	Angelica Blitch	My Boyfriend Is a Detective

We wrote stories for each other and sometimes interpreted the prompts in surprisingly different ways. I assumed "Somebody moves" meant that a character in the story would relocate (move to a different city, state, or country). Melissa told a story of a woman waiting by the bed of her comatose husband until finally, one day, his fingers moved. And what would you think "Somebody gets a new car" means? Melissa very sensibly wrote a story about a cancer survivor treating herself to a brand new bright red sports car. But I took it to mean . . . well, you'll see what I did.

If you compare the list above with the Table of Contents you will see that I sometimes had to write my stories out of order: stories written later about things that happened earlier. I also added three more stories because I was into the characters and wanted to fill out their story lines. I also kept wondering what would happen if a certain character experienced what was happening to one of the other characters. Or what if some of them were to meet each other? I even thought about writing a story in which one of my characters met one of Melissa's characters—but, no, she would not have liked that: narrative imperialism.

Writing stories was a huge, risky adventure for Melissa because she had never written a story for anyone before—she got a book out of the library and did some research on the internet to help her figure out how to go about it. But in a way, I had never written a story *for* anyone before either. I had written lots of stories but none of them had been intended for anyone but me to read. Still, I did it. Every story in this book was written for Melissa. Every sentence, every paragraph I would think, "Is Melissa going to like this?" That one overriding question determined every decision: I would think, "This might not be what I would normally do, and it probably wouldn't appeal to critics, but I think it's what she will like. So, if you like these stories, it just might mean that you are something like my dear wife, Missy Baby—which means that at least in some ways you are a wonderful person, lovely and lovable.

1

The Red Stapler

WHEN HE WAS FIFTY-SEVEN years old, James Haizlet could remember the name of every girl with whom he had ever been in love. It was a relatively short list that did not include many of the women he had dated or even one who had been his live-in domestic partner for a time. To be remembered as someone with whom he had been *in love* was special, and there were only seven who qualified. There was Cheryl Lee Vaughn in third grade—he could still remember every word that she had ever spoken to him (two: "why?" and "okay"). Then there was Diana Wooten, starting in fifth grade, and . . . well, there were seven in all.

He liked love songs. He knew that songs could be happy or sad, socially relevant or just for fun, but the best songs were almost always about love. One of the Beatles had wanted to fill the world with "silly love songs" and James thought there was nothing wrong with that (in case he'd like to know).

He liked love stories. Love poems. Love letters. He even liked lovebirds and loveseats; his favorite shape was the heart; his favorite saint was Valentine; his favorite gods were Venus and Cupid; his favorite plant was mistletoe; and his favorite airport was Love Field. When people would tease him about all this, he would just laugh and ask if they could guess his favorite score in tennis.

Basically, James Haizlet just liked love a bit more than most people his age—and it seemed to him that this had always been the case. Most of all James liked *being in love* and he claimed that he was still in love with all seven of the persons on his short list. He had been married for ten years to Number Seven (his Favorite and Final), but that didn't mean he had to stop being in love with the other six, if such a thing were possible, and it wasn't. Even the Bible said that "love never ends" and, though someone told him once "that isn't what it means," it remained one of the only two Bible verses he knew and he had decided that it was what it would mean for him.

Sometimes James thought that if he ever wrote an autobiography he would organize it into seven parts: seven distinct, identifiable stages of his life. Because, in his own mind, his life had never at any moment been defined by where he lived or by what he did from day to day. His life had never been defined by things like vocation, expertise, accomplishments, education, interests, or hobbies. No. In his own mind, the *essence* of his life at any given juncture had always been defined by "with whom he was in love." So there would be seven chapters, and he would not waste a single paragraph on any extraneous periods of his existence that didn't fit that chosen scheme. An autobiography, after all, should be the story of one's *life*, and James Haizlet did not think existence could properly be called *life* until and unless one was in love.

Thus, his story would not begin with birth but with third grade. The trick would be explaining the red stapler. Would anyone ever understand that? Probably not, which exposed the whole fallacy behind an autobiography. Nobody would get it. They might not even believe it: you're remembering it wrong; surely you were older (not eight? twelve?). Or, worse, they might think it was cute. Or sentimental. Or sappy. So, no autobiography. He wasn't really narcissistic enough for such a thing anyway.

Well . . . maybe someday he would tell the story, even put it into writing. But if he did, it would be for his eyes only. It couldn't, shouldn't, and wouldn't be something intended for anyone else to read.

* * *

Jimmy Haizlet loved his red stapler more than anything in the world (except, of course, Cheryl Lee).

He first saw the stapler at the Ben Franklin 5 and 10 in Reading, Pennsylvania, where his mother dropped him for an hour-and-a-half every Thursday while she did laundry next door. His family was in the up-and-coming range of lower-middle class but in 1960 most families in that economic bracket did not have washers or dryers in their houses.

So, Mrs. Haizlet lugged two baskets of clothing to the laundromat once a week. Once a month, she took two more, filled with bedding and towels.

Jimmy was eight years old and probably could have stayed home alone, but he liked going to do laundry with his mother as long as she let him go to the Ben Franklin and read comic books until the washing was done. In those days, most five-and-dimes had comic book racks that served as reading libraries for the children of loyal customers. Jimmy could sit on the floor and read the newest *Casper* and *Baby Huey* books as long as he didn't muss them up too much and as long as he put them back on the rack when he was done. Of course, when his mother came to collect him, she would be expected to buy him one of the comics and maybe pick up a few other things from the store as well.

In third grade, Jimmy liked the Harvey comics best: not just *Casper* but also *Spooky* and *Hot Stuff*; not just *Baby Huey*, but also *Richie Rich*. He was, however, quite ecumenical with regard to "funny books" (that was what his father called them). Indeed, he was somewhat proud of his broad-minded appreciation for diverse representations of the genre. He could read Westerns like *The Lone Ranger*. He liked comics based on cartoons like *Woody Woodpecker* and *Bugs Bunny*. He sometimes delved into the Disney universe of *Donald Duck* and stories from movies. And there was that whole other universe of *Yogi Bear* and *Huckleberry Hound*. Sometimes, he even read *Little Lulu* or *Nancy and Sluggo*. Though all of his friends read comics, he believed himself to be especially well-versed in the field—and not without reason, for none of his friends had parents who left them at Ben Franklin for an hour-and-a-half once a week.

But then, one Thursday, he saw the stapler. Some bigger boys were reading comics and so, after he finished just one, he wandered around the store, hoping they would leave. He looked at all the candy bars and thought about asking his mother to get him a pack of candy cigarettes instead of a comic this week. But then he changed his mind: candy was good short term but the comic he could read over and over again. Making this decision made him feel strangely mature. He was delaying instant gratification to obtain a more durable, long-term benefit—at some level, he understood this concept even without the vocabulary to articulate it.

Another aisle had school supplies and he wandered down it just to look wistfully at things he would never have. Jimmy always got no-nonsense school supplies. No lunch boxes with Peanuts characters, no notebooks with Tom and Jerry. Such frivolities were considered inappropriate for school by his parents, who seemed to think they might possess subliminal power to inhibit learning. Besides, Jimmy had just finished second grade in May and many of the supplies from last year were still sufficiently functional to be used again. So, it would be the plain, solid-color navy blue lunch box with its plain, solid-color navy blue thermos. He would need new notebooks, but they would come from a serious store like Montgomery Ward and would not have pictures on them. Ben Franklin was a five-and-dime after all, a store that sold comic books, which was not a proper place to buy school supplies.

Still, it was in this aisle that he saw it: a little red stapler that only worked with small staples, which had to be bought separately, though one box came with the initial purchase. The stapler was only three inches long and would fit in the palm of his hand. And it wasn't black or gray like all the other staplers in the world. It was bright red.

A few years later, these tiny marvels would become basic back-to-school supplies like plastic rulers, round-tip scissors, and miniature bottles of Elmer's glue. But in August of 1960 the small stapler was a new concept and the early models were far superior to their descendants. They were all metal, sturdy and shiny instruments that held up to expectations. Basically, they were the same as adult staplers save for two important differences: they were small, and they were red.

In any event, Jimmy had never seen such a thing before and he begged his mother to buy it for him. A stapler seemed like a very adult thing to own. The Haizlet household had only one stapler, on the desk of Jimmy's father, which was in a closed room that Jimmy was rarely allowed to enter. He had seen his father's stapler being used and had been told not to touch it. He might break it and, also, it was dangerous. He could put out an eye or staple his fingers together. His father talked about the stapler as if it were a loaded gun. It was kept on his desk, way up high, out of reach, in a room Jimmy couldn't even enter without adult supervision.

Now, here was a stapler for children, one that really worked—it wasn't just a toy. He could actually staple pages together with it! Up to this point in his life, Jimmy had never wanted to staple any pages together, but he was certain that, once the option became viable, he would want to do so on a regular basis.

Mrs. Haizlet would not buy Jimmy the stapler, deeming it superfluous and too expensive. Comic books were ten cents and he got one comic each week. The stapler was $1.29 and, though he lacked the arithmetic skills to determine how many comic books that would equal, he knew it would be a lot . . . maybe a hundred . . . so he offered his mother a deal: buy him the stapler and no comics for all of third grade.

She probably would have denied the purchase just to spare him the commitment to such a bad idea—an obvious and immature craving for instant gratification. Children his age were not able to understand the wisdom of more durable, long-term benefits. But, in any case, it was a moot point. She *had* to buy him a comic every week if she wanted to continue using the store as a day-care center on laundry day. Besides, even though the stapler was on the shelves for school supplies, it was in the same area as graph paper and slide rules, obviously not for third graders. And, she thought, it might even be dangerous. He could staple his fingers or something. Maybe put out an eye.

Jimmy went home that day with a fifteen-cent *Little Lulu* double-length special comic that was about her and her friends going to Paris. There was a joke where her best friend,Tubby, almost fell in the river and Little Lulu said that if he did then he would be "in Seine." Jimmy didn't get the joke but his father explained it to him and then years later in high school he knew how to pronounce the name of that river when no one else did. All because of the *Little Lulu* comic book.

But he also remembered where the stapler was and, for months, he would run over to see if it was still there every time his mother brought him into the Ben Franklin store. There had been eight of them, and then there were seven, and then there were six, and then there were five, and after school started there were only three.

Four months later, he said he wanted it for Christmas but his mother ignored the request, assuming that she knew his heart better than he did and that he would be happier with toys. But, then, she finally relented in February and bought him the stapler for Valentine's Day instead of a box of candy. It was red after all, and he had been begging for it for half a year. Also, there was only one left and it had been marked down to $.89.

From that day on, he looked for things to staple, collecting pictures from magazines and organizing them into groups. He quickly commandeered back copies of all the magazines in the house, piled them in his room, and began systematically paging through them to find pictures that went together—that is, pictures that should be together and *could* be together if somebody stapled them. He found six pictures of cakes and stapled them. Then, six pictures of animals.

He showed the stapler to Jim Bob Batey, a kid from school who did not understand the attraction. Jim Bob wasn't really one of Jimmy's friends; he was just the son of someone Jimmy's mother knew. When mothers were friends, they always thought their children should be also. Jim Bob was in third grade at Conrad Weiser Elementary School, same as Jimmy, but he was in a different class. They only saw each other at recess and hardly ever then. Still, when Mrs. Batey visited Mrs. Haizlet one weekend, she brought Jim Bob along and he discovered that if you opened the stapler and held it aloft, you could make it shoot staples like a gun. He shot staples at Jimmy and told him he should take it to school so they could shoot staples at girls. Then, when Jimmy said he wouldn't do that, Jim Bob tried to steal the stapler so he could do it since *he* wasn't chicken. Jimmy never showed the stapler to anyone else after that.

The family got *Life* magazine every week and *Look* every two weeks. They also got the *Saturday Evening Post* every week and, although it didn't have as many photos as *Life* or *Look*, it often had illustrations that Jimmy considered staple worthy. In addition, his mother got three monthly magazines, *Good Housekeeping, Better Homes and Gardens,* and *Ladies' Home Journal.* At first, Jimmy simply looked through the old magazines when new ones arrived, and he found himself waiting anxiously for the mail every day to see if maybe a new magazine would come, allowing him access to an old one. But then impatience got the better of him and he would look through the new magazines as well, finding pictures that he was going to staple when they became available. Then, he would be in a state of anticipation and he would have to guard the magazines from misuse. More than once his parents set their coffee cups on the pages and ruined pictures he had already planned on adding to his collections.

The staples would only go through six pages, so he had to sort pictures accordingly, and he became more and more discriminating as time went by. Not just "six animals" but "six ponies," "six puppies," "six kittens." He managed to acquire two boxes that would hold pages from the magazines and he used one for his stapled photo collections and the other for pictures that could be used for future collections if and when he found six that went together. By the end of March, he had used up all the staples that had come with the initial purchase and had to beg his mother to buy him a new box (for ten cents, instead of a comic book). She did, with an exhortation not to waste them this time.

It is safe to say that his parents didn't know what to make of this obsession. At first it seemed harmless enough, but they had not thought the fascination with stapling things would last more than a week. Or that it would dominate his attention to the degree that it did. Almost every day, he would shut himself in his room, going through whatever magazines were available, carefully trimming photos with scissors, organizing them into groups, evaluating and re-evaluating their worth (the six-to-a-set limitation required extreme triage), and finally producing stapled sets in which he apparently took great pride though he never showed them to anyone.

This latter happenstance (not showing the pictures to anyone) provoked his mother to conduct an investigation that she considered a justifiable invasion of his privacy. While he was at school one day, she went into his closet, looked through the two boxes of photos (stapled and pending), and made a horrifying discovery.

There were no pictures of cars or trucks (which he used to like so much) or sports or cowboys or Indians or dinosaurs. There were pictures of bunnies and baby chicks and lacy pillows and stuffed animals and . . . *God in heaven!* . . . dolls.

There were pictures of dolls! One set consisted of six pictures of baby dolls (like Tiny Tears). Another featured six pictures of Nancy Ann Storybook dolls (*Good Housekeeping* had run an article on them). Six dolls in six different outfits.

There were no pictures of boys his age riding bikes or playing ball or fishing or climbing trees. There *were* pictures of girls his age baking cookies and blowing bubbles and making posters and having tea parties. One set featured six pictures of girls wearing pink, and another set showed six girls in Easter dresses, with flowery bonnets. There were lots of pictures of flowers, or at least of flowery things.

Why had she bought him that second box of staples? Why? She was almost afraid to tell her husband but, of course, she had to. Neither one of them knew what to do except maybe talk to Pastor Wilson. And get Jimmy in Little League whether he liked it or not. And Cub Scouts. They just hoped it wasn't too late.

They couldn't tell him they'd gone into his room and seen the pictures but they knew they would have to talk to him, somehow, about his choice of subjects. They would have to talk to him. But, then, something else came up, causing that uncomfortable but necessary discussion to be postponed.

* * *

Two weeks before school ended Jimmy's parents told him that the family would be moving to Jacksonville, Florida. His father had found a new job, a *better* job where he could work in a building with air conditioning. And—this was the good news that they hoped would get Jimmy excited about the move—the house that they were going to live in also had air conditioning. In two rooms!

His parents spent a few days planning how to tell him about the move and his mother read an article in *Ladies' Home Journal* on preparing children for such potential traumas. They did all the right things, assuring him that although there would be changes, many things would still be the same. Their cat Felix would come with them and they would take Jimmy's bike and all of his clothes and toys and everything else that he owned. They told him that moving day would be fun because everything would be put in a big yellow van ("the biggest truck you've ever seen") with a green ship on the side. They told him that he would have a new room in their new house in Jacksonville that was bigger than his room in Reading. And there was a large white oak tree in the front yard. He would go to school in Jacksonville just like here (but different) and they would all still go to church, though it would be a new church with a new pastor. Most important, he would make lots of new friends. His parents understood that he might miss his Pennsylvania friends (like Jim Bob) but they said he could write letters to them and send them postcards. There were lots of children in the neighborhood in Florida where they would now live and since it would be summer, he would have lots of time to play with those children and get to know them.

Jimmy's parents talked to him for forty-five minutes, asking him repeatedly if he understood and if he had any questions. The entire time, as they went on and on about air conditioning and oak trees and schools and churches and friends and postcards, there was but one thought echoing and then booming in his mind: *Cheryl Lee.*

She was the only girl in the third grade with curly brown hair and probably the only one who would not be mean to him if she knew that he liked her.

When he walked back and forth to school from his home, five blocks each way, he daydreamed about rescuing Cheryl Lee from bullies or garnering her attention in some other unrealistic manner. In truth, Jimmy was a bit on the scrawny side and, had there been any bullies at Conrad Weiser Elementary School, he would have been in no position to rescue *himself* much less anyone else from their abuses. Still, this was what he thought about every day. And at home, when he watched TV, he translated every program into a story about Cheryl Lee. He was Popeye and she was Olive Oyl. He was Mighty Mouse and she was Pearl Pureheart. If a show was not subject to such mental reworking (*Mr. Magoo*, for instance, which featured no rescues), it had trouble holding his interest.

In school, everything he did was designed to please Cheryl Lee. Every time he drew a picture or read out loud or displayed an object for show-and-tell, he would look at her and wonder what she thought about whatever it was that he had said or done. Most of the time, of course, she thought nothing at all, occupied as most third-grade girls should be with drawing and talking and giggling with her friends, completely unaware that she was the constant preoccupation of a skinny boy with freckles.

What his parents didn't understand about the stapling was that all of the pictures were for her. He didn't choose pictures that *he* liked; he chose pictures that he thought *she* would like. Because some day, maybe, he was going to show them to her. He would sit in his room in the evenings, paging through this or that picture collection, pretending that she was there. He would show her six pictures he had selected just for her and tell her why he had picked them, what he thought she would like about them. He had a box almost full of stapled pictures that he was going to show her . . . someday.

This was a secret crush, of course. In those days, boys and girls his age did not generally talk to each other and they certainly did not officially *like* each other. The canonical judgment regarding girls among boys his age was that they had cooties. Certainly, if anyone had known how Jimmy felt about Cheryl Lee they would have teased him and—*much worse!*—they would have teased *her*. So, he didn't say anything or do anything. He just thought about her. And daydreamed about her: in class, on the walks to and from school, and at home in the evenings.

But now: moving to Florida! His parents could talk and talk but it didn't matter what they said. They wouldn't be taking Cheryl Lee with them, would they? Would she be packed in the big yellow van with a green ship on the side? And, if not, why did anything else matter? Who would rescue her from bullies if such need should ever arise? And would he be able to keep daydreaming about her once she was absent from his life? If he wasn't able to do that, would there be any reason to be alive? But surely he would be able to do it, wouldn't he? He resolved that he *would*. Even if he never saw her again, he would *always* daydream about her, every day for the rest of his life, because she deserved it. She was the sort of person who belonged in someone's daydreams.

After his parents ripped his heart out and destroyed his life, Jimmy assured them that he had understood everything they said and didn't have any questions. He went to bed and cried for an hour before he fell asleep and the next day he came to breakfast like a person in a trance. For the next week, he would hardly speak, moving about in a daze with little awareness of anyone or anything in the world about him. Horrified, his parents consulted their doctor, talked to Pastor Wilson, and reread the *Ladies' Home Journal* article in an effort to discover how things could have gone so terribly wrong. Pastor Wilson even paid the family a visit, ostensibly to bid them all adieu, but actually to talk to Jimmy. He sat with the child in his room and told him a story about Jesus getting lost in the temple and then he prayed a prayer out loud. He also asked Jimmy how he felt about moving to Florida and Jimmy said "Fine."

"Do you really feel fine?" Pastor Wilson asked, "Or is it bothering you?"

"No."

"You do feel fine?"

"Yes."

Jimmy sensed that, while Pastor Wilson would not tease him about his feelings for Cheryl Lee, he would not be able to understand those feelings either. On this point he was correct. Both the pastor and the boy's parents would have thought his crush on the girl was "cute" had they ever come to know of it—which, of course, was why they never did.

On the last day of third grade, Jimmy waited all day and watched Cheryl Lee carefully and then, when she asked if she could go to her locker to get something, he asked to use the restroom. Outside in the hall he approached her and handed her the little stapler, in its original packaging with a half-used box of staples.

"I want to give this to you," he said.

She took it from his hand and looked at it as if he might be playing some kind of a trick on her.

"Why?"

He froze, not having anticipated that question. Time stood still. His face turned bright red. Then he looked down the hall in both directions to make certain no one was watching. No one could hear. And then he did the bravest thing he had ever done, perhaps the bravest thing he would ever do.

He whispered, "I like you."

Cheryl Lee glanced behind her to see if anyone had heard. They were alone in the hall.

"Okay," she whispered, staring at the floor, and she put the stapler in her locker.

He would have given her his bike or his cat or his room or his mother if such had been possible. He had thought about giving her the stuffed rabbit that he slept with every night. He *would* have given it to her except that his affection for the rabbit was waning now and he liked the stapler better. He gave her the stapler because he loved it more than anything else.

Jimmy Haizlet loved his red stapler more than anything in the world (except, of course, Cheryl Lee).

* * *

In 2009, Cheryl Lee Robertson celebrated her fifty-seventh birthday with a collection of girlfriends at a Fridays in Pittsburgh. They were drinking margaritas and complaining about their bosses when one of the girlfriends happened to mention an incident involving a stapler at the insurance company where she worked. Someone had apparently removed a stapler from the boss's desk (unless, of course, he had misplaced it himself) and he got completely bent out of shape, fussing and fuming, even though there were at least a dozen of them in the supply closet. The next time he went to the bathroom, one of the secretaries, not her, but one of the other ones, got three staplers out of the closet and put them all on his desk so he wouldn't have to worry about *that* problem ever again.

They all laughed in response to this anecdote and then Cheryl Lee, who was on her third margarita said, "Did I ever tell you about the boy who gave me a stapler?" Of course, she hadn't, but now she did: when she was in third or fourth, or maybe it was second grade, one of the boys in school snuck up on her in the hallway and gave her a little toy stapler.

"Did he think you needed to staple something?" one of her friends inquired, laughing.

"I guess he must have," Cheryl Lee laughed.

"He said he liked me," she added a bit more seriously. "And then he left."

Everyone was silent.

"Story of my life," she concluded, laughing and lifting her glass.

And then they all laughed some more.

James Haizlet's birthday had been a month previous and his tenth wedding anniversary a month before that. He was also fifty-seven, and he lived in Pray, Montana now. He was married to a woman he sometimes called Number Seven—my Favorite and Final. But he still thought about Cheryl Lee from time to time and he still remembered every word she ever said to him.

2

Current Events

It was Wednesday, April 14, 1999. Angelika Blitch was anxious again—and if you had been asked to guess why, you might be forgiven for failing to identify Current Events as the chronic culprit.

Some of the other teachers at Bartlesville Elementary might have assumed the most troubling part of her job would be the simple fact that none of the children could pronounce her name—they tended to elide the all-important "l." But after sixteen years of teaching she was long accustomed to that. Of course it was only this year that they had finally come up with a nickname. The boys liked to call Mrs. Welch "Mrs. Belch" and Mr. Woermer, "Mr. Wormy," but no one had ever been able to think of an amusing variation on the name "Blitch." Until now. The most popular movie in 1999 was *The Blair Witch Project* and even though none of the first graders had actually seen the show, they had seen commercials for it on television and one of them (one of the boys) had come up with "Blitch Witch" as a hilarious appellation for talking about their teacher behind her back.

But she didn't care about that.

Closer to home on the anxiety meter, she was turning forty this year—unmarried and undated since high school. Perhaps undatable, given an aversion to makeup and makeovers in accord with the standards of her family's Free Methodist Holiness tradition. She was dowdy and she knew it, and now she would be a "dowdy old maid." How old did you have to be to be an "old maid"? She wasn't sure, but forty almost certainly qualified. And she could no longer deny it: She had gotten her first gray hairs; soon, there would be too many to pull out. But that would be a story for another time.

Even without makeup, she was a disappointment to her father. George Whitfield Blitch was the pastor of the Shidler Free Methodist Holiness congregation (a Bible church!) about an hour from Bartlesville. He eschewed the worldliness and "refinements" that had caused more traditional Methodist churches to disgrace the Holiness tradition. And now his daughter was teaching in a public school instead of a Christian one like the Pawhuska Tabernacle Children's Academy that she had attended (or, rather, one like that school *used to be*—it had moved left of his pleasure since her childhood, hiring people with who *knows* what ideas). If Angelika was going to teach in the world, he insisted, she should at least witness to the urchins and try to save their souls. That would be against the law, she told him. Whose law? he wanted to know. God's law? What did the apostles do when they were told, "Did we not straitly command you that ye shall not teach in this Name?" Did not Peter respond, "Whether it be right in the sight of God to hearken unto you more than unto God, judge ye, for we cannot but speak the things which we have seen and heard"?

She went home twice a month, driving US 60 for twenty-six miles to Pawhuska, right past the Big Boy near Lynn Avenue. Mama had warned her about who was working there now, in case she might accidentally stop. She hadn't eaten at a Big Boy for a very long time (maybe once in college?) and wasn't likely to start now. But thanks for the warning. Sixteen miles later, she took County Road 4020 for 2.5 miles to SH-11 and then in 5.6 miles she was in Shidler, temporarily raising its population to 421. She'd tell Daddy about all the wonderful things she thought she was doing at the school, things she was really *proud* of (but pride was a sin) and he would shake his head and mumble that she'd never find a husband (a godly one) out in the world, whereas if she'd taught somewhere like Pawhuska Tabernacle (or somewhere like it *used to be*) she'd be married with four children by now.

Any and all of this might cause anxiety. But what troubled Angelika Blitch most persistently, most regularly, in fact weekly, was Current Events. Every Wednesday, the children were to bring to class an article from the newspaper, or from a magazine, and three or four of them, as many as time allowed, would share the story they had brought with the class. This assignment was not her idea—all the grades did it. And so did other schools (at least some of them). Someone on the district school board or in the state legislature or somewhere had come up with the "recommendation" of devoting thirty minutes of school time every Wednesday to engagement with Current Events: encourage children early to become well-informed citizens, aware of the world around them.

Perhaps it made sense for the older grades, but most of the first graders couldn't even read a story from the newspaper, and none of them could understand one. No problem! she had been told. Their parents would help them to find a story, read it to them (or with them), and explain it to them. Family bonding over Current Events.

She sent letters home, suggesting what types of stories were "age appropriate" and where in the paper such stories were usually found. Hypothetically, they had a week to find a story—anything from any paper or magazine all week long! But parents were lazy and, every Wednesday, more than 80 percent of the class brought whatever the top story on the front page of *The Oklahoman* (or its rival *Tulsa World*) had been that morning. One Wednesday, several first graders took turns telling the class about how the Supreme Court had declared line-item vetoes unconstitutional—not a one of the students had any idea what that meant, nor (she suspected) did the parents who had quickly (perhaps in the car on the way to school) tried to explain it to them.

But that was better than the Unabomber. Honestly, she thought, how many Wednesdays is the top news story in *The Oklahoman* or *Tulsa World* about something comprehensible to six-year-olds or appropriate for them? So, last October, when Matthew Shepherd was beaten to death in an anti-gay hate crime, she tried to steer the children into a discussion of bullying and away from some of the observations the family bonding time had yielded in certain households ("boys aren't supposed to kiss boys"; "he wouldn't get kilt if he'd mind his own business"; "I think he tried to kiss *them* and that's why they got mad").

The last three months had featured several Wednesdays devoted to Bill Clinton and Monica Lewinsky and the impeachment trial—and the parroting of parental comments reached a fever pitch. Angelika Blitch tried to explain that some people thought Mr. Clinton shouldn't be president anymore because he told a lie and presidents need to tell the truth. Jerry Halter said the Publicans were the biggest liars on the planet and all the president did was have some fun. Timmy Folds said it wasn't just lying but he wanted to get rid of families and let people marry sheep or dogs or anything they liked. Mary Shoals thought that was a good idea and said she wanted to marry her dog if she could. Everybody laughed at her and said that then she would have puppies and she said she didn't care because she liked puppies. Angelika Blitch asked if anybody had brought in a *different* story for the day.

* * *

So now she was sitting at her desk, twenty minutes before the start of class. It was April 14, 1999 and she was staring at two front pages:

The Oklahoman: **UA FLIGHT 297 DOWN AT SEA—ALL LIVES LOST**

Tulsa World: **182 DEAD IN UNITED 297 CRASH**

A plane crash. That was what she had to look forward to. "Current Events" for Wednesday, April 14, 1999.

First she took attendance. Then they said the Pledge of Allegiance. She could already see the papers on their desks. Lots of big, bold headlines. Pictures of airplanes. Charts with flight paths. She took a deep breath.

"It's Wednesday, so we're going to have Current Events. Did everyone bring a story from the newspaper, or maybe a magazine?"

Several hands went up amidst murmurs of affirmation. She looked over the hands and selected one from a boy who hadn't spoken much this week.

"Bradley, do you want to share your story with us?"

"Yes ma'am," he mumbled over a chorus of groans from the unselected, and then he shambled to the front of the class, clutching half of *The Oklahoman*'s front page in his hand.

"My story is about this big airplane that crashed down in the water and all the people couldn't swim and they got dead." He held up the paper. "There's a picture of an airplane but not the one that crashed because that one is gone."

"Miz Bitch!" Tommy Walker wailed, waving his hand.

"Yes, Tommy?"

"That was my story too!"

"Me, too!"

"Same here!"

Suddenly lots of voices were empathizing with poor Tommy's dilemma. Imagine that! Lots of them had brought the plane crash as their story!

"Can you share anything else about it, Tommy?"

"No. It just crashed and they got kilt. That's all."

"Miz Bitch!"

"Yes, Albert?"

"My mom says they went to heaven. The plane went in the ocean and they all went to heaven."

"That's a nice thing to say."

"It could have been aliens or something," Teddy Samples volunteered.

"Teddy, you need to raise your hand first."

"It could have been aliens because it landed in a triangle and that's where the aliens are."

So far no girls had spoken.

"Okay, is there anything else about the plane crash?"

No hands. Silence. Rustling of feet.

"It is very sad, isn't it? Sometimes we get news that is very sad."

"It's a *little* sad," Tommy Walker said, without raising his hand. "But it's not *real* sad because they went to heaven."

Angelika smiled and nodded. She could hear her father prompting her, "Go on. Talk about heaven. They brought it up."

"Well. Did anybody bring in a different story?"

Rachel Collins raised her hand. Yes! One of the girls! Sweet, quiet Rachel Collins. Second to last row. Wanted to be a veterinarian.

"Please, Rachel! Share your story with us!"

She walked to the front of the room clutching a 5x7 piece of paper that appeared to contain nothing but a photo with a caption.

"My story is about . . . there's a zoo . . . in . . ." she walked over to Angelika. "What's this word?"

"Chicago," she said looking at the caption and the picture: a large polar bear with a small cub, in the water.

"In . . . where was it?"

"Chicago."

"In . . ." she stammered and hesitated. "There's this zoo in where she said and they have a big bear that is all white and it had a baby and the baby is all white too and it lives in the water."

"It's called a polar bear," Angelika added. "And that is a wonderful picture! Do you want to pass it around so people can see?"

"Uh . . . I don't want to pass it around because they'll ruin it."

"Oh. Okay. You want to keep the picture, and keep it nice. How about if we put it on the bulletin board and everyone can look at it when they get a chance? And then you can take it home after school."

"Okay," she said sweetly, and surrendered the photo. Then, as she was returning to her seat, she suddenly came back and said, "Oh, and I forgot. The baby bear's name is Snowflake, but I don't know what the mother's name is, but the baby's name is Snowflake."

"Thank you, Rachel!" Angelika enthused. "That is such a good story! And it is a wonderful picture! Thank you for sharing that with us!"

"Miz Bitch!" Terry Owens called, waving his hand.

"Yes, Terry?"

"Do you know if there were any Jews on the plane?"

"No, Terry, I don't know that. How would we know that?"

"Because Albert said they went to heaven and Jews don't go to heaven."

"That's not something to talk about in school. And we don't know . . ."

There was sudden hubbub of children talking to each other.

"Maybe we should talk some more about Rachel's story. Have any of you ever been to a zoo?"

"Mrs. Bul-itch!" Mary Shoals cried. "Albert's being mean!" Mary and another student had been trained by their parents to *try* to say the "l" in her name, which they did with melodramatic emphasis.

"Albert?" she asked "Are you being mean?"

"No. I didn't say anything."

"He says Jews don't believe in Jesus and that's mean because everyone believes in Jesus."

"It's not really mean, Mary. Jews have a different religion and they believe in God but they don't believe in Jesus like Christians do. It's not mean, they just have another religion."

"*I told you!*" Albert hissed at her and she made a face at him.

"Miz Bitch!" Now Kristen Morris was waving her hand. Another one of the girls.

"Yes, Kristen? Do you have a different story to share?"

"No."

"Have you ever been to a zoo?"

"No, but we saw this movie at church where people got raptured because Jesus came and they just disappeared, and some of them were driving cars and flying planes and then all the cars and planes started crashing."

Oh my, Angelika thought. Yes. I've seen that movie. It's called *Like a Thief in the Night* and my father shows it to teenagers to scare them into getting saved, or at least into keeping their shirts buttoned on dates, or . . . *it was not age appropriate for first graders!*

"I was just thinking it might not have been aliens like Teddy said but maybe the pilot got raptured and maybe that's why the plane crashed."

"I don't think we know why it crashed," Angelika said calmly. "We don't know yet, but the plane was probably broken."

"My mother put a bumper sticker on our car that says 'You better watch out because if there's a rapture no one will be in the car and it will go nnnh nnnh nnnh nnnh (weaving her hands back and forth to demonstrate) and then crash into everyone because there's no driver, so you better watch out.'"

Tommy Walker said, "That's a long bumper sticker."

"It *is* a long bumper sticker," Kristen responded defiantly, "so that's just how much *you* know."

"Miz Bitch!"

"Yes, Albert?"

"I have an idea."

"Okay. What is your idea?"

"Maybe since Jews can't go to heaven, they could fly the planes and then we wouldn't have to worry about pilots getting raptured and disappearing."

"Alright, I think we have talked enough about the plane crash. But you should not be frightened of airplanes, because they are very safe. This one was broken, but most planes, almost *all* planes, are very safe and the pilots are smart and brave and very, very careful. So, thank you all for bringing in your stories. And thank you, especially, to Rachel for the polar bear story and the picture. I'm putting it on the bulletin board and I want everyone to look at it before they go home."

They moved on to subtraction (with numbers one through ten) and played games with units of money and telling time (on an analog clock). Then they did a popular activity with the big screen and PowerPoint that involved "discerning patterns." The screen would show a cow, a horse, a pig—should the next picture be a shoe or an apple or a sheep? It should be a sheep because the pattern was "farm animals." Jerry Halter guessed "shoe" because horses wear shoes and Albert had to do a "do-over" for calling him stupid ("They don't wear *tennis* shoes, stupid!"). Then they did one that showed a wheel and a CD and a coin—should the next picture be a dinner plate or a book or a car? It should be the plate because the pattern was "things that are round" (two students guessed "car" because cars have wheels). The students were in teams and scored points and would have played all day. After lunch, Angelika read aloud to them from *My Father's Dragon*, and then they did Language Arts and worked on vowels, which was pretty boring, but then they worked together doing geography puzzles of the United States (with all of New England as just two pieces).

When the day ended at 3:00, all of the students hurried out, except for Rachel, who waited to get her picture. Angelika took it down from the bulletin board and thanked her again for bringing it.

"You're welcome," she said, taking the picture in both hands. "What do you call those people who are smart and brave and fly the planes?"

"Pilots?"

"Do they have to be boys or can they be girls?"

"They can be either. When I was your age, all pilots were men, but now there are women pilots too. Not very many, but some. I thought you wanted to be a veterinarian."

"I did but not anymore because they have to hurt animals and make them go to sleep."

"I guess they do sometimes. But there are other jobs with animals . . ."

"Can I tell you a secret?"

Uh-oh, she thought. Secrets were potential problems.

"I don't know if that's a good idea. Is it something bad?"

"*It's very, very bad.*"

Angelika blinked at the emphasis.

"You can't tell *anyone*," she continued.

"Well, I can't keep secrets from your parents, Rachel."

"My parents already know, but the other kids don't."

"Okay, I won't tell the other children," she said, and then immediately she knew what the secret was. She knew what Rachel was going to say. And still she winced as the little girl leaned forward and whispered it hotly in her face.

"*I'm a Jew!*"

"Oh! Oh, honey. That's not *bad*."

"Don't tell the other children."

"No. I won't. But . . ."

"You can't tell *anyone!*"

"No, but . . . oh! . . . is that why you want to be a pilot? Because of what Albert said?"

"I want to save people from the Jesus Monster when it tries to crash planes."

* * *

Angelika needed another forty minutes to get ready for tomorrow and then she headed home to an apartment, not a house, in a white neighborhood that had met with Daddy's approval. Sometimes she picked up food on the way but tonight she'd have a Cuisine-For-One from the freezer. And watch television—no cable, but several Oprahs on a DVR and one of them with Dr. Phil. Daddy didn't approve of Oprah or Dr. Phil—they were "new age." Angelika wondered if there would be any phone calls. Not to her—she didn't get phone calls—but to the principal, about religion in school. One or two parents might call and she'd have to see Mr. Hopkins tomorrow after class and explain why Jesus and heaven had been part of Current Events. He was pretty good at understanding. It was the kids, not her. It happened in *all* the classes. Still, the preacher's daughter who didn't wear makeup was always under suspicion. Well, another Wednesday was over, and she could go back to worrying about gray hair instead of Current Events.

It was Wednesday, April 14, 1999. Six days before the shootings at Columbine.

3

Jasper Gets a New Car

Algonkian Regional Park was crowded on the Friday after Thanksgiving. Some years it might have been too cold for that to happen. At times, there had even been snow, but not this year. This year the weather was a little chilly but tolerable and Washingtonians knew it might be their last chance to get out of doors for an afternoon in the park. It wouldn't be nice again until March, or maybe April.

Jasper was a Washingtonian—a more or less permanent resident of the DC area, to be distinguished from that portion of the population whose residency in the capital was dependent on the vicissitudes of political elections. Like many true Washingtonians, he cared little for the political environment or for the appeal the city held for its constant stream of tourists and other visitors. It was just a place to live and, from day to day, the cultural milieu that defined the area for outsiders whirled about him in a cloud of irrelevance.

That was part of the appeal of Algonkian Park. Tourists didn't come here, nor did politicians. It was a place for locals, mostly suburban whites including a good number of Virginians. Just eleven miles from Dulles Airport, the park was actually located in Sterling, Virginia, stretching out along the Potomac River for a good mile across from the Maryland border. It featured a boat launch, a golf course, a water park, and The Woodlands gathering center, which on this particular Friday was booked for weddings in both the morning and the afternoon.

Jasper liked the hiking trails and often walked them in the mornings to keep his heart healthy even though, truth be told, he did so much walking most days that he didn't really need the exercise. More to the point, he just liked the woods, especially in early hours of the day when there might be glimpses of wildlife. And, if he got a good start, he could still get to work by 8:00 or at least by 9:00. Now that he was "self-employed," he was busier than ever, but the hours were more fluid. Still, he had decided that today was a holiday and he would discipline himself not to work. There was plenty to do, lots of things he knew had to be done, but he was going to spend today at the park, just talking to friends and watching the river flow. The morning at least. He would spend the morning doing that, have lunch with Mickey, and then see about the afternoon.

Today, of course, the park was filled with families. Every picnic table, every shelter, was overflowing with mothers and fathers and aunts and uncles—and children, lots of children, laughing, playing, fighting, running. On Friday after Thanksgiving the park was a magnet for families and everywhere he looked there were images of before.

And yet the park also drew an odd cabal of men who couldn't imagine anything better to do on such a lazy day than sit around shooting the breeze. Maybe they didn't have families. Maybe they just didn't want to be with them. Nobody was asking, nobody cared. No one was working, no one intended to work. A handful of men were playing checkers on some little tables set up for just that purpose, but many were content to just sit on benches along the Potomac like Jasper and watch the river.

Jasper didn't even bother with a bench. He was seated in the grass, propped against a tree, deep in conversation with a couple of his best buddies, Samward and Ed, who he'd actually met on his morning hikes. Half a dozen lesser acquaintances were hanging out with them too, sometimes listening to their debates, sometimes just looking at the river or up at the sky, indulging whatever daydreams struck their fancy. They were waiting, perhaps, for Jasper to tell them a story. No one would admit that they looked forward to his stories like kids at bedtime. In fact, they groaned and berated him when he told them. They called him "Professor" or "Big Head." But the tales could be a momentary distraction on a day when no one wanted to actually *do* anything. Also, his park buddies did include a few men perceptive enough to realize that Jasper liked an audience and that it was considerate of people who called themselves his friends to indulge him now and then.

Two more buddies came over the rise. Emeril and Sasquatch.

"Hey!" Ed and Samward acknowledged their arrival, and then Ed added, "Jasper's got a new car!"

"Does he?" Emeril replied. "Well, yes, I guess it's that time of year."

"You got one last Thanksgiving," Sasquatch remembered. "What was it?"

"A Corolla Hatchback. But it was too small."

"He gets a new car every winter," Ed explained to the outliers.

"So what is it this time?" Sasquatch asked. "An Odyssey?"

There was a murmur of laughter. That *would* seem to fit. In fact, Jasper had joked one time about getting an Odyssey just for the name and then getting one of those specialty plates for the back that read ILIAD. Sasquatch remembered this but had not realized it was a joke, nor did he understand now why the others thought his suggestion was humorous. All the same, he liked it when people laughed, when they thought he was clever or witty.

"No," Jasper said, smiling. "But you're not too far wrong. It is a big one. One of those SUVs. It's called a Suburban."

"That's a Chevrolet," one of the men offered.

"Yep," Jasper agreed. "I didn't know much about them, but they got a huge cargo area. My friend Darius told me about it. Any of you know Darius?"

"You've mentioned him."

"He was a friend from before. You know, before I knew any of you. And we still keep up. Anyway, Darius drives a shuttle at Dulles, takes folks back and forth from the terminal to the parking and, so, he sees lots of cars. Sometimes asks the folks about 'em."

"We're gonna get a story here, aren't we?" one of the men said to Emeril. He was wearing a baseball cap and he'd been around but Emeril wasn't sure of his name. "He can't just say, I heard about the Suburban, I checked it out, and I liked it."

"No. Let him go."

"So," Jasper continued unabated. "Last Tuesday, Darius picks up this family named the McAllisters. They're parking in the blue lot, that's the cheapest one, four dollars a day, and they're going to the Greek islands for three months. A man and his wife . . . guess that's Mr. and Mrs. McAllister . . . and two kids."

"Does any of this matter?" the man in the cap asked Emeril.

"Just let him go."

Jasper ignored them. "Now, Darius says, they had a *ton* of luggage . . . so many bags in that storage area . . . the cargo space, they call it . . . and he has to haul them all out, one by one, and carry them to the shuttle. Just about fills the whole luggage area with just their stuff. They're just four people and the shuttle holds a dozen. It's *supposed* to hold a dozen, but now the whole luggage area's gone, so what's everyone else going to do? Hold their bags in their laps? The important thing however, what he noticed, was how much crap had actually fit in the back of that car, and he'd heard me complaining about the Corolla being too small, so he passed that tidbit on to me, told me about the Suburban and how big that cargo space was."

"Are these people just leavin' their car at the airport for three months?" one of the guys in the grass piped up. "I mean what does that got to cost them? A thousand bucks or something?"

"Where did you learn math?" Jasper responded. "I just said it was four bucks a day and three months. Does that sound like a thousand?"

"I wouldn't know. I don't have no calculator."

"Mercy! Say there's thirty days in a month . . . and three months . . . then we got ninety days."

"If you say so. You're the Professor."

"Twenty-eight," Sasquatch said, but everyone ignored him.

"Well you don't need college to know that thirty days times three is ninety days."

"Yeah, but you're smart and I'm stupid is what you're saying, and I still don't know how much it's costing them."

"I didn't call you stupid. Well, maybe I did, but I didn't mean it. You aren't stupid. I didn't meant that. You just got to think that if it's ninety days and four dollars a day, how much is that going to be?"

"Less than a thousand is probably your point."

"Yes, less than a thousand. Probably just about around 360, since nine times four is 36 and you just got to add a zero."

"Twenty-eight," Sasquatch said again.

"Well," the other man continued, "it's still three hundred and sixty dollars and that's just to park your car for a spell."

"I guess if you're going to the Greek islands maybe that doesn't seem like much."

"So why not leave the car at home and take a cab to the airport? Wouldn't that be less than $360?"

"Depends on where you take the cab from, doesn't it? What if you don't live around here? What if you live a hundred miles away?"

"And they don't have any friends to take them to the airport?"

"I don't know if they do or they don't. Do you want me to call 'em up in the Greek islands and ask them?"

"I expect not."

"I don't know the McAllisters, fool. I never met 'em and I don't plan to become one of their inner circle. I just heard about their car from Darius because he took them to the terminal and said what a big cargo space it had. And they tipped him five dollars . . . just five dollars for . . . I don't know how many bags . . . it was a lot . . . maybe a thousand."

"Probably," his mathematically challenged interrogator responded, refusing to be mocked. "Probably was a thousand."

"Anyway, if we can get back to the Suburban. It has three rows of seats like all of those big minivan type SUVs . . . like the Odyssey, if you want to know . . . but the second and third row fold right down into the floor, leaving this huge flat area. I mean, you could put a box springs and a mattress in there if you wanted to."

"Are you going to put a box springs and a mattress in there?" Sasquatch asked.

"Course not. But you *could* is what I'm saying. It's that big."

"Good, Jasper," Emeril interjected, with a nod to restoring civility. "Glad you found a car you like. What color?"

"Silver. I might have preferred a red one, but I kind of have to take what's available."

"I'd like to see it," Sasquatch volunteered.

"You may like to, but I don't think you will."

"Why not?"

"Oh, don't go there," Ed offered. "Jasper's mighty protective of his cars."

"I guess I am," Jasper said. "Don't expect you to understand, but it's respect. I'm going to keep it clean. Nobody's gonna get food on the seats or put their dirty shoes on the carpet or . . ."

"You think we're animals?" Sasquatch asked.

"I know *you* are. How do you think you got your name? It's my car and I'm taking *pristine* care of it. Respect."

"Twenty-eight days anyway," he mumbled in response."

"What?"

"February has twenty-eight days. You said thirty days in a month."

"That wasn't the point."

"There's a poem," Samward volunteered. "Thirty days has some month and something, something, and all the rest have thirty-one."

"Well that's not very helpful if those are all the words you know. And it's also not the point."

"He's always like this," Ed was explaining to some of the others. "Every year! New car! Nobody's allowed to get near it. Not even *sit* in it! I never even saw the last one. The Corolla."

One of the men who'd only been half listening said, "Has it occurred to anyone he might be making it up?"

Jasper didn't think he knew this man. He didn't know his name at any rate.

"What? Making up the cars?" Ed asked.

"Maybe. He's a bullshitter. You know him better than I do, but even I know that."

"He is a bullshitter," Samward agreed. "But the cars are real. At least the last two were. I saw the Mazda and the Corolla, both of 'em hatchbacks. Remember Jasper? The Mazda? I was there the day you got it and we put covers on the seats and mats down on the floor. I mean plastic mats *over* the floor mats . . . over everything . . . to keep it *pristine.*"

Jasper nodded. Yep, Samward was a good friend. Might let him in the car. Maybe, if anyone, it would be him or Ed. They understood about respect. Not Ed though, not *in* the car. Maybe just let him see it.

Darius was one of his friends from before. Only two of those left. Darius and Mickey. Darius was the one who gave Toffee and Taffy their names—twin girls, but not identical twin girls. "Toffee" because her hair was dark brown. "Taffy" because hers was light. They sounded like names for dogs but the girls loved those names and used them for each other, tried to make everyone else call them that too. And the dogs' names were Homer and Virgil, which were definitely not names for little girls.

"So . . . are any of the stories about cars, Jasper," Emeril asked him, "about new cars maybe?"

"Well, sure. I mean, they didn't have cars but they had chariots. Sort of the same thing but with *literal* horsepower."

By "stories" they meant myths: tales from Greek mythology. Jasper had read them all, not only from Bullfinch and Hamilton, but the original versions—and not just Homer and Virgil but Ovid, Hesiod, Aeschylus, Sophocles, Euripides. Not in the original languages, of course—he couldn't read Greek or Latin (like a real professor) but he had enough knowledge that at one point (before) he had taught at the community college and been invited to do programs at the public library.

"You must know the one about Phaeton," he said now. "I'm sure I've told it, and anyway it's famous. Everybody knows it."

"Best not to assume too much regarding our knowledge," Ed offered, egging him on. "Or our memories. Just 'cause you've told it wouldn't mean we 'member it."

"I might have been day-dreaming," one of the men in the grass said. "I only halfway listen to these things anyway."

"Yeah, well, Phaeton was the son of Apollo . . . or *a* son of Apollo I should say. Apollo was one of the gods. He's best known as the sun god who drove a fiery chariot across the sky every day—a very large chariot that literally held the sun in its open carriage."

"That's a big cargo space!" someone interjected, and drew a few chuckles.

"But Apollo, he also did other things. He was the god of music and he played a lyre . . . not a *liar* . . . not someone who tells lies . . . but, more like a guitar. He played this lyre and used it to seduce women."

"Very much like a guitar," someone offered. More chuckles.

"Yes. Think of him as a Greek god rock star, with lots of groupies. Apollo, he wasn't above getting a little human mortal nookie and there was probably at least one son of Apollo in every city or town. Anywhere the sun shined."

The men laughed.

"No one tells these stories like you, Jasper," Emeril said. "Not the way I learned them in school."

"No, but it's the way they really are told. I mean it's the way Ovid tells 'em. He likes to dwell on the sexy parts."

"I'm going to add that to my reading list."

"You should. But, anyway . . . back to the tale . . . this one boy Phaeton . . ."

"Weird name."

"Yeah, well he had a friend in school named Epaphus and he had another friend named Cygnus."

"God. These names! Is there going to be a test?"

"No, you don't need to remember the names. Just . . . I hope you'll all be mature and liberal when I tell you that his friend Cygnus wasn't just a *friend* . . . you know . . . he was . . . well, he was a lover."

"They did that back then?"

"They did it a lot, and thought nothin' of it. Phaeton liked girls, but he was also *friends* with Cygnus. But that doesn't have a lot to do with the story."

"I thought it was about a car."

"It will be if you can keep quiet long enough. So this other friend Epaphus, he was actually a son of Zeus, the Big Daddy god. If you've heard any of my stories before, they're a lot about Zeus. And Zeus was one horny dude. He impregnated goddesses and fairies and mermaids and earth women right and left. So Epaphus was his son by a woman named Io—that's another famous story I might have told you. Zeus had to hide Io from his wife so he turned her into a cow and . . . well, it didn't go well . . . not for her anyway. I'll tell you another time if I haven't already."

"Or even if you have," Sasquatch added, and the men laughed. Sasquatch smiled but looked confused. People often chuckled at things he said when he hadn't intended them to be funny. Jasper did like telling his stories more than once. That was all he meant.

"Anyway, here's the big difference. Apollo was a deadbeat dad. After he knocked up Phaeton's mom, he never saw her again. Didn't call. Didn't send child support. Can any of you relate? . . . Don't answer that . . . But Zeus for all his lechery was kind of different. He was proud of how much seed he'd sown and liked to have parties and show off the fruit. He'd invite all his sons—he always had sons, not daughters. Unless they were goddesses . . . but sorry I'm straying . . ."

"The car, Jasper. Get to the car."

"Yes, alright. So Epaphus is always talking about these parties and, one day, like in high school, he just mentions to Phaeton, sort of casual like, 'Yeah,' he says, 'goin' to another one with Dad this weekend. Party, karamu, fiesta, all night long. Probably be a bunch of nymphs there. They're always naked you know. And they like to cavort. Yeah, I'd have to say that cavorting is probably what nymphs do best, wouldn't you agree?'

"And Phaeton says, 'yeah, uh, I guess so.'

"And then Epaphus just keeps on: 'and the food! The food is, like, out of this world, and I mean that *literally*. You never had ambrosia, have you? Damn, wish you could come.'

"So now Phaeton has had enough and he says, 'Yeah, well, you know what? *My* Dad is gonna let me have the car this weekend. You heard about his car? *Four horsepower!* With the sun in the back seat. And I do mean the *sun!* You know, that big yellow thing in the sky that keeps everyone alive!'

"Well Epaphus just laughs out loud and says, 'Oh yeah, sure! Like he'd let you do that!' And then he tells everyone else and they all laugh about it, and Epaphus says he can't wait to tell all the naked nymphs what Phaeton said he'd be doing. 'We'll all be watching for you! Be sure and wave! . . . ha ha ha . . .'

"So you can almost guess the rest. Phaeton goes to Apollo's temple, where he just happens to be putting the moves on one of the priestesses and doesn't really relish the interruption. Sudden visit from a son he's never seen. But he can't really tell the priestess that, can he? So he's all, 'Welcome my boy, how is your life?' And Phaeton says, 'I want to borrow the car, Dad' . . . 'Oh no, that wouldn't be a good idea—it's got *four horsepower* and takes a lot to drive' . . . and Phaeton says 'Are you saying I can't handle it?' which is just what Apollo *was* thinking but he can't say so because he's trying to impress this priestess with what a good father he is, and he's also thinking, maybe if I didn't have to get up in the morning, we could have a little bonus round here in the temple. So he says, 'okay,' and hands Phaeton the keys (which is really the whip—you know, since it's a chariot—he hands him the whip) and he says 'Okay, don't scratch it and have it back by nightfall' . . . and by that he meant *literally* nightfall because, you know, it was the sun."

"Not gonna end well."

"No, of course not. Turns out four horses were about three too many for a teenager to handle and no sooner does that chariot start across the sky than it starts zigzagging every which way and dipping too low and rising too high. It roars so close to some parts of the earth that there end up being deserts, and it tears up so high in other places that there's still ice there to this day. Then it swoops down across Africa and burns all the people black . . . sorry about that Bernard but that is what the story says."

"Don't bother me," Bernard assured him. "Scorched black by the sun. Makes as much sense as anything else. I could have been a white man if not for that fool."

"Don't go discounting your heritage now. You're black and beautiful, Bernard—and you oughta be black and proud."

"The holy good Lord must know what he's doing," Bernard agreed. "I always say that."

Yes. He did always say that, Jasper thought. Darius and the kids. No, the chariot. There were so many interruptions. Sasquatch was muttering something about twenty-eight and February. But he wasn't stupid. Huge and hairy but not stupid. A little odd maybe, but not stupid.

"So, back to the chariot," he continued. "Apollo wasn't paying any attention because he was preoccupied with the priestess in the temple and when Zeus saw the chariot weaving all over the place he just thought Apollo must be drunk. He, too, had other things on his mind and he let it go until eventually that runaway sun car came swooping straight toward his party and all the naked nymphs stopped cavorting and started running about screaming and saying it was too hot and they were going home. Well that was that, and Zeus picked up a big lightning bolt and *zap!*... the chariot of the sun was struck by lightning! And Phaeton, well, he just got blasted right out of the sky. Instant cinders."

"Wohh! I can see why you're careful with your cars, Jasper."

"Good story," Emeril said. "Thanks for telling it."

"There's one more little note. You remember he had a friend named Cygnus?"

"The one who was a little light in his sandals?"

"Don't need to say that, bigot. He was just a friend who was more than a friend. Everybody had friends like that."

"You're saying back then everyone in the world was gay?"

"Maybe everyone still is and we're all just repressed. That's what some scientists think."

"Well then I'd have to say I must be *very* repressed."

"*Anyway* . . ." Jasper continued. "This guy Cygnus when he sees his friend get blasted like that, right out of the sky, he starts moaning. Just wailing, you know, moaning and moaning. And Apollo, he's still in the temple with the priestess and they hear all this moaning, not the kind of moaning they wanted to hear, and Apollo has to come out to see what's going on."

"Because the guy just happened to be right outside the temple."

"Yes, that's where he was. It's called literary license and you can look it up. So Apollo sees him and doesn't even think to ask about his dead son. He just says, 'Stop that racket!' And then he says, 'Don't moan like that until it's *your* funeral!' And then, you know what happens? The boy Cygnus turns into a big white bird, what we call a swan. And to this day swans are quiet their entire life until just before they die and then they let out a loud moaning wail. It's called a swan song."

"Is that really true?"

"Probably not. Most things aren't. Like ostriches sticking their head in the sand. But people say that about swans, so don't go spoiling the story."

"I bet they moan when they get it on. Like with a lady swan," one of the men in the grass suggested.

"Or just when they *want* to get it on, like, you know, when they're begging for it," another of them added.

"I've done that," a third contributed. "I don't mean for a swan, but when I'm begging for it."

"Well, anyway," Jasper interrupted again. "You've heard about cygnets, and that's why we call them that. The guy's name was Cygnus and he was the first swan."

"Wait! What have we heard about? Some kind of nuts?"

"Not nuts . . . *nets!* . . . cyg*nets* . . . don't you know what those are?"

The men all looked around at each other.

"They're baby swans," Jasper said, exasperated. "That's common knowledge. That's something everybody knows."

"Now he's calling all of us stupid."

"Cygnets! Baby swans!"

"It was a good story, Jasper," Emeril said. "And I learned something from it too. Now I know what baby swans are called."

"Like you're gonna remember!" one of the men said.

"I already forgot," another added. "Some kind of nut, I think."

Now they all laughed and Jasper got up, exasperated with them, and he might have gone off on them if Ed hadn't taken him by the arm and suggested they head over to the water park.

He looked at his watch to see how much time he had before lunch. He didn't want to forget his lunch with Mickey. It was only 11:00 so he said sure, just for half an hour or so. Samward got up to join them and all three headed over to the Volcano Water Park, which was really just a water playground with a six-inch-deep pool and lots of sprinklers and sprayers and mounted water guns so kids could splash around and soak each other on a hot day. Jasper liked to sit on a bench and watch brown-haired girls, but he knew a man couldn't do that for long, especially by himself, without parents starting to worry. It seemed a little less creepy when he had company and Ed and Samward knew this, so they'd join him sometimes. On a free day like today, you could just sit on the bench for half an hour watching the kids play in the water. The attraction was more popular in the summer but a lot of kids were braving the sprinklers today, with the sun hot overhead. They would dance about in the spray, squealing and screaming and then run over to parents or grandparents who wrapped them in beach towels while they shivered and chattered and then went back for another dousing.

He met Mickey at 1:00 at the Caravan Auto Shop, where he was assistant manager. Mickey would know all about Suburbans of course but he would be more interested in what was under the hood than in the size of the cargo hold. They headed over to a Friday's for lunch. Mickey was paying, and he picked the place because he said it had good food, though Jasper figured a big reason was the outdoor seating. Mickey always wanted them to sit outside even when the weather was a tad chilly.

Mickey was a friend from before. Sitting across from him, Jasper remembered Julie in the kitchen with chicken breasts in the oven and he and Mickey on all fours in the living room, den, and hallways. Toffee was sitting on Mickey's back and Taffy on his and they were charging each other with the girls giggling, each one trying to pull the other off her steed. Were they jousting? Was that it? Or just wrestling? He couldn't remember the details.

The food was good! He tried to have lunch with Mickey once a week and it was always a treat. The guy knew restaurants and where to find some good meals. Jasper ate a full slab of ribs, preceded by a salad and accompanied by a baked potato. Just butter on the potato. None of that sour cream—probably bad for the heart. The ribs were bad enough, but at least he'd gone with the baked potato instead of fries. He was trying to be healthy, though the ribs had proved too tempting.

He told Mickey about his morning in the park and how he'd told his friends the Phaeton tale.

"That's a good one," Mickey said. "And you tell it well. I bet you drew a crowd."

"Friends and hangers-on, I'd say. Met most of the guys hiking, you know, and it's just a good place for lonely old men to congregate."

"Well, you're not that old. And *lonely?* It sounds like you guys have each other at least."

"Yeah, they're like my *primary support group*," he said and laughed at himself. "Is that pathetic?"

"Not for me to judge. They're all men though. No groupies?"

"Not yet. I'm keeping my eyes open."

"There must be college girls who like Greek mythology."

"I guess there must be. They're probably at college though. And after hiking, you know, I may be too fragrant for their delicate sensibilities. No showers at the park. Still, I will keep my eyes open. Sasquatch says . . ."

"Sasquatch?"

"Not the real one. I haven't gone that crazy, like I think I'm seeing Bigfoot. Just a guy who's big and hairy so that's what we call him. Sasquatch says I should put a box springs and mattress in the back of my Suburban."

"Well, that could be nice."

"Coulda, woulda, shoulda. It's big enough. I could have a party. One or two naked nymphs. Maybe three. It's big enough."

"Now you're thinking."

"Gotta keep it clean, though. I mean, *pristine.* And nymphs, you never know where they've been."

"No. I've always said, that's the problem with nymphs."

"In the stories, they're always playful but not always nice. The wood nymphs were known for turning the heads of axes around to cause woodsmen to chop into their own backs when they hadn't asked permission to fell a tree. And if you tried to drink from a water source without asking first, the resident nymph might send a snake to bite you. But mostly they just liked to tease. They were always bathing naked in lakes and rivers, giggling and singing and splashing each other to attract attention and then when some hunter or someone would come by they'd scream and cry for their fathers—you know, the river gods—to punish the peeping tom."

"I've known college girls like that."

"Have you? Well, who knows? Maybe they *were* . . . anyway, the rule with nymphs was always, 'Beautiful but dangerous.' So don't let your guard down. There's this one story in particular about Salmacis. Do you know that one? Have I told you that one?"

The story took long enough that they had to have dessert. And coffee. Mickey picked up the bill and when Jasper protested, Mickey reminded him that he had picked the restaurant and had said he was paying before they even came in, so Jasper reluctantly allowed this, insisting only that the *next time* it was on him.

Then they headed over to the auto shop and Mickey gave him a few things for his new car: some thick blue covers that looked like large trash bags to cover the seats and some thick paper rugs for the floors. Also a few pair of the yellow booties he made his workers wear whenever they got inside a customer's car. It was a lot of stuff, but it squished or rolled up pretty compactly until it all fit in a single carrying bag.

And then, just before he left, he thought of something.

"Hey, Mickey," he called from the front of the garage bay. "Do you know what a cygnet is?"

Mickey was already stooping over a tire.

"What's that? A nut? Some kind of nut?"

"Not nut . . . *net* . . . a cyg*net*?

"I don't know. Is it some kind of net?"

"No. It doesn't matter. Never mind."

And so he was off, but it was still a little early. It was a holiday but he decided he could put in two or three hours of work and that would be alright. More than alright. Necessary.

So he didn't get to Dulles until 10:00 PM, around the time Darius finished his shift, but he wasn't there to see Darius and didn't want to get him in any trouble.

The silver Suburban was in the blue lot, Row 6D, right where Darius had said it would be. And he was right. They had forgotten to lock it. The jerks who had tipped Darius five dollars for a thousand bags. Still, one had to show respect. He pulled the blue bag covers over the seats and put the paper rugs down over the carpet. Then he set his dirty shoes down on one of the paper rugs, put on yellow booties, and climbed into the back. He folded the second row bench into the floor and spread one of his two blankets over the large, flat carpeted area. Keep it clean. Pristine. Because of *respect*.

He'd put in three hours of work and collected half a trash bag of bottles that carried a deposit. That was enough for five dollars, which would buy one of those big sandwiches at Subway. He'd probably be able to get another five dollars' worth in the morning on the way to Algonkian, eleven miles along the roadway, and then he'd be able to get a sandwich for Ed, too. Of course by then Ed would have found twice that much in the park, under the tables and in the trash cans, but Jasper knew that by the time he arrived Ed would have cashed in whatever he'd found and spent it on liquor. He'll eat a sandwich though, if I give him one, he thought. Long as I watch him—otherwise he might try to sell it to get another pint.

Well, it was bedtime. He took a picture out of his inside pocket and stuck it up on the inside of the window. A pretty brown-haired woman with two little brown-haired girls, one on either side of her. He rumpled his backpack into a pillow and lay down on top of the blanket, keeping everything clean so the rich McAllisters would never even know he'd been here. That was what he meant by respect and he couldn't trust any of his park buddies to understand why that mattered. Well, maybe Samward or Ed . . . no, not Ed . . . but maybe Emeril.

Anyway, he thought, pulling the second blanket over him . . . time for prayers. He remembered the people in the photo to the Lord and asked God (or the gods) to bless Mickey and Darius and the McAllisters and as many of the park buddies whose names he could remember. Ed and Samward were stretched out on benches by now, not ones by the river but over by the Woodlands where they were more secluded. And Emeril and Sasquatch were under the bridge. Bernard, too, most likely. But not me . . . not Jasper . . . Jasper's got a new car!

4

Tennis without a Net

FATHER MCCLOSKEY POURED THE brandy, a glass for him and a glass for his honored guest. They were seated comfortably in the rectory and would not be disturbed for the evening. A bowl of nuts, some cheese, and apple slices sat on the small table between their oversized chairs. He had offered the monsignor some port, but the brandy would suffice.

"So this is some sort of anniversary?" the monsignor asked.

"Some sort," McCloskey replied cryptically. "A fiftieth remembrance, I'd say."

"Fifty! What! Were you a child?"

"Well, almost. You know I've retired early. I'm sixty-two."

"So you were twelve?"

"Yes."

"I'm guessing it's when you received your call."

"No. Not to the priesthood at least. Not *that* call."

"Well. Shouldn't we have a cake? I mean, *fiftieth!* That's big, whatever it is. Why not a party?"

"It would be hard to explain to the guests."

"But not to me?"

"On the contrary. I expect it to be very hard."

"Well, I am intrigued."

"Good. At least we have that at the start. I fear I shall bore you with some philosophy before I'm done. How to hold your interest? Well, I'll put in some background that may seem irrelevant or even inappropriate, but which may eventually become illustrative. And, even if not, I suppose it may prove more entertaining than the rest."

"Why don't you just tell me? Short and simple. We are celebrating the anniversary of *what?*"

"Of a thought, Monsignor. The anniversary of a thought."

"How is that?"

"Fifty years ago today, I thought a *thought* that I had never thought before, and that *thought* would change my life. I daresay, it changed the lives of many others, though they don't know it. That thought changed, or at least affected, the lives of almost everyone I have ever known and loved. It affected them all because of what it did to me."

"You must tell me this wonderful thought."

"Other people exist."

The monsignor stared at him, waiting for more.

"That's it, short and simple. On October 3, 1971, I was sitting in math class, seventh grade, and I looked across the aisle at Debbie Peters and realized that there were other people in the world."

"Hmm. And this is worth a glass of brandy, fifty years later?"

"It is."

"I think you best give me the long version."

* * *

The long version would take most of the evening and, while it is uncertain that the monsignor understood the gravity of McCloskey's discovery any better when it was concluded, six glasses of brandy had been consumed and a tale that was alternately philosophical and entertaining had been told. We shall recount it here, noting first that John McCloskey, raised in Pennsylvania, had entered seminary in 1981, sure of his commitment to service but still in discernment regarding his call to ordained ministry. He had always appreciated women and had even thought that he was in love—there was a young woman in the nearby parish offices whose smiles and attention helped him to realize just what the cost of a commitment to the priesthood would mean. But eventually he got the assurance that this was what God demanded or expected of him and he took vows of obedience and celibacy, vows that he had kept faithfully for thirty-six years of active duty as a priest at St. Ignatius in Boston, Massachusetts. He had been beloved by his parishioners, had earned the respect of his peers, and had been highly regarded by senior ecclesiastical authorities, including the monsignor who sat with him now. He had retired just a month ago, on September 1, and had now arranged for an almost private commemoration of the thought that, he believed, had made his life and ministry count for more than he could ever have imagined. He was no saint. He'd had many failings (though not the ones lately associated with his vocation). But he had never forgotten what he realized that day in math class, and that had made all the difference.

"So, I was in math class," he told the monsignor, "and I was daydreaming about what we had done in Reading and Spelling the period before. We had been reading *Through the Looking Glass* and there is this one part where Tweedledum and Tweedledee show Alice the Red King. He is asleep and they tell her that if he wakes up she will vanish away and so will they. Why? Because he is dreaming, they explain, and we are his dream."

"Ah, yes. I know that part," the monsignor said, "though I might not have been able to tell you where it was found. I do have ten years on you, and have forgotten some references."

"No matter. At the time I was no big fan of *Through the Looking Glass* and I didn't think the story about the Red King was an especially good one, but I ended up thinking about it during math class all the same. Perhaps this was due to simple word association. My family had just moved to Hagerstown a year previous and my mother had taken a job at the Black-Eyed Susan Motor Lodge, where she worked from 9:00 PM to 1:00 AM several nights a week. It was an odd shift but one that did not interfere with what she took to be basic wifely duties. She was able to fix dinner and wash dishes and did not need to leave for work until I was getting ready for bed. The only drawback was that she often did not get to bed herself until almost 2:00 and was only able to get three or four hours of sleep before getting up to fix breakfast. A three-hour nap was required during the day, though I never noticed that housework suffered. The main impact on my life came with the weekend naps: Mom always worked Friday, Saturday, and Sunday evenings, and she slept every Saturday and Sunday afternoon. I was home then and had to be reminded or remanded not to make noise. "You'll wake your sleeping mother!" I was told. And *those* words would come to haunt me. As you may know . . . some years later when my mother was in a coma following that terrible accident . . . the one that took my father's life . . . she was in a coma and all I could do was wait for days, weeks, months, and years to see if she might wake up."

"She never did, though, did she?"

"No. Bless you for remembering. So, shall we call it irony? Because it seems like all I ever heard as a child was, 'You'll wake your sleeping mother! You'll wake your sleeping mother! You'll wake your sleeping mother!'"

"Tragic."

"Okay. Relevance? Perhaps this was the subliminal association that made me think about the sleeping king in math class. Or, who knows, maybe the story was just more interesting than integers. At any rate, I did think about the Red King and about what everyone had said. Some of the girls had thought it was funny that the king would be dreaming and we would be his dream, and one girl said she thought the king was God. None of the boys had much to say, partly because they thought *Through the Looking Glass* was a girl book (that is, a book about a girl). I may have thought that too—I don't remember. I do recall that Tom Kunze said the story was stupid, and Mrs. Edwards said maybe that was because he didn't understand it, and he said he didn't care about understanding it because it was stupid. Tom was always saying things out loud that other people would just think about; none of the teachers liked him very much."

"I would think not."

"At any rate, you must realize that while I frequently daydreamed in math class, I didn't normally daydream about anything related to Reading and Spelling. I mostly daydreamed about being a famous artist. I don't mean like Picasso. More like the guy who drew caricatures at the fairgrounds. I thought he was famous—everyone talked about how good he was—and I thought maybe I could be like him some day."

"That's aiming high," the monsignor noted with a smile. "But, you *are* quite the artist!"

"Thank you. It's my one talent."

"Not your only one?"

"Sadly, yes. Remember the parable: one guy gets ten talents, another five. I'm the poor slob who only got one."

"Aren't those talents a unit of currency?"

"Yes, of course, but you are ruining the joke."

"Oh. I'm sorry. I didn't know it was a joke."

"Well, like most jokes, it's not funny if one has to explain it. Or, well, perhaps it's just not funny. Still, I just have the one talent. I can draw."

"Cathedrals. You draw cathedrals."

"Yes. A whole series. Large paper. Colored pencils."

"I've seen them. Some of them. One at least. They are good. Or it was—the one I saw."

"Thank you. So, I've always had a knack for it. Drawing people or things in a style that is notably realistic."

"I like that. Much better than the modern stuff that doesn't look like anything."

"Picasso."

"For example."

"Well, I disagree with you. What I do is considered more craft than art. Exquisitely well-done, I hope, but the expressionists and the impressionists and, well, all of what you call 'modern stuff'—it is art on another level. I do not mean to disparage my talent, my *gift* let's call it, but art that is not mere representation requires something else. Something more. Something I don't seem to have."

"Yes, well, I am not a complete cave man. Monet did some fine cathedrals too."

"He did. And go easy on the cave men. They did paintings, you know—and not very realistic ones. I doubt it was because they lacked the ability to be more representational. They just lacked the inclination."

"Neanderthal impressionists."

"Cro-Magnon. But the point, Monsignor . . . the point, I suppose, is that realistic drawing and nonrepresentational art are different genres, like rhyme and free verse—both are poetry."

"Oh no! Do you know what Robert Frost said about free verse?"

"No. What?"

"It's like playing tennis without a net."

"Oh! Yes. Good joke. But, in fact, that is both ignorant and perceptive."

"How is it ignorant?"

"Because poetry is not just prose that rhymes. There can be many elements to poetry—assonance, alliteration, meter, rhythm, imagery, and other qualities that cannot be listed because it is the nature of poetry to defy definitions and confound boundaries, to expose rules that govern expression as arbitrary and dispensable. So, it is ignorant to imply that some poems are less *poetic* because they lack only one characteristic that is found in other poems. We might as well fault Dickinson for not using iambic pentameter. Could she have written 'Hope is the Thing with Feathers' in iambic pentameter? Maybe. Would it have been a better poem if she had done so? Nonsense!"

"Alright, alright! I yield! Can I just say I *like* poetry better when it rhymes?"

"What about the Twenty-Third Psalm?"

"Ah!"

"The Magnificat?"

"Okay. Yes. You've got me. I wasn't thinking of *that* kind of poetry."

"The Lord's Prayer. The Beatitudes."

"I have been filled with ignorance. But in company with Robert Frost. Good company, I must say."

"And 'Mending Wall' is free verse, you know—blank verse, I think he called it."

"Ah, so he's a hypocrite."

"It's also iambic pentameter—rare for him, I think. Still . . . 'tennis without a net.' I think that's also quite perceptive."

"So you said. Confusing."

"His point, I think, was that it can be easy to write poetry if you don't have to worry about rhyming. That wouldn't necessarily be true *unless* he means that if a poem doesn't rhyme, it needs to do something else."

"Something poetic."

"Yes. You can't just write a poem in the style of Frost or Longfellow but without the rhyming. I say, you *can't*, but obviously you *can* . . . and a lot of people do. Literary appreciation for free verse is taken as permission to just jot down lines without regard to grammar or punctuation and call it poetry when it's really just bad prose. That's what I suspect Frost was getting at, and it's true. A lot of free verse *is* just bad prose. Someone writes a poem similar to one that Frost or Longfellow would write—or Wordsworth or Guest or Browning or Dickinson—but then this person thinks, 'I guess I don't have to worry about rhyming; I'll just call it free verse.' But the point is, if a poem doesn't rhyme, it damn well better do something else. Something that makes it poetry."

"How did we get on to this?"

"Art. The analogy is to realistic drawing and nonrepresentational art. The latter is not easier, at least not when it's art. What I mean is, it may not be realistically representational but it is *something else*. Otherwise . . . well, maybe some fraud just does 'nonrepresentational art' because he or she can't draw very well. I suppose that happens, but critics spot the frauds. Usually. Or eventually."

"Alright. I'm getting a course in art history. Or theory. Or criticism. Or something. Also literary criticism. Or something. But this is all leading up to the immensity of your thought—your fifty-year-old thought."

"That people exist."

"Yes. An amazing realization. So where are we? Math class? The Red King? Oh, I know! You want to be a famous artist."

"Want to be? Well, that might be too strong. But I used to daydream about being an artist, like the guy at the fairgrounds."

"Did he draw caricatures? Cartoons of people?"

"No, not this guy. I've seen people do that too. But this guy, he just drew very realistic sketches of people. And he did it so quickly. It was truly amazing. At least, to me it was. I wanted to do that. So every day, just about every day, in math class or some other period, I would draw pictures of Linda Dobson."

"Linda. The one who really exists?"

"No, that's Debbie Peters, otherwise inconsequential, which is perhaps the whole point. Linda Dobson was just a girl I liked to draw."

"Was she pretty?"

"She must have been. Yes, I suppose so, but I wasn't, like, thunderstruck by her beauty or anything like that. There may have been prettier girls but I wanted to draw *her*."

"Did you have a crush on her?"

"I don't think so. I don't remember wanting to date her or kiss her or talk to her or anything. I just wanted to draw her."

"Hmm . . ."

"But she sat behind me, three rows back, and I had to know what she was wearing. Usually I'd try to look at her earlier in the day, to see her shirt or blouse or dress or whatever. And did she have earrings or things in her hair? I tried to see all that and remember, so I could draw her in math class."

"You were a strange kid, weren't you?"

"I don't know. I only . . . I mean, I have no basis for comparison."

"Did you ever know anyone else who did that sort of thing?"

"No."

"Strange, then."

"Alright. But . . . well . . . I can make it stranger."

"Oh, please do. Only let me steel myself with another of these."

The monsignor poured himself a second glass of brandy and then poured one for Father McCloskey as well. The latter took a deep breath, and then continued.

"This will be a little embarrassing, but it *was* fifty years ago. So, in the spirit of the occasion, let me tell it all."

"You said it would be boring."

"Not this part. I actually got paddled once for looking at Linda—the only time I ever got it except in Shop, where you could get paddled for not putting your tools up or for just about anything. But the shop teacher, Mr. Lorms, he didn't hit very hard. Our math teacher, on the other hand, Mr. Hilliard, if *he* gave you a lick—that's what they called it—well then you knew you had gotten one for days afterward. This would all be illegal now, of course. I'm not certain it wasn't then, but it was pretty common. And Mr. Hilliard, he was one of the strictest teachers in the school. Absolutely no talking in his class. So he thought I was talking to Patsy Rowland who sat behind me when, really, I was just looking back at Linda Dobson because I needed to see what she was wearing. I did it one day and got off with a serious warning. Mr. Hilliard told me to stay after class and then he said, "I saw you turned around in your seat and bothering Miss Rowland." That was how Hilliard did things. He didn't say anything to you at the time. He told you to stay after class and then, after everyone else was gone, he made you sit at a table with just him while he told you what you had done."

"And this was a public school. He would have made a good nun."

Father McCloskey smiled and sipped his brandy.

"Well, after the warning, I tried *not* to look back at Linda in math. But then, one day I did it again. Her shirt had some kind of pattern on it and I couldn't quite remember what it was. So, at the end of class, Mr. Hilliard said I had to stay. We sat at the table together and he told me what I had done and said that I had to go to the principal's office at the end of the school day. This always meant that you were going to get paddled, if you were a boy (they weren't allowed to paddle girls). I had to bend over and grab my ankles in the principal's office and Mr. Hilliard swatted my bottom one time, very hard, with a wood paddle. It hurt a lot worse than the ones I'd gotten in shop."

"So this was novel? The corporal punishment? You weren't paddled at home?"

"Nothing like that. And when I got home I looked at my bottom naked in the mirror and it had two red welts on it. It hurt so bad I couldn't even sit in a chair. I just wanted to lie on my stomach in bed. I didn't know what to do. I just lay in bed and cried because it hurt so bad and I didn't know what to do about dinner when I would have to sit in a chair at the table or else my parents would find out."

"Wait! The school didn't inform them?"

"Oh no, not in those days. I rather think they hoped the parents wouldn't find out . . . in case, maybe, some of them were liberals or lawyers or something. I don't know, but I suspect they counted on the child's shame to keep what had happened a secret. It worked in my case at least. I cried for half an hour and then decided to fake sick. I had to stay in bed for the whole evening, missing *Laugh-In*. My parents knew I had to feel pretty bad for that to happen, so they let me stay home the next day even though I didn't have a fever. They let me stay home under one condition, the usual condition, that I keep quiet and not wake my sleeping mother."

"She had worked the night before."

"Of course, and still gotten up for breakfast, which I didn't eat. And my bottom still hurt even when I sat in bed, so I lay on my stomach and read comics and then, when my mother went back to bed, I got out my tablet with drawings I'd done of Linda. Since she wasn't around for me to do a new one, I just decided I'd copy one of the old ones. I took this one where she was wearing a striped shirt with the top button open at her neck. I liked it a lot, possibly because the stripes curved around the curvy parts of her chest and I liked drawing them. And then I thought, as I was copying it, just to make it a little different, I would draw the shirt with two buttons undone."

"Oh."

"And then I drew a third one . . . and a fourth one . . . unbuttoning that curvy shirt one button at a time . . . with a brassiere and some cleavage showing . . . and then . . . well, I had the shirt unbuttoned but I never got it all the way open because . . . um . . . without going into too much detail, let me just say this was memorable because it ended up being the first time that I ever . . . you know . . . did what twelve-year-old boys do."

"Did you go to confession?"

"No. I didn't think it was a sin."

"I'm inclined to agree. But back then . . ."

"Then you're wrong, Monsignor. With respect. It *was* sin. I say so now . . . and I shall explain . . . but I've absolved myself long since. I've had to absolve *myself* because other confessors, like you, would not detect the need for it."

"Is that why you've brought me here? To critique my modernism?"

"No. I promise that's not it. Just stay with me."

"Let's continue then."

"I'll tell you something I've never told a living soul. This is a bit of a detour, but that day yielded enduring associations. The pain in my backside and my first experiences of that kind of pleasure. I know enough psychology now to understand it, though not to overcome it . . . not that I would even want to do that . . . but the association . . ."

"Are you telling me you have a spanking fetish?"

"That would be a conventional diagnosis. Not to act upon . . . I mean, I've never . . . and I would confess to you if I had . . . I'm sure there are women who provide such services, but I've never done that. I might have, though . . . the flesh is weak . . . I might have if not for . . . well . . . do you know what 'sweet dreams' are, Monsignor?"

"Of course I do. Or, to be more honest I should say, I *did* know once. It's been a while."

"Well mine . . . not always, but sometimes . . . they feature a woman with a paddle."

"Not Miss Dobson, I hope."

"A twelve-year-old? No. No, nothing like that. A woman my age actually."

"A sixty-year-old woman with a paddle?"

"It's my fantasy, not yours. And it's not just *any* woman. It's . . . oh, it doesn't matter."

"I don't care if it's Hillary Clinton."

"It's not."

"But I don't care. These are dreams. If they have no effect on your waking life, let your conscience be clear."

"It is, Monsignor, I assure you. Otherwise . . . well, I told you, I've never told this to anyone before. If my conscience were not clear, would I not have told my confessor?"

"Perhaps. Unless you thought him too liberal."

"I could find a conservative. Could I not find a confessor to prescribe penance for such dreams?"

"Easily, I fear."

"But I desire no penance. Dreams are not sinful and though I find the content a little embarrassing, I admit it without shame. Actually, it feels good to say it out loud, to speak of something I have never told anyone."

"Good. Now you have done so."

Father McCloskey poured another brandy. His third. And he refilled the monsignor's glass.

"And now back to my story. I had finally learned not to look back at Linda in math class—not even when Mr. Hilliard had his back turned. So, now, when I daydreamed I looked off to the side. To my left was Chuck Kettleborough, a fat kid who was bad at sports, and to my right was Debbie Peters, who wasn't super pretty but she was better to look at than Chuck. And on the day in question . . . October 3 . . . fifty years ago today . . . I was daydreaming about the Red King and I looked at Debbie and a thought flared into my brain like a missile searing across the night sky. The thought was so invasive, so unwelcome and uninvited, that it had to come from some place outside my own consciousness. It was a *revelation,* a realization that I have never quite been able to put into words, but the best I can do is to put it this way: *she exists!* . . . she exists *apart from me!* . . . she is a person, an actual person with a life of her own, and not just a character in my story."

McCloskey paused and looked at the monsignor, who asked no question but waited for more.

"The revelation," he continued, "the unwelcome and uninvited *thought* that invaded my brain, is simply that there *really are other people in this world.* Our human tendency, I suspect, is to imagine that we are the Red King, that our life is a dream in which many so-called 'other people' have roles of varying significance. But it is *our* dream, and we assume or just imagine that if and when we awake . . ."

He paused and then asked with a touch of desperation, "Do you see what I mean?" And he paused again, studying the monsignor's face, and continued, "I looked at Debbie Peters that day—a minor, almost inconsequential character in my life—and it struck me that she was just sitting there thinking things that had nothing to do with me and that when the bell rang, she would get up and go out in the hall and go on to do things and say things and think things that I wouldn't even know about. Don't you understand? From my perspective, my life is a play or a story and she is one of the characters, but in reality, when she leaves, when she's off the stage or whatever, she's still real and her life goes on. And here's the thing: to *her* I am just a character in *her* story. To her, I don't really exist. You know, I'm only important to the extent that I impact her life in some way. I think of her as a character in my story but to her it's the other way around."

"Heavy stuff for a seventh grader," the monsignor said, responding to McCloskey's outbursts at last. "This was 1971. It sounds a little like things I might have heard people say around that time. But not twelve-year-olds. More like college students, who were smoking something."

Father McCloskey sighed. The explanation always got lost like that, caught up in philosophical mumbo-jumbo that others didn't understand. And the monsignor was right. It *was* the kind of thing two stoners would say to each other, nodding their heads at the heaviness of it all. But for Father McCloskey, the revelation was more practical than philosophical. Perhaps when he brought the tale full circle . . . .

"So," he began.

"Wait," the monsignor interrupted. "I didn't mean to make light of it. Obviously, this . . . um . . . *breakthrough* . . . was very important for you. But do you really think that, as a result, you became more enlightened than the rest of us? On an intellectual, or philosophical, or psychological plane?"

"Well, I could surely be wrong about that. But I have thought about it a lot, believe me. I have different theories and don't know which one is right."

"Let's hear them."

"Alright . . . one possibility . . . you know that there are people who are not able to comprehend the significance of others in any way that does not relate to themselves."

"We call them *narcissists.* An extreme psychological malady."

"So let's say that my so-called great revelation was simply the discovery of something that everyone knows—everyone but the true, clinical narcissist, that is. Maybe that day in math class, I was the only person in the room who didn't know the truth about other people. What I'm saying is, maybe I was a true, clinical narcissist and then I just got transformed and became like everyone else."

"Faith healing? A miracle?"

"Sure. Why not? By a divine, unanticipated blast of God's grace, I was cured of narcissism. That would be something worth commemorating, wouldn't it?"

"I guess it would."

"Fifty years ago . . . it happened! Otherwise, I might have lived my entire life as a narcissist. I might have spent the last fifty years thinking only of myself. Maybe I would have learned how to fake it—compassion, empathy, whatever—but I would have evaluated the worth of every human being in terms of how they might serve my interests, benefit my life. But, thanks be to God, I was miraculously and instantaneously healed. No psychiatric analysis or years on the couch. Just *bang!* a bolt from the blue and I became like everyone else in the room. My narcissism was gone and I was able to embark on a life devoted to others. To *serving* others. Not completely free of selfishness, of course, but willing to make sacrifices, to renounce my own interests in order to be of benefit to others."

"To love."

"Yes! To *love.* Do you know my definition of love?"

"I would like to hear it."

"Love is being a character in another person's story."

"Sounds . . . a little Hollywood."

"Did I miss my calling?"

"Oh, no."

"If I love you . . . and I do . . . I don't regard you as a character in my story. I regard myself as a character in yours . . . a character who might be a blessing to you, if you want that . . . but only if you want it . . . and, in any case, a character who will not intrude . . . a character who might just fade away or vanish altogether, if that's how your story develops."

"All these literary references."

"Yes. Story is my metaphor for life. More than a metaphor, probably."

"Well, then, is *this* story done?"

"If it is, we can just drink a toast to my transformation fifty years ago. To the day I was miraculously healed of narcissism, enabling me to live as one who is genuinely aware of the authentic existence of other people."

He raised his class and the monsignor raised his. They both took a sip and then the monsignor interjected, "But that's not what you really think happened . . . is it?"

"It *might* be. I grant that. It is one alternative."

"Apparently you think there is another."

"The other . . . and I fear this will sound vain . . . but another possibility is that I had a genuine revelation regarding something that many people . . . most people? . . . don't really know."

"Come on, John . . ."

"They think they know it. That's obvious. Everyone might *say* that there are other people, but what they mean is that there are characters in their story, people who interact with them for better or worse. They will tell you, of course, that there are other people in the world, but they don't act the way they would if those 'other people' had value or worth apart from them. They know it on one level but they don't really get it—not in any way that has existential significance."

"All you're saying is, people don't live the way they should."

"But *why?* Why don't they live the way they should?"

"Maybe they're all narcissists. Me too? Maybe we all are—except for you and the enlightened few."

"I'm not claiming that. I'm just wondering out loud. I think it is best not to speculate on levels of awareness that others might or might not have—specific others, I mean. I'm not the most *woke* person around, I know that. But do you remember the pictures? The drawings?"

"Hard to forget them."

"I went home that day and destroyed them. All of them. I didn't even look at them. I just tossed the tablet and got rid of them all, and I never did another one."

"Good for you."

"But *why* did I do that?"

"Guilt?"

"No. I didn't feel the least bit guilty. I still don't."

"Well, then . . . fear . . . afraid you'd get caught? Your parents might find them."

"That would have been sensible, but no, didn't even occur to me."

"Why then?"

"Don't you see? I quit drawing pictures of Linda Dobson for one reason only: it occurred to me that perhaps she would not have liked me drawing pictures of her—and that her thoughts and feelings on the subject mattered."

"Hmm . . . yes, so *that's* why it was a sin."

"Because she exists. Like Debbie Peters, she was an actual human being who existed in the world. Imaginary girls, or women I should say, they can be characters in my stories—they might exist for my amusement and I can draw as many pictures of them as I like—but Linda Dobson had a life with qualities and characteristics completely unknown to me, with value and purpose that had nothing to do with her positive or negative effects on my life. I had to ask myself, if I am a character in *her* story, what ought my role to be? A kid who draws pictures of her and . . . well, you know, kind of enjoys them. No, I thought. That's not a character she wants populating her narrative."

"Some girls might not mind actually."

"And I could be happy to oblige them . . . *could be* if I knew which ones . . . but I wouldn't actually want to see them in the flesh . . . and it's simpler to just go with imaginary ones."

"So you still draw these pictures. Unclothed women?"

"Imaginary ones? Of course. The female form is nature's masterpiece, superior to any mountain or canyon or sunset."

"Superior even to cathedrals, I guess?"

"Well, yes. Obviously—and I think everyone knows it. I have a portfolio that someone will find it when I die. It's mostly Aphrodite . . . Venus for the Romans, you know. She's been the favorite with most artists. Aphrodite and her friends—Athena, Hera, Persephone. Not Artemis, though. She wouldn't have liked it."

"No?"

"Don't you know the story? Some poor slob walked into a clearing one time when she was bathing. He turned away as quick as he could, but she turned him into a stag and sicced his own dogs on him. The price for having seen what was not meant for mortal eyes."

"Hmm . . ."

"But Aphrodite was immortal and probably the nakedest woman who ever lived. Quite the show off. I think she would be gravely disappointed if anyone drew her vested."

"So you spent your boyhood drawing Greek goddesses."

"Well, then, it was more Wonder Woman and Supergirl. But eventually, sure . . . goddesses, nymphs, fairies, dryads."

"Eve?"

"No. Well, a couple of times. I mean, she's *probably* imaginary, but who knows? I like to imagine she isn't."

The monsignor smiled at the irony.

"In any case, it sounds like you discovered ethics. At age twelve."

"The basis for ethics at least. Think about the Golden Rule."

"Do to others as you would have them do to you."

"I would say, Try to be as good a character in other people's stories as you want other people to be in yours."

"I doubt that would have caught on. Forgive me, but I believe our Lord said it better."

"I'll not argue with that."

"Well," the monsignor said, realizing the evening had come to a close. His glass was empty and he shouldn't refill it. "Well, John, you are always interesting to me."

"How's that?"

"Well, you inspire me. You fascinate me. You intrigue me. And you challenge me. I mean this from the bottom of my heart, John . . . I think my life is richer for having you in it."

* * *

Father McCloskey thanked him for the compliment and for his visit. And after the monsignor left, he sank back in his chair. His glass still had one more swallow.

He thought for a moment about people who had lives . . . who had them now or had them once . . . Debbie Peters and Linda Dobson and Tom Kunze and Chuck Kettleborough and Patsy Rowland . . . Mr. Hilliard and Mr. Lorms and Mrs. Edwards . . . Robert Frost and Emily Dickinson . . . Picasso and the guy who did caricatures at the fairgrounds . . . I have been a totally insignificant, or nonexistent, character in their stories, yet those stories are real all the same—vital and lively and full of meaning (without me). I know this because of the revelation. I *know* it.

And then he thought about what the monsignor said when taking his leave. That was a nice compliment he thought, but an interesting way of putting it. His life is richer for having me in it. That's who I am for him: someone who is *in his life*. A character in his story.

Just an expression. But does he know? He does, I'm sure. Maybe everyone does.

"Well . . . fifty years ago today!" he said, raising his glass to commemorate what he called "the revelation"—an uninvited, perhaps unwanted thought that had changed his life and unknowingly impacted the lives of many, many others.

5

Lightning Club

THE RAIN HAD JUST started when she got to the eighteenth hole but that wasn't going to stop her. She was twenty-six, single, athletic, physically fit, but relatively new at golf. She was at the course alone because she needed extra practice if she ever wanted to hold her own with the men at the firm where she hoped for minimal advancement. She didn't expect to beat them (indeed, that might be a bad idea) but if she could just not be embarrassingly bad they might invite her once for how she looked in shorts and then invite her back because she could actually play the game. But for that she would need practice and she wasn't going to let a little rain be the ruination of what had been her best game in a month. Not when she was already at the eighteenth hole. In ten minutes, she could be in the clubhouse: a locker, a shower, a change of clothes. She raised her club for the tee and the world exploded.

Blinking . . . slowly . . . like waking up from a very deep dream . . . she felt hot all over . . . like a fever . . . or more like a sunburn . . . it was raining . . . so she was outside . . . and she was on her back . . . did she get hit by a truck?

There was a face . . . she blinked . . . shook her head . . . looked . . . a young boy . . . no . . . two . . . three . . . four . . . faces . . . the faces of four boys in a circle around her . . . looking down at her like doctors over an operating table . . . their eyes huge. . . their mouths hanging open . . . what? . . . she tried to speak but couldn't . . . they were just looking at her. . . and she didn't even know that she was naked.

* * *

Glenda Watson was the *second* person in Jacksonville to be struck by lightning in 1962. The first had been James McConnell, just four months previous. This was remarkable but not completely extraordinary since in those days a good number of people were struck by lightning each year in the United States. With stormy summers, Florida accounted for considerably more than the per-state average.

Less than 10 percent of those struck would die, but the experience could still be catastrophic. At the moment of the strike, the air temperature around the victim often soared to 50,000 degrees Fahrenheit. This was but a flash, lasting less than a millisecond, but it was enough to burn away the victim's clothing. Such was the embarrassing result for the aforementioned Miss Watson, but she was actually quite fortunate insofar as a full millisecond of inconceivable heat would have burned away several layers of her skin as well. This was more common: victims of lightning strike were often left lying on the ground, with their clothes incinerated and first, second, or third degree burns over their entire body. Ear drums would sometimes explode, internal organs might fail or be permanently compromised, and metal jewelry would melt and then instantly re-solidify, fused into the person's body in a manner requiring surgical extraction. Memory loss was common, in addition to other neurological anomalies, such as Parkinson-like twitches or muscle spasms that might plague the victim for the rest of his or her life.

But such details were usually kept out of media reports, and the cases of James McConnell and Glenda Watson were moderate and mild, respectively. When the story of McConnell made the front page of Jacksonville's main paper, *The Artisan*, in May of 1962, Jimmy Haizlet brought the details-free article to his fourth-grade class for Current Events. Several of the other children brought the same article and it said that Mr. McConnell was camping and got struck by lightning but didn't get killed. In fact, contrary to popular belief, the paper said, most people struck by lightning don't die. Mr. McConnell was in the hospital getting treatment and they didn't know what the lasting effects would be.

Billy Thompson always knew more about everything than anyone else and he told Jimmy what "lasting effects" meant. They were waiting to see if he had super powers because that's what happens when you get struck by lightning. You get super powers, like Lightning Lad in the Legion of Super-Heroes. Lightning Lad could shoot lightning bolts out of his fingers and Jimmy knew all about him but he hadn't known how Lightning Lad had actually gotten those powers. Billy Thompson said he *thought* it was because he got struck by lightning when he was nine years old like them, and later he would say that he was *pretty sure* that was it, and still later he would say that it was definitely the case.

Jimmy had just started reading *Legion of Super-Heroes* this year because he was in fourth grade and *Baby Huey* and *Casper* were for little kids. Actually, he still liked those books too, but not *Wendy*, since it was for girls. He would read *Wendy* if he didn't have anything else, but *Casper* was better and now that Jimmy was in fourth grade he also read the grown-up comics like *Archie* and *Superboy* and *Legion of Super-Heroes*. There was kissing in the *Archie* comics but not in the others and the *Archie* ones could still be pretty good.

In any case, that was why he decided to get struck by lightning. Billy Thompson told him and Tommy Garrett and Boonie Brill that *usually* when people get struck by lightning they get some kind of super power, though it might not always be the same as Lightning Lad. Sometimes they could shoot red beams out of their eyes and make things blow up, or make themselves grow super big like Colossal Boy. Tommy wanted to know if, sometimes, you could fly and Billy didn't want to mislead them so he said there were no known cases of that, but it was possible and, in any case, some people struck by lightning could turn invisible, which was even better. Jimmy started thinking about what he could do if he could turn invisible. He could always win at hide-and-seek. He could listen to people's secrets and know almost as much about things as Billy Thompson. He could ride his bicycle down the street and people would think it was a ghost. And he wouldn't have to be afraid of bullies.

After the McConnell incident, there were school safety programs on lightning strikes and four of the children at Westwood Elementary paid closer attention than they had paid to anything in school ever before. Jimmy even took notes and there was a poster on the wall of the classroom and he copied everything it said on to a tablet. The school year was ending and the boys had decided that they would get struck by lightning that summer. That way, when they started fifth grade they would all have powers, but they would keep them secret. They called their group the Lightning Club and met at Billy's house almost every afternoon to plan how to make it happen and to talk about what they would do with their powers.

The Legion of Super-Heroes had nine or ten people in it, or maybe even more, so Tommy wondered if they should have more members in their club as well, but Billy said they should start with just four and then maybe next summer, they'd find four more. Jimmy said that there were girls in the Legion of Super-Heroes and so he wondered if . . . but all three of the others were horrified at this thought and told him that girls had cooties and they couldn't be in the club even if they did have powers, which was very, very rare.

Jimmy wondered about this because there was Phantom Girl and Saturn Girl and Triplicate Girl and Shrinking Violet in the Legion—and that was four girls. Almost as many girls as boys. Still, if Billy said it was rare for girls to get powers he was probably right because he knew these things. Also in the Justice League, which Jimmy didn't read but he knew about, there was only Wonder Woman, so that meant Billy was right. Then he thought about it some more and realized that the Legion of Super-Heroes was in the future, in the thirtieth century, and the Justice League with Superman and Batman and Wonder Woman was right now so that explained it. Maybe in the future girls would be able to get power the same as boys and in a thousand years there might be almost as many women with power as men. But that would be when there were flying cars and time travel, not now.

Jimmy had actually been thinking about one particular girl named Diana Wooten who had blonde hair and smiled. He knew from *Archie* and *Superboy* that when you got in high school it was okay to like girls but he realized it wasn't okay in fourth grade and if girls thought you liked them they would be mean to you. All girls were mean to boys who liked them except Cheryl Lee, who lived in Pennsylvania and had never been mean to anyone. He had given her his stapler when he moved. That had been in third grade and now he was going to be in fifth, but he still thought he might go back to Pennsylvania and marry her someday.

Saturn Girl was in the Legion of Super-Heroes and she had blonde hair like Diana and Jimmy thought she was pretty. That was a huge secret: he would never tell anyone that he thought Saturn Girl was pretty—also Supergirl, and Betty from the Archie comics. They all had blonde hair. He didn't want to kiss them or anything like that, and he was going to marry Cheryl Lee in Pennsylvania even though she had brown hair, but it had to be a secret that he thought the comic book girls looked pretty (the blonde ones) or people would laugh at him.

When they met for the first time, Billy called the club meeting to order and said that he was the president and the first business was making a list of how to get struck by lightning. Jimmy had notes from the safety program and the poster, so Tommy said he should be the club secretary but Billy said only girls could be secretaries. For one moment, Jimmy thought that then Diana could be their secretary and if secretaries could get struck by lightning, she might end up getting powers after all, but he didn't say anything. Meanwhile Billy had gone off on a tangent as to how the only reason Wonder Woman was in the Justice League was that they needed a secretary, but the Lightning Club could do without one. Also, Wonder Woman was just a copy of Superman with powers that weren't as good. Tommy said he liked her costume and Boonie said same here, and then Jimmy realized that he did too. Sometimes he would sit on the floor in the 7-Eleven and look at comics before buying one and though he had never bought *Justice League*, he had paged through some of them and looked at the pictures. Wonder Woman didn't have blonde hair but, for some reason, he still liked looking at the pictures of her, probably because of the costume. Then Billy said they were all retarded because she didn't even have a cape.

Eventually, they got back to business and listed all the rules for *not* getting struck by lightning:

- Stay inside until thirty minutes after no more thunder.
- Indoors: Stay away from telephones and electric stuff.
- Also bathtubs and sinks.
- Outdoors: don't go up high like a hill.
- Stay away from tall things like trees and towers.
- Open areas (not sure what that means).
- Things in the water like boats.
- Stay away from windows and doors.
- Stay off porches.
- Don't lie down on concrete (also no concrete walls).

Then, they studied the list to figure out what to do. The best thing about living in Florida if you wanted to get struck by lightning was that it rained almost every other day around 3:00. There wasn't always lightning but lots of times there was, so you just had to figure out how to get hit by it.

The very first rule indicated that outside was better than indoors, so they agreed to get together at Billy's house every day and go outside whenever it rained. Billy's parents were gone until 5:00 every day and he didn't need a babysitter since he was going to be in fifth grade. There was a pretty tall tree in his backyard, so almost every afternoon the boys would change into swimsuits and if it started raining, they would run out and sit under the tree. They would get really wet from the rain and hear the thunder overhead and even see big lightning bolts. Jimmy didn't think sitting in the rain was much fun, and the lightning and the thunder was scary, but then Billy would talk about the powers they would have and what it would be like to go back to school in the fall.

At first Jimmy just thought about being invisible but then he thought maybe he would like to shoot things out of his fingers or eyes. He would have to keep it a secret but he thought maybe he could show Diana behind the shed at recess and she would keep it a secret too. Then he started imagining how some mean kids would be picking on her and he would tell them to leave her alone and shoot lightning bolts at them and they would all run away screaming and scared. Then she would smile at him and ask him if he wanted to be her boyfriend and he would say yes but only if it was a secret.

Probably everyone in the Legion of Super-Heroes had got struck by lightning. Sun Boy could light things on fire, which was kind of cool, but not as good as others. Chameleon Boy could turn into a table or a dog or anything at all and no one knew it was him. That was a good power, but when he wasn't turning into anything he was orange and had stalks sticking out of his head. Billy said he was an alien and those were antennas like TVs have. Jimmy knew that if he was orange and had antennas everyone at school would laugh at him but Billy said "The lightning didn't turn him orange and give him antennas, stupid." It was because he was an alien—he was already orange with antennas, and the lightning just gave him powers because that happens when aliens get struck by lightning the same as people. So then Jimmy thought turning into a table or a dog would be okay if he didn't have to be orange and have antennas the rest of the time. But there was another hero named Bouncing Boy who could swell up really fat and bounce around like a beach ball and nobody wanted to be him or get his power. It was very rare, Billy said, because Bouncing Boy was almost never in the comics since everyone knew it was a stupid power, but you don't get to pick which power you get. That was the thing with lightning and that was why you had to be brave or everyone would do it. You might get invisibility or you might be Bouncing Boy.

Billy Thompson knew more about everything than anyone else and Jimmy learned a lot from him that summer. They had a big discussion one day about which was better, Hi-C or Kool Aid and it wasn't an argument because everyone agreed that Hi-C orange was better than orange Kool Aid, but red Kool Aid was better than red Hi-C. Also there was grape Kool-Aid which was okay but there was no grape Hi-C. No one in the entire world drank green Kool Aid. Tommy Garrett said that he thought there was yellow Kool Aid that looked like pee but no one had actually seen it and they weren't sure if that was true. If it was, no one would ever drink it. But back to the matter of orange Hi-C, and to Billy knowing things, everyone thought that Tang was better than either Hi-C or Kool Aid, and only Billy knew why. He said that John Glenn had brought it back from outer space and it had space dust in it that was orange and probably came from the sun. If you drank enough of it you could float around in the air like an astronaut. Billy had tried this one time when he was left home alone. Instead of eating lunch, he drank an entire pitcher of Tang, which was a lot of work, and then climbed on a chair and jumped off to float but landed splat on the rug. He didn't cry because he wasn't a baby but he decided they must take the floating powder out of the Tang they sell in stores so that only the astronauts could have it. The government did things like that all the time.

Another day, Tommy Garrett said he had heard that there was a magazine named *Playboy* that had pictures of girls without their clothes on, but Billy said it was a lie. The magazine did exist, that much was true, because you could see copies of it up high behind the counter at Rexall Drugs next to ones like *True* and *Argosy* and it looked like there were pictures of girls on the cover, but they were in pajamas. Tommy said he knew a fifth grader (now going to be a sixth grader) name Evan who said his older brother told him that their uncle had been in the army and had a copy of the magazine and the brother (but not Evan himself) had seen one of the pictures and the girl wasn't wearing any clothes. But Billy said people got put in the electric chair for things like that and then Tommy said that maybe she had been holding a towel or something. Evan wasn't sure because he hadn't seen it himself. Billy said some of the other magazines at Rexall Drugs were better because if you stood back from the counter and looked when the druggist was busy you could see the covers had pictures of men fighting bears or Nazis and rescuing girls whose clothes were all torn by the bears or Nazis but they were still wearing clothes, just torn ones. This was much cooler than girls in pajamas having slumber parties. Also, Billy said there was a magazine they didn't sell at Rexall Drugs because it was probably illegal and it was called *National Geography* and it had pictures of colored girls from Africa and no clothes because people don't wear clothes in Africa. He hadn't seen it but he had heard about it. It wasn't the same thing though because colored girls don't look like real girls.

And then Billy said that he knew a secret that he wasn't going to tell. The other boys begged him and asked him, *what about?* and it took a long time but he finally said that it was about what girls look like without their clothes. He knew a secret about *that* but he wasn't going to tell because it was the biggest secret in the entire world. They begged him to tell them and he said it was a *huge* secret that no one was supposed to know. But they begged him some more and he finally told them: they have fur like teddy bears or gorillas. No they don't, Tommy said, because they wear shorts and T-shirts and you can see their arms and legs. Billy said he was a moron and didn't know anything. They shave all the fur off of their arms and legs but not everywhere else. Did you ever go to a swimming pool? You see girls there in swimsuits and the suits are specially designed to cover up their fur because *everywhere under the suit is fur.*

This was when Jimmy realized that Billy was the smartest person in the world. It all made sense, the more you thought about it. He knew that his mother shaved her legs just like his father shaved his chin. And he had seen men with big hairy beards like the men on the box of Smith Brothers Cough Drops. That was what men's chins would look like if they didn't shave, and that was what women's arms and legs would look like if *they* didn't shave. They would be completely covered with hairy ape fur and that's why they shaved places men didn't. But they might not shave under their swimsuits because they were lazy and then everything you didn't see would be ape fur, like Billy said, or a lot of it anyway. He wasn't sure about *everywhere*—that could be an overstatement. Maybe they wouldn't have fur on their stomachs. Or backs—how could they shave their backs? But Billy was mostly right about the arms and legs at least, and maybe more. Now he wondered if this was why girls had cooties, like everyone said, because of the fur.

Jimmy was going to ask about the cooties but first he had to say something else. He told them that when Billy mentioned the swimming pool, he had suddenly remembered that one time he was at the pool and there was thunder and everyone had to get out of the water or else they would have all gotten struck by lightning. Now Billy said that Jimmy was *so stupid*, he couldn't believe how stupid he was, because he hadn't said this earlier. Jimmy said he just forgot, but Billy said that it was his fault they had wasted two whole weeks sitting under a tree and no one had been struck by lightning, not even once in two entire weeks!

Then Tommy said there was a book in the middle school library that used to have paintings in it. Evan's older brother said it had paintings of girls with no clothes, and one of them standing on a sea shell, but now all those pictures had been torn out by older boys and not even Evan's brother knew who had them. Billy told him to shut up about pictures of girls because he had already told him what girls looked like and the swimming pool idea was much more important. If Dum Dum Jimmy had told them about it two weeks ago they wouldn't have wasted all this time. And, besides, everybody knew there were books with naked paintings in them but they were at great big libraries, not schools, and they were kept in a secret vault and you needed government clearance to look at them.

The problem, of course, was how you could be in the swimming pool and get struck by lightning when they made everyone get out of the pool. That was the whole problem. Billy said grown-ups were always trying to keep you from getting struck by lightning because they didn't want kids to have super powers. This made a lot of sense to Jimmy because he knew his parents wouldn't want him turning invisible or having a secret girlfriend he had saved from bullies (or from bears or Nazis who tore her clothes, which was a new idea he would be thinking about a lot from now on).

They figured they couldn't go to the public swimming pool because of the guards and grown-ups who didn't want them to have powers, so they would have to use a pool in Billy's backyard. Some rich people had great big swimming pools in their back yards and Billy said they could get struck by lightning anytime they wanted, but the only pool Billy had was a little plastic one. You had to blow it up and fill it with a hose and it was for babies. You could have put two or three babies in it but only one big person their size. So for a few days, Billy would sit in the baby pool by himself whenever it rained while the other three boys sat under the tree, but it didn't work and nobody got struck by lightning.

Fortunately, Billy had a birthday at the end of June and he cajoled his parents into getting him a bigger swimming pool from a brand new store called K-Mart. The pool was green and made out of hard plastic and you didn't need to blow it up like the baby pool. It was way bigger and it just sat in your yard all the time and you filled it with a hose. You had to tip it over whenever you were done so mosquitoes couldn't make babies in it and you'd leave it upside down and then fill it up again the next day. K-Mart was the biggest store in the world, Billy said, or at least in Florida, and it was one of the most expensive, but his parents had taken him there and there were shelves and shelves and shelves full of toys plus the green plastic swimming pool.

Now all four boys could sit in the same pool every time it rained and they could all get struck by lightning together. Tommy wondered if that meant they would all get the same power and Billy told him he was stupid and didn't know anything. People always get different powers, everybody in the world knew that, especially if they read comic books. Tommy said he *did* read comic books but Billy said he had read more, in fact he had read all of them, and that's why he knew so much and was the president.

In mid-summer, James McConnell was released from the hospital and there was a story in the newspaper. There was a photo of him in a wheelchair and he didn't have any hair. The newspaper said he had been peril-ized and couldn't walk. Also, he was deaf. Billy explained that this was going to be his secret identity. Lots of times when people get super powers they need to have secret identities and being in a wheelchair was a good one. Still, Jimmy worried a little bit about getting deaf or peril-ized and wondered if maybe getting struck by lightning was a bad idea. But then Billy reminded him how Benjamin Franklin went outside and flew a kite so he could get struck by lightning. Did he get deaf or peril-ized? No, he was the greatest American who had ever lived and he won the war and killed all the British because he had some kind of super power. He also had a secret identity named Poor Richard. This was all true. It was history. Jimmy remembered learning it in school, though Billy remembered some of it better than he did. Still, it was only now that he realized why they named those five-and-dime stores "Ben Franklin." They sold red staplers at those stores, but they also sold superhero comics, so they named them after the guy with super powers, the one who got struck by lightning. This was all true and you couldn't argue with facts.

Meanwhile, he had been wondering if maybe he could get the power to walk through walls, like Phantom Girl, and what he would do if he had that power. He was afraid to ask because Billy might say he was stupid, that it was a girl power and everybody knew that. There were good things about being friends with someone as smart as Billy but you always had to be careful not to say things that were stupid. Jimmy never fought with Billy, but Tommy did. The biggest fight was when Billy said *The Flintstones* wasn't realistic because they had a pet dinosaur and in real life the dinosaur would eat them. Tommy had a whole book on dinosaurs, plus some toy dinosaurs, and he said he knew more about dinosaurs than Billy did, which made Billy really mad. Then Tommy said there were dinosaurs that didn't eat people, just plants, and you could ride on them and everything. They fought about it for a long time and then Tommy went home. Billy said they were going to kick him out of the Lightning Club but they didn't really do that and Tommy came back the next day. They didn't talk about dinosaurs any more though, which was hard because *The Flintstones* came on every week.

Jimmy's favorite shows were *The Flintstones* and *Yogi Bear*, which the TV always said was in color except that no one in Jacksonville had a color TV. They actually said *Yogi Bear* was in "technicolor" and Billy said that meant it had new colors that scientists had only just discovered and that you couldn't see anywhere else in the world. Jimmy wanted to see them because old colors were good but he'd seen them all his life. Still, Billy said they only had color TVs in places like Beverly Hills and you couldn't live there unless you were a movie star or found oil in your back yard. Jimmy suggested that maybe they could look for oil in their yards instead of trying to get struck by lightning and Billy said they'd do that next summer, after they got powers.

Jimmy also liked *Dennis the Menace* and one time they talked about how cool it would be if Dennis the Menace got struck by lightning and got super powers. They started making up whole episodes with Dennis turning invisible or growing super big like Colossal Boy or shooting lightning bolts at Mr. Wilson, and everyone agreed that these ideas were better than the ones actually on television. Boonie said there could also be one where he could run super fast and Jimmy hadn't even known you could get *that* power. Boonie didn't say much, but when he did, it was always worth hearing.

But when August arrived, they *still* hadn't gotten struck by lightning and wondered if they ever would. Also, sitting in the pool while it thundered and rained was boring, so they wondered what else they could do. Billy said many times that the pool was too small and they needed to go to the big public pool but the grown-ups guarded that one to keep kids from getting powers and there was nothing they could do about it. There was a big swamp about half a mile away and that might have worked but the grown-ups had put alligators in the swamp to keep kids from getting powers there. Jimmy asked what would happen if the swamp got struck by lightning and all the alligators got super powers and Billy said that was exactly the kind of thing that could happen and that was why there needed to be a Lightning Club with kids who could save the world when it did. Who was going to fight invisible alligators if not them? Jimmy hadn't known they would be fighting invisible alligators. He had just thought about winning at hide-and-seek and protecting Diana from bears and Nazis. He also wanted to know if the alligators would be able to shoot beams out of their eyes and blow things up and Billy said of course they would, at least some of them. Then Tommy asked about the fish and Billy said he was stupid because there was no such thing as super fish. He had read every comic book ever written and not a single one said anything about super fish. Tommy said he'd never read one with super alligators either, and Billy said that *he* had but he didn't say which one.

As August drew to a close, all hope of being struck by lightning seemed lost. But then Jimmy's parents took him to a big city library and left him in the children's section for two hours while they did something downtown. He could pick out four books to take home. He picked them real fast and then went to look for the room with magazines that had pictures of girls with no clothes on. They called them periodsicles or something that sounded like popsicles so you wouldn't know they were magazines, but he found them anyway and after half an hour he found the one called *National Geography.* It just had pictures of bridges in China and things like that. No naked colored girls, so that must have been a lie. Billy was probably right about the *Playboy* one too. Another boy had told them it just had pictures of girls dressed like bunnies. Jimmy looked for it anyway but the library didn't have it. They didn't even have *True* or *Argosy* or any of the magazines from behind the counter at Rexall Drugs. They only had magazines nobody wanted or ones that everybody already had like *Good Housekeeping* and *Ladies' Home Journal.* He noticed those—and, for just a moment, remembered how he had scavenged such publications for photos he could staple . . . once upon a time . . . so long ago it seemed.

Jimmy wandered out of the periodsicles room and thought about asking a librarian if they had any books with paintings in them, but he was afraid they might call the police or tell his parents, so he just went back to the children's section. And there he found it: a book about lightning! He paged through it and looked at all the pictures and it mostly just said what they already knew, but there were two pages where it said across the top, "The Worst Things You Can Do in a Lightning Storm." And there were two pictures: one showed a man fishing, casting his line with the fishing pole way up high, and the other showed a man on a golf course—in an *open area* (he remembered the poster)— holding up his golf club.

He took the book home and brought it to the club the next Monday. They had been almost ready to give up. School was going to start and they still wouldn't have super powers. But now, here were two new ideas. Two very good ideas. They didn't have fishing poles and they didn't have golf clubs, but now, at least, they knew what "open areas" meant. And there was a golf course about a mile away.

* * *

The last Tuesday in August came six days before Labor Day, one week before school started. Billy Thompson, Tommy Garrett, Boonie Brill, and Jimmy Haizlet arrived at the Windsor Parke Golf Course just as Glenda Watson was finishing the seventeenth hole. There were dark clouds overhead and other afternoon golfers had timed their play to be in the clubhouse before the inevitable showers began, as they did on many afternoon around 3:00. The boys saw Glenda and watched as she headed to the nearby eighteenth hole. They ran to the spot she had vacated, and arrived just as the rains started. They cheered and ran about in circles, happy to be in an open area with thunder rolling overhead. They were getting soaked and there were no adults at hand to chase them away. And there was lightning in the sky!

The blast that struck Glenda's raised club was accompanied by a flash of unbelievably bright light and a boom louder than fireworks. The boys saw it. They saw the bolt of lightning streaming straight down from the sky right where the woman was. Or had been. She was gone! Invisible? Had she turned invisible?

They ran the fifty yards to where it had happened and there she was, lying on the ground . . . and . . . she was lying on her back . . . her red, pink, nude body in bright green grass. They gathered around her in a circle, staring down at her . . . wide-eyed . . . slack jawed. They looked at her. She blinked at them and they looked some more. And then Billy spoke.

"Do you have powers?" he asked the naked woman.

She blinked . . . still dazed . . . so confused . . .

"What?" she asked.

"Do you have powers?"

She lay there . . . breathing . . . for another thirty seconds . . . and then, looking up, possibly at them, she said, "Get . . . help."

"What?" Billy asked, still mesmerized by the sight of her. He was wondering what had happened to her clothes and he was fascinated by what she looked like and he was confused as to why a woman with super powers would need help.

"Get . . . help . . ." she repeated. "Clubhouse . . . go . . . help . . ."

And then, as if coming out of a trance the boys looked up . . . and looked at one another.

"She needs help," Tommy said. "Like a doctor or a hospital."

And three of them, Boonie, Tommy, and Billy turned and ran toward the clubhouse, a hundred yards away. Jimmy started after them but then thought it wouldn't take four, and someone should probably stay and watch over the woman, and that someone could be him.

The woman didn't speak to Jimmy and he said nothing to her. She just lay there staring up at him. Her eyes found his and they locked. She made no effort to roll over or get up or even to cover herself. She just lay there, naked in the grass, staring into the face of a nine-year-old boy who was . . . well . . . looking at her . . . just looking . . .

Her skin was the color of a sunburn.

She had no cooties and very little fur.

* * *

Three men from the clubhouse arrived in a golf cart. They knelt beside the woman and asked her questions: What was her name? Did she know where she was? How many fingers am I holding up?

One of the men was a doctor, and an ambulance had already been called. The three boys had burst into the clubhouse screaming that a naked woman had got struck by lightning and taken her clothes off—a somewhat confusing message, but the doctor had heard the "struck by lightning" part and ordered the bartender to call an ambulance, while he and his two friends commandeered the first available cart. Unfortunately, they hadn't arrived with anything to cover her and since they were wearing golf shorts and shirts, no one even had a coat to drape over the woman's body. Then a second golf cart arrived with three more men, but they hadn't brought anything either, so they spent their time hanging about in case they might be useful and trying not to look at her. After about fifteen minutes someone decided that two of the men could take their shirts off and drape these over her chest and crotch, which was something, but then the ambulance arrived and the men retrieved their shirts before the paramedics set to work.

Glenda was placed on a stretcher and taken to Duvall County Hospital, where she spent four days in observation and was then released, an extremely fortunate victim of what was classed as "a mild occurrence of lightning strike." Her main suffering was the equivalent of a bad sunburn over most of her body, but she also experienced memory loss related to events immediately before and after the strike. Indeed, she did not recall playing golf at all that day. She just remembered being at her home in the morning and having lunch . . . and then she was in the hospital, with some vague recollection of being loaded and unloaded from an ambulance . . . and she thought she recalled *eyes* . . . someone looking down upon her from above. This someone, she and her Presbyterian friends realized, must have been an angel, and the kindly doctor from the golf course told her nothing to contravene that assumption.

No one from the hospital or the golf course thought Glenda needed to know how many people had seen her naked—or, indeed, that she had ever been naked. So, she went home a little miffed at Duvall County for having disposed of what had been a new outfit and new shoes—they told her that someone in the emergency room saw burn marks and just threw everything away once she'd been put into a gown. She'd had to call her sister to bring a complete set of clothes before she could check out when they were done with her. "They threw out *everything!*" she railed. "I mean, did my *underwear* have burn marks?" But she was grateful to be alive and she would never forget those penetrating eyes . . . eyes that did not look away even for a moment.

"Someone was watching over me that day," she said, whenever she recounted the miracle. "You can think whatever you want, but I *know* . . . someone was watching over me."

The Artisan focused on the four young heroes who, according to the doctor from the golf course, may have saved the woman's life. These quick-thinking boys—fifth graders!—had immediately sized up the situation and taken decisive action. They had remained calm and, first of all, determined that she was alive and responsive. Then, they had run the full distance of a football field to seek the aid of adults and to ensure the enlistment of medical personnel. Most important, they had made no attempt to move the victim, not even to help her sit up—an error that could often result in spinal fracture. The doctor said he was sure they must have received some training in first aid or emergency response from their school or, maybe, the Cub Scouts. Sure enough, one of the four, William "Billy" Thompson, confirmed that he knew all about those things. In an interview with *The Artisan*, he explained that he had learned everything there was to know about lightning strikes and he also knew a lot about the first aid and emergency response and spinal fractures that the doctor had mentioned. Accordingly, he had quickly taken charge in the situation and instructed his friends as to what they should and should not do.

Jimmy did not remember hearing any precise instructions along those lines, but there had been a lot going on and he had probably just forgotten in the excitement. The doctor had also spoken to Jimmy personally and said that what he did—keeping the woman focused, her eyes locked on his face—*that* was the most important thing he could have done. Otherwise, she might have tried to sit up or roll over, or do something that could damage herself before the paramedics arrived. In fact, Jimmy remembered, that was what the paramedics did too. "Look here," one of them told the woman, pointing to his eyes. "Look at me! Keep looking! Right here!"

The doctor said, "You did exactly the right thing, son, looking her in the eyes and keeping her focused." Then he paused . . . smiled . . . and said, "You were looking at her *eyes*, weren't you, son?"

"Yes, sir."

"Good. I thought so."

The more pressing question, of course, was whether the woman had received any super powers and, if so, what they were. Billy thought it was obvious and explained that her super power was making her clothes disappear. Tommy asked, then how come she didn't make them come back again so they wouldn't need to put shirts over her, and Billy said it was because she hadn't learned how to do that yet, but by now she could. If she were in the Legion, she'd be Naked Girl and she'd be able to make her clothes appear or disappear anytime she liked. Or more likely she'd be Costume Change Girl because she could probably make *any* clothes just appear or disappear on her body whenever she pleased, and so she might be good at disguise or at least changing her appearance. Tommy thought this was a stupid power and didn't see how it would help to catch bank robbers or defeat aliens but Billy said, well that was the thing with lightning, you didn't get to pick which powers you got, and girls didn't usually get powers as good as the ones that boys got. Jimmy stayed out of the discussion but he thought privately that making her clothes disappear was way cooler than flying or turning invisible. He even thought maybe they could ask her to be in their club except that she was old and might not want to be their secretary. In any case, she didn't have cooties, whatever Billy said. Jimmy knew that for a fact.

The Artisan ran a picture of the four boys on the front page the week before school started, with tributes to their bravery and wisdom from the golf course doctor, and from Tommy's Cub Scout leader, and an expression of gratitude from Glenda Watson herself (who didn't remember them but was glad they had been there to fetch the help she needed). And so it was that Billy Thompson, Tommy Garrett, Boonie Brill, and Jimmy Haizlet entered fifth-grade as heroes. They had not gotten struck by lightning and they did not have super powers, but they were heroes nonetheless. The picture from the paper was on several bulletin boards around the school and, on the very first day, the principal talked about how proud Westwood Elementary was of them, listing all four boys by name over the loudspeaker during morning announcements.

Later that day, at recess, Diana Wooten came up to Jimmy and asked him if he was afraid when the lightning struck the woman and he said no because he read comic books and knew how to be a hero. She asked which ones, and when he said *Legion of Super-Heroes* she said her brother had that one and she'd read it too. He told her she looked like Saturn Girl because she had blonde hair. She laughed and smiled at him and he fell in love with her. But then she asked him if he wanted to go behind the shed and kiss with tongues. He shook his head and ran off to play with his friends and never told anyone about it.

6

Slippery Slopes

LIKE THE SCOPE COMMERCIAL, she thought. She was still angry and sad, maybe a little depressed. But she took her present out of the trash where she'd tossed it two days ago and folded it into a hollow of her suitcase. She wrapped it in clothing, not to keep it from breaking but to keep it from being seen.

She knew right where she would put it: that little spot behind the doorframe in her old bedroom closet, a cubbyhole where the shelves didn't quite meet in the corner. It was where she'd kept her medicine her senior year of high school—easily accessible but not easily detectable. She'd be there for two weeks, in her parents' house in Shidler. She'd be in her old room, sleeping in her old bed.

She had called it her "medicine." Drugs. I was on drugs back then, she thought. There were different forms, but she liked pills. She hadn't thought about those pills for a while, about how she could trick her father by hiding her "medicine." The old fool, she'd thought at the time ... *but she had been so awful!* ... and that one time when he had turned around in the entryway! She remembered that most of all. Was high school like that for everyone? She was so ashamed of who she had been and of what she had done and yet she didn't really feel *regret.* She almost wished she had done more—but only almost. Does it count as repentance to be ashamed of what you don't regret? Anyway, that spot in the closet was still there, empty for twenty-two years. And now, Angelika thought, I have something new to put there. She was going to like doing that. She was going to like putting it there, having it there. It was the worst present she'd ever gotten, but she was going to like having it there, hidden in her bedroom closet for two weeks.

Angelika Blitch taught first grade at the Bartlesville Elementary School. She liked her job—most of it, except for Current Events every Wednesday—and she thought she was good at it. She thought she was good enough, actually, that sometimes she was *proud* of herself, though she knew Christians shouldn't be proud. Every visit home was a reality check on that score. She wanted to tell her father the things she was doing at the school, the things that she was proud of . . . but there was no point in trying. She should have learned that by now.

Well, it was Christmas break, 1999, and she was facing the new millennium with frank acknowledgment that she was now a "dowdy old maid." She had turned forty in September and for several months had been plucking gray hairs from the side bangs of her already drab chestnut brown hair. It was cut (but not *styled*, definitely not *styled*) as conservatively as possible to frame her aging, no-makeup face. Makeup, like perfume, jewelry, and hair styles, was worldly—and, of course, only whores dyed their hair. First Peter Three Three. She had heard that over and over again. "Let it not be that outward adorning of plaiting the hair, or of wearing of gold, or of putting on of apparel." Rather: "let it be the ornament of a meek and quiet spirit, which is in the sight of God of great price." She had been whipped more than once because of 1 Peter 3:3, when she came home talking about another girl's clothing. Or earrings (with *pierced ears!*). Being *covetous* of sinners.

By now, she was used to no makeup, perfume, or jewelry. She had attended a women's Bible college where such things were forbidden and where she had been surrounded by peers who claimed "the natural look" was not only more godly but actually more attractive. Of course, most of these peers were prettier than she was. They had faces that didn't need much help. Her skin had been plagued with acne all through adolescence. She had gone through a lot of Clearasil (at least that was allowed—it was a little controversial, but could be construed as medication, not make-up). The pimples were long gone but they had left her with a face pocked by acne scars, the kind of face never featured in posters at the college promoting the beautiful no-makeup natural look. Still, by the time she got out of college, feminists were promoting what her Holiness parents and peers had said all along: strong, self-confident women do not need to alter their appearance just to please men, to fit some artificial standard of beauty.

According to the internet, there were lots of women these days who didn't use makeup, and *some* of them must have faces like hers.

In any case, she could live with being "plain." She'd always been "plain," but now the gray hair seemed unjust, and every time she went home made it worse. It wasn't that Mama looked young. She was fifty-nine and even more committed to eschewing vanity than her daughter. But *she* didn't have gray hair! That's what made it so unfair! I'm forty, Angelika told herself. I can accept looking like Mama when I'm fifty-nine, or even having gray hair *then*, but I'm only forty . . . *only* forty! And then, staring at herself in the mirror, grabbing hairs with tweezers and plucking them out of her scalp, she said it out loud: "I look older than her! That's the truth! I'm only forty and I look older than my mother!"

Thrashed, is what her father called the whippings. He was pastor of Shidler Free Methodist Holiness Church in Shidler, Oklahoma, and he had dedicated his life and ministry to upholding the way of holiness so many others had abandoned. So, he had been compelled to thrash his daughter when she sinned, quoting the Scriptures as he lay the leather strap across her bare bottom. There were marks there now. They looked like the stretch marks she'd seen on some women who'd had babies, but they were on her butt not her belly, scars from when he'd gone too far. He'd say it. He'd admit that with a mumbled apology ("Went too far this time, but you drive me to it"). And when she reached puberty he said it was no longer proper for him to gaze upon her nakedness—she had to grant him that much—so he tried turning the whipping duties over to her mother. But Mama wouldn't do it, or couldn't do it, or didn't do it right, so he had to inflict the pain on a different part of her body—usually the palms or backs of her hands, striking them with a bamboo whip he'd bought at the Christian book store, a strip of bamboo with a handle that had some Scripture verse on it. "Withhold not correction from thy child; thou shalt beat him with the rod and deliver his soul from hell."

So, she got whipped for being covetous, for liking clothes or jewelry or glitter or lipstick—things she saw in magazines or on TV or on other girls her age. They were all marks of vanity that led to wantonness and coquetry. But she also got whipped (or thrashed) for *talking back* and for *trying to be funny*. And for *being reckless* (spilling her milk) and for *lying* (saying she got a B instead of a B minus, and then *again* for saying she had just forgotten about the minus) and for *thieving* (taking a snack from the pantry without asking). She got whipped for lots of things, but most of the time the whipping involved slippery slopes. There were lots of slippery slopes, things that might not seem bad in themselves, but what would they lead to? You want to go bowling and it doesn't seem like there's anything wrong with bowling, how is that sinful? But what does it lead to? That's the point. What does it lead to? It's like the women want to wear their skirts above the knees and you think, alright, but then they want them shorter and shorter and pretty soon they won't be wearing anything at all. Do you see, it's a slippery slope and that's why we have to thrash you sometimes because we don't want you sliding down the slope.

Dancing led to sex. Make-up led to harlotry. Bingo led to gambling. Social drinking led to drunkenness. Bowling led to . . . well, she was never sure what bowling led to . . . worldliness and general frivolity most likely . . . but in any case, there were *lots* of slippery slopes. Lots of things that led to other things.

He'd preach about slippery slopes in his sermons and talk about them in his Bible studies. He was very good at finding them but admitted with tremendous humility that he had sometimes been taken in himself. "Twenty years ago women wanted to go out and get the jobs that the men had. And I thought, alright, that's not a problem as long as their children are grown and raised. A woman can be a dentist or even a bank president, I didn't care, I was very liberal. And now look! We've got girl *soldiers*! And the Methodists, the other Methodists not us, are having girl *pastors*. They just decided to ignore the Bible on that one. And young people don't even know what's a man and what's a woman anymore and we're seeing what that means, aren't we? Aren't we finding out what that means? We should have known better! It was a slippery slope, is what it was."

Slippery slopes! Every time he said it, she would smile to herself and think about Billy Booker and the medicine in her closet.

Shidler was about an hour's drive from Bartlesville and as she headed home she had to pass through Pawhuska where, her mother told her, William Booker now managed the Big Boy restaurant on US 60, just past Lynn Avenue. She normally went home twice a month and every single time she would drive right past that Big Boy on the way there and again on the way back. It always gave her a little wince of guilty memory. She'd given it four years of contrition while attending Bartlesville Christian Women's College, and, she thought, that should be enough. Truth be told, she didn't feel all that contrite anymore, but still, there was always just a little wince of guilt on US 60, going both ways, twice a month.

William (Billy) had moved away but now he was back and divorced with kids in some other state. Her mother told her this and even made reference to him as Angelika's "high school sweetheart."

"Oh Mama . . . *chauffeur* is more like it!"

"I always thought there was just a bit more to it than that."

"Well, maybe. Just a little."

"Your father sure did like him. He was planning your wedding. He was going to do it of course, with lots of readings about wives submitting to their husbands. Anyway, he was so disappointed when it didn't work out."

"There wasn't really anything to *not* work out."

"I guess, he just hoped you'd take it to the next level."

Oh, goodness, Angelika thought. Billy would have taken it to the "next level," that's for sure, but not what Daddy was wanting. And, in any case, the reason Mama told her about Billy being back was to *warn* her in case she might stop at the Big Boy sometime by mistake. He hadn't gone into the ministry like he'd said he might. And he was *divorced!*

* * *

Angelika had gotten the pills ten days after the Tulsa trip. They had turned out to be completely unnecessary but Billy Booker had seen her breasts and she knew that once a boy saw your breasts, babies could result. One thing led to another.

The Tulsa trip was organized by the Pawhuska Holiness Youth Fellowship. There weren't enough teenagers at any of the Holiness churches in Shidler or Pawhuska to have a decent youth group, so some of the Wesleyan, CMA, Disciples, and others had combined forces. Daddy was always suspicious of ecumenicity and the Tulsa trip was all about visiting Oral Roberts ministries, which also gave him a caution. "What parents would name their child that? I mean, I guess you can't blame *him*. It was his parents gave him the name, but he could go by another, couldn't he? What's his middle name, is what I want to know." Still, he let his darling daughter go on a bus ride to the big city and that was where she met Billy Booker who was from a Holiness church in Pawhuska.

She didn't even see him on the way there but he sat next to her on the way home. He had been following her around during the day and chatting her up. He had even sat with her at lunch and laughed at things she said. Her father would have whipped her if he had known that, and even her mother had told her boys don't like it when girls try to be funny. But she had thought *he* was funny and she sensed he was just trying to be nice when he laughed at things she said because she knew she wasn't actually clever or witty. He had an oafish face and wasn't very good looking, but you could probably call him cute, or at least cute enough for her, since she was plain. None of the boys at Pawhuska Tabernacle High School had ever even talked to her or so it seemed. Surely that wasn't true but so it seemed. They never talked to her and none of them had ever sat with her at lunch or laughed at things she said.

And when they started on the way home, Billy sat next to her on the bus. He had a blanket big enough for both of them and it was dark. The bus rumbled on for a while as the students chatted noisily with each other, but then things quieted down. Eventually, Mrs. Crumble, the sponsor, went to sleep way up in the front and then Billy put the blanket over both of them and he put his arm around her shoulders and nuzzled her neck and started kissing her. Her heart was racing and she was terrified that someone might see and tell on them. Also she was afraid that she was doing it wrong. She didn't know how to kiss. She *knew* that she didn't know how to kiss, so she thought she was probably doing it wrong. And while she was still worrying about not knowing how to kiss, she felt his hand underneath the blanket rubbing her stomach and then it was rubbing one of her arms and then it was rubbing her chest and, if she hadn't been 100 percent sure whether she was sinning before, she knew she was now.

They went on sinning for another twenty-five minutes and then the bus made a pit stop and she committed the worst sin of her life, what was *still* the worst sin she had ever committed and probably would remain that until the day she died. In the rest room, she stared at herself in the mirror and looked at her chest . . . the hills over which his hands had been roaming. He had been holding them . . . first one, then the other . . . one arm around her shoulders but the other hand free to travel all about underneath the blanket, on top of her shirt . . . his fingers feeling the straps and cups of her thick cotton bra and pushing against the soft flesh that rose above it.

She went into the stall, took off her shirt, took off her bra, and put her shirt back on again. She stuffed the bra into her purse and came out to study her chest in the mirror. You couldn't really tell, not just by looking, especially if it was dark. Not by *looking* . . . but he wouldn't just be looking, would he? . . . surprise! . . . surprise! . . . surprise!

Back on the bus, he sat several inches away from her for the first five minutes, almost hanging over into the aisle until everyone was settled in and Mrs. Crumble (they called her "Grumble") had quit craning her head around, checking to make sure no one was drinking alcohol or fornicating in the aisles. But after she went to sleep, he slid over, put his arm around her shoulders, pulled the blanket up over them, kissed her on the cheek, slid his hand under the blanket and up . . .

"Ahhh!" he gasped, almost too loud, muffled only by her mouth on his. She giggled softly, her lips quivering against his lips. And now his fingers were finding things. "*My God! Oh my God!*" he whispered in her ear.

He liked the surprise! He touched her breasts through her shirt and squeezed them and *played with them* all the way home, his hand under the blanket, on top of her shirt. At one point he started unbuttoning that shirt and she grabbed his hand through the blanket and tried to whisper, "*No! Not that!*" but what she heard come out was, "*No! Not here!*"

When they got back to the Disciples of Christ parking lot, the passengers took turns calling their parents from the church office and Billy had a suggestion. "Tell them we're still on the way back but it'll be another hour . . . hour and a half . . . and that I'll bring you home."

She broke into a sweat while she was on the phone, lying to her mother . . . a harlot in the church office with no bra under her shirt. What a thrashing this could bring! She was so scared . . . so terrified! . . . but when she walked out and saw Billy waiting, looking at her anxiously, she burst into a grin and exclaimed, "*Yes!*" and he whooped with joy or excitement as they ran, skipping, toward his car.

"Where are you two going?" Mrs. Crumble (Grumble) asked.

"It's okay," she said. "My parents said he could bring me home."

She glowered.

"I'm her *cousin!*" Billy exclaimed.

"Oh . . . well . . . then . . . alright . . ."

So many lies! Angelika was laughing as the car pulled out of the church parking lot and she was still snickering ten minutes later when Billy pulled into a shady, dark area of Hensel Park where she had heard bad boys took bad girls. The car had hardly stopped before she opened her door and bounced out, laughing, pulled open the door to the back seat, and climbed in. By the time she'd gotten seated he was already coming in through that same door and climbing on to her lap, facing her, and then, without even kissing her, he started undoing her buttons . . . one, two, three, four . . .

She thought: *I'm going to have naked breasts with a boy! . . . I'm going to have naked breasts with a boy! . . . I'm going to have nake . . .* and then he pulled her shirt open and she saw his face. His eyes were huge and hungry. His mouth gaping open. She had never seen a look like that ever before and she would never, ever forget it. He was looking at *them* . . . like he had never seen anything so . . . *wonderful* . . . she squealed with excitement.

I did, didn't I? she thought now, driving along US 60. I squealed when I saw that look. I actually *squealed.* And she laughed softly, to herself, at the memory.

* * *

Two days later, she had talked to Pastor Harper from the Pawhuska Holiness Youth Fellowship. He had been on the Tulsa trip and seemed *way* cooler than Grumble Crumble. A lot of the girls thought he was cute and half of them were in love with him.

She had been in hell for two days. God! *She was a whore!* And she felt so guilty . . . so terrible. She swore she would never, ever do anything like that ever again. She had prayed and prayed and promised God, never, ever again! No boy or man would ever see her breasts ever again in her entire life . . . well, at least not unless she got married . . . if she even *could* get married now. And she would never even speak to that boy Billy Booker again . . . never see him or go on any more trips if there was any chance that he might even possibly be there . . . or *anything*. So that was all settled and over and done with.

But the consequences? *That* was what she needed to know now. Was she going to hell? And what about poor Billy? Was *he* going to hell too, for something she had done? It hadn't been his fault, since he was a boy. It was *her* fault. She was the one who tempted him, arousing the lust that boys can't help or control. Loose women did things like that and it wasn't the boy's fault. Like poor David in the Bible who saw some girl taking a bath on the roof of her house, of all places. It wasn't *his* fault what happened next, and of course God had to kill their baby to punish them.

In any case, she wasn't going to mention Billy to Pastor Harper or tell him any details . . . nothing about *who* or *where* or *when.* She just needed to know if she was going to hell. And, if so, could she get saved all over again? Or did she maybe need to get rebaptized? She could do that if she had to, as long as her father didn't know (because he'd want to know *why*).

"So . . . I'm just asking . . ." she said to Pastor Harper, who actually *was* kind of cute, "and I'm not saying it's for me . . . it's just a question . . . like an *academic* question . . . and some of us were talking and we were just curious and wondering . . . I mean, a whole bunch of us were wondering, not just me . . . do you go to hell . . . does a *girl* go to hell for just . . . you know . . . above the waist? . . . just above the waist?"

"No," he said immediately. "No she does not. Not if she believes in Jesus Christ, who died for her. It is a sin, but she can repent and pray and be forgiven."

"Okay."

She looked around and wondered if she could leave.

"Is that all you wanted to know?"

"Un-huh," she nodded . . . he *was* cute . . . and then she thought that she really should say something else.

"Is it a sin?" she asked, apparently unaware that he had just said it was.

"Yes. Yes, it is. And you have to think, would a godly man want to marry you if he knew you had allowed another to take that pleasure in your nakedness?"

Pleasure in my nakedness, she thought, rolling the words around in her head . . . that's what the bad boy Billy had been doing all right . . . the boy she was never going to see again . . . he had been taking *pleasure in her nakedness* . . . a *lot* of pleasure! . . . but it was wrong! . . . *very, very wrong!* . . . and now she looked at Pastor Harper again and tried to focus.

"Is it . . . in the Bible?" she asked, not really wanting to know, but just to stay a little longer so he wouldn't think "going to hell" had been her only concern. And because she had blushed before and stammered so much, she felt like she had to let him know it really was just an *academic* question, just something that a whole group of them had all been wondering about because they wanted to understand the Bible and God and stuff better.

"Well, that's interesting," he replied, settling in for a longer discussion and relishing the chance to enlighten her. "There's nothing about that part of the body . . . the, uh, bosom . . . in the Bible *per se* . . . except, well, the Song of Songs, which is about marriage . . ."

Some of the girls on the Tulsa trip said he was really smart and used words that were Latin or French or something . . . words like *per se* . . .

it sounded like French but it might be Latin . . . like *à la carte,* which meant ice cream or something . . . he wasn't married so he had probably never taken pleasure in anybody's nakedness, unless maybe he had and then repented, and she wondered if he ever thought about it . . . taking pleasure in someone's nakedness . . . and she also wondered if he knew that all the girls were in love with him and what did he think about *that*? . . . and . . . what did he think about *her?* . . . was he wondering right now if maybe it *wasn't* just an academic question and if she really had done something . . . somewhere . . . with someone . . . above the waist stuff . . . with *pleasure in nakedness* . . . and was he thinking about that part of her body . . . the, uh, bosom . . . and wondering whether her bosom was *per se* or not . . . the ones in the Bible might not be, but maybe hers was . . . she hoped it was . . . Billy probably thought it was . . . but he was terrible and bad and she wasn't even going to think about him anymore . . . or about anyone ever again taking pleasure in her nakedness . . . .

But the pastor was still talking . . .

". . . in the general area of lust and arousal. So one might even make a case that viewing or touching a woman's chest would not have to be sinful *per se* but the problem is what it causes, inspiring lust and arousing concupiscence, and also what might follow, because one thing leads to another."

"Like a slippery slope?" she asked, picking up on his last five words.

"Yes!" he responded, very impressed with her, and she smiled and felt proud of herself. "Yes, that's exactly it. The way of holiness is like a narrow path and one does not usually leap into the pit of immorality like jumping off a cliff. One *slides* into that pit, slowly but surely, doing what might seem only a little bit wrong at first. But it makes no difference whether you leap or slide. If you end up in the pit it's all the same."

Daddy had been a youth pastor once. A long time ago, before she was born, George Blitch had been youth pastor at some Methodist church (a regular one). Maybe he'd been kind of like Pastor Harper, though it was awfully hard to imagine half the girls being in love with him. Mama was, though. Well, sort of. She had been in the youth group and now she would talk about how she had a "girlish crush" on him even then, but of course he was all respectful and proper, a very godly man, which was one of the things she had liked about him. Three months after she graduated, he had asked permission to court her and a year later they were married. It was hard to imagine Daddy that young, but of course, knowing Daddy, he would have been proper in his courting.

* * *

Four days after talking to Pastor Harper, Angelika told Billy that he had called her breasts "slippery slopes" and Billy thought that this was the funniest thing he had ever heard.

"I like 'em slippery!" he exclaimed and that made her giggle.

She was in the back seat of his car and he was taking pleasure in her above-the-waist nakedness. They were at Hensel Park but her parents thought they were at a Pawhuska Holiness Youth Fellowship discipleship event. Billy had come by the house to pick her up and had come inside to meet her parents (father). That was when he made a little speech.

"Pastor Blitch, I understand that you might be concerned about your daughter riding with me, unchaperoned as it is, so I just want to tell you that I believe it will be best for her to sit in the back seat while I'm driving and that way there will be no appearance of anything improper, you know, I mean the appearance of her being with a young man of her age and without a chaperone. It is what I would want if I were a godly father of a godly family."

George Whitfield Blitch had been impressed by this and told the young man William so. William responded with deep gratitude and respect and said that he hoped to be a pastor of a Holiness church himself someday, if God would grant him the grace, and he knew that these discipleship events would help him to prepare for such a calling, just as they would help his daughter to discern God's call on her life. At this, George Whitfield Blitch was almost overcome and said that she certainly could use some guidance in that regard, she certainly could. And then, when he turned about in the entryway, Billy had suddenly reached over and grabbed her breasts with both of his hands, squeezing them, and then he quickly let go and folded his hands in front of his body again just as Daddy turned back around. She was standing there completely flushed, almost panting, as Daddy opened the door and sent them on their way. *That* was what she remembered more often than anything else. That one unforgettable moment had actually been more exciting and more fun than anything they ever did at the park. And all these years later she was so ashamed to admit: that one moment in the entryway (behind Daddy's back) was the single best memory of her youth and adolescence.

The Pawhuska Holiness Youth Fellowship met every Thursday for Discipleship Training. Billy and Angelika supposedly went every week but never attended a single class. She would laugh and giggle as he chauffeured her to the park, giving him orders from the back seat like a rich woman in a limousine, and then when they got there, he would get in back and make out with her for two hours, kissing and petting and huffing and puffing and taking off her shirt and fumbling with her bra. He called her "Angie" and sang the chorus from a Rolling Stones song to her (*"An-an-gee! . . . An-an-an-gee! . . ."*). And he said his second favorite song was the Doublemint Gum commercial and he would sing it too ("Double my pleasure, double my fun") and ask her, Do you know who I think of whenever I hear it? . . . and she would giggle and ask *Me*? . . . and then he said, Guess what the *double* part means? and she giggled some more and thought that it was the single wittiest thing that anybody had ever said.

Teenagers! . . . . Angelika thought now, passing the sign for the Pawhuska city limits . . . so silly . . . so immature.

He called her breasts "slippery slopes" and one time he brought baby oil and made them really super slippery. And another time, a little packet of honey from a restaurant.

"Do you think they're *per se*?" she asked him and he assured her that they were. "You have a pair of *per se* titties!" he told her. "That's what you have . . . *per* se titties!" And she blushed and giggled, even though he had cussed.

Twelve Thursdays and then the year wound to an end. Their tongues had tangled all around in each other's mouths and their bodies had squished together a lot but . . . thinking back now . . . it had been mostly above the waist stuff. Mostly. My pants stayed on, she thought. She could be proud of that. They were frequently open, unbuckled, unzipped, and he did get his hand down there. But her pants never came off completely.

And he had put *her* hand on the front of *his* pants. He did that over and over and over again until she finally gave up and just left it there, her fingers sprawled across the big lump. And wow! did she remember *that* . . . the lump in his pants! . . . underneath her hand, her fingers and . . . oh! . . . one time he wore khakis and she saw a wet spot near his pocket "Did something leak?" she asked, and he said, you know how girls get wet down there, the same thing happens with boys, and she had believed him. It was years before she realized what had really happened, but by then she was old enough not to be disgusted, just mildly amused. It happened every week probably; she only saw it when he wore khakis.

Twelve Thursdays in the spring of 1977. High school was about to end for both of them; she'd spend the summer at home, but he was going into the Army and he told her, what with all the wars, he might not ever see her again, he might even get killed. He told her to think about, no pressure, but just *think about* maybe giving him a special graduation present that he would remember for the rest of his life. She said she needed to remain pure and he said there were other things she could do. She didn't even want to think about what those things might be. So there was no graduation present but he did tell her, on the last Thursday, that he would remember her and her slippery slopes for the rest of his life. He would never forget her . . . or *them!*

And then he was gone.

She looked out the window at the Big Boy as she passed it. Halfway home. It was almost exactly halfway between the school in Bartlesville and her parents' house in Shidler.

Divorced. Two kids somewhere.

No one else had ever called her "Angie" . . . not before . . . or since.

* * *

Bartlesville Christian Women's College had been like four years of penance. She had gotten right with God and repented of those twelve weeks of sin. There was chapel every day and a revival every semester and many of the preachers were quite persuasive. At first she just had to repent of what she'd done with Billy but then later she had to repent of not really being sufficiently sorry for it, of sometimes remembering it fondly (at least some of it), of almost (but only almost) wishing she could do it again. Every revival found her at the mourner's bench, sobbing and pleading with God to take her back and make her holy, *really* holy, so that she would *hate* who she had been and what she had done.

But despite the repentance for old sins and a dearth of opportunity for new ones, she kept taking the unnecessary pills. She had gotten them ten days after the Tulsa trip, three days after the first time they didn't go to Discipleship Training. She had driven to the place her father called Planned Infanticide in Bartlesville and they had given her a three-month supply, no questions asked, with absolute assurance that, since she was eighteen, it was *against the law* for them or anyone else to tell her parents. And she hid them in that little cubbyhole in her closet. Every morning, she would hold one in the palm of her hand and look at it and think about the bamboo switch from the Christian bookstore and say, "Here, Daddy . . . look at this . . . I got it at the abortion store . . . and that godly young man named Billy Booker grabbed my tits behind your back and he puts his hand down my pants when you think we're at the Bible study."

Now, at the women's college, she hid the pills from her roommates and still took one every day. There was no reason to do so except . . . *she liked taking them!* And four times a year she would make another little trip and pick up another batch, enough to last three more months.

Sometime after talking with Pastor Harper she had read the entire Song of Songs to find out what it said about bosoms, which wasn't much, just that some are like towers and some are like grapes and some are like roes and some are just walls. Basically, it was just an old-fashioned way of talking bra size, no doubt something boys came up with. She wasn't sure what roes were but they sounded better than grapes or towers or walls and so that's what she decided she had. Maybe roes were some kind of flower, or maybe it was supposed to be rows, like two of a kind. She knew the King James was the only Bible God liked, but it had a lot of weird words in it. There weren't supposed to be any errors, but some things were misspelled: "colour" instead of "color"; "favour" instead of "favor." Maybe "roes" instead of "rows."

Her father used the phrase "roes and hinds" sometimes in sermons or prayers that she didn't understand. She couldn't remember anything he'd actually said about "roes and hinds," just that he used the phrase. Once she found out that "roes" were breasts, it seemed pretty obvious what "hinds" would be and so, for a few years she had thought "roes and hinds" meant "breasts and butts" and that it was a biblical way to talk about "T and A" without cussing. At forty now, of course, she knew better, but she had smiled perversely a few weeks ago when she was home and Daddy was saying, "God keeps his eye on the roes and hinds and is always looking out for them."

Anyway, back in college she had decided she had roes and she was kind of proud of them even though that, too, was sinful. And finally one time a teacher at the college said the bosom verses in the Song of Songs meant no one was supposed to see your breasts until your wedding night, and that was all those verses meant—the point probably being that your husband wasn't supposed to know if you had grapes or towers or roes or walls until then, which might be a good idea. And then he would be the only man in the world to have ever seen them. This interpretation was probably right because the teacher got paid to know these things but the main thing she got out of it was that, in her case, it was too late. She had already sinned so much that she'd ruined herself.

Most of the girls at Bartlesville Christian Women's College were virgins and those who weren't had done the ceremony to become "renewed virgins," which was when Christ restored your virginity in a spiritual sense, and you could actually say you were a virgin and not be lying. You could even tell a boyfriend or potential husband that you were a virgin and it would be the spiritual truth. She wondered if you could do that for just above the waist, so that her husband, if she found one, would never have to know. She did know that some of the girls had messed around with boys even more than she had, and a few of them even had boyfriends they might see now and then and do some of the "other things" to which Billy had alluded. They'd have to repent afterwards but they said it was worth it. They were all prettier than her, except for the fat ones. In any case, there were no boys at Bartlesville Christian Women's College so if you really wanted to be holy (and she did), that was a help. No kissing. No dating. And absolutely no need to keep taking the pills—but she kept taking them anyway.

She didn't give them up until she started teaching at Bartlesville Elementary, first grade, a public school. She was twenty-two and had gotten over her daddy issues. That was all in the past and not even worth thinking about. So . . . the pills. The current supply ran out and she just didn't get any more. Now that she was out in the world, she realized how drab she truly was . . . how plain . . . how unappealing. The whole idea of birth control pills was comically or tragically ridiculous. She had no life outside the school other than a trip every other week to visit her parents in Shidler. Most of the teachers were women and the only men were married—except for Lawrence, who was black, and Mr. Ansel (third grade) who she kind of figured was gay.

"Oh Gosh! I bet it was him!" she suddenly thought. The one who gave her the present! That would make sense in so many ways!

In any case, one thing was sure: it had been a long time since she had inspired any lust or aroused any concupiscence in anyone . . . anyone at all.

She invested herself in the children—completely! They weren't just her job, they were her life. She helped them to learn some arithmetic and language, a little reading and spelling, life skills like counting money and telling time. But most of all, she helped them to feel good about themselves, and to plan ahead, and to do their best, and to keep trying, and to believe they could do and be just about anything. They couldn't pronounce her name but they all seemed to like her and she liked them. She *loved* them.

She thought about them and worried about them and prayed for them every night—many of them by name. And she would tell Daddy this. When she came home twice a month, she would tell him what she had done for the children—how she'd made up games and created posters and helped this one learn his numbers (when he was way behind) and another one to feel so proud of the pictures she drew that now she would share them with the whole class. "But what about their *souls*?" he wanted to know. He didn't like that she was teaching in a *public* school. He didn't like that she was just doing what any pagan could do, teaching children to read and write and draw pictures when the Lord was about to return and they would all end up in hell. Imagine that a house is on fire and you are going around straightening pictures on the wall instead of shouting the alarm. She was *wasting time* he told her one weekend . . . *wasting time!*

* * *

She was home for three days before she took out the present. She had thought about just sticking it in the closet, in the little space where the pills had been. But then she decided to tell her mother. So she got the little present out of her suitcase and told her mother about the Secret Santa program. She had gotten Mrs. Garner's name. That was the art teacher, so she went to the Bartlesville Art Museum and got her a mug that had a pretty design on it and said, "*earth* without *art* is just *eh.*"

"I didn't know if she'd like it or not, and maybe she goes to the art museum all the time and already has it, but at least I tried, and I wrapped it up and put it in the lounge as her gift from a Secret Santa. And I picked up the present someone had left for me—a small box—and I took it home and unwrapped it . . . *and this is what they gave me!*"

She hadn't wanted to cry but she choked on those last words and started sobbing as she pulled the box out of the bag she'd stuck it in . . . a ten-dollar box of L-Oreal Paris Superior Preference Self-Styling Hair Dye (chestnut brown).

"Oh!" he mother gasped. "That's . . . that's so *mean!*"

"No, Mama!" she sobbed. "No, it's not! I wish it was. I wish someone was being mean, but I don't think they are. I think they're trying to be *nice.*"

"It's an odd way of showing it."

"It's like the Scope commercial, Mama, don't you remember? You give your boss a bottle of mouthwash because no one wants to tell him he has bad breath! That's supposed to be a nice thing to do, but do you think there was ever a single person anywhere in the world who liked getting an anonymous bottle of Scope for a present?"

"Who would do such a thing?"

"There's a teacher at the school . . . I think he's the kind of man who notices women's hairstyles and things . . ."

"You mean like a *fetish*?"

"No, just the kind of man who notices those things, and he's very nice. Maybe it was him, but I don't know."

"It was a dumb thing to do."

"I know it was, Mama, but that's not the point."

"And what is the point?"

And then she broke down completely, bending over at the waist and *bawling* like she hadn't done since she was a little girl.

"They feel *sorry* for me, Mama!" she sobbed. "They feel *sorry* for me! Because they think I'm pathetic! And I *am* pathetic! And if the nice people feel sorry for me, what do you think the mean ones do? *Laugh at me?*"

"It's not as bad as you think."

"You can say that!" she erupted angrily. "Go look in the mirror, Mama! What did *you* look like when *you* were forty? Go look in the mirror! How many hairs did you pull out today?"

"Not a one," she said calmly. "But I won't talk to you like this. I'm going to leave you for a little bit. I need to make a phone call. And then I'll be back."

Angelika sat on the bed and cried and then forced herself to stop and got some Kleenex and wiped her face and blew her nose and sat back down. And then she started crying again. She had to stop feeling sorry for herself but how could she when *other people felt sorry for her!*

Her mother didn't come back for twenty minutes and by then she was under control. She'd gotten up and washed her face and decided the matter was settled. There was nothing more to say, but then Mama came in carrying a small cloth bag. It was a knock-off on those expensive Vera Bradley bags and looked like one of them but had probably come from Family Dollar.

She seated herself a few feet from the bed where Angelika was sitting, no longer sniveling. She took a little jar of Vaseline out of the bag and wiped some of it on a Kleenex.

"You never look at me, Angelika," she said.

"Yes I do, Mama. What do you mean? I'm looking at you now."

"You never *look* at me!"

She wiped the Kleenex across her cheek and held it up. It was brown . . . tan . . . completely smeared as if with paint.

"Mama!" she gasped. "What's that?"

"Poor dear! Are you really forty and you don't know what *foundation* is?"

"Yes! I know what foundation is! I'm not *stupid,* Mama. It's . . . is it makeup?"

"Not really, but kind of. Well, I guess, technically, it is."

"Mama! You're wearing makeup! *What?!* What does Daddy say?"

"Silly! I hide it under the sink in the bathroom. Just about every woman in the church wears foundation. He thinks it's what female skin looks like."

"Mama!"

"Oh, honey, your father's such a good man, but he *is* a bit of a fool. You know *that,* don't you? And a woman can't be married to a man like that for forty years without learning a few tricks."

Tricks, she thought.

"But . . . he'd have to notice it some time."

"Did you? You never look at me. Why would he? Well, alright, one time, he saw something and asked if it was Clearasil and I said, kind of, just a little skin problem, it'll go away, don't worry."

"Oh, Mama," she gasped . . . and then she giggled.

Her mother reached in the bag and pulled out a tube of something tan, and handed it to Angelika.

"What does that say?"

She read the label, "Cover Girl Foundation Undetectable"

"Did you get that? Undetectable!"

"But if its undetectable, what's the point?"

"Heavens! How did you get to be forty? Keep reading."

"instant dewiness leaves your face looking toned, smooth and natural"

And then her mother pulled another bottle out of the bag.

"This is called *primer.*"

And another.

"This is called *concealer.*"

And a jar.

"Creams are more natural than powders. This is *blush*, for the cheekbones and the bridge of your nose."

"Mama. I can't believe this."

"Oh! I've been a bad mother I guess . . . I just thought . . . I thought you didn't care. I mean, in college you were all about the 'natural look.' Ironically, that's what they call this stuff. It's a whole line of makeup: *the natural look*. No matter. We'll get down to it tomorrow. They sell all this at Belle Vita."

"Mama . . ."

"Now, I want you to toss that hair dye in the garbage."

"Okay," she said and thought, or maybe I'll just keep it in the closet.

"Because you would never be able to do a decent job by yourself and tomorrow we're going to Bartlesville. To the Belle Vita Beauty Salon. I just called them and they've got no business because of the holidays. I've been going there once a month for twenty-two years and it's time you found out why my hair's not gray."

"*Mama!* . . . but what if? . . . doesn't he know? . . . *dying your hair?!* . . . I mean . . . that's big!"

She had heard it so many times:

Only whores dye their hair . . . the epitome of vanity and the Bible forbids it . . . why change what God gave you? . . . do you know better than God? . . . only whores . . . first you change your hair color and then what? . . . what does it lead to? . . . that's what I want to know . . . what does it lead to? . . . these women who get their hair dyed and they get phony bosoms because they don't like the way God made them . . . and then they get their face all lifted and next thing you know they decide they want to be men . . . or the men would rather be women . . . it's all a slippery slope, is what it is . . . only whores . . .

"For real?" she asked. "Doesn't he notice?"

"The first time my hair was worse than yours and I was terrified. I waited for him to be out of town for three days and then I went, hoping by the time he got back maybe he wouldn't remember what I looked like. Do you know what he said?"

"What?"

"I worried. Oh, I worried about it. And prayed . . . for three days. Then he came home and he didn't say anything. I'd had it styled and colored . . . *styled*, did you hear me? . . . and *colored!* . . . well, he didn't say anything and I just waited . . . waited for the boom to fall. He'd never hit me, but I figured this was what would do it. Then finally at dinner, he was just staring at me, and do you know what he said?"

"What?"

"He said, 'Did you get your hair cut?'"

Angelika laughed out loud.

"So I said, 'Yes I did, dear, thanks for noticing.' And I've been back once a month ever since."

"Why didn't you ever tell me this?"

"Like I said, I thought you didn't care. Also, I couldn't risk you saying anything."

"I wouldn't have."

"In an outburst or something. Besides, I thought you'd figure it out for yourself. You were pretty good at tricking him sometimes."

"What do you mean?" she asked.

But Mama just shook her head.

* * *

They got into the beauty parlor at 9:00 AM the next morning, after the hour-long drive from Shidler through Pawhuska and right back to Bartlesville, from whence she had come four days before. Angelika's mother had simply moved her monthly appointment up a week and the beauticians were delighted to make time for her daughter. They did not actually have a dearth of appointments "because of the holidays" as Mama had indicated—if anything they were busier than usual on that account. But they went out of their way to accommodate 1) a longtime customer, and 2) a potential future longtime customer. Three women were working at Belle Vita that morning and one man named Tony. He smiled when Mama told them Angelika was a teacher at Bartlesville Elementary and said he knew another one of the teachers there. Angelika thought she could guess which one but didn't say anything. Bartlesville was not a big city after all, not like Tulsa, and it was possible for people to know other people for all kinds of reasons.

They spent three hours on her hair and nails and makeup. Nobody had ever trimmed her nails before and they looked the best they had ever looked. She didn't get them polished of course, because *only whores . . .*

Tony not only put makeup on her but told her about each product, one by one, and showed her exactly how to use it and how not to overuse it especially if you didn't want it to be showy. She wouldn't look like she had any makeup on at all; it would just look natural but that was the whole point, Tony said, because natural doesn't mean "looking like you've just been attacked by a dozen crows." She felt stupid, like this was what they usually did with fourteen-year-olds, but then the women all joked about her getting the Shidler Holiness Special because apparently there were half a dozen women from the Blitch church who went there, sometimes with Mama. They all got treatments that their pastor wouldn't notice, indeed that their husbands might not notice, though, as it turned out, the husbands didn't care.

Her hair was styled in what they called a "shoulder bob" that wasn't too different from how she usually wore it except that now it actually had shape and what Tony called "bounce"—instead of just hanging there like "some dead animal squatted on your head." And they colored it—a chestnut brown tint similar to her natural color but "richer and livelier" (Tony said). And, of course, there was no more gray.

She looked at herself in the mirror and could not believe what she saw. She was almost pretty! Almost. But she couldn't believe Daddy wouldn't scream when she walked in the house. Scream and run to get the bamboo switch that he hadn't used for more than twenty years but (she assumed) he had hidden away somewhere just in case it was needed. But Mama assured her, "He knows we're getting haircuts. We just went to 'the barber' is what I tell him . . . the 'lady barber'!"

But it was Mama who screamed when they were driving back through Pawhuska and Angelika pulled off US 60 just past Lynn Avenue and into the Big Boy parking lot.

"*No-o!* Angelika! No! You will not go in there!"

"I'm just curious, Mama . . . and he might not even be here."

"Well, I'm not going in. I am not."

"Sit in the car then," she replied, getting out of the driver's seat. She headed for the restaurant and didn't even look back. Inside, a pretty high school girl greeted her and asked how many were in her party. Only then did she turn around and see Mama climbing out of the car.

"Two. But it will be a moment."

She scanned the restaurant . . . and saw him . . . in back by a door talking to someone in the kitchen . . . standing sideways to her. He was chubby and halfway bald, still a little oafish looking, wearing a white shirt with a conservative necktie . . . dress shoes . . . khaki pants . . . *don't think about that!*

Her mother came in and a less-pretty high school girl walked them to a booth and gave them menus. She took their drink orders for two sweet teas and departed. Angelika was looking at Billy when he turned. Their eyes met and she looked down at the menu, but she could tell he was walking toward them. She studied the menu . . . and suddenly he was there.

"Angie Blitch! I don't know if you recognize me, but . . ."

She looked up and smiled.

"I recognize you, Billy."

"Billy! No one's called me *Billy* for a long time."

"No one's called me *Angie.*"

"No? Well, *Angelika* . . ."

"I didn't say not to."

Now he was flustered.

"Oh . . . okay . . . and this is your mother, right?"

"It is. Mama, do you remember Billy Booker from the Youth Fellowship?"

"Of course I do," she said coldly.

"It's good to see you again, Mrs. Blitch," he said, though he had never met her and was seeing her for the first time. "I trust your husband is well."

"Still thundering."

"That he is. I hear now and then. We get folks from Shidler of course. Shidler, Pershing, Wynona, Burbank. And, Angie, I have heard that you are a schoolmarm now, is that true?"

"It is. Seventeen years at Bartlesville Elementary. I teach first grade."

"When I heard that, I thought . . . *yes!* . . . she would be so good at that! It just seemed right, you know."

"It did?"

"And is it the most important job in the world? It is, I think. It is the most important job in the world."

"Well, I like it, most of the time."

"Okay, I'm going to move on and leave you to your lunch. But I just want to say, I am glad you stopped in. I had hoped you would. I mean, I thought about calling when I moved back here, but I didn't want to be forward, and I won't be now . . . just . . . I want to say . . . it is good to see you. The years have been good to you and I hope you know that you have the most important job in the world. I am very proud of you!"

He moved on, as he had promised, just as their teas were delivered.

"So!" her mother said. "We see what has become of our sweet Billy!"

"Oh, Mama! Don't be mean! So he lost his hair and got a belly. He's forty years old!"

"That's not what I mean. And *he is divorced!*"

"I'm not marrying him, Mama."

"I should hope not!"

She paused a moment and then resumed. "And he kept . . . well, you know . . ."

"What?"

"You don't know?"

"What?"

"Oh heavens, Angelika! He kept looking at your *chest!*"

"He did?"

"He most certainly did! Here you are with a new hair-do, and *that's* what he wanted to look at!"

7

Jasper Gets a Hobby

He was definitely heading toward them. One of the bums from the east side of the park. Roberta glanced at the tables and saw the young couple was still there—a man in his twenties and someone who was probably his wife (though who knew, these days?). Otherwise, Mrs. Gibson, Shondra's mother, was the only other adult in the area.

It was awkward but she decided to ask the man if he could stick around a little longer. She pointed to the approaching stranger, still fifty yards away, but heading right toward them . . . probably harmless, but Mr. . . . ? . . . I'm sorry, what was your name again? . . . oh yes, Taylor . . . Mr. Taylor? . . . if you could just? . . . for the girls?

It was the first Sunday in March and Girl Scout Troop 2770 had set up two tables in Algonkian Park to sell cookies. Roberta Blankenship was the troop leader and she was the one who had thought this might be a pleasant and potentially profitable spot for cookie sales on a Sunday afternoon. Other troops were set up outside grocery stores and strip malls. The park was indeed more pleasant, but apparently the day was not going to be profitable. Only a handful of folks had wandered by, though about half of these had yielded to the allure of impulse buying, charmed no doubt by the undeniable cuteness of ten-year-old girls in Scout uniforms, laughing and playing in a sun-drenched tract of the grassy woodlands. Eight girls had come out and there were currently two at each table, the other four chasing each other around the trees, playing some sort of game. They wanted to go over to the Volcano Water Park and jump around in the sprinklers but they were in uniform and no one had brought swimsuits. There were more tables and chairs in the van but they wouldn't be needed. There just weren't a lot of people in the park today and the cookie sales would be disappointing.

Right now the Taylors (if they were a couple with a shared name) were the only customers and they'd gotten one box each of four different varieties. Mr. Taylor was no great physical specimen and probably did not relish the idea of being an impromptu bodyguard for two women and eight little girls, but he couldn't really say no in front of the third woman, who was probably his wife or girlfriend or at least potentially one of those. Terry and Shondra had just finished selling the cookies to the maybe-Taylors while, at the other table, Petra had given up on cookies long ago and was teaching Peggy Thatcher how to paint kindness stones. She was quite the artist and had finished three of them: two ladybugs and a sailboat. Peggy's rocks were just rainbow stripes, not pictures of anything recognizable but still pretty and Roberta hoped that the Taylors wouldn't think anything specific was meant by the rainbow design. The girls were only ten.

In retrospect, she should have had a father come with them, but she had thought the park would be more crowded and then there would have been safety in numbers. Besides, this park did have a pretty good reputation. Not many coloreds, and the bums hung out way over on the east side, down by the river. They probably slept under the bridge every night after spending whatever they'd earned on booze after a hard day of begging. God knows what they ate. Or where they used the bathroom. Well, the park did have restrooms—so maybe . . . .

What do you call them these days? "Bum" was probably not PC . . . but what? . . . hobo? . . . tramp? . . . derelict?. . . vagabond? . . . domecilically challenged bohemians?

Well, it didn't matter because this particular whatever-you-called-them was close enough now to speak to her but he kept coming closer rather than calling from afar. Roberta thought about the lepers in the Bible who were supposed to yell, "Unclean! Unclean!" when anyone got within ten or twenty yards of them, so you could give them a broad circle and not be infected. They knew better than to just walk right up to you. Unless you were Jesus, she supposed. They could walk right up to him. But Jesus wasn't here and this unwashed free spirit seemed intent on making *her* acquaintance.

He was unshaven with wild, untamed hair tumbling over his ears and collar. Six feet tall and dressed in clothes that had perhaps never been laundered: jeans and a nondescript sweatshirt, the latter visible through an orange plaid flannel shirt that hung loosely over his body like a jacket. There was what looked like a stocking cap sticking out of one of his pockets but now, five yards away, he reached into his other pocket and extracted a relatively clean five dollar bill.

"Good morning, Ma'am. Have you got any of those Tagalongs? Or Samoas?"

* * *

The State of Virginia had enacted a bottle bill in 2012 after being rated one of the worst states in the US for both recycling and litter. Jasper had found spots where discarded bottles or cans tended to accumulate (along roadsides, picnic areas, anywhere teenagers gathered for outdoor parties) and it wasn't difficult to come up with five dollars' worth in a twenty-four-hour period. That was currently enough for a "footlong" at the Subway across from Algonkian Park, conveniently located next to a 7-Eleven that took the bottles. But he'd had a sandwich just yesterday and the day before that he'd eaten a really big meal at an Applebee's courtesy of his friend Mickey from the auto shop. Mickey was one of his only friends from before, and they had lunch together every Friday at an actual restaurant—almost anywhere with outdoor seating since it was still a little cold to be washing in the river and he might not have been welcome indoors. In any case, he could probably get by today with just a box of cookies, or maybe he and his friend Ed could pool some afternoon bottle money and get a sandwich to split this evening. Toffee liked the Tagalongs, and Taffy, the Samoas. He figured he'd get one of those today and the other in a week. He'd only eat a couple—cookies were probably bad for the heart—but then he could pass the box around down by the water when his friends gathered to hear one of his stories.

He was completing his purchase, one box of Tagalongs from two lovely young ladies in green and white uniforms when he glanced over at the next table and saw the round rock painted to look like a big, round ladybug. He lurched to attention, startled as though lightning had struck the heart whose health he was sometimes committed to protecting.

"That . . . that rock!" he exclaimed, hurrying to the table in a manner that put all of the adults on red alert. Then he saw that there were two of them. Two ladybug rocks, plus another rock with a sailboat, and a couple with rainbows. He pointed at one of the ladybugs. "Are you selling these? How much are they?" He had no money, but could return the cookies. Toffee and Taffy liked ladybugs. If they were here, they would beg and plead for these rocks with ladybugs on them. One time they had caught real ladybugs in the garden and kept them in a jar with holes in the lid. That didn't turn out so well, but they also had ladybug pillows, and matching ladybug sheets on their twin beds, and ladybug curtains.

"It's not for sale," the little girl said. She had dark brown hair, like Toffee, but also brown skin, light brown, not Hispanic, but maybe mixed. "It's not for sale, but you can have it."

"No. Oh, no, I wouldn't want you to do that." Jasper never accepted handouts. Someday he was going to start paying for the weekly lunches with Mickey and keep on doing it until they were even. "You don't have to do that. I won't let you give it to me for free. I want to buy it."

"Not allowed," she said. "They're kindness stones. Do you know what those are?"

"No. No, I don't."

"Kindness stones are rocks that get painted pretty and then we hide them around the world. We put them in parks and places so people can find them and be happy. No one is ever allowed to sell them or buy them."

"I never heard of such a thing! They must take a lot of time. Do they? Are they a lot of work?"

"No. Painting them isn't a lot of work. It's just fun. But *getting the rocks* . . . that's the hard part!"

"Ah!"

"Look," she said. "See, the rocks have to be all smooth . . . round and smooth all over . . . and also kind of small. You can do bigger ones but small is better."

"They're river rocks."

"I don't know what they are, but I have to look for the rocks and that's the hard part."

"So then you get the rocks . . . and you paint them . . . and . . . you just give them away . . . you just put them places . . . ."

"Yup. Just put them on the ground or under a bench or on a table or wherever. Then people find them and smile or pick them up or just look at them or maybe they take them home."

"It's okay to just *take* them?"

"Sure. If you see one and you want it, you just take it and it's yours. But then if you get tired of it you take it someplace and leave it for someone else."

"What if I kept it forever? Would that be greedy?"

"No," she giggled. "I don't think so. Maybe you could paint one of your own to make up for it, and leave that one for somebody else to find."

"I'm not an artist like you."

"I'm not an artist," the other girl chimed in. "Look at mine, they're just stripes. Petra's the artist and she does bugs and boats and kittens and things . . . flowers and clovers . . . I just do stripes."

"I like yours!" Jasper said. "I like the stripes! They're like a rainbow."

"Thank you. They're not as good as Petra's."

"Oh! Is it a contest? I didn't know it was a contest!"

"It's not!" she said. "It's not a contest, but she's just a better artist. Everyone knows that."

"I think that if someone is walking through the woods and sees one of your rainbow rocks, they will definitely smile and pick it up and maybe take it home. They might even keep it forever."

"Oh! Do you think? I hope so."

"I think these are great," Jasper said. "I like all of them but most of all I would like a ladybug. Still, the thing is, even though you said I could have it, that's not how it's supposed to work, is it? Maybe if you hid it some place and I *found* it, that would be better. I could just be walking along and find it, you know. And then I could pick it up."

"Okay!" she said, and jumped up. She took one of the rocks and ran to the trees where the other girls had been chasing each other and walked around for a while and then came back.

"That one's hidden," she said. "But you better be quick or somebody else will get it."

"You didn't hide it very hard?"

"No, it's an easy one."

Clutching his Tagalongs, Jasper walked away from the tables, where Mrs. Blankenship and Mrs. Gibson were still eyeing him a bit suspiciously. The Taylors, however, had decided it was safe to move on. He walked over to the trees where Petra had been and walked about underneath them, scanning the ground like a kid on an Easter egg hunt. It wasn't quite as easy as she had implied. He walked about looking and looking, and then, sure enough, after about five minutes, he saw it: the little colored rock with a ladybug lying between two roots at the base of one of the trees.

He grabbed it up and emerged from the small copse to see the Scouts at their tables. They had no customers at the moment. Petra and Peggy were painting rocks. The other two girls were sitting at the cookie table talking with some of their idle friends who were now standing by the table with them, bored. He heard one of the girls say she wanted to paint rocks but Mrs. Gibson said there weren't any more. Then they asked if they could go to the water park because nobody wanted any cookies.

As he was leaving, he caught the brown girl's eye and held up the ladybug stone.

"Look what I found under the trees!"

"That's a nice one," she said, smiling.

"It makes me happy," he replied and dropped it into his pocket. Then he headed over to the east side of the park to share a story and some cookies with his friends.

* * *

Exactly one week later, Troop 2770 was back, hoping for better luck. Roberta Blankenship had gotten permission to set up in the area every Sunday of the month and, even though that now seemed like a bad idea, there was no obvious alternative. There were more than 4,000 troops in the Nation's Capital Girl Scout Council, so the grocery stores and strip mall locations had all been taken—at least the ones in any part of town where Roberta would be willing to take her girls. And, besides, the park was at least a pleasant, out-of-doors location. The girls could run about and get plenty of sunshine and exercise. This time, however, she made sure they had a man as one of the sponsors. Peggy Thatcher's father it was (he must have named his daughter after the British prime minister). That scare with the cookie-and-rock bum had left Roberta flustered all week. She'd told some of her friends about it and they all said she should cancel the event. Algonkian wasn't what it used to be. But, for the girls, she summoned some inner fortitude and, with Mr. Thatcher along, she thought things would probably be alright.

They did a little better this time. After two hours, they had sold forty boxes of cookies. And then she saw him again—the same man staggering toward them. He was tiny in the distance, the length of a football field away, but she could tell it was him. Same orange shirt, and this time, he was carrying something. There were more customers around than before, and Mr. Thatcher was there, so she wasn't worried, just slightly annoyed. Men who slept on benches had no call to be presenting themselves to members of civil society as though nothing was amiss, much less chatting up ten-year-old girls who (she'd heard them say) thought he was "sweet" and "nice" and "funny."

But here he came, with his big box. That's what he was carrying—a box. And as he came closer, she saw that it was a liquor box, of course. Dewar's Scotch Whiskey—not that he or his friends could afford a case of good liquor. He probably just got the box from the 7-Eleven. It was full of something heavy enough that he swayed from side to side as he walked. At least she hoped it was the heavy box that was making him sway from side to side. He was wearing exactly the same clothes as before. And then when he got really close, he set the box on the ground, reached in his pocket, and pulled out another folded five dollar bill.

"I'd like a box of Samoas please, Ma'am. The Tagalongs were very good."

Then he went to the cookie table, leaving the box where it was, and Roberta walked over to glance inside. She gasped. It was half full of rocks—small, smooth, round stones exactly like the ones Petra painted. There must have been 200 of them. And then she heard Petra calling behind her. She turned and, sure enough Petra was standing up at the painting table and waving, calling to the bum who was getting his Samoas from Kathy and Penny.

There were four girls at the painting table this week, but they only had twelve rocks. Petra's father had taken her somewhere yesterday to look for potential kindness stones but she was very picky with regard to what would work. They had gone to a gully where she'd found some good rocks before but this time she'd only gotten a dozen round ones that could be deemed suitable, though they weren't really what she wanted. Nevertheless, she had divided them evenly between herself and Peggy and the two new girls and by now each of the four had finished two kindness stones and each of them was working on her third and last. Jasper waved and greeted her and then, holding on to his Samoas, went to retrieve his box, carried it over to her table, and set it down in the grass.

Total bedlam ensued when Petra and her friends saw what he had brought them. The girls were screaming and squealing and running back and forth showing the other girls and the adults the rocks and *how many there were* and *how they were perfect.*

"Where did you get them all?" a delighted Petra squealed.

"In the river," Jasper responded. "They're river rocks."

He had spent a couple of days wading in the chilly shallow area of the Potomac, turning over bigger rocks and looking for the little ones, and some of his friends had helped him. He had showed them the one with a painted ladybug and told them that was the size and shape they were going for, though he expected a little variety might be welcome . . . bigger, smaller, fatter, some narrow ones . . . but not *too* different. It hadn't taken that long, with the water low. They piled the good rocks under a tree and then Jasper had gotten the box at the 7-Eleven.

Mrs. Blankenship was somewhat humbled. She thanked Jasper and said it was a nice thing to do. And then all the girls wanted to paint rocks. They set up extra tables and, pretty soon, girls were seated around them, painting kindness stones at Petra's direction. There were eleven girls all told, so two unhappy ones had to sell cookies in half-hour shifts while the other nine painted. Peggy Thatcher and her father went to a Target to get more paint, with *exact instructions* from Petra as to the type and brand that worked best.

Jasper sat under a tree a little ways away. He was somewhat aware that he might have an odor not everyone appreciated, though he *had* taken a bath in the river this week (and washed out his clothes as well). The girls would run up to him one by one and show him their finished stones, and he would ooh and ahh over their nascent artistic talent and remarkable accomplishments.

"Why this looks like something that would go in a museum! I don't know who will find it, but if one of those . . . what do you call them? . . . museum curators—those are the folks who decide what goes in museums—if one of them is walking along in a park and sees *this* under a tree . . . well, next time you visit the Smithsonian, you might just see your rock there, on display."

The girls giggled and said he was silly. Most of them tried to do ladybugs or flowers, copying Petra's designs. A few of them had the skill to produce original images of bunnies or unicorns with painstaking detail. Two girls said they didn't know how to paint anything so they just splotched colorful blotches on their rocks, but Jasper praised these as *abstract*.

"You know that's probably the most famous kind of art in the world right now. *Abstract!* Have you been studying with some famous artist? No? How did you learn to do it? There are entire museums with nothing but art like this, and they're always the great big buildings because it's the most popular art in the world. People study forty years to do *abstract* art.

They go to the university and get a PhD and here you just sit down at the table and do it like you were born to it. Does your Scout teacher mom know she's got abstract art *geniuses* in her troop?"

By 4:00, they had done forty rocks. Only half of them were dry but Jasper said they could leave the others on a picnic table and he'd get them in the morning. Then he would put some of them along the hiking trails where he walked every morning. His friends could put a few more in other areas. They get around a lot, he said, and could handle some of the *distribution* of the kindness stones. Also he'd see to collecting more rocks by next week, if the girls wanted to do it again—and they did!

Mrs. Blankenship thanked him again. She thought maybe she should offer to pay him something, but she knew better than to give money to a vagrant so she just suggested he take some cookies back for his friends. He said, No Ma'am, he had the Samoas and that would be enough. He was trying to take care of his heart and the other boys, well, they ought to do so too, and he didn't want to encourage them otherwise. The cookies were good . . . *very good* . . . but no one should eat too many of them.

Now Jasper had a hobby. The Girl Scouts painted stones every Sunday and he made sure they had enough rocks for the activity. The number of Scouts increased as word got out but they still couldn't paint more than sixty in an afternoon and the yet-to-be painted rocks began accumulating until they had a few hundred extra, and this gave Roberta Blankenship an idea. She contacted the council, told them what was going on, and plans were made for a council-wide Kindness Stone Crusade the last Sunday in April (which would also be the final day for cookie sales).

In preparation for the big day, one of the fathers, who was a manager at Lowes, got fifty blue buckets for Jasper's crew to use instead of cardboard boxes. There was likely to be media coverage and all those buckets had Lowes' name prominently displayed. Jasper and a few of his buddies—Ed, Samward, Emeril, Sasquatch—showed up for the troop's weekly painting program on Sunday, April 1. They met the girls who, to Roberta's chagrin, were very impressed with the large and hairy Sasquatch. He tried to explain his name to them because only Petra knew that it was another word for "Bigfoot" and the rest suggested he should call himself Wookie instead. He allowed that he would consider this. After collecting the fifty empty buckets, the men carried them to their spot down by the river (near the bridge). They probably could have filled them, but it was determined to put just one hundred rocks in each bucket (one-fourth full) so they wouldn't get too heavy . . . and if they could put one hundred rocks *exactly* in each bucket, that would help keep track of how many rocks went to each table at each location on the big day at the end of the month.

The buckets were ready by mid-April, stored behind sawhorses in what had been Troop 2770's painting area, and covered with a tarp. But by then, the council said they were expecting an even bigger turnout and it might not be enough. Fifty more buckets were obtained and the Algonkian crew went back to work. Some of them crossed the bridge to pick up rocks on the Maryland side. Mrs. Blankenship worried if anyone over there would start complaining about "rock stealing" or if some environmental group would suddenly object to vagrants depleting the Potomac of its natural riverbed, but nothing like that happened. The men strolled along both sides of the river for two miles, concentrating on shallows, but occasionally squatting in deeper water to pull up handfuls of rocks that could be hauled to the shore in a bucket and then sorted for keepers. Four miles of riverbed (two miles on each side) allowed for ample collection without any noticeable ecological impact and by the last Sunday in April, they had 100 buckets filled with a total of 10,000 river rocks, just waiting for members of the Nation's Capital Council of the Girl Scouts of America to turn them into kindness stones.

Half of the council's 50,000 Scouts were juniors, the girls in grades four and five (the ones who sell cookies). But for this event, Cadettes (grades six through eight) were also invited, so it was not surprising that more than 1,000 girls participated in the council-wide Kindness Stone Crusade on April 29. Parents had driven buckets around to different parks, also transporting selected member of Jasper's team to those locations as representatives of the Rock Collection Crew. Ed took ten buckets to the Seneca Regional Park; Samward took ten to Fred Crabtree Park; Emeril, five to Sugarland Run Stream Valley Park; Sasquatch, six to Claude Moore Park; and Bernard, eight to Lake Farifax Park. Many of these men were offered money by the Scout leaders who were grateful for the time and effort they had put in to help the girls, but all of them refused, saying kindness stones were about *giving* something for others, not getting anything for yourself—all except Ed (*damn him*, Jasper would say) who accepted twenty dollars and then had the driver take him back to Algonkian and drop him at the 7-Eleven, which sold cheap liquor that tasted awful but had a high alcohol content. An hour later he was passed out drunk under a tree, unconscious for the rest of the day.

The plan was for individual troops to take charge of distributing the stones all over the metro DC area, in parks and other spots where passersby might be surprised to happen upon a pretty painted rock. They could just note it and smile. Or pick it up and look at it. Or put in their pocket and keep it, if that's what they wanted. Some children might even collect them, but no one should be greedy: if you keep more than one or two, it was suggested, you might think about painting a rock yourself and leaving it for someone else to find.

Jasper and his crew had made one request—well, really, two. First, Bernard and five African American transients known to him were going to get ten buckets full of finished, painted stones and distribute 1,000 of them in parts of the city where the mostly white Girl Scouts were unlikely to go. "Po' kids gonna love these things," Bernard said, "and they need pretty stuff most of all." Second, another ten buckets filled with an additional 1,000 painted stones would be left with Jasper and his men for them to distribute. He knew exactly what he wanted to do with them: take them right to the most traveled and visited part of the city and leave them for the tourists and politicians, especially the latter (who always seemed to need cheering up). They would leave the stones at night to be found the next day, along the mall and at the monuments and outside the courts and office buildings—just a couple dozen each time, so they'd be a little rare. A couple dozen, once a week, every week for the next year.

Algonkian Park was ground zero for the event, with dozens of tables set up—plus ten more off to the side for the cookie sales. Given media coverage, crowds of people were expected to come out to watch the girls painting their rocks and many of these spectators would no doubt want to load up on cookies (before they became unavailable for another full year). Two of the local TV stations were on hand. They interviewed Roberta Blankenship who was directing the whole affair and they interviewed Petra, "the little girl who started it all." She turned out to be Native American, and that added a significant element of human interest to a story that already had tremendous appeal. It was also revealed that she had put her initials on the backs of all the rocks she'd painted over the last two months and in the next week two of those rocks would sell on Craigslist for $500 a piece; soon, however, Petra-knockoffs would begin showing up and, with no means of authenticating which were the genuine articles, the value of stones she maintained should never be bought or sold would rapidly decline.

Roberta Blankenship explained to the TV cameras that she had gotten the idea for the event when she saw the wonderful stones little Petra was creating, and that she had thought this could be something for the whole troop, and then for the entire council. The real "aha!" moment, however, was when she got the idea of asking homeless men who slept in the park if they would help by gathering the necessary rocks from the riverbed. The TV interviewers were impressed beyond measure with the image of this brave woman going to the disreputable east section of the park—an area that many men, not to mention single women, would normally avoid—and calling upon the men there to commit themselves to acts of kindness and generosity, to show their devotion not only to the wonderful young women of the Girl Scout Council but to people in the world at large, people who, after all, were not unlike them in that, whatever their status in life, they had worries and problems and could always use a reason to smile. She had felt like Jesus going among the lepers, not that these men were lepers, she wasn't saying that, but they were often *treated* like lepers, the downtrodden and the forgotten of our world. And wasn't' it wonderful to give *them* a chance to give something back to society instead of just *taking*? And, oh yes, she allowed, "I did bribe them with a couple boxes of cookies! I mean, who can resist Tagalongs and Samoas?" The interviewers laughed at that, and both channels played it as the final line before they cut back to their studios for some amusing banter among the Channel 3 and Channel 6 family news teams.

Both channels wanted to interview Jasper himself but he was nowhere to be found. "He is a bit camera shy," a man named Emeril told them. The woman correspondent from Channel 3 asked Roberta if he might be "an illegal" and the latter assured her that he wasn't Mexican but, who knows whether he could be wanted for *something*? She didn't want to get him in any trouble, though, and the correspondent agreed that would not be good for the story—perhaps it would be best not even to talk about him too much or else *The Washingtonian* would have some follow-up reporter track him down and try to turn a sweet, inspiring story into a scandal. Instead, they gathered a few of his friends—Jasper's crew, they called themselves—into a covered area with benches and did a quick interview with them, with Bernard seated front and center between Samward and Emeril, and Sasquatch and a couple others in the back.

Jasper was deep in the woods, as far from the frenzy as he could get. He'd always hated being a focus of attention, unless of course he was telling stories, and then he always figured it was the story, not him.

So he was deep in the woods, sitting on the ground, his back against a tree. He was holding a photo in one hand—a picture of a brown-haired woman and two brown-haired girls—and a little stone with a painted ladybug in the other. And he was weeping.

"Fool!" he cursed himself. "Fool! This is a *happy* day! Good things are happening today." But he couldn't stop crying until he stuffed the picture and the stone into his shirt pocket and tried to focus on a story he might tell the boys in the evening after this was all over.

It ought to be a story about rocks, he figured, and the tale of Decaulion and Pyrrah would probably work best. "What kind of names are those?" he could hear 'em complaining . . . so maybe they could just be Decca and P *something* . . . what would work? . . . Pee-Pee . . . the boys would like that.

There was this man named Decca and he had a girlfriend called Pee-Pee . . . he could hear the chuckles and ribald suggestions as to how she got that name . . . good, that was an improvement.

Now all this happened after a big flood and they were the only two people left alive.

"What about Noah?" Sasquatch would say, and he'd have to tell them that there wasn't any Noah in this story and then there'd be a little detour.

"Are you saying the Bible is wrong?"

Well, he'd have to say, this was a different flood at another time in a different part of the world, and these two folks, Decca and Pee-Pee (heh heh heh they'd all giggle like immature girls), they sat on a big wood chest and survived the flood.

"What, there weren't any boats?" somebody would complain.

No, this was before boats were invented, but someone had a big wood box and Decca and Pee-Pee sat on top of it and no one else thought of doing that so they ended up being the only people left in the entire world.

Jasper realized this didn't make any sense, of course. If there were wood chests, there would have been boats, but that *was* the story and sometimes you just had to go with it. Literary license and what not.

"What about the animals?" someone would ask, and he'd have to say, This story isn't about animals. It's gonna be about rocks if you'll just let me tell it. Maybe the animals could swim or maybe they climbed trees, I don't know and it doesn't make any difference.

And then somebody, probably Sasquatch would say, "I always wondered that about Noah, how come he took the animals that could swim. The Bible says he took two of every kind, and I always thought, even the ducks? Why'd he take ducks?" And I'll have to tell him to shut up about Noah, this doesn't have anything to do with Noah (just because his father was some damn fool preacher who beat the shit out of him every single day till he ran off, he's always gotta go on about the Bible this or that—but I won't say that to him, of course).

Anyway, if we can get back to the story, Decca and Pee-Pee they don't know what to do. I mean, you might think it's pretty obvious what they could do if they want more people in the world, but they wanted there to be a lot of people right away, not just, you know by the normal route, so they went to the oracle to ask what to do.

At this point Sasquatch might try to say something about Adam and Eve and how for the first generations everyone must have had sex with their brothers and sisters or cousins 'cause there weren't nobody in the world except their brothers and sisters and cousins (he'd said that to his father one time and got the shit beat out of him) and I'll have to shush him up.

Also they won't know what an oracle is, so I should just say it's a fortune teller (though it really isn't) and the fortune teller didn't drown, on account of being on a mountain or something . . . what I go through telling these guys anything! . . . what I go through, just trying to tell them a story about rocks!

So, anyway, the oracle tells them to cast the bones of their mother over their shoulders, and they wonder how the hell are they going to do that? Are they supposed to go dig up their own mothers? And then Pee-Pee who, in spite of her name, seemed to have the most brains of the two goes, "Oh, it means Mother Earth!" And the "bones" of Mother Earth are rocks and stones. So then, to make the long story short, Decca and Pee-Pee go all over the place. They go to all the parks just like us, picking up rocks and tossing them over their shoulders. And everywhere a rock lands a new person sprouts up.

While Japer was figuring out his story, the young woman from Channel 3 was prepping an unusual group of men for the on-camera interview. Before they started, she tried to find out a little more about the absentee ringleader—just for background.

"Does Jasper have a last name?"

"None of us have last names, Miss. We're like Madonna or Cher."

"Or Fergie."

"Or Prince."

"Okay," she smiled. "But you know Prince isn't a real name. Or Madonna. I don't know about Cher. Do you know if *Jasper* is his real name?"

"Course it is! But my name's Sasquatch and that might be a surprise to my parents, may they rot in hell."

"Down, boy."

"Try to imagine," the woman from Channel 3 suggested, "or try to *remember* that all the Girl Scouts are going to be watching this, seated around the TV with their parents."

"I ain't going to tell no one to rot in hell when I'm on the TV. I ain't a total fool. Or maybe I am, but I ain't gonna do *that*."

"You will if you mention your parents."

"Well I just won't mention 'em then! I ain't a total fool. Well, maybe I am. No socialologist would have to study me long to figure that out, but it don't mean I'm gonna talk about my parents, may they rot in hell, when I'm on the TV for the Girl Scouts."

"Well, okay. That's good," the woman from Channel 3 said. "But back to Jasper. Do you know why he isn't here? I'm not asking for the TV cameras and we're not going to get him into any trouble, but do you know if maybe he's wanted for anything?"

"Wanted by who? College girls? I can think of somethin' they might want him for."

"No," she responded, still smiling. "I mean, wanted by the police?"

"Have they made bullshittin' a crime yet?"

"Are you kidding?" she asked, with a laugh. "In *this* town? Washington, DC?"

When they got on camera at last—and she'd explained it wasn't live and they could always edit—she asked them about the rock collecting and about their plans for distribution. And then, in a grand climactic "reveal" she announced that Channel 3 was going to treat them all to a meal at one of DC's finest restaurants. They could take some time to talk it over and decide which . . .

"Subway," two or three of the men said at once.

"Subway?" she asked.

They all nodded, and it appeared the entire group was in agreement.

"They got these big sandwiches for only five dollars. It's a special though so we gotta do it fast."

She nodded her head and reminded them that they could pick any restaurant they wanted and that the TV station was paying for it. They could have the restaurant close down except for them if they were concerned about other customers. They could have the whole place to themselves, or at least a room.

Subway, they said, and it was unanimous. Then Emeril volunteered that Subway did have little bags of tater chips and big Pepsi's, though that would be more than five dollars. The woman from Channel 3 assured them this would fall within the station's budget and they were all delighted and said they'd appreciate it.

"Also," Samward said, "I'd like to get a sandwich for my friend Ed if I might because he's done as much as any of us but now he's drunk . . . oh, wait . . . can I do that again?"

She told him to count to five and start over.

"I would like to get a sandwich for my friend Ed, too, if I might. And a Pepsi and some tater chips. Ed, he's been one of the main ones and done as much as anybody but he can't be here right at this moment on account of because he's indisposed."

Eventually, Channel 3 would decide to give each of the men a $50 Subway gift card—twelve cards in all for the dozen men identified as participants in the project. Ed and two of the others sold theirs for $45 each, which they spent at the 7-Eleven, and then they disappeared for three days. But the kindness stones did get distributed, in places both likely and unlikely, and they probably brought close to 10,000 smiles to around 10,000 people.

Very little was said on camera about Jasper, though his name did come up, and the Channel 3 correspondent asked Roberta Blankenship *why* she thought he did it.

"He just said, 'They liked ladybugs.' That's all I know."

"Who did? Who liked ladybugs?"

"His friends, I suppose . . . or maybe just folks in general. I don't know but when I asked him 'why are you doing this?' that was all he said . . . 'They liked ladybugs.'"

8

Photographs and Memories

Coffee table books go on the bottom shelf. Not on the coffee table, Father McCloskey thought, smiling. Not these books.

He was reorganizing the rectory in a manner appropriate for his retirement. He'd been retired for three months but hadn't gotten to the bookcase yet. Now, half the volumes were in a box marked "Donate," but these three books were definitely keepers. Their size (9 x 12) made them too tall for vertical shelving, but they could lay horizontally on the bottom shelf with some other books stacked on top of them. Neither prominent display nor easy access was necessary, but he did like having them close.

They were picture books: collections by his favorite photographer, all out of print and only one available on Amazon. None of them had sold very well and he didn't know a soul who would appreciate them the way he did. There was nothing embarrassing or rude about them. Oh no, they weren't *that* sort of photos! They were just *particular*. You had to have a certain interest.

Well, he hadn't looked at them for a while. Now was a good time to take a break and page through the volumes one more time.

* * *

Open Hands: Muffler Men in New England and on the National Road (Kallos Press, 1988) was a study in American kitsch. A thin volume, it contained fifty full-page, full-color pictures of fiberglass behemoths that had dotted roadside landscapes during the 1960s. On the facing page for each photo was a description of the sculpture: its origin and history (initial use, subsequent re-uses, and ultimate destiny), plus, a critical assessment of the work's distinctive features and artistic merits. All of this was done a little tongue in cheek, but respectfully. And clearly, reading between the lines, one could easily regard the stories of the Muffler Men as stories of American popular culture and, so, as stories of America.

The photos were preceded by a brief introduction for the totally unenlightened. Muffler Men were large statues made of molded fiberglass intended for use as advertising icons. Most of them were about twenty-five feet tall and, though they were constructed (for the most part) in Venice, California, they were distributed throughout the United States, especially along Route 66 and Route 40 (the National Road). They were very colorful and no two were alike: there were cowboys, lumberjacks, businessmen, Indians, pirates, cooks, Vikings, astronauts, and more. Among the most curious variants were a fifteen-foot Amish man who stood over a diner in Lancaster, Pennsylvania and more than a dozen giant women (wearing short skirts or swimsuits) who had once been displayed at Uniroyal tire stores around the country.

The statues came to be called Muffler Men because many of the most prominent ones were bought by car dealerships or auto parts stores and were installed holding full-sized car mufflers in their open hands. But that moniker was somewhat misleading. In actuality "Muffler Men" statues with the typical open-handed pose were used by a wide variety of businesses and they could be seen holding any number of large items: footballs, hot dogs, tires, chain saws, camping gear, and so on. The Big John grocery store chain had more than a dozen that each held four overflowing sacks of produce.

The sculptures were lightweight, eye-catching, and relatively inexpensive ($1,000–$2,000). Thousands of them were produced but they were not especially sturdy and many proved unable to survive the elemental conditions of the outdoor settings in which they were placed. Further, construction of freeways made the use of such icons less fetching than they had been when cars passed the establishments on two-lane highways. And then, during the 1970s, businesses came to rely more on neon signage to attract attention. Nevertheless, many of the surviving Muffler Men were repainted and refurbished to enjoy second lives as sentinels for amusement parks, sports arenas, and miniature golf courses.

All this from the book's introduction, which was illustrated with half a dozen stock photos for historical purposes. There was, for example, an old publicity shot of the very first "Muffler Man": a fiberglass sculpture of Paul Bunyan created by Bob Prewitt in 1962 for Flagstaff, Arizona's Lumberjack Café. It was featured briefly in the 1960s counterculture film *Easy Rider*. Then, when the restaurant got new owners in the late 1970s and became Granny's Closet, the now inappropriate statue was sold to Northern Arizona University, where it stood at the entrance to their regionally famous Lumberjack Stadium.

The bulk of *Open Hands* (after the intro) was devoted to high-quality photographs of fifty selected roadside monuments. McCloskey, who knew a bit about art, considered the prints to be spectacular, quite apart from any interest in the specific content. In each shot, the photographer had found the perfect angle, the perfect lighting, the perfect scope and focus to depict the so-called Muffler Man in a manner that was striking and specifically appropriate for its given theme.

On page eleven, there was an impressive looking cowboy Muffler Man erected in the early 1970s at Cowtown Rodeo in Woodstown, New Jersey and the photo was taken in such a way that the cowboy's pistol was aimed directly at the viewer. The picture had to have been taken from a ladder or something to get that perspective.

Likewise, the photo on page seventeen showed nothing but a close-up of an enormous, goofy head, a face that readers of *Mad* magazine might assume to be that publication's cartoon mascot and cover icon, Alfred E. Neuman. The face was splattered, furthermore, with what appeared to be splotches of colorful gore: red and purple and yellow and green. A smaller photo on the facing page revealed that, in fact, this peculiar "Muffler Man head" was perched atop a tall lead pipe, like a gruesome head on a stake. The text explained, first, that an entire line of "Half-Wit Muffler Men" were produced in the 1960s, enormous statues of the gap-toothed grinning redhead who was usually considered to be a hopelessly out-of-it dim bulb, but might also be regarded as a sly imp or spaced-out bohemian. Some of the Half-Wits were dressed as hillbillies or vagabonds and all were intended to be comical. To avoid copyright disputes with *Mad*, the company that produced these statues claimed the figure had been inspired by Mortimer Snerd, a ventriloquist dummy from the 1940s who also had a goofy aspect, but most knowledgeable observers thought the image looked more like Alfred E. than Mortimer. In any case, very few of the Half-Wit Muffler Men had survived. In 1981, after a fire at Atlantic

City's Million Dollar Pier, the guillotined heads of two such sculptures were sold to the owner of some rural property just south of I-195 near Jackson, New Jersey. He put them on poles to be used as targets for a paintball course. Given all this, what struck McCloskey was the ironic pathos that the close-up of this paint-splattered head conveyed. It aroused sympathy for the poor fellow who had become a cavalier object of ridicule. Decapitated, his body lost or demolished, he was now doomed to offer his face as target practice for people who wanted to splatter him with sludge or slime and then laugh because they thought this made him look even stupider than before. And through it all, his frozen idiotic grin beamed blissful ignorance of his fate. What a photo! Father McCloskey thought. And how was it taken? From a crane, perhaps? The photographer literally had to come up to the subject's level and look the poor Half-Wit in the eye. And now, we have to do so as well.

But then on page fifteen, there was a photo taken from the ground looking up: this one showed an enormous lumberjack holding an American flag. Accompanying text on page fourteen explained that this "Bunyan style" Muffler Man could be seen in Cheshire, Connecticut. It was moved from some unknown location to be erected on the front lawn of a lumber business in the early 1980s. The town of Cheshire, however, had a law that no signage can be more than seven-feet high and the sudden appearance of a twenty-six-foot advertising icon put the town elders up in arms. But was it a "sign"? The potential court case was avoided when the lumber company replaced the lumberjack's axe with a horizontal pole from which hung an enormous American flag. The company maintained that, "You can build a flagpole as high as you want." The town let it go and even the elders now seemed to regard the patriotic Bunyan as an official landmark. This was all interesting, but Father McCloskey admired the aesthetics of the image itself: the photo allowed the colors of the flag to balance the frame with the figure's own bright red pants and blue shirt. Further, looking up from the giant's feet, everything was foreshortened in a way that emphasized the figure's height and the flag's dependence (hanging down, rather than waving from a vertical pole). Whatever you make of pop art or kitsch, this was good photography.

And so on. McCloskey flipped through the pages and turned at last to the back flap of the dust jacket. And there she was: Audrey Phillips, the author and photographer. Audrey at age thirty, thirty-three years ago. Curly hair and hazel eyes. Calm, tranquil eyes. A soft mouth that used to laugh at his jokes. He had known Audrey when he was in seminary, studying for the priesthood. If not for . . . well, if not for *God* . . . who knows what might have happened?

The month after he graduated and was ordained, she had left her position with the parish office and embarked on this project, making the most of a college degree (artistically, if not commercially). She had majored in graphic design, focusing on photography. The book had been privately published and sold at Stuckey's and Nickerson Farms along Route 40, marketed to purveyors of Americana who might or might not be able to appreciate creative or cultivated aspects of photography as an art form. Only 600 copies had been printed. And Audrey Phillips would never know that he owned one of them.

* * *

Bronto Butlers (Kallos Press, 1996) was an experiment in postmodernism. At least, that was how Father McCloskey understood it. The idea for the book (according to its foreword) arose out of the same kind of fascination with popular American culture that had informed Phillips's first volume. As a child, she had liked the green dinosaur signs at Sinclair filling stations and as an adolescent she had noticed that the stations displaying those signs tended to be more interesting, more Americana, a few steps closer to the soil, than the encroaching megamall truck stops and ubiquitous convenience-stores-with-gas-pumps that were refining travelers' service station options. In fact, the signs themselves all but disappeared, replaced by Arco or BP or other boring brands with mundane logos. But eventually she discovered that the Bronto Sinclairs were still alive and well out west, in Montana, Colorado, Wyoming, and Idaho. So she headed to those regions to photograph the stations as though they were an endangered species.

The bronto-sign Sinclairs were mostly in small towns and, as a photographer, Phillips soon found herself drawn not only to the stations but to the men who ran them. They were crusty, small-town American men, with interesting faces. And so, in *Bronto Butlers*, she was able to display a collection of high-quality portraits of these men, quintessentially American men who were indeed facing extinction. Some of the pictures were head-and-shoulder shots, but quite a few captured the men *in situ*: in the garage looking under the hood of a car, at a desk going over receipts, even pumping gas (some of them still did that!).

What made *Bronto Butlers* noteworthy, however, was the turnabout Phillips had hit upon spontaneously at her very first shoot. The station owner, probably flirting with her, asked if he could take a picture of her. Sure, why not? And then, that was what she did at every stop. How postmodern could you get? *Bronto Butlers* was a photography book in which the photographer became the *subject* of the photographs. Phillips had used a digital camera that had just come on the market (Eastman Kodak's EOS DCS) and she had edited all the photos on a computer with Adobe Photoshop. This technology was so new that most of her gas station "butlers" found it incredible (Where does the film go? When can you get these developed?). She plugged her camera into her laptop and showed them all the pictures with no waiting—the photos she had taken of them and the ones they had taken of her. Not only that, but she cropped the photos and adjusted them for light, saturation, color, and so forth. The end result? The photos these gas station attendants had taken of a professional photographer were of a comparable quality with that photographer's pictures of them.

This, Father McCloskey thought, was an experiment in post-structuralist art, like Fish's "Self-Consuming Artifact." An art book of *professional* photography that deconstructed the very notion that some photography should be considered "art" or even "professional." It was also a dire prophecy: if anyone can do this (and do it this well), what does that mean for an industry? Why should a school hire someone to take the kiddies' photos? Why should a church employ some company to produce their new directory? If there's a message here, it might be, "A new world's a'comin'—sell your stock in Olan Mills!"

He thought this was brilliant, but it wasn't what made him like the book so much. No, this time, that came down to simple content. Accompanying the fifty-two photos of quintessentially American men were fifty-two photos of the woman he had last seen at his ordination. Guess which ones he liked best? Here was Audrey Phillips at thirty-eight, hair still curly (though quite a bit longer), eyes still hazel (calm and tranquil), mouth still soft (wide lips). Here she was sitting in a car at the pumps, airing a tire at the self-serve, shopping for gum at the cash register, even sitting on a toilet in the ladies room (Ha! Ha!). His favorite was one from the waist up in which she was smiling beautifully and holding a green plastic brontosaurus in front of her chest, the long neck and tail underlining the curves of her breasts like an underwire bra.

She must have sent a copy of the book to *American Photographer* because they published a short review: Father McCloskey had the page here, tucked inside the back cover. Three stars out of five. They indicated the potential for the work to be perceived as "self-indulgent" but suggested the "turnabout" could also be considered an act of humility or respect. Did it convey empathy with the subject? Or was Phillips making some kind of artistic statement about technological threats to her profession? Or, was it just a joke? In any case, the review included a tiny duplication of the Bronto-under-the-breasts photo side-by-side with Phillips's portrait of the man who had taken it. That might have helped sales, but only 1,000 copies of the book were ever printed. Father McCloskey assumed that Audrey had bought at least fifty-two of them herself and given them to the men who participated in her sophomore project. Who knows what became of the rest? They were never on Amazon. Did she sell them out of her car? Send a few to relatives?

Of course, he had one. She would never know that.

Thirty-six years at St. Ignatius and he had done a lot of good. God had done a lot of good through him. It had been the right decision, and he was sure she would agree.

* * *

Hellish Beauty (Kallos Press, 2002) was the thickest of the coffee table books. It was definitely the best, though not necessarily Father McCloskey's favorite. As with *Open Hands,* there was only one picture of Audrey, a tiny snapshot on the back cover flap. Age forty-four. Still lovely, but not much of a photo. Anyway, this volume *was* sold on Amazon and it had done reasonably well for its market: a first printing of 5,000 copies and then, two years later, a second printing of 3,000 more.

He opened the book to a dedication page. This was the only one of the three books with a dedication page. It said:

For James & Kimana
Congratulations on your fourth anniversary
Invite me back for your fortieth

That was the dedication page. Father McCloskey didn't know James or Kimana.

The book was almost all photos, incredible full-color, full-page displays of hellish beauty and of regular beauty too. But there were also a few pages of full text and, although these weren't by Audrey, he had to admit that he enjoyed them—more than he wished, actually.

So, he flipped past the title page to a little essay he loved.

The Discovery of Hell

By Ranger Jim

In 1829, when he was only nineteen years old, Joe Meek discovered hell. He was hunting beaver pelts with some friends one day when the whole group was set upon by Blackfoot Indians. Two of his buddies were killed and the entire party was scattered. Meek fled in terror, alone, and for four days he headed south hoping to catch up with a horse or a mule or another of the survivors. On the fifth day, he ascended a large hill and coming over the crest beheld a sight that he knew only from the Bible. It was hell, laid out before him as far as the eye could see. The air was thick with the stench of sulfur and, as he would later write in a published report, "The whole country was smoking with the vapor from boiling springs and burning with gasses issuing from small craters, each of which was emitting a sharp whistling sound."

Before Meek's incredible discovery, most clerics and theologians had assumed hell was located somewhere underground, secreted away in the bowels of the earth where no human being could just happen upon it. But there was no denying that this was it. There was the lake of fire, several miles across, a boiling cauldron awaiting the souls of the damned. Matthew's Gospel declares that on the last day,

> *The Son of man shall send forth his angels, and they shall gather out of his kingdom all things that offend, and them which do iniquity; And shall cast them into a furnace of fire: there shall be wailing and gnashing of teeth. Then shall the righteous shine forth as the sun in the kingdom of their Father. Who hath ears to hear, let him hear (Matt 13:41–43).*

Of course, the lake is also described in the book of Revelation, where we learn that the devil himself will ultimately be thrown into it (after being bound for a thousand years) and there he and the beast and the false prophet will be tormented day and night forever and ever (Rev 20:10). And then at last anyone whose name is not written in the Book of Life will be cast into the lake of fire as well (Rev 20:15). Meek was not a reader but by the age of nineteen he knew his Bible and he also knew Dante, who spoke of this lake and its environs.

But the lake was not all. Hell was enormous, as of course it would have to be to accommodate all of the damned from creation to present. It stretched on, endlessly, to the horizon. Mesmerized, Meek was tempted to explore. From the top of his small mountain, he scanned the region for any sign of Satan or the demons. Finding none, he gingerly descended, a cloth over his face to stifle the sulfurous fumes. He wandered unmolested throughout the terrain, taking notes and drawing diagrams. The first human to visit hell—the first white man at least (who knew what truck the Indians might have with devils?)—he hoped also to be the first to return from thence. And like a good explorer he hoped to do so with maps. It was very dangerous. The ground itself was unstable, for in places there was but a thin crust of earth pasted over a fiery pit. More than once, Meek almost slid into perdition before his time. And, of course, the entire area was booby-trapped. Sometimes, without warning, the earth to his left or to his right would explode as though struck by cannon-fire and spray scalding water at him as he attempted to give berth to the fire-pits. It was a Scylla-or-Charybdis scenario: be burned or cooked. He chose the former and escaped with minor injuries. Then, the devil stepped up the assault and sent a billowing tower of boiling water up from the earth as high as a flagpole, obliterating everything in its path. Still, somehow, he made it through: he traveled across hell and came out the other side, with crude maps and drawings to document the experience.

Meek was found by a search party some days later, wandering traumatized in the desert. His accounts of hell were disregarded as "lurid and intolerable" by some and yet were eventually confirmed by others, who braved the Blackfoot and the devil to climb that hill and behold something of what Meek had witnessed.

Theologians and clerics were most troubled by two of Meek's assertions. First, he claimed that hell was empty. The absence of demons was difficult enough but, by most doctrines, there should already have been a large number of tormented souls cooking in those fiery pits. Some scholars, of course, argued that none would be punished until after the Great Assize, but this was a minority position. Did Meek's report give credence to that view? More likely, if he could be trusted, he had seen but a small corner of Hades.

> *He had traversed an as yet uninhabited quarter, while the demons were occupied abusing the damned elsewhere.*
>
> *But another of Meek's claims regarding hell was even more troubling: he said that it was beautiful. Despite the sulfur and the smoke, he said, this landscape, like nowhere else on earth, was as colorful and livid and pleasing to the eye as anything he had ever beheld. The ground itself was painted with the colors of a sunset and the waters that bubbled in the cauldrons of fire were of a spectacular and constantly changing hue. If not for the constant danger of being boiled alive, Meek said, "I could spend eternity there and call it heaven."*
>
> *Disclaimer: Ranger Jim has a knack for making good stories better. While Joe Meek's initial observation of Yellowstone as a place of "hellish beauty" is basically correct, there is no indication that the park's discoverer ever believed he was actually in the realm of the damned [A. P.]*

Ha! Father McCloskey chuckled at the disclaimer. Ranger Jim's no literalist, but he does know how to spin a yarn. And Yellowstone *is* a place of hellish beauty. To prove the point, he turned the page and, immediately after the little essay there was a brilliant two-page spread showing one of the national park's bubbling hot springs. Yes! It *did* look like hell and . . . *yes!* . . . it *was* beautiful. Undeniably beautiful. Exotic. Like nowhere else on earth (at least nowhere that Father McCloskey knew about). What a photo!

And then, page after page, there were extravagant pictures of an extravagant landscape: geysers and waterfalls, canyons and ridges, sunsets and spectacular starry nights. There were stunning photos of rock formations, flowing streams, and all sorts of flora: cottonwood, junipers, pine, sage. And, of course, there were remarkable photos of bison, bears, elk, mountain goats, bighorn sheep, foxes, coyotes, even a moose with her newborn calf. The book was all photos of Yellowstone National Park, one of the most photographed places on earth, but these pictures were exquisite. They must, Father McCloskey thought, be equal or superior to whatever competing volumes have to offer. Anyone wanting a coffee table book devoted to one of America's top tourist attractions would certainly be pleased with this one. Even given the eighty-dollar price tag.

About halfway through, there was this:

The Halloween Horror:

Ranger Jim Addresses the Boy Scouts

On October 31, 1996, Ranger Jim spoke to a group of Boy Scouts gathered around their evening campfire. It was Halloween. He had told them earlier that Yellowstone was initially misidentified as a displaced corner of hell. Now, the Scouts had specifically requested a "scary story" from the park's history.

"Today is October 31," he began, "and I want to tell you all about something that happened 128 years ago on this very day, in the year 1870.* It happened nearby, over on Blacktail Deer Plateau where you boys were this afternoon. You remember—near the Mammoth Hot Springs?"

The boys nodded their heads. Yes. They had just been there.

"A man by the name of Jack Baronett came on to that plateau, looking for a friend who had been lost a few weeks earlier. His dog picked up a scent and began tracking something that left strange scuffle marks in the sand. Baronett thought it might be a wounded bear. I'll read you now what he reported.

At this point, Ranger Jim opened a tattered book he'd wrapped in torn leather to disguise the fact that it came from one of the park's gift shops. It looked like it could actually be 127 years old—possibly, the very diary of Jack Baronett, its pages covered with his own scribbled handwriting. Ranger Jim read in an ominous, echoey voice:

> My dog began to growl, and looking across a small canyon to the mountain side beyond, I saw a black object upon the ground. My first impulse was to shoot from where I stood, but it was moving so slowly, I thought I might move in closer for a better shot and a closer look. I crossed over to where it was, and had no difficulty overtaking it. Then I saw that it was not a bear at all, though what it *was* I could not tell! It did not look like any animal that I had ever seen, and it certainly was not a human being. I went up closer still. It was making a low groaning noise, crawling along on its knees and elbows, and trying to drag itself up the mountain.

Ranger Jim read these words by the flickering firelight and when he paused for effect, the Scouts were hanging on every word.

"What was it?" someone asked.

"It was Jeffrey," another volunteered, referring apparently to one of their number. There were scattered guffaws and one boy tried to push whoever had spoken off of the log on which he sat. A Scoutmaster sought to restore order.

"What do you think it was?" Ranger Jim inquired.

"Bigfoot," a couple responded in near unison.

"A buffalo," someone else suggested and got scolded for being unrealistic. "If it was wounded," he continued, in a vain attempt to support his answer, "if its legs got broke or something."

"The truth may be less interesting," Ranger Jim continued. "But it's much more scary."

He paused to let that thought sink in.

"Jack Baronett had found that which he had come to seek. Do you remember what he was looking for?"

"Gold?"

"A buffalo?"

"Bigfoot?"

And then a voice near the back said more quietly, "His friend."

"That's right," Ranger Jim said, waving his hand toward the boy who had been listening. "He had found his friend. Thirty-seven days earlier, Truman Everts had come to Yellowstone Park on a camping trip much like the one that you are on right now. He was with a group that explored the park's Grand Canyon where you're going to go tomorrow. Then, the next day he went off with a partner and together they climbed a mountain, leaving early in the morning and returning to camp at nightfall. Everyone in the group thought he was the best explorer in the bunch, so they thought nothing of it the next day when he decided to go off on his own. Having a partner would just hold him back. He was faster and stronger and a better explorer than all the rest. Normally, no one was ever supposed to go off alone, but Truman Everts was the best of the bunch, they thought, so they let him go."

"What happened to him?"

"A lot of things could have happened. He could have met a bear or been attacked by wolves. He could have been gored by bison or trampled by an elk. In those days, he might even have met up with some unfriendly Indians. But the truth is much simpler. Less exciting perhaps, but a lot more scary. He just got lost. For thirty-seven days he wandered around lost. He couldn't find the camp and he couldn't find his friends. There was nothing to eat but grass and berries, so by the time Jack Baronett found him, he weighed only fifty pounds. He was a full-grown man, but he weighed only fifty pounds."

"Gaw . . ." the boys exclaimed at this revelation, whispering to each other about how much *they* weighed, always more than fifty pounds.

"It had been bright and sunny when he went off on his little adventure, so he was dressed in warm summer clothes. He wore those clothes for thirty-seven days. The snows came, the rivers froze with ice. His hands and his feet became black with frostbite and fell off of his body."

"Ooh . . . gross . . . ."

"He crawled about in the snow on all fours, like some kind of wounded animal, no hands, no feet, digging for something, *anything* to eat. He ate worms and bugs that he dug out of logs with his teeth."

"Ooh . . ."

"And then he lost his mind. He became sick with a fever and his brain quit working as it should. He no longer knew that he was human and when his friend Jack Baronett happened upon him, growling and dragging himself through the snow, he had no idea that he was being rescued. He had to be trapped like a wild animal and carried back to the camp where they forced him to drink tea from a spoon."

* *Actually the story related here occurred on October 6, 1870. Ranger Jim is no literalist. [A. P.]*

Well, that will teach the little buggers to use the "buddy system," Father McCloskey thought. And of course the photos on the following pages showed the vastness of the Yellowstone wilderness, an area in which the best of explorers could easily get lost.

But Father McCloskey couldn't help noting the date of this Halloween talk . . . 1996? That was six years before the book was published. Was she there, to hear this talk? Was she there with Ranger Jim, five years before the book was done? Well. The book must have been a *lot* of work, if she spent five or six years on it. A lot of time spent at Yellowstone. A lot of time with this Ranger Jim.

Most of the pictures in *Hellish Beauty* were full-page spreads without any unnecessary text—no caption was needed to tell you the bison were standing in a vibrant green meadow or the bear was climbing a tree with her cubs. But other pictures had entire paragraphs of commentary.

This one was significant: a spectacular view of an unusual wall of rock that actually resembled a fort or stockade. The accompanying text read:

> Sheepeater Cliff is a geological formation of columnar basalt that can only by accessed by an unmarked trail in the park, sometimes identified as "a secret hike." The cliff is named for a tribe of the Shoshone Indians who were displaced from the area, moved to the Wind River Indian Reservation in Wyoming in 1878 when the US government decided to turn their homeland into a national park. The Shoshone were a peaceful, nomadic people who traveled in relatively small family groups. They would replicate their journey each year, visiting the same spots to collect plants almost on the very day that they ripened and to re-visit the favorite haunts of various small animals—both those that they wanted for food and those that they simply liked to observe. Different family groups referred to each other by names that designated the primary diet: the Seed Eaters, the Bird Eaters, the Rabbit Eaters, and so forth. The Sheepeaters became known as the most peculiar of the Shoshone because they did not accept horses when white men arrived. They preferred dogs and kept large ones to pull their travois sleds and assist them with hunting. Even stranger, they were pacifists who eschewed warfare and would have nothing to do with guns, not even for hunting. The Shoshone were famously friendly to white settlers. Sacagawea, a Sheepeater woman, served as interpreter for Lewis and Clark. Unfortunately, many settlers interpreted passivity as weakness and the literature of the day generally portrays the Sheepeaters as feeble-minded primitives ripe for exploitation. In 1868, 250 noncombatants, including children, were killed for no apparent reason by soldiers in what became known as the Bear River Massacre.

So, the book was informative as well as picturesque. It had been sold in the Yellowstone gift shops; perhaps, it still was. The final page was, again, given to Ranger Jim, who apparently could also serve as a chaplain:

Ranger Jim Leads Earth Day Devotions

> On April 22, 1997 Ranger Jim led an Earth Day devotional service for tourists gathered in an outdoor clearing he designated as a temporary chapel. The service consisted of two readings, followed by the performance of an original song.

FIRST READING

from the Wisdom of Ben Sira (Old Testament Apocrypha)

All human beings come from the ground, and humankind was created out of the dust.

In the fullness of his knowledge the Lord distinguished them and appointed their different ways.

Some he blessed and exalted, and some he made holy and brought near to himself; but some he cursed and brought low, and turned them out of their place.

Like clay in the hand of the potter, to be molded as he pleases, so all are in the hand of their Maker, to be given whatever he decides.

SECOND READING

from the Book of Bokonon*

God made mud.

God got lonesome.

So God said to some of the mud, "Sit up!"

"See all I've made," said God, "the hills, the sea, the sky, the stars."

And I was some of the mud that got to sit up and look around.

Lucky me, lucky mud.

I, mud, sat up and saw what a nice job God had done.

Nice going, God.

Nobody but you could have done it, God!

I certainly couldn't have.

I feel very unimportant compared to You.

The only way I can feel the least bit important is to think

of all the mud that didn't even get to sit up and look around.

I got so much, and most mud got so little.

Thank you for the honor!

SONG

"Lucky Mud" (composed by Ranger Jim—with apologies to K. Vonnegut)

First Verse

A long time ago, the ancients say
God would sit and play with clay.
Piles of dirt and muck and crud
Nothing but God and lots of mud.
For millions of years he was a lonely Lord
And then, at last, our God got bored.
He took some slop and he took some slime
Mixed 'em together and said, "It's time!
Most of my mud has to stay on the ground
But this lucky mud gets to walk around."

Refrain

Lucky me! Lucky mud!
Earth and rain, flesh and blood.
Lucky mud! Lucky me!
I'm so glad I get to be!

Break

Volcanic ash, the earth's own crust
Soot and soil and lots of dust,
Sand and silt, grit and grime,
Sludge and ooze and slop and slime.

Refrain

Lucky me! Lucky mud!
Earth and rain, flesh and blood.
Lucky mud! Lucky me!
I'm so glad I get to be!

Second Verse

God spoke to me when I was dirt
And now I'm more or less alert.
I get to work and I get to play,
Laugh and love and hope and pray.
I get to hurt and I get to heal,
Taste and touch and think and feel.
I get to hear and I get to see,
Eat and drink and poop and pee.
I get to learn and I get to doubt,
Sing and dance and jump and shout.

Refrain

Lucky me! Lucky mud!
Earth and rain, flesh and blood.
Lucky mud! Lucky me!
I'm so glad I get to be!

Second Break

Ashes to ashes, dust to dust
All things pass, all things must
But here and now, ain't it great
For mud to have such lucky fate?

Refrain

Lucky me! Lucky mud!
Earth and rain, flesh and blood.
Lucky mud! Lucky me!
I'm so glad I get to be!

**The reading from the Book of Bokonon is actually from the novel* Cat's Cradle *by Kurt Vonnegut. The "Book of Bokonon" is a fictitious work sacred to a fictitious religion that features in Vonnegut's novel. [A. P.]*

Oh, good song! Father McCloskey thought. Could be a hit and Kurt might not even sue. No, really. It is a good song. I'll grant that.

But . . .

But . . . the thing is . . .

Cat's Cradle had been Father McCloskey's favorite book when he was in seminary. He had raved about it several times over lunches with Audrey Phillips. He had told her all about Bokononism, the satirical religion Vonnegut created to poke fun at religious certitude. The Bokononists questioned the usefulness of truth and promulgated a religion that identified with its own falseness. They warned against reliance on their most trusted doctrines and they celebrated the dubiety of their most cherished ideals. Hilarious—but also provocative, and strangely inspiring. It was a postmodern religion, a self-consuming artifact (or artifice). And Father McCloskey had told Audrey Phillips all about it at least twelve years before Ranger Jim led this devotion. She had heard about it from him.

It was *my* thing, he thought. It was *my* thing! Where did *he* get it? Did he get it from *her?* Well, she got it from *me.* And why was he getting things from her anyway? Six years at Yellowstone for this book? It took *six years*—with Ranger Jim helping out of course.

Well, that was it for this book. All but the inside flap on the back cover. There was the too-small picture of Audrey with a couple lines of identification:

Audrey Phillips

Audrey Phillips is a professional photographer who appreciates all forms of beauty be it hellish or heavenly. Her previous publications include *Open Hands: Muffler Men in New England and on the National Road* (Kallos Press, 1988) and *Bronco Butlers* (Kallos Press, 1996).

And there was this:

Ranger Jim

Ranger Jim has worked for Yellowstone since 1979. He lives in Pray, Montana and has learned to move among the elk in a way no one else has ever mastered. He plays guitar rather badly (four chords) and exaggerates profusely. The tourists love him all the same. His wife Kimana is a Shoshone Indian, a Wakonda priestess of the Sheepeater tribe.

Father McCloskey closed the book and placed it with the other two on the bottom shelf of the rectory book case. Now all three of his coffee-table books were lying horizontally on the bottom shelf. He stacked a few other largish volumes on top of them.

So Ranger Jim found himself a wife, he thought. A Sheepeater. Well, there is someone for everyone, so they say.

Someone for everyone.

They do say that.

9

Wear Your Love

Fall 1963–Fall 1966

WHAT HE WANTED WAS a dinosaur. Like many youth of his generation, Jimmy Haizlet was fascinated by dinosaurs and the attraction was intensified by being shared with a boy named Tommy Garrett, his best friend throughout the redoubtable years of middle school. It was a bond, a big thing they had in common, though Jimmy's interest in the prehistoric was a little more scientific than his friend's. Tommy collected plastic and rubber models of the beasts without regard for accuracy of depiction. Jimmy was more discriminating.

An alligator was like a modern dinosaur, Tommy said. Actually, it was more like a modern Dimetrodon, Jimmy knew, but it was in the Paleozoic ballpark. Gators and crocodiles and caymans, they were hold-outs. You couldn't get much closer to owning a dinosaur than that, unless of course you had a monitor lizard or an iguana. But the pet store did not sell monitor lizards, and iguanas were not only expensive but famous for escaping.

Pet options were severely limited in the Garrett household, so it fell to Jimmy to get an alligator that they could both regard as their very own almost-dinosaur. Jimmy's father was initially supportive of the idea, but his mother was sensible: "What do you do when it gets big?" That question ended discussion, for Jimmy and Tommy looked at the baby alligators in the tank at the pet store and could not come up with an answer. So, they got a turtle.

A turtle, Jimmy's father insisted, was also something like a dinosaur. Like an ankylosaur basically. And turtles were reptiles that had been around for a long time. What Mr. Haizlet didn't get, and what the boys didn't really want to tell him, was that the *reason* they found dinosaurs so fascinating had less to do with their antiquity than with their capacity for violence and destruction. They were monsters, literal monsters that had actually existed, not just in movies, but on this planet, even in Florida, stomping about the countryside, tearing things from limb to limb. Brontosaurs and ankylosaurs had their place, but the really cool dinosaurs were the ones with *teeth*. Still, a turtle was better than nothing.

They called their acquisition Flagg because of the red stripe on its face (and they spelled it with two "g's" because that looked cool). Jimmy quickly forgot that Flagg had come into his life as a compromise. He doted on the turtle, cleaning its tank daily, feeding it pellets and an occasional goldfish, and playing with it in ways he would not have anticipated were possible. He would lift Flagg out of his aquarium every day and let him run about on the floor, sometimes constructing obstacle courses for him to negotiate. As the months and, eventually, years, went by, he would buy his turtle ever larger tanks and after each move Flagg would grow. And grow. And grow.

At present, however, the most wonderful aspect of turtle ownership was the discovery that the chelonian was of peculiar interest to Diana Wooten, the girl with whom Jimmy had been in love since the beginning of fifth grade. For three years, Diana had tolerated and teased him, flirting with him, but enjoying his devotion without reciprocation. But now, as they entered ninth grade (high school!) together, she became enchanted by Jimmy's exotic pet and actually stopped by his house a couple of times to watch Flagg swim in the tank, eat fish, and crawl about the living room. Finally, she got a turtle herself, a red-eared slider like Flagg but only a third as big. She named it Shelly and placed it in a ten-gallon aquarium with a filter that Jimmy had recommended. After that, he was invited to her house to see the set-up and to offer advice that would ensure Shelly's health and happiness.

And then Jimmy made his move. He suggested that Shelly might be lonely. He knew Flagg was! At the pet store, all the turtles had been in one huge tank, two dozen of them at least. So, maybe, she could bring her pet over some day . . .

"Like a playdate!" she exclaimed.

Yes. Yes, he agreed, excited at the prospect of her coming to his house for something that might be described with words like "play" and "date." And then, for three days, he could think of nothing else: she was coming Saturday morning. She had been there before, but this might be different. For one thing, his parents would not be home. They would be alone in the house and he kept playing out scenarios for what they might do while the turtles swam around together. They would watch them, of course, for a while, but then? Maybe they could sit on the couch and watch TV or something. Lots of scenarios played out in his mind. For three days, he thought of nothing else. She was so blonde and beautiful and he had been in love with her for three years. Three years! And never more than now.

But when Diana dumped Shelly into the large tank in the Haizlet den, Flagg immediately soared through the water, grabbed one of her legs in his mouth and pulled her under. Diana screamed but, laughing, Jimmy assured her, "It's okay, it's okay, they're just playing." But as Flagg swept back and forth under the water, dragging the smaller turtle by its leg, Diana continued squealing anxiously and then exploded, "She can't breathe! She can't breathe! He's drowning her! She can't breathe!" Jimmy suddenly realized that this could actually be true and he ran into the kitchen, returning with a large wooden spoon, which he stuck into the tank, smiting Flagg on his exposed head to make him release his hold. And then, abruptly, the turtles separated and Flagg spun off to one side of the tank while Shelly sank to the bottom. And there she lay, flat in the gravel with her neck and legs splayed out completely, long and floppy. They weren't pulled into the shell at all. They were hanging out, way longer than anyone would have thought. Her neck and three legs and . . . horribly, Jimmy saw the fourth leg lying in the gravel at some distance, off by itself, slightly bloody and completely severed. Diana was screaming and Shelly's head was lying in the gravel without hint of movement. There was no question that the playdate was over and that Diana's pet was dead.

Diana sobbed and cried but it is possible that Jimmy knew the greater sorrow. An intended act of kindness had caused heartache to someone he loved. Before his very eyes, his beloved pet had turned into a vicious fiend. This was a pain beyond anything he had ever imagined: to be the cause of someone else's suffering, with *something he loved* serving as a source of torment *to someone he loved.* After all the times he had fantasized about protecting Diana from bullies and rescuing her from various dangers, it had turned out that the only one she needed to be rescued from was him. How could that have happened? He had intended no evil. How could something so awful result from his only wanting to be good and kind and friendly? A good God would not allow it. A God who cared. Or, at least, a God who cared about *him*.

And so, at the age of fourteen, Jimmy Haizlet turned amateur theologian. He spent that afternoon lying in bed, staring at the ceiling, and repeating a mantra: "God hates me. God hates me. God hates me. God hates me." It was the first time he said these words out loud, but it would not be the last. He had actually been introduced to the possibility of such a deduction in church. Sort of. He didn't usually pay much attention to Scripture or sermons, but one time a line from a Bible reading had caught his notice. Somewhere in the Bible God said, "Jacob I loved, but Eeh-saw I hated" and Jimmy thought, shame on you God, you shouldn't hate anyone. Whoever this poor Eeh-saw guy was, Jimmy felt sorry for him. First, his parents named him after the sound a donkey makes (why not "Oink" or "Cock-a-Doodle"?). Was that why God hated him, or did he do something really bad? Well, whatever it was, Jimmy thought, lying in his bed on that Saturday afternoon, whatever it was, now I know how he felt.

Whether or not God hated Jimmy Haizlet, one thing was certain: Diana Wooten sure did. And Jimmy accepted that this was his fate, to be in love with a girl who hated him. He not only accepted it, but reveled in it, developing an entire philosophy of life that explained it all and sustained him from day to day. It might have been called Adolescent Existentialism 101:

1. the purpose of life is to be in love; and,
2. the condition of being "in love" can be defined as a spectrum of pain ranging in intensity from "familiar ache" to "constant torment."

In his sophomore year, many of Jimmy's friends began dating and by his junior year, *most* of his friends were dating and quite a few of them had girlfriends. The school regularly had dances and even the guys who didn't usually date would ask someone to go to a dance or maybe they would just go alone and meet a girl there. But Jimmy Haizlet didn't date and he didn't go to the dances. He didn't even go to the junior-senior prom. It wouldn't have felt right. He never tried to explain this to anyone but, basically, he just thought it would be *wrong* to date anyone else when he was so in love with Diana. It would be *unfaithful*, like cheating on someone. He couldn't bring himself to be *unfaithful* to Diana, whatever she thought of him. He preferred to stay home and listen to favorite songs on vinyl LPs and 45s. It was the end of the sixties and there were a lot of good songs.

Years later, if you had mentioned his name to almost anyone at the high school's twenty-fifth reunion (which neither he nor Diana Wooten attended), they would have said, "Haizlet? Jimmy Haizlet? Was he that guy who was in love with a girl who hated him?"

But to be fair, he did have other interests: science, science fiction, fantasy, and comic books. As for the first of these, he continued to be interested in science that had to do with the prehistoric world, but also now, with outer space. Not coincidentally, these were areas that often provided inspiration for fantasy and science fiction. And although he wasn't much of a writer, he liked making up fantasy or comic-book-style stories in his head and thinking that maybe he would write them all down someday. He actually composed a whole series of comic books (in his head) featuring the exploits of a superhero he called Naked Girl. She could blink her clothes off and suddenly be stark naked and the bank robbers would be so startled that they dropped their guns. Plus, once they saw her they couldn't take their eyes off her and they would literally freeze where they were, staring at her but unable to move. The cops would come and take them away and say, "Thank you, Naked Girl!" and then she would blink her clothes back on again. Someday when he found an artist, he thought, the two of them could create a whole new line of graphic novels that were tasteful (she'd have to be standing behind things a lot) but more mature than the comics that were just for kids, and he would tell the artist that Naked Girl should look exactly like Diana Wooten. That way, when there was a movie he could recommend her for the part and it would be her big breakthrough in Hollywood and maybe she wouldn't think he was such a nerd *then*.

Sometimes he realized that none of this was ever going to happen.

* * *

Spring 1970

Ben Stewart and Todd Meiner were quite possibly the sort of adolescents that roots rocker Jonathan Rundmann had in mind when he composed his song "Tired, Tired, Tired," though that would actually be thirty years later, around the turn of the millennia:

I'm so tired of teenage smokers
Standing on the corner, goin' nowhere slow
Passin' round a lighter, cussin' and complainin'
I don't want to hear it, I don't want to know.

It was in the company of these cussing and complaining smokers that Jimmy Haizlet would embark on a memorable trip to Florida State University in Tallahassee when his senior project, and theirs, were selected by Wedgewood High to represent the school at a regional science fair.

Jimmy's study of trilobite fossils was classed as an entry in the broad category of Life Sciences. Laura Swanson was supposed to represent Wedgewood in Chemistry but withdrew at the last minute due to a schedule conflict (Bowie concert). Ben and Todd shared honors for a contribution to Physics that had something to do with electrical impulses. Their display was quite fancy and involved batteries, lights, and a number of dials and switches. Jimmy didn't quite understand what it was about and, to tell the truth, neither did Ben or Todd. The latter's father was a physicist and the boys made no secret of the fact that Dr. Meiner had done most of the work on their project. Mr. Stewart (Ben's father), on the other hand, had the distinction of owning a 1968 Dodge A100 van (buff colored with Gulfstream II corporate airplane interior and no windows), so it fell to him to drive the three boys with their display boards and assorted paraphernalia to the Florida State University campus in Tallahassee where the extravaganza was to take place. Wedgewood had made reservations there for the four of them for two nights and, even before Mr. Stewart had decided not to stay, Ben and Todd had declared that they would be roommates, sticking Jimmy with the adult. Mr. Stewart, however, had compassionately determined that a night in a cheap motel would be preferable to bunking in a dorm room with one of his son's schoolmates. Jimmy's parents would come up the next day with the Meiners and return that evening with the projects in Mr. Stewart's van. The Meiners would take over the motel room and drive all three boys home to Jacksonville on Sunday afternoon.

The fair itself ran from eight to five, all day Saturday. The boys would sit at their respective tables and explain their projects to judges in the morning. Then, after a two-hour lunch break, the displays would be open to the public and students would be expected to sit at their tables again and talk to anyone who came by until 5:00. After that, there would be a banquet of sorts in the dining hall, where ribbons, awards, and certificates could be presented.

Thus, the fair was really just a one-day event but the boys had to arrive Friday to set up and they had to stay over until Sunday because then there would be a campus tour and other events sponsored by the university in an attempt to capitalize on the presence of prospective students who they assumed to be of extraordinary caliber. Nobody in the Wedgewood group actually cared about the Sunday program, but the institution was granting free room and board to those who stayed the extra night, so that was the deal.

Ben and Todd had complained a good bit about the fair being on a weekend, such that they did not even get out of school to attend, and a good bit more about having to stay over on a Saturday night for no good reason whatsoever. Dr. Meiner decided unilaterally that his son could skip school on Monday and Tuesday as a reward and once that was declared, Ben gained sufficient leverage to wheedle the same arrangement with his father. Otherwise, there was a good chance that Wedgewood might have gone unrepresented in the Physics arena.

Mr. Stewart was an affable man who did not smoke, cuss, or complain, but he was also quite open-minded with regard to issues of free speech and Jimmy discovered immediately that Ben and Todd talked almost the same way around the adult as they would have talked had he not been there. The father gained some points in Jimmy's mind for managing to instill such a rare degree of trust or camaraderie in the parent-child relationship. Or was it just a lack of respect? In any case, it did unfortunately mean that the two-and-a-half hours spent with Ben and Todd would be almost as tiring as it would have been with no adult present.

"Tolkien, eh?" Mr. Stewart said, noticing Jimmy's book (*The Two Towers*) as the latter climbed in to the shotgun seat in front. Ben and Todd had already claimed the two rear benches (which faced each other) and they were busy setting up their Mercury cassette recorder and digging through a cardboard box of tapes. For the next two hours they would be blaring Iron Butterfly, Deep Purple, Black Sabbath, Led Zeppelin, Mountain, and Vanilla Fudge. Jimmy would have preferred the Beatles, Peter, Paul, and Mary, or even the Monkees. Actually he had just acquired two new albums in the last three months, records that he would prize for the rest of his life: *Bridge over Troubled Waters*, by Simon and Garfunkel, and *Déjà Vu*, by Crosby, Stills, Nash, and Young.

The famous 1960s had just come to an end and although there weren't many actual hippies in Jacksonville, Florida, Jimmy had been caught up and transported by all the attention to love and peace and flowers and happiness. It was almost as if the world had caught up with him, as if people under thirty had decided to embrace the values he had espoused all along. He loved Donovan's *A Gift from a Flower to a Garden* partly for the name and partly because he thought "Wear Your Love Like Heaven" was the most beautiful song ever written. And now he was perhaps the only person in America who thought the best song on *Déjà Vu* was the album's closer, a song called "Everybody, I Love You."

But there would be no flowery celebrations of love and peace in the van on the trip to Tallahassee. Robert Plant screamed about squeezing his lemons and Ozzy Osbourne roared about Satan worship and Lucifer's love affairs. "N.I.B. means Nativity in Black," Ben explained to Todd, "and the song is all about the devil doing it with an earth woman." He was wearing a T-shirt that showed the famous Woodstock logo with a dead dove hanging from the guitar, pierced by an arrow and dripping blood.

"That's the one with the Ents, isn't it?" Mr. Stewart asked Jimmy regarding his book. "It's about Sauron and Saruman."

"It's about fairies," Ben volunteered from the back. "And little gay elves who do each other in the butt." His father glanced back at him, seemingly more surprised that his son had been attentive to the conversation than by the content of his remarks.

"It's required reading for freaks and squares," the boy continued. "And for queers and Star Trek fans."

"He should not be reading that book if he ever wants to have a girlfriend," Todd affirmed.

"Unless he wants to *be* someone's girlfriend," Ben added, and they both snickered.

Todd continued the thread.

"Next he should read all the Narnia books about talking Jesus lions."

"And the Oz books and Peter Pan. The library has a whole section called Books for Fairies."

They went back to venerating Ozzy, apparently unaware that the second song on the album ("The Wizard") was about Gandalf.

"Well," Mr. Stewart said to Jimmy, ignoring them, "I really liked the whole series. I read them twice. That's a bit of a commitment for someone your age, though."

"I like long books," Jimmy replied.

"What else have you been reading?"

"I read this book called *Dune.* And I liked *The Lost World* by Sir Arthur Conan Doyle."

"The Hardy Boys . . ." Todd chimed in from the back.

"Nancy Drew," Ben continued and they guffawed at each other's cleverness.

"Well, Tolkien's a good read," Mr. Stewart said, continuing to ignore them. "Did you get to the Ents?"

"Yes. They're cool."

The van continued along the highway and, for some time Ben and Todd swapped out tapes. They debated the competitive merits of songs and sounds and Ben said that the name Black Sabbath came from a movie that Ozzy liked. Ben had seen the movie and he thought it was pretty good, but not like *The Wild Bunch* or *Night of the Living Dead.* Not that good. And then, as a coda, he opined, "I just saw the worst movie ever made."

"And I know it had to star Jerry Lewis," Todd volunteered.

"But it didn't. It was worse."

"How can it be the worst ever and not have Jerry Lewis?"

"It starred Mary Poppins and it was about this nun who was desperate to get laid but no one would do her because she was such a twit, so she marries this rich Nazi and makes all his kids sing songs from Romper Room and the Mickey Mouse Club."

"Are you talking about *The Sound of Music*?" Mr. Stewart inquired from the front.

"The Sound of Puking is more like it."

"That's a classic musical. The songs are all by Rodgers and Hammerstein."

"Who were gay lovers," Ben concluded and then chortled at the quickness of his repartee.

"I don't think so," Mr. Stewart responded. "But . . . well, it's music from another era . . . not rock and roll."

"Roger and the hammer guy."

"Hammerhead. Hammerfoot. Hammerbutt."

"What was his name, Dad?"

"Hammerstein."

The two exploded in laughter, as if the real name was funnier than anything they might have come up with.

"He's like the love child of Thor and Frankenstein," Todd offered after a moment for reflection . . . and then he shrugged as if to indicate, okay, not one of my better ones. But Ben continued anyway . . .

"He used to get queer with his lover and say, 'Oh, Roger! Let's write songs about how gay we are and then see if we can find anyone lame enough to sing them.'"

"So tell me who they found."

"Five girls who a) couldn't sing, and b) were such twits no one would ever want to do them. I mean, one of them was like two years old, but even the other ones, you would never want to do them."

"Were they real dogs or something?"

"No, but they were all like young versions of your grandmother and they wore matching dresses made out of the living room curtains."

"Now you're lying."

"I am not. They took down the drapes and made dresses out of them. And the nun decided she was Shari Lewis and taught them all these bubblegum puppet songs that the Cowsills would have rejected. Lamb Chop and Wing Ding . . ."

"Like yummy, yummy, yummy, I've got love in my tummy."

"Like that, yeah. I'm surprised they didn't do that one. Anyway, do you remember that stupid song Mrs. Elkins made us do in music . . . 'Doe, a Deer, a Female Deer'?"

"Sometimes in my nightmares. My junior high nightmares."

"They sang that song."

"Now you are definitely lying."

"They sang it twice."

"Liar."

"They sang it and everyone clapped and applauded like they didn't even realize that they had just heard the single worst song ever written and then, I mean, I was praying to God to kill me or to just lobotomize me right there on the spot to end my suffering before anything else could happen, and then they sang it again."

"Wow."

"And then this teenage twit sings this song to her boyfriend that's like, 'I'm sixteen, and a slut, slut, slut,' but it's to the tune of a dog food commercial."

"Did they get it on?"

"That song would have turned him gay if he wasn't already, which he was. So he just sings it with her and they skip around their clubhouse and then have a tea party or go play with their Barbie dolls or something."

"Okay, music critics," Mr. Stewart interrupted. "This is from before the Beatles, you know. It's not rock and roll."

"There wasn't any music before the Beatles," Todd responded. "Not really."

"What about Elvis?"

"No one likes Elvis except fat women."

"Fat women at laundromats—that is his entire audience."

"Really?" Mr. Stewart replied. "Well, I did not know that. This is quite enlightening. What about Frank Sinatra?"

"I don't know anything by him."

"Um . . . 'Fly Me to the Moon' . . . 'My Way' . . . 'The Lady is a Tramp.'"

"Never heard of them," Todd responded.

"It's a Disney movie about gay dogs," Ben explained.

"No, it isn't," his father countered.

"Anyway, the Beatles are wimps," Ben concluded. "Except John. Paul is a wimp. George, who knows, but he's like a Mormon or something. And I think Ringo's a drag queen."

Mr. Stewart looked over at Jimmy, as if to avoid the temptation of further involvement with the backseat conversation.

"So, how's the book?"

"A bit slow actually. Hard to concentrate."

"Ah! Well . . . any instances of elfin anal intercourse yet?"

"No. But I've got a hundred pages to go."

* * *

They got to the university around 6:00, too late for the dining hall if they wanted to get everything set up before dark, and they did. They spent the next hour finding the right building and then unloading the van and transferring materials to designated spots where their different projects should be placed. The exhibits had to be carried down a flight of stairs and then arranged on the cafeteria-style folding tables the school had provided (one for every two projects). Jimmy was pleased to note that the displays for Life Sciences and for Physics were housed in separate rooms. Mr. Stewart helped Jimmy get his work set up first and then tackled the more difficult task of last-minute wiring on the Physics exhibit (so that the various lights and switches would actually work). Dr. Meiner had provided him with a brief instruction sheet, no more complicated than your usual stereo set-up but a little daunting for an assistant manager of a pool supply company, which is what Mr. Stewart was on most days. Ben and Todd sat off to the side and talked about a friend of theirs who was supposed to be cool but had gone to see Three Dog Night, marking him forever as a total dweeb.

Next they found the dorms and their assigned rooms. It was actually a suite of two rooms with a bathroom between them. Each room had two twin beds, two desks, and two empty dressers, but no television or "anything else that the world's crappiest motel would probably have." While Ben and Todd were listing these deficiencies and bemoaning their fate at spending an entire weekend in what was essentially a homeless shelter, they discovered that most of the school's regular students had vacated the campus for spring break, during which time the fair had been strategically scheduled. Ben lamented that his intention of bagging some college babe would now, perhaps, go unfulfilled, and Todd observed that the mere fact that the school had so many empty rooms available was a bit of a red flag that any potential student who didn't have dog turds for brains would be likely to notice. Indeed, they were staying on the third floor of the building's west wing, which was now occupied in its entirety by other male high school candidates for the science fair. The lower two floors contained locked rooms of the FSU students who were on spring break. Female fair participants were similarly housed on the third floor of the building's east wing. Florida State had been a women's college until 1947 but the current building had been constructed since then with a design that allowed for minimal co-ed occupancy: one could not reach the female-occupied east wing from the male-occupied west wing (or vice versa) without going through the first-floor lobby and using keys that were distributed only to persons of the appropriate sex. Ben opined that while such separatist measures would never prove insurmountable to the motivated, they were pretty much unnecessary considering the type of dweebs and dweebettes who would be attending an event like this. His father noted from a pamphlet left on the desks that there was to be a dance in the gymnasium that night.

The foursome piled back into the van to find some food. After passing up two fast-food establishments that, according to the backseat, specialized in serving barf and diarrhea, they settled on a Whataburger that had closed its indoor seating but still had a drive-through.

The advertised dance started at nine and ran until twelve. It was 10:15 when Mr. Stewart dropped the well-fed teenagers off in front of the gym. He wished the boys well with the fair the next day and drove away. The strains of the Carpenters' "Close to You" could be heard wafting from inside the building. Ben and Todd had produced cigarettes from somewhere and were already lighting up. Then, turning, they both headed toward the dorm.

"You're not going in?" Jimmy called after them, noting that they seemed to make such decisions in sync, through telepathy or something, and that they hadn't included him in whatever their plans or lack thereof might be.

They looked at him incredulously, glanced at the open doors to the gym from which the melody emanated and then, covering their ears, made faces that conveyed their assessment of what the morons in charge of the dance apparently thought might qualify as aural entertainment. Of course. Bacharach/David would be only one step removed from Rodgers and Hammerstein.

So, alone, Jimmy wandered into the gymnasium. The dance was pretty lame, he had to admit. There were about thirty-five people there, and only four couples were really dancing, boyfriends and girlfriends holding onto each other and swaying or at least hugging to the sounds of a song they possibly liked. Other folks were standing around talking and in one corner some girls were dancing (sort of) with each other, sliding back and forth in rhythm to the tune without actually touching. There was no live band but just a table with a big stereo and one of the college's senior students was playing selections from what was possibly his personal record collection.

Jimmy toured the perimeter of the room while "Spinning Wheel" by Blood, Sweat, and Tears blared out of the speakers. The girls who were dancing with each other were a bit more energetic in their movements now and he noticed that one of them was extremely cute. She was slender with long straight hippie hair like Cher and Joni Mitchell and Buffy St. Marie. She was wearing something sparkly. Her breasts bounced as she moved and she seemed to have a really pretty face. And then he suddenly realized that she had seen him looking at her. She turned away, ignoring him, and then she looked back and smiled. Her eyes seemed sparkly too, as they caught the beam of a flashing strobe light that someone had strung up from a basketball backboard. She probably wore contacts.

Her face was so pretty! Thirty years later, he would think the singer Dido might look a lot like her, if only she let her hair grow. He almost wrote to Dido to suggest she grow her hair long but then he thought that, considering the song she did with Eminem ("Stan"), Dido might be the least likely celebrity on the planet to appreciate mail from a possibly obsessed fan. Still, he would like all of Dido's songs (except for the one with Eminem) and they would be a soundtrack for remembering this weekend.

But that would never have happened if not for Sly and the Family Stone. Jimmy was already heading for the door when, against all odds, the senior said he was going to play a twofer of "Hot Fun in the Summertime" and "Everyday People," bouncy songs that Jimmy really liked. Okay, he thought. I'll give it a chance. The sparkly girl was talking to her friends, sliding on the floor, showing them one of her moves. He walked toward her and it was a long walk because he realized when he had gone a little ways that she and all of her friends knew he was coming long before he arrived, and still he had to walk on and on while they glanced his way repeatedly and pretended not to know or care that he was approaching . . . and then *finally* he was there.

"Do you want to dance?" he asked, realizing immediately after he said it that he had addressed the entire group of girls and there was no way for the cute one to know he was talking to her. But apparently there was no mystery in that regard because they all knew who he meant and she responded immediately.

"Sure," she said, and took his hand and walked with him, leading him across the floor away from where her friends were standing. All he'd done was ask her to dance and now she was holding his hand. He was sure that he had held hands with girls before but this somehow felt different—not like holding hands in a prayer circle at church or for some other social or friendly reason. Her hand was warm and moist and soft and smooth and he couldn't help but realize that it was covered with girl-skin, the same skin that went underneath her clothes and covered her whole body. But no sooner had he begun to realize that he was in physical contact with naked girl-flesh, than she let go and turned to face him.

"Um . . ." he said then, realizing there was a problem.

She looked at him and understood.

"Do you know how to dance?" she asked.

"No," he shook his head, feeling stupid.

She smiled.

"Well, basically, you just bounce around. Can you do that?"

"I don't know. I . . . I don't think so."

"Do you know anybody here?"

"No."

"So, it doesn't matter if you look silly since there's no one to impress."

"Well . . . you."

"Okay." She smiled. "I won't look." She shut her eyes tight. "Okay. Now. Start bouncing or something."

He looked at her pretty face and then down at her sparkly shirt.

"Are you doing it?"

"Un-huh," he lied, staring at her chest. "A little bit." Round, sparkly hills. On her chest. Round, sparkly hills.

"Okay . . . watch me!" she said (unnecessarily) and started swinging her body around to the music. Now her breasts bounced underneath the sparkly shirt and he watched them, mesmerized, and then looked back toward her friends, who were laughing and talking about him. She stumbled into him and he laughed. She looked ridiculous, sillier than he possibly could if he did the same thing, which was apparently the point.

"Are you dancing?" she asked.

"Yes," he lied again, and then started moving his hips just a little bit.

"'Cause if you're not, you are making me look pretty silly and I don't want you to do that to me."

"No, I'm dancing. I look bad. Worse than you."

"Can I look?"

"No, not yet." He tried to dance a little bit but couldn't when he was watching her, which seemed a lot more important. The strobe light was reflecting off her sparkly shirt and her curves were moving underneath it, like rolling sand dunes beneath a galaxy of twinkling stars. Rolling, bouncing hills. Bouncing with the music.

The song ended and she opened her eyes a split second after he looked up. God! He thought. She almost caught me. Indeed, there was a flicker of a questioning look but then she laughed and said, "That was a practice dance. Now you gotta do one for real." The next song was the previously announced "Everyday People," and he found it pretty easy to move to, so they both danced (or at least bounced around and shook their bodies) to it, eyes open, watching each other, and he tried not to think about how socially relevant and meaningful the lyrics were, which had once been what made him love the song but which had nothing to do with dancing in a gym with a sparkly girl. She said things like "That's pretty good," and "See how easy it is," and "This is fun, isn't it?"

Then the student put on "Hey Jude," which was a slow song and Sparkles (his name for her) came up close to him and wrapped her arms about him. Her breasts touched his chest. Then he put his arms around her and they hugged each other close and her breasts squished against him so that he could *feel* them touching him. He could *really* feel them and could even tell what size they were—small-to-medium, though he didn't know that (and for the rest of his life he would think that these were what perfect breasts felt like and that anything larger was too big). A hard lump formed in his pants and he was terrified that she might feel that. They started swaying softly to the music, not really dancing but just walking slowly about in circles, keeping to the rhythm but mostly just holding onto each other's bodies. She put her head on his shoulder and nuzzled his neck with her nose and mouth and she rubbed her hands in gentle circles across his shoulder blades and back. He did the same to her and he could feel the straps of her bra underneath the sparkly shirt. She slid one hand down to the small of his back and pushed the lower part of his body closer to hers and the hard lump in his pants pressed tight against her, right at her waist and he thought, oh my God, now she's going to feel it for sure! He expected her to push him away at any moment and probably yell and maybe hit him, but they kept dancing through all the "Na Na NaNaNa Nah's" until the song ended and then the student DJ went for something by Booker T. & the M.G.'s.

"I don't like this song," she said. He shook his head to indicate a similar judgment and she took him by the hand and they walked farther from the speakers where they could just talk. That was when she told him her name was Dana and she was from Gainesville. She had a cat named "Fleabag," which he thought was a funny name, and she told him some stories about this cat who lived indoors and was afraid of mice, and how he had become a primary object of her affection. Then they danced to a couple more tolerable numbers and he held her body close to his again for "Helpless" from Crosby, Stills, Nash, and Young's new *Déjà Vu* album. After that, the DJ put on "Tighten Up" by Archie Bell and the Drells and it was just like telepathy how they both moved immediately away from the dancing area to where they had talked before, but then she pointed to a door that led outside and said loudly over the music, "Let's go make out, okay?"

That definitely sounded okay, though he wasn't 100 percent sure what it meant. Kissing, he thought. "Make out" means kissing, right? The door led to an outdoor enclosed area where there were a few tables and benches. Four couples were scattered about, as far from each other as possible, their mouths locked together and their hands exploring each other's bodies. The sparkly girl he now hoped to marry led him to a bench where they plopped down side by side and, immediately, she put her mouth on his. Her lips were soft and parted and, just like that, he was kissing one of the prettiest girls in the world and her tongue was in his mouth . . . and then they were suddenly interrupted by one of her friends calling her from the doorway. Breaking from his embrace, she got up and went over to talk to whoever it was. She fidgeted there and fussed, obviously displeased with the message or the messenger, and then she tramped back in a very different mood.

"Sorry. I have to go."

"Okay." He was disappointed, but of course, not surprised.

"It's my sponsor. Mrs. Gingrich. She says she wants us all to get together now, tonight, to go over stuff for tomorrow. Really she just wants to ruin our evening. She never wants anyone to have any fun."

"I'm sorry. I like being with you."

"No, really. I'm not blowing you off. I thought, you know, you could love on me a little, but now . . . well, this is a bummer."

"Okay."

She kissed him on the mouth and said, "Thanks for asking me to dance with you." He didn't know what else to say so he told her she was pretty and he liked her sparkles. Then she walked away. Her friend was holding the door and as they went into the gym he heard her say, "He was looking at your tits. The whole time you had your eyes shut, he was looking at your tits." Jimmy waited a couple of awkward minutes alone in the outdoor patio with the kissing couples and then he went out through the gym to return to his dorm. His mind overflowed with questions and thoughts, including what, precisely, "love on me a little" might mean.

Thirty-two years later, when he was fifty, James Haizlet would make a list of "The Twenty-Five Best Songs of All Time." Number one, of course was "Wear Your Love Like Heaven," but it is noteworthy that "Everyday People," "Hey Jude," and "Helpless" were also on the list.

* * *

Jimmy's folding travel alarm was set for 6:30, not because he needed an hour and a half to get to his display table but because he wanted to get into the shared bathroom before Ben or Todd laid claim to the shower. He needn't have worried. He had not seen either of them the night before and he did not hear from them now. In fact, they would not arrive at their table until a little after 9:00 (an hour into the official judging period). So, although he did not particularly care about breakfast, he ended up leaving his dorm dressed and ready a full hour before he was due to appear in the exhibit hall. He wandered the campus a bit and went by the cafeteria on the off chance that Dana might be there. She wasn't. Eschewing the eggs, pancakes, and grease-soaked sausages, he scarfed down a bowl of Lucky Charms and then wandered over to the hall, arriving just as the doors were opened.

Unlike his co-representatives of Wedgewood High, Jimmy took this fair seriously. He really believed in the importance of his project. He had worked hard on it and he was proud of the work that he had done. He realized, of course, that such enthusiasm marked him as a nerd or square or something like that, but he was not embarrassed that he had been selected from his peers as one whose work in this area was exemplary. In fact, the previous night, in a pause between dances, he had almost launched into a summary of his work, under some illusion that his sparkly partner might be impressed to learn the man who had requested her company was an amateur authority on paleontological arthropods. God, he thought now. How close he had come to ruining everything. If he had followed his instincts, been true to himself, the all-important (but very short) make-out phase of the evening would likely not have transpired at all. There was a lesson to be learned.

The truth is, he found trilobites to be intrinsically fascinating. The Paleozoic sea creatures ruled the earth for some 200 million years, making them quite possibly the most successful life form ever to inhabit the planet. Fossils had been discovered in almost every part of the globe and over 10,000 different species of the creatures had been identified. Distant relatives of horseshoe crabs and centipedes, they came in one basic shape but many sizes. Most were only three to six centimeters in length, but the big ones grew to sixty to seventy centimeters. They were intriguing for many reasons, but it was their ability to adapt to such diverse climates and circumstances that raised some particularly piquant possibilities. If life should one day actually be found on another planet, Jimmy surmised, it would not likely be the humanoid aliens of sci-fi fame. It would not likely be intelligent (i.e., self-aware) beings at all. It would probably be something similar to trilobites.

That was the crux of his project: *The Evolutionary Success of Class Trilobita and its Implications for Speculation Regarding Extra-Terrestrial Life*. He did not claim, as he had to explain repeatedly, that there were trilobites in outer space. Rather, he suggested that the trilobites that had once existed on earth (and only on earth) were a more likely approximation for what scientists should hope to find elsewhere than were humans, mammals, reptiles, birds, or any of nature's other less successful experiments. In part, the conclusion was simply statistical. If scientists on some other planet had been searching for life on earth at random points during its four billion year existence, they would have been far more likely to have found trilobites than mammals. But beyond that, factors contributing to the trilobites' titular "evolutionary success" were worthy of note. Most earth creatures (e.g., humans) have very specific biological requirements with regard to such things as environment, temperature, atmosphere, food supply, and energy (light). Such beings are unlikely to have analogues on other worlds where such conditions are rarely (if ever) duplicated. But trilobites were less finicky; they demonstrated an ability to make do and a capacity to survive conditions that would send other creatures packing.

The judges began coming by around 8:30 and Jimmy displayed his materials and discussed his passion to them in individual conversations that inevitably had to compete with conversations at adjoining tables. The high school junior who shared his table had a moronic project dealing with the intoxication of ants (he gave them beer and observed the effect on their work habits) and that, at least, seemed to make Jimmy look good by comparison. There were a lot of judges because, in addition to the official awards presented by the fair itself, various sponsoring agencies were giving out prizes. The chain of Noodle Kidoodle stores offered gift certificates for students in each division and the Lions and Kiwanis clubs both had representatives roaming the exhibits to select projects for special honors. The branches of the military were there as well and Jimmy thought he might have a good shot at the fifty dollar Air Force prize, seeing as how this fair had no category for Space Science and his was one of the only ventures to deal even remotely with that field. But he was hoping for one of the major awards: the fair's official team of judges chose projects in each division for first, second, and third prizes, and gave everyone else what Ben and Todd called "Loser Awards" (officially known as "Certificates of Merit"). Back home, Jimmy hadn't been sure what his chances might be, but he'd toured the displays the previous night while Mr. Stewart was occupied with his son's work, and he didn't think many of them were as good as his. Most were somewhat gimmicky, often relying on a single process that could have been copied from a catalogue or some mechanism constructed from a kit. He suspected that most of the projects had been presented elsewhere in almost identical formats by countless other students at countless other fairs. By contrast, he was presenting an original thesis, substantiated by research and evidence that some people in the scientific community might actually take seriously.

The judges seemed to ask basic questions that he could have answered even before working up the project itself. He explained repeatedly that the name *trilobite* means "three lobes" and derives from the segmentation of the creatures' bodies into three parts: a cephalon (head), thorax, and pygidium (tail). They had numerous pairs of legs on the thorax and four more pairs on the head. These legs had gills. Trilobites lived 570–240 million years ago during the Paleozoic era. But all of this was basic. He wanted to explain in more depth that these creatures had in fact existed (and thrived) for eons under conditions that scientists allow could exist on other worlds (or moons) within our galaxy. "So do you think they would have come to earth on a meteor?" one professor asked him. "No," he explained, clarifying his position in a voice that perhaps showed a little too much patience. "There's no reason to think that trilobites ever existed anywhere but on earth. But their survival here has implications for what kind of life forms might be found elsewhere."

"Are they bugs?" a young woman asked. She was a student at the university and a member of the Science Club, which was also giving an award. She was five years older than Jimmy, but young enough and attractive enough to necessitate suppression of an instinctive urge to flirt. Ben and Todd would be less successful at such suppression when she visited their table, but the disastrous impression they made on her mattered little, as she was really only interested in chemistry projects. Jimmy could understand how a chemistry major might not be sufficiently informed to distinguish all the classes of arthropods (Trilobita from Insecta) but he couldn't help but think that *bugs* was a rather unscientific term.

"They're not, but they look a lot like insects, don't they?" he responded. "Actually, when they were discovered, some scientists thought that they were the ancestors of insects. A guy named Handlirsch speculated that their lateral lobes eventually became wings, allowing them to leave the water and lose their gills. But now everyone agrees that insects and trilobites must have had some common ancestor, probably from the Cambrian period."

"Un-huh," she responded, nodding, and then moved on.

Jimmy also spoke to a distinguished gentleman with white hair, who carried an unlit pipe as though it were a prop to aid his impersonation of an Oxford don. This man sat with him for considerably more time than would seem to be a normative allotment and Jimmy had the opportunity to show him somewhat extraneous pictures in a book from a box beneath his table. They displayed drawings that looked like illustrations from some fantasy comic book: a segmented creature with five eyes on stalks that emerged from its head and spiked pincers on the tip of its tail, and an oddity with fourteen legs and with seven tentacles growing out of its back. These, he assured his inquisitor, are not fanciful depictions of imaginary extra-terrestrial aliens or even of *lusus naturae*, but scientific representations of animals that actually lived on this planet, though they bear no resemblance to any living organism today.

"Are they trilobites?" the gentleman asked, though he surely knew that they were not.

"No, these are from the Cambrian period. This one is called Hallucigenia, a great name I think, since it looks like something you'd have to be on drugs to dream up. And the one with five eyes is Opabinia. They weren't as successful as my trilobites, but they help to illustrate a part of my thesis, that life on another world would probably not be humanoid but, to our reckoning, something utterly fantastic."

"Do you have any fossils of these?"

"Oh no, those would be rare, and they would all be in museums. Actually, they're mostly in the Smithsonian, because they were discovered by a man named Charles Walcott who was one of the directors of the Smithsonian Institution."

"Ah!" the adult seemed surprised. "You know about Charles Walcott?"

"Yes. He did excavations in what's called the Burgess Shale in the first part of this century. It was important because he found there the first fossils that linked single-cell organisms to more complex ones."

"That's right," the man confirmed, betraying his own apparently specialized knowledge and interest in the subject. "I'm glad to see someone your age with a sense of scientific history."

"Well, Walcott is pretty interesting. He used to camp out in the Rockies every year, way up in Canada, with his whole family, and hunt fossils along old Indian trails. It was quite an adventure a hundred years ago. Also, I'm intrigued because the man didn't have much education. He came from a poor family and just worked his way up, learning what he had to know as he went. But, you know, he ended up teaching at Harvard."

"I don't know much about that part of his life."

"Well, then, here's some trivia. Do you know how he got started in becoming a scientist? When he was a boy, like in 1860 or something, they were trying to push a wagon out of the mud and the wheel kicked up a flat rock that had a fossil on it. He picked up that rock and kept it and, well, over time he just got fixated on it and had to find more rocks with pictures on them . . . that is, more fossils."

"Really?"

"Guess what the fossil was?"

"A trilobite?"

"You got it. He ended up being the world expert on trilobites. He found one that had an injured eye and wrote a paper about how it had been hurt. He studied trilobite eggs. He was the first person to figure out that trilobites had legs, which don't show up in most fossils. And that they could roll themselves up in balls for protection like armadillos or pill bugs."

"What?"

"Woodlice. I call them pill bugs."

"Because they look like pills?"

"When they're rolled up they do."

* * *

After lunch in the dining hall (where once again he searched in vain for Dana), the exhibits were opened to the general public and Jimmy sat at his table for three hours, talking with visitors, most of whom were parents or siblings of the other students. He repeated many of the same points from the morning ("No, they're not bugs." "No, I don't think they came here from outer space.") and began to grow noticeably tired and cranky. And then, around 4:00, his parents arrived and spent a few minutes praising his display and drilling him about the morning. He recounted with genuine pride the impression that he believed he had made on the judges and his parents were congratulatory and pleased. Then he suggested they all check in on Ben and Todd, whose parents had also just made the trip from Jacksonville, and when they moved into that room, he seized the moment to look for Dana. She would be there, in the Physics room, having put together something to do with lightning rods (and eventually he hoped to tell her what he knew about lightning strikes which, he believed, would provide material for an interesting narrative). He scanned the room and spotted her. All the way across the hall, she was standing with her friends and teacher (Mrs. Gingrich!). She was wearing a skirt and a green blouse. It wasn't sparkly, but she still looked beautiful. They were all getting ready to leave, to go out the door on the other side of the room. Then, she looked in his direction and she saw him, standing there, looking at her. She lifted one hand and wiggled her fingers as her entire troupe exited out into the hall. And then she was gone. He hadn't even gotten to see her project. And she hadn't seen his. He had wanted to show it to her. Well, maybe if it won a ribbon, he'd have to leave it up for photographs and he briefly imagined how she would come by while he was posing for the newspapers and then he would take her aside and tell her about trilobites and ask some intelligent questions about lightning.

There was a banquet and he sat between his mother and father, eating salad and chicken and green beans—nondescript cafeteria food—and then the awards were presented. All of the prizes given by special groups were read first, starting with Life Sciences. Jimmy didn't win the Air Force prize; that went to someone who'd built a little machine to launch a ball into the air and a receiver to catch it. He didn't win any of the other special honors either, but that wasn't surprising. Next were special group prizes for Chemistry and the girl who had come out on the porch last night (to fetch Dana out of his arms) won something. He watched her return to her table and noted the general location of where that group must be seated.

The important awards, the ribbons presented by the fair's own judges, were next. For Life Sciences, third place went to *Effects of Carcinogenic and Non-Carcinogenic Smoke on Botanical Growth Rate*; second, to *Does Growth of Mold Under Diverse Temperatures Vary with Grain Composition of Bread?*; and, first, to *The Effect of Antibiotics on Gram-Positive and Gram-Negative Bacteria*. He was disappointed. Shut out. Nothing. Well, at least, the drunk ants didn't win. He really, *really* hoped Ben and Todd would not take home any of the ribbons. But they did. Third place in Physics. God. They got their ribbon and their parents congratulated them and then his parents and he himself congratulated them while they rolled their eyes and made it clear that they didn't care.

"And now the losers," Ben quipped to Todd as a stodgy middle-aged woman proceeded to recite a roll call of all the remaining science fair participants, and practically every student in the room moved in a steady alphabetical stream to a table in front of the dais to receive a "Certificate of Merit." And then something odd happened. The names jumped from Hailey to Healey, omitting him entirely. There was some murmured discussion between his parents and then his father whispered loudly to him, "Well, I don't get that" and "It's some kind of oversight" and "Don't worry, we'll make sure you get it." Jimmy's embarrassment burgeoned with every comment and he attempted to fend off the invasions with dismissive remarks that he realized sounded a lot like those of his Wedgewood classmates. "It's no big deal." "Just forget it." "Dad! Forget it! I don't care." But he did care. The certificate was the sort of thing he would like to put in the souvenir box he kept in his closet, and he had earned it, and he *should* get it.

When the banquet was over, the students were all supposed to return to their tables and dismantle their displays. Everything had to be out of the exhibit hall by 9:00. On their tables, they would find an envelope with copies of the judges' scoring sheets and remarks. Jimmy's mother accompanied him back to the building to do this while his father headed for the front of the room, determined to talk to somebody about the missing certificate. He would get an answer about the same time that, 1000 yards away, Jimmy opened his envelope in the basement of the exhibit hall and saw the word "DISQUALIFIED" stamped in red ink across a photocopy of his entrance form. There was an official-looking letter accompanying this, and it read:

> Project 5026 (*The Evolutionary Success of Class Trilobita and its Implications for Speculation Regarding Extra-Terrestrial Life*) is disqualified from competition in the 1970 Northern Florida Regional Science Fair. The reason for this disqualification is that the project is primarily a research study and lacks the essential experimental component as indicated in the "Principles and Guidelines" for the fair's Proposal and Design Manual. Projects are not simply to report on past findings or to summarize scientific research but are to involve the student in a controlled experiment by which a proposed hypothesis can be tested in accord with scientific method and conclusions drawn on the basis of empirical results. Read the rules!

The last remark, seemingly unnecessary and cruel, prompted an immediate chain of thoughts. Of course, he *had* read the rules, and so had the teachers and administrators at Wedgewood High who not only thought his project merited inclusion in their local fair (which followed exactly the same Principles and Guidelines) but thought it to be the best of all works submitted in its division. And, yes, he realized that his project was research-heavy, but it *did* present a hypothesis and it *did* test this through what he (and others) considered to be an experimental component. It was not a *laboratory* experiment, he would grant (like feeding beer to ants or growing mold on bread) but it involved testing a theory with a different kind of evidence, the sort of evidence that paleontologists and space scientists must use. Some scientists don't have their subjects available to them. Trilobites, unlike ants, are long gone. Extra-terrestrials, perhaps, do not even exist. Neither trilobites nor extra-terrestrials are subjects for lab experiments, but in the fields of paleontology and space science, statistical projection based on a reasonable accumulation of data sometimes takes the place of empirical results.

Well, he wasn't actually sure if such an argument would work. Either way, he realized what they were saying was, "You shouldn't have been here at all." The letter didn't just say that he had not won anything this time; it effectively took away what he thought he had won previously.

His mother who had been visiting with Mrs. Meiner came over now and he handed her the envelope. She let out a quick gasp when she saw the word DISQUALIFIED, and then she continued to shake her head as she read the accompanying letter, muttering her disbelief and disagreement. Then his father came in, fuming. He had already seen a copy of the letter and he now assured Jimmy, a bit too loudly, that they would appeal this decision, get letters from the teachers and administrators at Wedgewood, and that he would *personally* make certain that this thing did not stand.

"Dad, I don't care," Jimmy said. "I really don't care."

"Can you just drop it?" his mother pleaded with the fuming patriarch. "You're making things worse."

This did not calm Mr. Haizlet down, but it did quiet him, and the family unit found temporary distraction in the business of dismantling the rejected project to carry its components out to Mr. Stewart's van. By now, however, many other projects were already heading up the stairs, so there would be a bit of a wait before the human log-jam cleared. Jimmy's project would have to be one of the last to leave the room, except of course for the three Life Science winners, which would indeed remain up for newspaper photographs after the room had been otherwise cleared. Likewise, Ben and Todd's project had to be left up for similar photos to be taken later on in the Physics room, which meant that Ben and Todd themselves and Mr. and Mrs. Stewart and Dr. and Mrs. Meiner were now all congregated at Jimmy's table, where his disqualification letter had been passed about to all. Jimmy knew that this was taking too long, that it would soon be too late, if it wasn't already, to pop over to the Physics hall and catch Dana before she left. And he knew that if he excused himself, say, to go to the bathroom, and went over there by himself, everybody here—all of the parents—would talk sympathetically about him *right in front of Ben and Todd* while he was gone. Mrs. Stewart and Mrs. Meiner would admonish their offspring to be sensitive to poor Jimmy and not say anything that might hurt his feelings because even though he was being big about it, he had to be really heartbroken, and his father would tell everyone about how this fair had meant so much to Jimmy and how he had really hoped that he would win something because he had never won anything before. But Dana might still be in the building. And she was leaving. Forever.

"I need to go to the bathroom," he said at last, and wandered out through the door no one was using and down the hallway, and then he actually sprinted what seemed like forty or fifty indoor yards to the other side of the long building. The Physics hall looked a lot like the Life Sciences wing. Only three projects (including Ben and Todd's) were standing, pristine and unmolested, on their tables. Others were down and most tables were empty. A small horde of students and parents were clumped in the corner, vying for the stairwells. But she wasn't there. She'd already left. She was gone.

Once his project had been securely loaded into the Stewart's van. Jimmy asked his parents if he could maybe please go back with them that night. There was room in the van and he was 100 percent certain that he was never going to go to Florida State and he didn't care about the campus tour in the morning. Yes, his father reminded him, but the more campuses you visit the more of an idea you get of what you *do* want. Plus, the high school would get charged for his room and board if he didn't show up at 10:00 the next morning for the tour and program. That was the deal.

"Anyway, I'm sorry things turned out the way they did," his father said in conclusion, awkwardly broaching the topic they weren't going to discuss. "You had a good project and you should be proud of it."

"The point isn't to win things anyway," he responded in possible agreement. "I mean, the whole point is to learn things, and I learned a lot by doing this."

"Well, that's very mature of you," his father concluded, and Jimmy could not help but remember what someone smart said one time about maturity. That it was "the art of hiding our base tendencies."

When he returned to his dorm room that night, he went to bed unusually early and just lay there looking at the ceiling and repeating, "God hates me. God hates me. God hates me. God hates me." Then, eventually, he read *The Two Towers* and finished it, discovering the conclusion (with Shelob!) to be as absorbing and as thrilling as most readers, though the rhetorical effect may have been blunted somewhat by the occasion of his mood. Finally, tired and deflated, he turned out the light and began to catch up on the sleep he'd missed the night before. He awoke sometime around midnight with the strange sensation that someone was in his room. Someone was. It was Dana and she was sitting by his bed. There was enough light coming in through the windows to see she had changed into the sparkly shirt from the night before. It looked like she was wearing stars. She was wearing the night sky. She was wearing heaven.

"Hi," she said, grinning.

"Uhh." He rubbed his eyes and tried to adjust to the moment. "I was dreaming."

"You were snoring."

She slid into the bed beside him and he rolled over on top of her. Their mouths locked, their tongues entangled. They kissed several times while he groped her chest and gradually realized that he was awake and that there actually *was* a girl underneath him and that his hands really were massaging her breasts.

"I can't believe this! You're in my bed!"

She smiled.

"Are you going to stay?"

She shrugged her shoulders and smiled.

"I want you to stay, please. I've been looking for you all day."

"Here I am."

"I want to love on you a little," he said.

"Really?"

Her eyes sparkled.

* * *

A picture of Ben and Todd was printed in the Jacksonville paper, holding their ribbon and certificate as if they were *proud* of their accomplishment. Thus, they became the inevitable butt of jokes among the Westwood clique of teenage smokers, which gathered every morning across from the school to cuss and complain for awhile before the first bell. The boys tried to transcend this embarrassment by assuring peers that they really couldn't care less about any retarded science program and that they only went to the thing because it was a chance to check out college babes, plus they got to miss school for two days. Eventually, they would both claim to have gotten to second base with a couple of co-ed first years (unaware that, given FSU's history, a "co-ed" was technically a male student). Still, when friends and enemies implied they were now worthy of inclusion in circles of respectability detrimental to their preferred reputation, they would try to change the subject as quickly as possible, often by swearing that they had seen Jimmy Haizlet crying when his Bugs in Space thing got tossed for being so lame. ("I kid you not. There were real tears. You would of thought someone had torched his Pooh bear or something.")

It took Jimmy three weeks to find an opportunity for calling Dana. Long distance phone calls were an extravagance in the Haizlet household. They could only be made evenings and weekends when rates were cheapest—and, of course, they could never be made by him without parental permission. But, finally, one Saturday he found himself alone in the house and seized the opportunity. He realized he would have to explain the charge when the bill arrived, but figured maybe he could think up something to say about following up with someone on getting a certificate for the science fair. That was still a subject that earned him sympathy and there might not be too many questions. In any case, he *had* to call her and, sure enough, she answered.

"Hi, Dana."

"Hi."

"This is Jimmy, from the science fair thing."

"Oh, hi! That was fun. How are you?"

"Okay. I keep thinking about you and I want to see you again."

"Well, yeah. I would think so."

He laughed.

"Can we do that? Can I see you again?"

"Do you have a car?"

"No, but I can borrow one, probably."

"From your parents?"

"Right. I could come to Gainesville. Or, you know, if there's nothing you want to do there we could just pick someplace else."

"Hmm . . ."

"Like Disney even. And we could spend the day, you know, riding roller coasters and stuff."

"I like roller coasters. I like stuff."

"Do you like me?"

"Sure. So how does this work?"

"Well, it's not real thought out, because I didn't know if you . . . I mean maybe you had a boyfriend or something."

"No boyfriend."

"Can I be your boyfriend?"

"No. I see lots of guys."

"But maybe for one day?"

"Yeah, maybe you could be my boyfriend-for-a-day. Probably."

"Ooh. Okay. So going from Jacksonville to Orlando, Gainesville is almost on the way."

"Not really. I don't think."

"But it *could* be . . . and I could leave real early and get you and then off we go."

"Alright, well, this could work. I mean, the Disney thing. But I want to talk to you about something first."

"What?"

"Like why do you want me to do this with you?"

"I like you. You were a lot of fun, at the fair and all."

"But this is going to be different isn't it?"

"That's alright. I want to get to know you better."

"You're not crushing on me, are you?"

"No."

"I don't want you crushing on me."

"I'm not. God, no, I would never do that."

"Do you know what it means?

"What?"

"Crushing on someone."

"Sure."

"Okay, because I go out with lots of guys, but none of them are allowed to crush on me. That's just sort of a rule I have right now."

"I won't. I didn't before, did I? I mean, I didn't even try."

"You don't know what it means, do you?"

"No."

"Okay. I didn't think so. Crushing on me is when you get all obsessive and think you're in love with me and that I'm the most important thing in the world and the best thing in your life."

Oops, he thought. Too late!

"You don't want to be the best thing in my life?" he asked.

"No. We live a long way apart and you're not my boyfriend, except maybe for a day."

"We could do this more than once."

"That's not the point. The point is thinking you're in love with me just because, you know, your hormones squirt all their adrenaline into your emotion gland or something."

He resisted the temptation to comment on this amazing description of the endocrine system. And she was still talking . . .

"If I'm the best thing in your life and you only see me every now and then, you'll be pathetic."

"Okay. But. What if I don't mind?"

"Being pathetic?"

"Yeah."

"I can't have guys crushing on me. Not unless I don't like them and don't care about them. I like you so I don't want you to be pathetic."

"Okay. I won't crush on you. I promise."

"Are you in love with me?"

"No," he lied.

"You see, even if I like you, you are not going to be the best thing in *my* life, okay?"

"Okay."

"I like other guys and I do stuff with them and have a lot of fun with them."

"That's alright," he lied. "I mean, that's good. It doesn't bother me at all."

These other guys, he thought . . . how many of them would give up everything they have for you, or drop out of school for you, or die for you, or kill for you, or be pathetic and miserable forever for you, even for the rest of their lives? I would. In fact, I will. I actually will. I know I will.

"Do you date much?" she asked then.

"Some," he lied.

"Do you go out with lots of different girls?"

"Sure. Well, you know, a few."

"What do you do when you go out?"

"Oh, just stuff. I'm probably not as popular as you."

"Have you had even one date with any girl since the science fair?"

"No."

"This year?"

"No. Not really."

"Well, see, that's why you think you're in love with me."

"No . . . it's because . . . you're *lovely* . . . I mean, how could anyone *not* be . . . ?"

"Jimmy . . ."

"You're *really, really* lovely!"

"That's sweet, but . . ."

"Your eyes sparkle. Do you wear contacts?"

"No."

"Your eyes sparkle in the light."

"They don't, actually. You just think they do because you're in love with me."

"I can prove this. I saw your eyes sparkle. In the gym, before I was in . . . before anything else happened and I didn't even know you."

"You were looking at my eyes?"

"Yes."

"I think, actually, you were looking at my . . . my shirt."

"But that was when your eyes were *shut*."

"Well, okay, they were. A valid point. I'm going to grant you that one."

"Your eyes sparkle."

"I guess they must. But now I'm going to make a deal with you, okay?"

"I know. No crushing."

"I'll do this Disney thing or whatever but only after you start dating some other girls."

"Alright. But. What if they won't go?"

"They will, if you're not pathetic."

"Um . . . might be too late."

"No, we're still in the sixties. Basically. Free love. Fun love. Do you know what that means?"

"I think so."

"It doesn't mean sex, or not just. It means enjoying all the good stuff about love without all the bad stuff that hurts. The hippies were the first people on earth to figure that out."

"Are you a hippie?"

"I guess not, but I learned from them. I don't do drugs, but I like love and I don't think it should hurt. Also paisley. I like paisley. I'm wearing paisley right now."

"Panties?"

"Shirt."

"Sounds nice." Jimmy liked paisley too. It reminded him of paramecia or something you'd see under a microscope, but he didn't think that would be a thing to say at the moment.

"So," Dana continued, "if you go out with some girls and make out with them and stuff, pretty soon you'll be cured."

"Cured?"

"Of the crushing thing . . . the obsessive thing that hurts and keeps love from being free or fun."

"I don't know if that will work with me," he said.

"What? Do you think you're going to be an old man someday, like you know, eighty years old, still moping about all pathetic and crushing on me?"

"No," he laughed. And thought . . . maybe. Actually, yes, that sounds like me.

She laughed too and it sounded like bells that fairies might ring when dew falls on fresh grass.

"Of course not," she said sweetly. "It just takes a little time to get the hormones in check. A little time and maybe a little adventure. So take some time, have some adventures, and then call me back so we can get together without me hurting you."

* * *

Jimmy never saw Dana again, but he never forgot her. And he never "got over" her, or even understood what that might mean. Like Buddy Holly (and then Linda Ronstadt) Jimmy Haizlet found it was easy (it's so easy) to fall in love, but he never did discover how to fall *out* of love, nor did he understand why anyone would want to do that. At some point, he would share all this with a therapist who seemed to regard the inability to fall out of love as a disorder or syndrome or some kind of emotional defect, as something that should be "cured" (to use Dana's word). But why would anyone want to be cured of loving? Because it hurts, the therapist said. But, to *stop loving*? That would just be *wrong*!

Jimmy thought about Dana every day for a long time—and then not every day, but still frequently. And decades later, even after he had found and married his final Number Seven, even then he would lie in bed at times and think about the girl in a sparkly blouse, with eyes that sparkled in the light. He would think about *that night . . . in his bed . . .* but mostly he would remember being in the gym and watching the curvy hills roll under her blouse as she danced, like waves under the night sky, cresting to shore. And he would think about how her small-to-medium breasts felt pressed against his chest when he held her close. And how her laughter sounded like fairy bells and how she said things like "free love" and "fun love" and "love on me a little." He would lie in bed sometimes and remember these things and sing softly but out loud, "Still crushing after all these years." He sang it to the tune of the Paul Simon song: "Still crushing. Still crushing. Still crushing after all these years."

10

My Boyfriend Is a Detective

Friday, May 19, 2000

Now she would have to hurry. The ceremony began at 7:00 and it was already 5:20. She was only an hour from Bartlesville but had to stop in Pawhuska to pick up William and she would really like to get to the school early. They wouldn't have time to eat. Maybe a pizza afterwards, like at 8:30 or 9:00. They'd be starving. She should have brought some granola bars or something. She should have thought of that.

But she had thought of almost everything. This was always her favorite night of the year and tonight would be no exception. And then tomorrow and Sunday. And then . . .

Monday! The first day of summer break in the year 2000. Maybe she would go by the school to do some of the necessary "clean-up." Take down posters, bring things home. But that could all wait till Tuesday if necessary. In a way, she had been preparing for this Monday all her life and she knew that it could be a big disappointment, but, still, she was so excited!

Maybe William would have some granola bars. If she had a cell phone, she'd call him now so he could find them. Or maybe they could just stop at a gas station. She *was* going to have to get a cell phone now, she realized.

Until recently she'd had no one to call, but her life had begun to change five months ago thanks, she had to admit, to the unexpected intervention of her mother. That would be the mother who, right now, she never wanted to see again. But that would pass. She *would* see Mama again. Daddy too. She would see them again and have a few things to say to them. But by then she would be a different person. How different might depend on Monday.

* * *

Angelika Blitch taught first grade in Bartlesville, Oklahoma. She loved her job (most of it) and she thought that she was good at it. Her parents didn't seem to care but now, for five months, she'd had a "platonic friend" named William Booker with whom she had dessert or appetizers twice a month, and when she told *him* about her teaching and her students, he listened and told her how committed she was, and what good ideas she had, and how fortunate the kids were to have her. Of course, he wanted to get into her pants (as the young folks would say). She knew that, but the interest in her work was genuine and the praise sincere.

She had known William for a short time twenty years ago, when they had spent a few evenings in the back seat of his car, but then they had gone their separate ways. Now that he was back in the area and managing the Big Boy in Pawhuska, she had developed the habit of stopping in to see him every two weeks when she returned to Bartlesville after visiting her parents in Shidler. She would arrive around 3:00, when the Sunday brunch was ending and he could turn things over to assistant manager Nathan. They would head out to the Applebee's or Panda Express or one of the other spots on Lane Avenue and continue with what they called "catching up."

Nathan always grinned like a Cheshire cat, assuming they were off to a motel, or at least to William's apartment. But it hadn't been like that. William might have *wanted* it to be like that, but he had read the signals and he had respected them. She wanted a friend, not a boyfriend. This meant that they never talked about "old times," though of course every now and then, a potentially embarrassing memory would intrude. Like when they got biscuits at the Cracker Barrel and the waitress brought jelly but he asked if he could have some honey. "I love honey," he exclaimed when it arrived and suddenly they looked at each other and knew that they were both remembering that time he brought a packet of honey on one of their dates to enliven the back seat activities. But neither one said a word or cracked a smile. It was just, "So, uh, how were your students this week?"

That couldn't last and eventually things got a little flirty but she discovered she didn't mind being flirted with (for what seemed like the first time in her life) and for five months now their Sunday afternoons had been filled with learning things about each other that they probably would not have learned if they'd spent the time at a motel doing what they'd done in his back seat (and more). He read mystery novels and adventure stories. She liked creating "pattern games" for the children and teaching them 2 + 2 + 2 arithmetic and reading out loud from books like *Charlotte's Web* and *My Father's Dragon*. And, of course, "the Carol mystery" had afforded them some continuing moments of distraction and entertainment.

What if she *hadn't* stopped by that Walmart on that particular day at that particular time? Had it all happened for a reason? Been arranged by some unseen, guiding hand? She'd have to ask Daddy what he thought about that!

Sunday, January 2, 2000

Flashback four-and-a-half months. Angelika had spent the Christmas break visiting with her parents in Shidler, and was heading back to Bartlesville for the start of the new school term. It was a new millennium. They had survived Y2K, and her whole life seemed new and fresh. She had gone to a beauty parlor over the holidays and was wondering if anyone at Bartlesville Elementary would notice the difference. And so she was full of optimism when she stopped at the Big Boy where she and her mother had briefly spoken to William Booker a week previous. But this time Mama was not with her, and this time, she had called in advance to let him know she was coming. He turned the restaurant over to assistant manager Nathan and the two of them sat in a booth for three hours just catching up.

He told her about his marriage (after he'd moved to Montana) and he told her about the divorce, and about the two kids living now with a remarried ex-wife. Their names were Daniel and Matthew, ages eight and four. They had just been with him for Christmas and they would be back for more time during the summer. He'd gotten married in 1990 after a stint in the military and the woman was a Shoshone Indian—Sheepeater tribe. "Did she eat sheep?" Angelika asked, hoping to be witty. "Not then," he said. "Now maybe. Mutton."

So they had two kids. Daniel was named for the courageous prophet, and William had wanted to name the second boy "Amos" because his favorite Christian rock band was a group called Daniel Amos. His mother forbade it (wisely, Angelika thought). "*Amos?* Why not *Jethro*?" she had protested. So they named the baby Matthew after the Gospel with the Sermon on the Mount. But already by then, his wife was rediscovering her Shoshone roots. She wouldn't let Matthew be baptized and, indeed, she performed some ritual on Daniel that would cleanse him of his previous ablution.

Basically, William said, his Indian wife embarked on a spiritual journey that took over everything. She worshiped Wakonda now, the Sioux god (or spirit-power) of nature. And then she hooked up with some park ranger who fell for it all as well. Basically, she converted him. At the time Billy had thought the guy just wanted to get into her loin cloth, so to speak, but he really did take to her religion with a passion. Plus, he had some screwy ideas of his own. He called it Bokononism and he'd gotten it out of a science fiction novel. It wasn't even a real thing. It was just a made-up religion from some book he'd read. Anyway, the two of them were married now and they led this Bokononist Wakonda cult that contained only two other members—his kids.

Wow, that was quite a story. Of course, Angelika had known the bare facts (divorced, two kids). They were the main reasons she had not stopped in to see him sooner. In fact, she had driven right past the Big Boy every other week for two years after Mama warned her that "Billy" was back, that he was managing this place, and that he was *divorced*. It was definitely the reason Mama had disapproved of their stopping in for lunch after the trip to the beauty parlor. And it was the reason her parents could never know about this stop now—or any future ones. Whatever the circumstances, divorced men were not candidates for marriage, and unmarried women (Christian women) had no business socializing with men who were not potential husbands.

So they did not talk much about the past. Instead, William told her some adventures he had managing the Big Boy, replete with humorous anecdotes of customers and employees. He was not just interesting, but funny and lively and she wanted to listen to him. And she told him about her students and what she did with them, with a few anecdotes concerning parents and the other teachers and the school administration. And he wanted to listen to her!

This was remarkable. She had never considered herself to be funny or lively or interesting, but this man wanted to listen to her. She had a new look physically, and now she had to wonder if maybe she was improving in other ways as well.

Sunday, January 16, 2000

The Carol mystery began innocently enough on her second stopover in Pawhuska. She was running a little early and stopped by the Walmart on Lynn Avenue to pick up a few groceries. She was in the produce section, looking at bananas, when a women's voice cried, "Carol!"

She turned and there was a woman about her age. Blonde, dumpy, short.

"Oh!" the woman exclaimed, embarrassed. "I'm sorry. I thought you were somebody else."

That was all. That was nothing. From behind, someone thought she was somebody else. Not worth thinking about. Except that it *wasn't* all.

When she got to the register, the woman taking her groceries looked at her with amazement, not from behind but straight on, and she said, "Oh my gosh! For a moment, I thought . . . you look just like someone else who comes in here."

And then a voice spoke up behind her.

"Doesn't she, though? She looks like Carol *something (did she say a last name? If so, Angelika would not remember it).*"

It was the blonde, dumpy woman. The short one.

Angelika looked back and forth at the two of them.

"Do you *know* her?" the blonde said. "Are you related?"

She shook her head. She wasn't related to anyone except Mama and Daddy.

"Well you sure do favor her."

She didn't know what to say. And then she did.

"Is she pretty?" she asked.

"Yes," the blonde laughed "Carol's very pretty."

And Angelika moved on, thinking, that was witty! I was witty! I *am* improving. I said something witty, like a person who's funny and interesting.

And that was why she told William about it twenty minutes later. She wanted to impress him with her witticism. But he missed it. He was more struck by the mere fact that she looked like someone else.

"A doppelgänger!" he exclaimed. "You have a doppelgänger!"

"A *what?*"

"A doppelgänger is a double of a person. If you read science fiction, you'd know all about them."

"Well, I don't, so enlighten me."

"There was some philosopher, I don't know who, but hundreds of years ago, and he had this idea that every human being on the planet has an exact double somewhere. But since the world is so big, they never meet. So that was the basic idea. But then, of course, people asked, what if they did meet? And there was this famous *Twilight Zone* where a woman kept seeing herself all over the city, shopping, getting on the bus, eating at a restaurant, and I think she went crazy or something."

"So this is all make believe."

"Well, yeah. But there are people who really believe it. Famous people. That poet Shelley, his wife wrote *Frankenstein*, he claimed to have met his own doppelgänger and he told her about it, and then he was going out to meet him again. He told his wife that's where he was going and he went out and never came back. Turned up drowned."

"The dope-all gunger killed him?"

"That's the rumor."

"So I shouldn't look for Carol. She might kill me."

"She might."

"Do you believe this stuff?"

"No, but it's fun. Dostoyevsky believed it. He wrote a book called *The Double*."

"Have you read it?"

"No. Too much for me. As a general rule, if I can't spell an author's name, I don't read his books."

"Okay, well, I think you've solved it. There's a double me out there."

"You should try to find her."

"No. I don't think so."

"I could help."

"How?"

"Hang out at Walmart. See if your doppelgänger shows up."

"Okay, but don't tell her about me. I don't want to turn up drowned."

Sunday, January 30, 2000

Two weeks later, William had another theory.

"Remember Carol?" he asked.

"My doper-gangon?"

"Doppelgänger. But there's another possibility. What if she's your *clone*?"

"Wow. That makes more sense," she said, trying to emote masked but still evident sarcasm.

"She could be. They're cloning dinosaurs now, you know."

"In movies, right?"

"Yes. Have you seen it?"

"No."

"How is that possible?"

She shrugged her shoulders and said, "The truth? I don't think I should tell you."

"Why not?"

"Maybe . . . you can't handle the truth."

He laughed, impressed that she had answered a movie question with a movie quote.

"That's good. You're pretty witty, Angelika."

She was pleased but had no idea *why* what she had said was witty.

"Pretty witty," he repeated. "That rhymes, doesn't it?"

"It does. Like Plain Jane . . . or . . . I know . . . Silly Billy!"

He smiled. "Actually, some people used to call me that."

"Oh. Does it hurt?"

"Not when you say it."

"Anyway . . . it's kind of the same thing, isn't it? A dobal-gunger and a clone?"

"No. A doppelgänger would be someone who just *looks* like you. A clone is science and it's someone who *is* you—physically at least. Exactly the same."

"Okay, but how did they do this? Make a clone of me? Wouldn't I know? I mean wouldn't I have to go to the clone lab or the hospital or something?"

"Not if they're good. All they need is, like, a tooth or a strand of hair or something."

"Well, alright, I think you've solved it."

"There's also another possibility."

"Yes?"

"Maybe you're the clone."

"Oh my! Wouldn't I know?"

"No. Maybe Carol went to the clone lab and you're the result."

"So my parents would have gotten me from a lab. Or ordered me through the mail or something."

"Like Amazon but not books. Some kind of Secret Science Amazon."

"Mmmh. I can't see Daddy going along with that. He's not big on science."

"No, but maybe it would be a better way to get a baby. You know, a more holy way than the usual."

"Oh! Yes, I could see him thinking that."

"If people could have babies without taking their clothes off."

"He would be all for it."

"So, whoever's the original, don't you want to meet your clone sister?"

"*Oh!*" she said pained. "You just said the S word."

"What?"

"*Sister*. All my life, when I was growing up, that's what I wanted more than anything in the world. A little brother would have been okay, too but . . . a *sister!*"

"You're an only child."

She nodded. "I begged my parents to get me a sister, before I knew what that involved. And even after."

"I have two brothers and one sister," he said. "And maybe I didn't always appreciate them, but yeah, it's good."

"I had an imaginary one," Angelika recalled.

"Was her name Carol?"

"No. That would be creepy, wouldn't it? But, you know how some children have imaginary friends?"

"I did. He was an elf."

"Well, I had an imaginary sister. Her name was Heidi, after the girl in the book, and we had tea parties and played games and talked about Mama and Daddy together. I told her all my secrets and made up pretend secrets for her to tell me."

"Hmm . . . I can't do anything about your sibling deficiency but, speaking of secrets, if we could perhaps return to the appalling fact that you have never seen *Jurassic Park*. I have heard the reason is something I might not be able to handle, but I am willing to take that risk."

"I've never been to a movie theater, William. Daddy thinks their worldly."

"Well, yeah. I grew up with that too, you know. Holiness. Even the supposedly good movies have bad words and scantily clad women and suggestive situations."

"Right. Also, the theaters themselves are pits of iniquity."

"Do you believe that?"

"No. I guess not. But I've never been."

"You know you can watch movies on your television now. There are these things called DVDs."

"Are you making fun of me?"

"No."

"It *sounds* like you're making fun of me."

"Well . . . a little . . . but we should go. I will take you to your first movie. Whatever you like and . . ." He caught himself in mid-sentence . . . "and . . . it will be a total non-date thing."

"I don't think we should do that."

"We can leave an empty seat between us."

She just looked at him.

"Or bring Nathan as a chaperone."

"Still making fun of me."

"But . . . okay . . . maybe . . . but I'm trying to figure it out. And I *didn't* suggest we get a DVD and watch it at my apartment. Did you notice? Did you notice that I didn't suggest that?"

"Yes."

"Do I get points for not suggesting that?"

"I think so."

"How many?"

"Three. And then, minus two for making fun of me."

"Yes! I am ahead!"

Sunday, February 13, 2000

Two weeks later they forgot about Carol and she told William more about her teaching and why she loved her job. She found a creative way to begin.

"How well do you know me, William?"

"Not very well. I mean, pretty well, but you still surprise me."

"So if I asked you, what is my favorite day of the year? What would you think?"

"Christmas."

"Nope. That's everyone's. And very obvious. My favorite day is graduation."

"First-graders have a graduation?"

"No, silly."

(Silly Billy, she thought.)

"I mean, *high school* graduation. I always go and it is my favorite night of the year."

"You like the speeches. Or what?"

"I see my children all grown up. Well, kind of grown up. I've been teaching first grade for eighteen years, so by now, every year some of my first graders are graduating."

"You still remember them?"

"All of them, I think. Definitely most. People don't move much in Bartlesville. You know that. So every year at graduation, I see the students and maybe one out of four, or one out of five, I say, *one of mine!*"

"That's amazing, Angie. I'm impressed. God, I'm so proud of you."

"Don't say *God* unless you're praying. But so far I have had three valedictorians and four salutatorians."

"I am impressed. And thankful to God, who I was just now talking to and telling him that I was proud of you."

"Oh, see I thought '*God, I am so proud of you*' would mean that you were proud of God."

"Well, I am. I'm proud of God for what he has done with you and that's what I was telling him. But, back to the kids . . . you keep track of them after they leave your class?"

"I do. There's a little Jewish girl in second grade now and I am paying close attention to her. And the editor of the Cat Chat . . . that's the middle school newspaper . . . the editor is a girl I had six years ago. I taught her how to read and write. Not all by myself, but I helped. I taught her to write sentences and now she's the paper editor."

"You are incredible. I hope you are proud of yourself."

"I think I am—and that's why God gave me Daddy, to keep me humble."

William wanted to know more about her actual teaching and she told him about the pattern games she created for the children. She spent lots of time on these and they were, perhaps, her favorite thing. The kids liked them too.

"I show them three pictures and the point is, what do they have in common? Then I show them more pictures and they have to pick the one that fits the pattern."

"Are these, like squares or triangles and things?"

"Actually, that *is* one of them: a square, a tall narrow rectangle, a short wide rectangle . . . and then do you pick a triangle or a circle or another thing with four sides?"

"A parallelogram?"

"Yeah. And that's the right answer because the pattern is things with four sides."

"And the kids like this?"

"Not that one so much, but . . . here's a cat and a dog and a hamster . . . now you need to pick: fish, bird, or bunny?"

"I'd go with the bunny."

"Why?"

"They're all mammals."

"Right, and if they don't know what mammals are they could just say things with fur."

"Give me another one."

"I show them the pictures . . . you know, on PowerPoint . . . so, I'd take the bird from before and put it with a butterfly and an airplane, and what would you expect?"

"Something that flies."

"Excellent. So if there's a train and a turtle and a hot air balloon?"

"I pick the balloon."

"You might just pass first grade, William Booker."

"I love that you do this for them. I've told you, I think you have the most important job in the world—and you are so good at it, Angie! You are so very good at it!"

"Thank you."

"I like the whole idea of these games. They're fun and they teach children how to think. We didn't do anything like that when I was in school. It was more just memorizing."

"But you learned how to think."

"Somehow. Yes, I believe I did. It's one reason I like mysteries. I like looking for patterns, connecting dots. Just, you know, putting two and two together, making the pieces fit."

"Do you do puzzles?"

"Like jigsaw? Yes! I have one set up right now in my apartment. On a card table."

"Same here," she said, and realized he was the first person she had ever told. It seemed the definition of pathetic: the lonely forty-year-old woman sitting in her apartment doing a jigsaw puzzle. It was embarrassing, and she would have been ashamed for anyone *else* to know.

And then . . . like with the honey . . . they both knew what they were both thinking. They were thinking, "That's something we could do together!" Angelika had a sudden mental flash of her and William in their old age, sitting around a card table, both of them with white hair, hunched over a table in what must be *their* apartment. She shook her head . . . *no! . . . that wasn't going to happen!*

He was divorced. For whatever reason . . . it didn't make any difference . . . Mama and Daddy would never, ever tolerate her being with a divorced man. They would disown her. They would *almost* disown her if they knew she were here now, eating pie at an Outback with him.

Sunday, February 27, 2000

Near the end of February, she stopped by the bank before heading over to the Big Boy. The only ATM was indoors but she wanted some cash so that she could pay for her own food. It was barely inside, in what amounted to an entryway and as she was punching in numbers a woman exiting from the lobby exclaimed, "Oh Carol, you've lost . . ." then stopped herself. Angelika had turned around and the woman scrutinized her, studying her face.

"Sorry," she muttered. "You're not Carol are you?"

"No. But what would I have lost if I were?"

"Weight," she said. "You would have lost weight." She started out the door, but Angelika couldn't let her get away.

"Wait!"

"Yes, weight . . . but never mind . . . I'm sorry."

"No, I mean the other kind of *wait* . . . hold up, just a moment, please."

The woman turned but looked annoyed, embarrassed by her mistake and not wanting to prolong the conversation with a skinnier-than-Carol stranger. Angelika decided to abandon the ATM without getting her money yet and make it quick.

"I just wondered . . . you're not the first . . . this Carol, I guess I look like her."

"A little."

"What's her last name?"

"I . . . I don't remember. She's in my book club. I see her four times a year. We're not friends or anything . . . but *why?* . . . sometimes people just look alike and there's no reason to . . . you don't really need to know that." She turned to exit. "Sorry to bother you," she called as the door closed behind her. And then she was gone.

She decided *not* to tell William.

He began the conversation with tales of the high school girls he hires. He had to fire one of them. They always seemed so irresponsible, but he wanted to help them along. He tried to be a good boss.

"I probably put up with too much: not showing up for work, leaving early, things like that. I'm always trying to give them another chance."

"Because they're pretty?"

"I don't know. I hope not, but who knows? Just because I'm a softie, I guess. They do take advantage."

"That they will. I was never pretty, but I saw the others do it. Pretty high school girls look at middle-aged nice men as though they're standing on the corner passing out All-Purpose Permission Slips."

She changed the subject only slightly to talk about discipline in the classroom—what she needed to do when a child misbehaved. Time-outs and take-aways were the primary forms of punishment, but of course the goal was to avoid punishment altogether by setting clear expectations, offering positive incentives (enforced by peer pressure), and allowing "do-overs." A student never had to go to tTime-out or have some privilege taken away if they restated what they had said or re-enacted what they had done in a more appropriate manner.

"I'm not sure that would work with teenagers though," she concluded.

"What about spankings or paddling? Do they still do that?"

"Not in our district. It's still legal in Oklahoma schools but only with older kids, and it's been phased out in Bartlesville Public. Of course, the schools where we went . . . you know, the Christian ones . . . they're still big on hitting."

William said that he got paddled a couple of times in school, but way more at home.

"My dad had a flat wood paddle, just like the one at the school, and we'd have to bend over and *whap!* he'd give us a 'lick' right on the butt.

Sometimes two or three licks. And it *hurt*. I got to tell you. It hurt for hours. Sometimes, you could still feel it the next day."

"Daddy called it *thrashing*," Angelika said. And then she told him about the leather strap on her bare bottom and, when she got too old for that, the bamboo cane on her palms or on the back of her hands.

They compared notes on what the offenses had been. William's were all pretty predictable: fighting with his siblings, not cleaning his room or doing his chores. But then, as Angelika related her list of what warranted a whipping she realized for the first time that it was longer and more ambiguous than anyone would have suspected.

"I think you win," he told her as she tried to spell it out. "It seems like you had it pretty rough."

She nodded. "I have scars."

Suddenly he got very serious.

"What?"

"Scars. He went too far. But he knows it and he's said so."

"Scars, Angelika? Where?"

"On my bottom."

"I . . . my . . ." he stammered . . . "I'd like to take a strap to him!"

"Oh!" she gasped as if she were impressed. "Thrash a sixty-six-year-old man. That's brave, Mr. Booker."

"I don't mean for real. I just mean that what he did was terrible."

"Yeah. I wish I hadn't told you."

"Okay. Don't feel that way," he said, trying to relieve the sudden tension—something they hadn't experienced in the last two months. "I want you to feel free to tell me *anything*. I just don't know how I'm supposed to respond."

"Make light of it," she said.

"Angie! It's not the sort of thing to make light of."

"I don't know. It strikes me as pretty good material for immature humor. And it's over. It's past. It's not something I want anybody to get serious about. So, you should say, *Scars on your bottom?* . . . and then make some dumb joke."

"Like . . . do you want me to examine them for you?"

"Yeah, like that."

"Okay. Are you sure they're really scars, Angie? Maybe they're something else?"

"Like what?"

"Some kind of marking. I don't know, but they're probably not scars."

"I think they are."

"If you like, I could examine them for you, and let you know what I think."

"That's very thoughtful of you, Mr. Booker, but it won't be necessary."

"By *examine,* I mean in a totally detached and completely professional way."

"I know you do. I would never doubt it. But it won't be necessary. Thank you for your consideration, though."

"Mmmh . . . wait . . . I just thought of something else . . . this could be very useful information."

"How is that?"

"Well, we know there's a Carol clone out there who looks just like you."

"Oh my. Her again."

"So what would happen if she said that she *was* you? If she started showing up and doing things and claiming she was you."

"That would be a problem."

"And how would we know? We could get you both together, but if you look exactly alike, how do we know which one is really you?"

"Oh, now I see where you're going. You're going to have us drop our drawers."

"Drop your drawers and turn around. The one with scars on her bottom is the real Angie, and the other one's an impostor."

"Well, that's good thinking. Thank you, Mr. Booker. I knew I could count on you."

Good save, she thought. Back on track, keeping it light and not bogging down in anything too serious. Plus . . . now . . . there would be no need for a mood-killing explanation if and when he ever did see . . .

No! . . . No! . . . No, Angie! . . . Stop it! . . . she told herself, shaking her head so abruptly William wondered what was wrong . . . *Just stop it!*

"So," she said out loud, "you're still worried about Carol. Still looking for her."

"I'm not obsessed, but whenever I'm at Walmart, I look around. If there are any women about your size and shape, I look a little closer."

"Are you sure you're looking for Carol? Or is this just an excuse to look at women?"

"Oh Angie, trust me. There isn't a man alive who doesn't find excuses to look at women who look like you."

She just smiled and said nothing. He was flirting, trying to see how much she might allow, before shutting him down. And she didn't know how much that would be—or should be. No one had ever flirted with her before.

Then she told him about the bank.

Sunday, March 12, 2000

They were eating nachos at the El Jalisco restaurant on John Dahl Avenue. Nachos with a pitcher of sweet tea, though the waitress had tried to tell them about the beer—a fine selection on tap.

"Do you drink alcohol?" William asked her, once they'd been left alone.

"Never tasted it."

"That's pretty unique. I was brought up a teetotaler, of course, but I had a bit of beer in the Army. I'll admit I like it, but I'm still not much of a drinker."

"Holiness guilt?"

"I don't think so. More just Holiness culture. You know? When you're brought up a certain way, you just sort of go with that. Unless you rebel."

"So you haven't rebelled? Against your upbringing?"

"Well, I've changed some. I'm just regular Methodist now, but I think a lot of it stays with me."

"I get that. But your dad wasn't your pastor."

"No—and I suppose that *would* make a difference."

"I don't agree with him on everything. Or most things."

"But you still want to please him."

"I think so. Yes. I guess I do."

"So, then, just to take an example—do you think there is anything actually *wrong* with a person drinking a beer with a plate of nachos—or a glass of wine with some chicken marsala? Do you think that person is sinning?"

"No, of course not. That would be judgmental. You can have beer if you want."

"I don't. I'm just trying to think this through, to understand you, but also, just for me. I *used* to think such a person was sinning, but I don't anymore. Now, like you, I would think that is judgmental."

"But Daddy, he thinks you start with one beer and then, what does it lead to? It's a slip . . ."

She caught herself and stopped . . . looked down at the table.

"A *slippery slope*?" he asked, and they both burst out laughing.

"Yes," she said, recovering and blushing. "That is what he would call it."

Another shared memory from high school . . . from the backseat of Billy Booker's car.

"Ah yes! Slippery slopes!" Billy said, shaking his head and chuckling. "I had almost forgotten."

"You hadn't."

"No. That would be impossible."

"Shall we move on?"

"Sure."

"Do you want to hear a funny story about my dad?"

"Of course."

"Alright. My Mama has told me this one, about how they met. It's hard to believe, but Daddy was young once, and apparently he was pretty cute."

"I can see that. I mean, he's old and fat now, but there's a nice-looking man under all that."

"Yeah. I've seen pictures."

"You take after him, you know."

"Really? Well, anyway, he was the youth pastor at a Methodist church in Bartlesville."

"Not a Holiness?"

"No, just a regular Methodist, what he calls *liberal* Methodist these day. Of course he had been raised Holiness, but he took this job at a regular Methodist church because, well, you know, he never went to a seminary or anything, so it was just what he could get."

"That must have been hard. On him, I mean, but maybe also on them."

"I guess it was. At some point, there was a lot of trouble. His Holiness standards didn't go over."

"Telling Methodists, don't drink, don't dance . . ."

"Don't wear makeup, don't go to movies, no jewelry, can't date without a chaperone . . ."

"That was my upbringing. Remember Pastor Harper?"

"At Youth Fellowship? Yes. I suppose Daddy was like him."

"But more uptight I would think. Pastor Harper was kind of cool."

"Maybe more uptight, but I don't know. Mama says he tried hard to please them. He tried to *compromise*."

"Wow. Not a word I would ever associate with your dad."

"So they had a bowling team."

"Bowling?"

"A girls' bowling team. Maybe there was a boys' team once but the guys didn't stick with it. The girls did, though, and my dad was like the sponsor or chaperone or something."

"Not the coach?"

"Oh heavens no. He doesn't know anything about bowling, but he had to, like, be the sponsor for the girls' team and be there for all their practices and games and tournaments."

"Doesn't he think bowling is evil?"

"Not exactly evil, but . . . you know . . ."

"A slippery slope?"

"Exactly. It's one of his favorite examples. All my life I've heard, *It may not seem sinful, but what does it lead to? That's what I want to know! What does it lead to?*"

"What *does* it lead to?"

"Well, I've never been completely sure. Frivolity and worldliness, I suppose. And they serve liquor at bowling alleys. Anyway," she continued, ticking off items on the fingers of her right hand, "short skirts lead to nakedness . . . dancing leads to sex . . . one beer leads to drunkenness . . . makeup leads to harlotry . . . pop music leads to rock and roll . . . rock and roll leads to devil worship . . . it's all about those slippery you-know-what's."

"This didn't go over at the Methodist church?"

"No, but for a while I think he tried to go along with as much as he could, or so Mama says. And she was on the bowling team."

"Your mother *bowled?*"

"She did! And I don't know if she was good but she wasn't too bad. They always beat the Lutherans and the Presbyterians and some of the other Methodists, just not the Baptists."

"Well, sure . . . I mean . . . Baptists!"

Angelika was smiling, telling a story that, for her, was full of amusing images of her parents as she had never known them. And yet, images that seemed to fit with who they were now, with who they had become.

"I just try to picture Daddy at the bowling alley."

"It's like trying to picture him at a dance hall."

"It is. But, of course, he was the *chaperone*. So his main job was making sure there were no boys around."

"Ah, yes."

"And no drinking."

"Right."

"They went on out-of-town trips. Daddy would drive the church van and the girls would be in a couple of rooms at a Best Western or something, and Daddy thought it was his job to make sure no boys came knocking and that, you know, no one tried to stay up late or leave their rooms or have a party."

"Oh God, I can see that."

"Are you telling God this?"

"What?"

"You said, *Oh God*, so I assume you are telling God this."

"Oh, yes . . . I was . . . that's exactly what I was doing . . . telling God that I could see it. But now I'll just tell you: I can see it! George Blitch patrolling the hallways or parking lot or sitting up in the lobby. On the lookout for *boys!* . . . or *booze!* . . ."

"Or just one of the bowlers out after curfew! I can see it too. But the mere fact that he was *there* . . . taking them to the tournaments . . . going to the lanes . . . he was *trying*, you know."

"He might have bowled himself."

"He did. Mama says the girls talked him into it, and he was terrible. Of course he was. He'd never done it before. Ball in the gutter. I don't know how many times he tried it but I sometimes wonder, maybe *that's* why he's got such a thing against bowling. Not to discount the frivolity and liquor licenses but also . . . he was bad at it!"

"Not just that," William volunteered. "He wasn't just bad. He was *worse than girls*. They may have laughed at him."

"Oh, William! Yes! Of course they did. High school girls? You don't think they'd laugh at their pastor throwing gutter balls?"

"Oh, well. That's it then."

"Yeah. I hadn't thought it through before . . . but, yeah . . . the girls made fun of him . . . and then he decided bowling was evil . . . hmmm . . . poor Daddy! . . . but, anyway, Mama says she had a 'girlish crush' on him. Remember all the girls being in love with Pastor Harper?"

"Are you confessing?"

"No, but I could see it. Anyway, Mama had a girlish crush on Daddy the youth pastor but, of course, he was all proper and respectful and if he noticed her he didn't let on. Not till after she had graduated and then, a few months later, he requested permission to court her."

"He went to her father?"

"I suppose. I never hear that part. Her dad . . . my grandpa . . . he's gone now and was never really a part of our life."

"Didn't like George?"

"No, probably not. Because, you know, even though he tried, he did not fit in. He wasn't really Methodist. He was Holiness through and through and it would have just been one thing after another."

"Right."

"I think those were hard times. It wasn't just theology. He was less educated than the other two pastors. Less educated than most of the church members. And he was a bit more . . . rustic?"

"I understand that."

"So I don't know exactly what happened. Mama says he quit but I think maybe he was fired. She says there was a lot of trouble at the church. His Holiness standards were just way too high for the rest of them and eventually the liberals and the educated folk thought they were too good for him."

"That's your mama talking?"

"Yes, but I sure can see it. I've been there. Forty-year-old virgin who doesn't drink or dance . . . doesn't even go to movies . . . people can be cruel."

"I know, Angie."

"So, Mama says, some people left the church because of him. And folks were saying terrible things about him, but he moved to Shidler and started a Free Methodist Holiness church and that seemed to be just right. That was where he belonged."

"Just no more bowling teams."

"No. And he's been preaching against frivolity ever since. Frivolity and vanity and every sort of sin."

"I think it must have been hard to be his daughter. At least sometimes."

"It was. It still is. But . . ."

"You still want to please him, don't you?"

Angelika nodded her head.

"I do."

And the sadness in William's eyes told her that he knew what that meant as far as he was concerned.

Sunday, March 26, 2000

Two weeks later, she told him another story about her father—perhaps her favorite from younger years.

"Think anniversaries!" she said, right after they'd ordered salads at the Olive Garden.

"Oh no! Is it our anniversary . . . of something?"

"No, silly." (Silly Billy.) "Not us."

"Good, 'cause I didn't get you anything."

"Think anniversaries in general. What is the most important anniversary of all?"

"Wedding?"

"Yes, but which one?"

"Um . . . twenty-five, I guess."

"That's right. I mean, maybe fifty if you live that long, but for most it's the twenty-fifth wedding anniversary. That's the big day!"

"Alright. I passed the test."

"So now I want to tell you about my parents' twenty-fifth wedding anniversary."

"Let's hear it."

"First, you have to get why I can always keep track. I mean, do you know when your parents' wedding anniversary is?"

"Uh, yeah. It's in June . . . the latter part . . . maybe June 23. I think that's right. I have it written down somewhere. It's not like I send them cards or presents."

"You could call them and say congratulations."

"I could. Never have. Probably should. Good idea."

"You could say, 'Thank you for getting married and having me!'"

"Right. I should do that."

"But do you know how long they've been married?"

"Um . . . not off the top of my head. I could figure it out."

"Right. But see my birthday is September 21 and my parents' wedding anniversary is November 21—so that is always easy to remember."

"Ah! Convenient!"

"And since I was born in their first year, I always know which anniversary it is. This year, I'm going to turn forty-one. So two months later, they'll celebrate number forty-two."

"You came along, what, ten months in?"

"They were quick! Married November 21, 1958, and then on September 21, 1959 . . . ten months to the day . . . boom! . . . there I was!"

"They *were* quick."

"Pent-up Holiness, you know!"

"I do, indeed."

"But just me. No little brother. *And no sister!* It still makes me so sad. If they could crank me out that fast . . ."

"Anyway . . . you've got the anniversary math down."

"Right. It doesn't usually matter, but the year I turned twenty-four I suddenly realized, 'Oh my goodness, in two months it's Mama and Daddy's twenty-fifth wedding anniversary!'"

"Thank God for easy math."

"Thank him for lots of things, William. But I wondered, should I do something for them? Should I buy them something? The thing is, I was so busy with work then. It was just my second year of teaching and I was up every night making posters, planning class for the next day. I know, it's not a good excuse, but I think I was the busiest I had ever been, except for maybe my first year. I didn't even go home as much. Home being their house. The plan was to see them every other weekend, but sometimes I just had to stay and work."

"So, did you neglect the anniversary?"

"Not just me, but, yeah, basically. The time just went by and I thought about it for a minute every once in a while. I asked one of the other teachers and she said that when her parents had their twenty-fifth she and the other kids all went in together to send them on a cruise. Well, I didn't think Daddy would want to go on a cruise. And there were no other kids to go in with me on anything. And I didn't have any money!"

"I get it. This is nothing you need to feel bad about."

"I know that now, but suddenly, the anniversary was a week away and I hadn't done anything, so I called Daddy to see what the plans were and . . . *nothing!*"

"Nothing?"

"Oh, they were going out to dinner."

"So, he's not big on anniversaries."

"*It was their twenty-fifth!* I kind of went ballistic. Not before, but after. Before, I just told him, 'Daddy, you should do more than that!' But the next time I came home, after the anniversary was already past and I asked, what did they do, and he said, we just went out to dinner, then I went ballistic. I told him she had been his wife for twenty-five years and he had to treat her better than that! He should have made her feel special!"

"I'm sure that went over well."

"He didn't know what to do. He'd never seen me mad at him. I mean, expressing it. A few years earlier, I would have been thrashed just for talking back. Now I was practically yelling at him. I told him he should take her on a cruise and he muttered something about casinos and floating brothels."

"Does he have something *against* anniversaries?"

"I guess maybe he did . . . parties . . . boasting . . . who knows? But I said, well if not a cruise, why not something at the church? Why didn't you let folks put together a celebration for the pastor and his wife? With a cake? Are cakes sinful now, Daddy? Do *they* lead to something? You don't think the people at church would have wanted to do that? And you don't think Mama would have wanted it? To feel special after twenty-five years?"

"So how did that turn out?"

"I'm getting to that. But, first . . . and you have to realize how huge this is . . . how *unique* . . . he was kind of sheepish and he acted like . . . *maybe I was right*. Did you hear that, William? Did you hear what I just said? *Daddy thought that maybe I was right!* I mean, he said that he did think parties were worldly. And he couldn't endorse frivolity. But maybe something at the church? Maybe that *would* have been a good idea."

"Wow! That is memorable!"

"Of course he said it was too late, and I said it *wasn't*. They could do it a month late . . . but by then it was almost Christmas so nothing happened."

"So, the special part, the *memorable* part, is that you yelled at him and he said you might be right."

"He didn't actually say it, in so many words, but he thought it because . . . and this is the part I love . . . one year later . . . do you know what he did?"

"Had a party at the church?"

"Exactly! He wouldn't have called it a *party* but that's what it was. And you might think it would be a twenty-sixth anniversary celebration, but since nobody does that, it was a "twenty-five-plus-one." They had the Fellowship Hall all decorated in silver and there was a silver punch bowl and napkins and stuff that had *Happy 25th Anniversary* or *25 Years Together!* on them because, you know, that's what was available."

"So instead of a month late, it was a year late."

"Right. Twenty-fifth wedding anniversary celebration, one year late. That's my dad!"

"Did people think it was their twenty-fifth?"

"Oh no. They weren't fooling anybody. It was 'twenty-five-plus-one.' To me, that's the funniest part. There was this big sheet cake from the bakery that said '25 Years Together' in frosting on the top—that's what the store had and it costs more to have one designed special. So, Daddy got that one and had someone from the church (maybe Mama, I don't know) get some frosting and put *+ 1* next to the *25*. It looked really jankey, as the kids say, but there it was: *25 + 1 Years Together!*

"But no one made fun of him?"

"Oh they all did. A little bit. He can take a little bit, and he joined right in himself. Talked about courtin' Mama, and Mama said she didn't really need any courting, she'd picked him out before he even knew who she was. Everyone was laughing and having a good time. It was exactly what it should be, only a year late."

"So this is a happy memory."

"One of my favorites. Because it means he *can* come around. Maybe he'll decide movie theaters are okay or teaching at a public school isn't so bad."

"Or . . . who knows what?"

"Exactly. Who knows what?"

Sunday, April 9, 2000

They had been meeting for over three months, so she decided to tell him her secret. If it *was* a secret.

"Look at my face, William," she said. "Look close. What do you see?"

"Pretty eyes . . . pretty lips . . ."

"My skin. What do you see?"

"Pretty skin . . ."

"Can you tell I'm wearing makeup?"

"No . . . but . . . okay . . . yes. I guess you are. I mean . . . I don't know much about it. Some kind of powder or something?"

"It's called *foundation*. And *primer*. And *blush*."

"Okay. Yes. I've heard of those things."

"Holiness says no makeup."

"Oh, yeah. I knew that, heard it growing up but never paid much attention. It didn't really apply to men."

"Right. I've noticed a lot of the rules don't apply to men. Though it's the men who make them."

"Cruel world."

"But my point is, what I'm wearing is called *subtle makeup*. Or some people call it *the natural look*."

"Not red lipstick or green eyeshadow."

"No. It just covers up bad stuff and makes me prettier but it doesn't look like I've got anything on."

"Are you prettier when you don't have anything on?"

"Not when it's makeup we're talking about, gutter mind. So Holiness says no makeup . . . but here I am!"

"Does your father think it's okay? The subtle stuff?"

"I'm sure he doesn't, or wouldn't if he knew about it. It would be one of those slippery things. But that's just it . . . *he doesn't know!* I wear makeup and Mama wears makeup and all the women in the church wear makeup and *he doesn't know!* He thinks it's what skin looks like . . . female skin."

"Ah! Yes! Now I get it! And Mama's in on it?"

"She's been doing it for years. Decades!"

"And you?"

"About four months."

And then she told him all about her trip home last Christmas. Her hair was tuning gray and her face had all these acne scars but Mama took her to a beauty parlor and Daddy just thought she got a haircut. She related this as a humorous anecdote, one that William would especially enjoy. After all, it showed that she was less of a "stick in the mud" than he might otherwise assume. Less hopeless anyway. But when she finished, he seemed obsessed with the chronology.

"So *when* did you do this? Your hair and all?"

"You remember the day Mama and I came here for lunch?"

"I will never forget it."

"We came from the beauty parlor. That was the day. The very day."

"And after that, people thought you looked like Carol."

"Yes. The first time I went home . . . oh, I see what you mean . . ."

"It's the hairdo, Angie."

"I have her hair?"

"Think about it. Who does your hair?"

"Tony at Belle Vita. Very nice man. But maybe . . . the kind of man Daddy might not approve of."

"So, no need for me to be jealous?"

"I think not."

"Well, does Tony come up with a totally new hairstyle for everyone he sees? Or do you think he has favorite styles that he uses over and over?"

"I think there might be a book of them."

"So maybe he has a client named Carol and her hair is . . . what color is your hair?"

"Chestnut brown."

"So there's a Carol with chestnut brown hair and then you come in with the same color and he thinks, I'll give her a Carol-do."

"He made me look like someone else."

"Mystery solved."

"Could be. I'll ask him this Thursday. Anyway it makes more sense than the clone thing . . . or the doppol thing."

Sunday, April 23, 2000

She waited for William to finish his latte. They'd ended up at a Starbucks now, having made the rounds to most of the restaurants Pawhuska had to offer. She waited for him to finish before dropping the bombshell.

"Well, I know who she is."

"Who *who* is?"

"Who do you think?"

"Oh. Carol?"

"Yep. I'll tell you if you promise not to stalk her."

"Why would I stalk her?"

"It's what you would do. You have to drop it now, alright. No tracking her down or spying on her or anything like that."

"Do you have a name?"

"Her name is Carol Walker. She probably lives in Wynona. That's what? Ten miles south?"

"Yes. Can I go online and find a picture?"

"That seems pretty stalky."

"Come on. Don't you want to see a picture of her?"

"Well, sort of. But only if it's right there and you don't need to hunt around."

"Yes! I'll show it to you next time. In two weeks."

"But nothing more."

"Agreed."

"I mean it, William. Nothing more."

"I'm not creepy."

"No. Well, you're *probably* not creepy, though I still don't know that for sure. And . . . listen to me! . . . she's just some random woman with my hairstyle. Or actually, I have *her* hairstyle. And the woman at the bank was right. There's no reason for me to know anything else about her."

"So it *was* the hair."

"You were right. You solved the big mystery. You rescued me. You saved me. You're my hero."

"Are you making fun of me?"

"Un-huh," she nodded. "I won't have to lie awake at night worrying about the clone and how I might have to drop my drawers to prove my identity."

"You can keep your pants on."

"Thanks to you! It is such a relief! Turns out, it was just a hairdo."

"Tony?"

"He confessed, eventually. At first, he didn't get it. I asked him if he'd made me look like someone else and he got defensive. I told him I didn't *mind*. It wasn't a criticism. I was just wondering. And then I said people in Pawhuska kept calling me Carol. Well, that did it. The name."

"He knows her. He does her hair."

"He *did* her hair. He used to work for a shop in Wynona, three years ago, and he did Carol Walker's hair. He's moved but, you know, maybe she kept the same style."

"So, anyway . . . he made you look like her."

"That's not what he would say. He claims I already *did* look like her and that's why he did the same hair."

"Why?"

"Because, he says, it worked with her features . . . her nose and mouth and ears and whatever . . . and then when he looked at me and saw the same color hair and similar features, he thought, well that one 'do' worked with Carol's face, it worked really well, so I'll try it with this one.

And it *does* work, he said. He hasn't seen Carol Walker for three years but he just bets we're two peas in a pretty pod."

"That sounds like a direct quote."

"From the lips of Tony: 'two peas in a pretty pod.' And the Carol mystery is solved. You did it and now you have to drop it."

Sunday, May 7, 2000

He didn't drop it.

Two weeks later, he was anxious. He had thought about calling her. He had an envelope with some stuff in it.

"I've been doing investigative research," he said.

"Oh no, William," she said, immediately exasperated with him. "I asked you . . ."

"Not . . . not *her* . . . or not just . . . I mean . . . I do have a picture . . . do you want to see it? . . . but the patterns . . . and dots . . ."

"What? . . . What are you talking about?"

"You know . . . those pattern games you play with your children . . . a bird and a butterfly and a plane . . . I like those things . . . like the anniversary and bowling and Carol . . . I like putting things together . . . connecting dots . . . making pieces fit . . ."

"You're babbling, Billy," she interrupted, and then corrected herself. "I mean, William."

"Research. But you're going to get mad."

"Oh gosh, Billy, why? What have you done? You're like my best friend . . . my only friend . . . I don't want to get mad at you. Just put it away and don't tell me. You've been stalking her, right?"

"No. You're going to get mad. But it's worth it."

"What could be worth that? This has been the best year of my life, maybe. Don't change things please. Whatever you've done . . . I don't want to get mad . . . nothing is worth that."

"This is."

"Alright then," she sighed, giving up and wishing she had never heard of Carol . . . never gone in that Walmart . . . or that bank . . . never told William about it . . . or told him what Tony had said. "Alright . . . tell me."

Saturday, May 13, 2000

She did get mad. And although she did not go home the next weekend, she did drive to Pawhuska. She drove there but didn't go to the Big Boy. She didn't even see William or tell him she was in town.

She went to the Walmart. She had to get a prescription filled and pick up a few things for the next weekend. Of course there was a Walmart in Bartlesville, eight minutes from her apartment but she drove half an hour to the one in Pawhuska, two blocks from the Big Boy. Why had she come here? She wasn't even sure. She wasn't looking for Carol. She was pretty sure of that, though she couldn't help glancing around at the customers, just in case. It would have been like a thing from God if the woman had suddenly appeared. Too much for coincidence.

That's probably why I'm here, she thought, just to give God a chance. But no, there was no divine intervention and she knew now what she had to do. Just wait a little longer.

Friday, May 19, 2000

On Friday, the last day of class, she left Bartlesville Elementary almost as soon as school was out. She'd had another week to think it through and there was time for this quick trip before the graduation ceremony that evening. All the stuff to do at the school—taking down the posters, cleaning the classroom, packing up stuff to bring home for the summer—that could all wait until Monday, or, probably Tuesday.

Who celebrates their twenty-fifth anniversary a year late? William had asked himself. Why would anybody do that? Because of frivolity, she said. And then he "came around" a year later.

"Uh-huh," William grunted, unconvinced. And then he showed it to her . . . a public record . . . available on-line . . .

George and Sarah Blitch weren't married on November 21, 1958. They were married on November 21, 1959. Not ten months before she was born, but two months after.

At first, anniversaries wouldn't have been a problem. Not until she learned some easy math. Then she might wonder, why is your eighth anniversary two months after my eighth birthday? At any rate, by the time she was twenty-five, they had to have a big Silver Anniversary Celebration with an absurd cake that said "25 + 1." Because you can't have a twenty-fifth wedding anniversary when your daughter's already twenty-five years old. *And was that just for her?* Most of the church members were old enough to remember. *Did everyone know but her?*

In any case, the bowling mystery was solved. He was always saying, *it don't seem like there's anything wrong with bowling . . . but what does it lead to?* . . .That just never seemed to fit . . . what *does* bowling lead to, Daddy? . . . . or what *did* it lead to? . . . it led to *me* . . . didn't it?

And there was a whole lot of trouble at the church back then. I bet there was, but it wasn't because his standards of holiness were so high. *She was in high school!* He was the pastor and Mama was in high school! And, by the way, Mama, you said there was a *lot* of trouble . . . that's what you said . . . a *lot* of trouble . . . what constitutes a *lot*, I wonder . . . what constitutes . . .

But now she had arrived . . . . 614 Suffolk Avenue in Fairfax, Oklahoma.

The middle-aged woman gave a start when she opened the door, as if, for just an instance, she thought she saw someone she knew.

"Are you Margaret Thomas?" Angelika asked.

"Well yes . . . yes, I am."

"And you have a daughter named Carol . . . Carol Walker?"

"I do . . . oh my God! . . . is everything alright?"

"Yes . . . yes . . . I didn't mean to frighten you. My name is Angelika Blitch and I think you knew my mother. . . Sarah Blitch . . . used to be Sarah Wilson?"

Now she looked flustered . . . on the verge of denying it . . . but then she surrendered.

"That was a long time ago."

"Yes. You were a member of Cross Roads Methodist Church in Bartlesville. You were on the bowling team, weren't you?"

"What do you want, Ms. Blitch?" she asked coldly.

"The girls' bowling team . . . the *high school girls*' bowling team . . . out-of-town trips with my father as the chaperone . . . George Blitch?"

"What do you want?"

"I just . . . out of respect . . . I thought I should give you a heads up . . . I'll be seeing Carol on Monday in Wynona and I just thought . . . well, if there's anything you'd rather have her hear from you than from me, I want to give you that chance."

"You're a fool," she said suddenly. "And our lives are none of your business. Why would you want to bother good people with your foolishness?"

"I'm going to see her on Monday."

"She'll want nothing to do with you."

"That may be. I'll respect it. But I know one thing for certain. I know she'd rather make that decision for herself than just have you make it for her. I'm sure of that."

"Did your parents put you up to this?"

"My parents are liars. But my boyfriend is a detective."

"Well, you're a fool, Angelika Blitch," she said, looking her up and down as she closed the door. "A pretty fool, I'll grant . . . but a fool nonetheless."

* * *

And now she had to hurry. Bartlesville High School was a little more than an hour from Farifax and it was already 5:20 PM. Graduation was at 7:00 and she needed to stop in Pawhuska to pick up William. He was going with her. He was going to sit with her and watch the high school seniors graduate and she would tell him which ones were "hers"—her first graders from eleven years ago. She had wanted a sister for forty years, but wouldn't think about that anymore till Monday. Tonight was her favorite night of the year.

Maybe they could get some granola bars before the ceremony, but by the time it was over they would be starving. And then she would just suggest they get a pizza or something and take it to her apartment. This would be unexpected. He was assuming she'd drive him back to Pawhuska after the ceremony. He would be thinking about how he had to get up early the next morning to open the Big Boy. But he wouldn't *say* anything, not if he had the chance to actually get inside her apartment. He'd be thinking, this is a step . . . pizza in her apartment and, who knows what we'll do the next weekend . . . or the next. And then she would show him the *Jurassic Park* DVD she'd rented and the player she'd borrowed from the school. They could watch it while they ate. He'd be excited to hear that . . . so pleased . . . and yet *worried* . . . because how late would it go? . . . and he really did have to get back and get up early.

She wouldn't say a thing. She would enjoy his consternation. Eventually, maybe he'd use the bathroom. Maybe he'd see the spare toothbrush she'd gotten at Walmart, along with three pair of men's underwear and some T-shirts. Maybe he'd see those in there on the shelf. She'd gotten them a week ago when she picked up her prescription. The pills. They were in the bathroom too, right out in the open. Would he know what they were? Amazing you could get them at Walmart now. She'd picked them up a week ago, when she'd asked Nathan if he could cover the restaurant this weekend.

But she wouldn't say a word. He was the detective—let him figure it out.

11

Jasper Is Rich

Yeni Navarro was strolling briskly across the mall on Seventh Street, heading toward her office just south of the Air and Space Museum. An obvious person of importance, she was accompanied by two men in suits who possibly looked like Secret Service agents, causing the mob of tourists to divide on both sides of the sidewalk and ask each other who she might be as she strode majestically through their midst like Moses passing through the parted waters of the Red Sea.

The secretary of education was rarely on television and, so, was rarely recognized. She did not merit Secret Service protection; the men accompanying her were senior staff, young men whose careers had probably attained their lifetime pinnacle, at least in terms of prestige and salary.

Just before they got to Independence Avenue, where the Arts and Industries building was on her right, she caught a glimpse of a small, colorful object propped against the railing of the side staircase that led to an entrance for official personnel only. She almost kept going, then did a double take, looked at it more intently, and walked over, ten yards out of her way.

"How cute!" she said, looking at a small stone, propped against the rail as if on display. It was painted with a picture of a poodle.

"Yes ma'am," a senior staffer replied, affirming the stone's cuteness.

"Some child must have lost it. I suppose someone set it up here in case they come back."

"No ma'am. It's a kindness stone."

"What's that?"

And then they told her the local news she had missed three months previous, having been out of town for a few weeks. The Girl Scouts had an event where they painted 10,000 stones with pictures and designs and then placed them all around the area for people to find and keep. Or pick up and put some place else. The whole idea was just to make people smile.

"Well, it worked for me," she said. "Did you know I have a poodle?"

"No ma'am."

"The Girl Scouts put it here?"

"No ma'am. Bums."

"What?"

"Bums. I mean . . . the homeless. They kinda took charge of distribution, around here at least. They got buckets full of rocks from the Girl Scouts and every Sunday, after dark, they come to the mall and put a couple dozen of them in different places for people to find. Tourists and, uh, politicians."

"Why do they do that?"

"To make them smile. The tourists and the politicians."

"No, I mean, why would homeless people do the distribution? Why not the Scouts?"

A staffer shrugged.

"Someone pays them, I imagine."

"Gives 'em booze, maybe," his colleague joked.

"But you don't know?"

"No ma'am."

She picked up the kindness stone and slipped it into her side pocket. "Find out."

* * *

About a month after Ms. Navarro's fortuitous discovery of the poodle-painted rock, Jasper was getting ready to tell a story to his friends at Algonkian Park. These men (Jasper and his friends) were in fact the "bums" who traveled to the Washington mall every Sunday evening to plant two dozen kindness stones in various locations where tourists or politicians might happen upon them. They needed to take the Metro to do this, but Darius and Mickey (two of Jasper's friends from before) had donated Metro passes for some of them to make these weekly trips. Ed and a couple of the others would have sold their passes to buy liquor at the 7-Eleven, so Jasper had appointed himself keeper of all passes and kept them in an inside pocket with his photo of Toffee and Taffy.

Sasquatch had requested a story about a cat, but Jasper said he'd have to think on that one a while. The Greek myths didn't feature cats as much as the Egyptian or Persian ones. The only tales that came to mind were stories of Chimera or Sphinxes or the Nemean lion, all about cats who were monsters and got slayed by heroes. That wasn't what Sasquatch had in mind. Instead, for today, he thought he would relate an homage to the big man's appetite: while none of the men were well-fed, Sasquatch claimed to be always hungry. He was also the only one of their number who regularly ate out of trash cans, grossing the others out by consuming picnic leftovers that he claimed "hadn't got too ripe."

During these warm months, some of the men (including Jasper) slept on benches and tried to find enough deposit bottles during the day to purchase sandwiches from the nearby Subway. Others were more inclined to beg, sitting at intersections with unconvincing "Will Work for Food" signs. Sasquatch scrounged trash cans and dumpsters, and at night he liked sleeping on the ground under a bridge with his friends Emeril and Bernard. The latter said it was better to sleep "on the holy good Lord's good earth" than on some man-made park bench, but in Sasquatch's case that point lacked relevance because no bench would have held him. At 6'6" he weighed about 290 pounds and, though he wasn't fat, he was wide. He was also abnormally hairy, which even apart from his animal habits might have been sufficient to account for his nickname (it was, they all assumed, a nickname, but if he had any other name there was no one alive who knew what it was).

Sasquatch had acquired a large cat named Purty a week after the big Kindness Stone Crusade at the end of April. Purty was smoky gray, with very long hair, and she slept with Sasquatch under the bridge at night, accompanied him on garbage runs, and found his lap whenever he sprawled in the sun for a nap during the day.

"Why's he call her Purdy?" one of the men had asked when Sasquatch and the feline were absent. "Sounds like a boy's name."

"It's not pur-*dee*, it's pur-*tee*," Jasper explained. "And he's very proud of that name because he thinks it's clever. Sasquatch doesn't often think of himself as clever, but he thinks he hit a peak with that name."

"Well it's too clever for me, I guess."

"Don't you ever hear him talk about what a 'purty' cat she is?"

"Yeah. So, what, is *purty* just a hillbilly way to say pretty? What's so clever about that?"

"What do cats do? What noise do they make?"

"They meow."

"What else?"

"They hiss at you."

"What else?"

The men looked at each other and shrugged.

"They *purr!* Cats *purr!*" Jasper exclaimed in exasperation. "So she's a pretty cat, but instead of callin' her *Pretty*, he calls her *Purrty*. Am I the only one who got that?"

"What is he, six?"

"You can ask him that when he's here."

"He's a six-year-old girl."

"You can tell him that."

"Don't think I will. But I ain't never heard that cat purr. Heard it hiss and growl and spit, but ain't never heard it purr."

"Anyway he thinks he's clever and he's very proud of himself for being so smart, though apparently I'm the only one who got it."

Those conversations had taken place when Sasquatch was not around. At present, however, the large, hairy man was sitting in the grass with his back against a tree and the large, hairy cat was stretched out across his lap, looking larger, if not hairier, than ever.

"Is that cat going to have more babies?" one of the men asked, just as Jasper had been gearing up to tell his story.

"I guess she is," Sasquatch answered, scratching his pet behind the ears. "She does like her lovin'—and she's right popular with the boys."

Emeril confirmed that this thesis was congruent with all the yowling that went on under the bridge some nights when he was trying to sleep.

"She's such a purty cat," Sasquatch continued. "I'm going to get her one of them collars that's pink and has diamonds on it. They're not real diamonds but she won't know."

"I give a girl a ring like that one time," Samward volunteered. "Before I come into my present context, this was. It cost me twenty-five dollars and I told her it cost twenty-five *hundred* dollars. She found out though."

"Was she a cat?" Jasper asked.

"No, she wasn't a cat."

"So that's not exactly relevant to our current conversation, is it?"

"I'm just saying, sometimes they find out."

In fact, last May Sasquatch had actually called his cat Scruffy for a week and thought it was unusually chubby but then Scruffy had kittens, at which point her name was changed to something more appropriate for a young lady. For the Fourth of July weekend, Sasquatch had gotten a box from the 7-Eleven and a sheet of cardboard on which Jasper had scrawled "FREE KITTENS FROM A PURTY CAT." All eight of the babies went home with impulse-buying parents whose children had begged and squealed in ways that reminded Jasper of Toffee and Taffy.

"I'll be needin' another box afore long," he said now. "Hope some of 'em are black and I can give 'em out easy for Holler-ween."

Jasper had decided to tell them the story of Erysichthon and Demeter but he knew better than to use those names and had just decided to call them Eric and Demi. He promised the boys that this was going to be a tale that was "extremely gross." They liked gross, though they liked sexy better. Maybe he'd think up a sexy one for next week—one with a cat—but the Tale of Hungry Eric would have to do for now.

"So this story is about a rich man named Eric. He had a big house and servants and was used to getting everything he wanted, but his wife had passed and he didn't have any sons to inherit from him. All he had was one daughter. A young lass he called 'Messy.'"

In the myths her name was Mestra.

"Now Messy, she was a special girl because she'd got in good with the god Poseidon at some point—that's a different story—and he gave her the ability to change herself into anything she wanted. She could turn herself into a snake or a dog or . . . yes, a cat! I mean, she's not going to do that in this story but I guess she could. She could change herself into a cat or anything she wanted."

Sasquatch smiled at this and kept scratching Purty behind her ears. The cat was spread out across his legs and looked close to purring.

"This sounds like superheroes," one of the men said. "One of the X-men could do that. Or X-women. They got movies about 'em now but I ain't seen 'em. They got lots of X movies now but they ain't what you would think that means. They's about superheroes. Anyhow I ain't seen 'em but I read the comic books once, a while back."

"I read the Hulk and the Conan. They didn't have chameleon women though."

"All fascinating," Jasper interjected. "But not relevant to our current story."

"It might have been a good one if they did. What if the Hulk or the Conan met this woman who can change herself into things? That might have been a good one."

"What if she, like, changed into the Hulk and then he'd have to fight himself?"

"That would have been a good one. They should have hired you to write them stories."

"So Eric was this rich man" Jasper persisted. "And there was a big tree in his yard that he wanted to chop down because it blocked his view or something. Maybe he just wanted the wood." I should have had the reason figured out, he thought. I'd do better at telling these things if they'd just shut up and let me tell them. "Anyway he tells his servants, go chop down that tree, but none of 'em will do it because the tree was special to this goddess named Demeter . . . um, Demi . . . this goddess named Demi."

"Like that girl that married a ghost?"

"Yes," Jasper said. "A lot like her, I imagine."

"I saw that one," another man interrupted. "When I was . . . you know, back . . . when I watched a TV sometimes."

"I saw it too," Samward added. "But I was only like ten or something. It was a hunnerd years ago. She's a *purty* girl, that one. Not as *purty* as Squatchy's cat, but a *purty* girl nonetheless."

"I don't know. If I had to pick between the cat and the ghost girl, I think I'd take the girl. Just sayin' if it was me."

"Wait, was she a ghost? You couldn't do nothin' with her if she was a ghost."

"She wasn't a ghost, fool, she just married a ghost."

"Oh in that case, you might have a chance, I s'pose, less there was competition."

"That's the truth. I never done too well when there's competition. Options tend to tell against me."

"I'm trying to tell a story here," Jasper erupted. "Does anybody care? Do you want to hear it or not?"

"We want to hear it, Jasper," Emeril said. "These clowns . . . you just need to talk right over them."

"Alright then. Eric, he gets so frustrated with his servants, he just grabs an ax and goes out and cuts that tree down himself. And the goddess, Demi? Well, she is mad! So she calls up a friend, a spirit named Limos who used to live inside that box Pandora opened. I told you about that one. Limos used to live in there, but Pandora let her out. That box held all the bad stuff in the world and Limos—her name means 'Famine', and of all the bad things, she is one of the worst. Well, anyway, Demi the beautiful ghost goddess was so mad about Eric chopping down her tree that she sent Limos to visit Eric in the middle of the night.

"You got to picture this now because Limos is beyond ugly and horrible. She looks like one of these zombies you might have seen on a TV or something. She is a crooked old hag with all her bones showing and her skin all yellow. She's naked with long saggy breasts and she looks to be a thousand years old. Bony fingers. Hair like steel wool. And she comes creeping into Eric's room in the middle of the night. Right up to his bed. And she puts her putrid mouth right over his and kisses him long and hard. Just breathin' her foul breath right into him. He wakes up with a horrible start and she's gone."

"Okay, this is gettin' pretty good now."

"This one's kinda scary. Gonna give me nightmares."

"I like it when there's nekkid women, but usually they're young and pretty."

"And when Eric woke up, he was *hungry!* Limos had breathed famine and starvation right into him and he was hungrier than he had ever been before. Hungrier than you, Sasquatch, and that's sayin' a lot. He got up and started eating. And he ate all the next day. The servants just brought him more and more food, and he ate and ate but just got hungrier. Eventually, he'd eaten all the food in the house and then he ate all the livestock, you know, the animals outside the house. The cows and the sheep. He ate a couple dogs, some mice, and some rats. They didn't have any cats, though, so he didn't eat them. But still he kept eating. Every day all he did was eat."

"Did he get fat?"

"No, he didn't even get fat. He didn't gain a pound, but he ate and ate and ate. And sure enough, eventually, there wasn't nothin' left. He had eaten it all. He sold everything he had to buy more food and then he ate that too. The servants all left. Time went by and all there was left was him and his daughter Messy . . . and he was still hungry."

"He's not gonna eat *her*, is he?"

"See, that would be one way the story could go. I told you it was gross, and that would be pretty gross, wouldn't it?"

"Sure would."

"He did think of it. Remember, she can change into things. So Eric thinks about sayin', 'Hey Messy, how about you change into a big, fat sow? Or a steer? Or somethin' really tasty?' But then he gets a better plan."

"Good . . . 'cause I was startin' to worry about her."

"He tells her to change into a supermodel. The most beautiful girl in the world. And when she does that, sure enough, some fool comes along and wants to marry her. But, you see, back then, if you wanted to marry a beautiful girl, it cost you a bit."

"What do you mean *back then*?"

"That ain't changed none."

"P'raps it's still that way, but they had a name for it. Called it a dowry. So some rich fool wants to marry Messy who looks like a supermodel and Eric says, you can have her if you give me a cow and two pigs and six sheep. Transaction completed and off they go. The happy couple. But after they go a ways, Messy turns into a fish or a fox or a horse or something and comes gallopin' back. She's right back at her home with her dad and her husband is too embarrassed to say he couldn't keep a woman so he never says nothin'. But it don't matter because by then Eric has eaten up all the dowry animals. And guess what?"

"He's still hungry."

"You're a genius. So they do it again, but his time Messy looks twice as beautiful and Eric wants double the number of edibles. And, well, it goes on and on. He keeps marryin' her off and eatin' up the dowry and she keeps comin' home until finally one day he marries her to a young man who's kinda cute and less a fool than the others and she thinks 'Hmm, this one's not bad' and she lets him sleep with her and then she thinks 'not bad at all!' And so she falls in love and forgets all about her poor old dad, which is exactly what young girls are supposed to do.

"And here's where the story gets gross. Eric is still hungry and now there's no more animals to eat. And no more coming. He would have gone through all the garbage in the land and eaten it, ripe or not, except he'd already done that. I mean, he was a garbage eater to put our Sasquatch to shame. But now even that's gone and he's still hungry. What is he going to do?

"Well I'll tell you. He sits there one day, looking at his bare naked foot and thinking, Hmm! . . . there's meat on that! So, he looks at it for a day or two and then he gets an axe and chops his foot off. Puts it on the grill. Barbecues it good and eats it up. Then he chops off the other one. But he's still hungry and hankerin' for calves or thighs. Maybe some shoulder or rump roast. The story gets a bit sketchy here, as to how he kept doing it once he ate his arms and couldn't wield an axe. Maybe he just bit into himself as best he could. But what they say . . . and why would they lie? . . . what they say, is that when folk finally came around, they didn't find nothing but teeth. A pair of chattering teeth lying on the very spot where that special tree used to grow. Eric had ate himself all up and there wasn't nothin' left but teeth. And those teeth were chompin' up a storm because . . . you know what? . . . *they were still hungry!*"

"Wow! That was a good story, Jasper."

"It's pretty gross, alright."

"You think it's got one of those morals to it?"

"Don't eat garbage maybe," one of them suggested, looking at Sasquatch with his cat.

Jasper thought a moment.

"I'd say, the moral, if there is one, might be . . . don't piss off a goddess."

"How do you know which ones . . .which women . . . are goddesses?"

"Don't think you can know for sure. So maybe you just shouldn't piss off women in general."

"Someone should have told me that before I bought that ring," Samward said. "The twenty-five dollar one."

"Here's some Mormons . . ." Ed said then.

Two men in suits with white shirts and ties were walking in their direction.

"Ought to have bicycles if they're Mormons," Bernard objected. "Mormons always got bicycles. That's how you spot 'em."

"Maybe they parked 'em. In any case, we don't want any. Mormonism or Jehovahs or whatever it is. We don't want it, that's for sure."

The men in suits kept coming, across the grass toward the river, until they arrived at the area where the bums . . . the *homeless men* . . . were lying about under trees. One of them was as large as an ape and he had an enormous cat in his lap. They didn't eat cats, did they?

"Does one of you answer to the name of Jasper?" the man on the right asked.

There was a predictable, dead silence. The men looked at the ground. At the river. Not a one of them looked at the men in suits.

Then Samward said, "Ain't nobody here by that name. Nope, there isn't."

And the others piped in.

"Never heard of the man."

"And if there was, he wouldn't want nothing to do with none of you."

"We're all saved here. Or lost. Either way, we don't need what you're selling."

"We have a message for a man named Jasper," the man on the left explained.

"Well, he ain't here to receive it."

"God don't want him and the devil won't take him. So peddle your Mormon shit somewhere else."

"I'm not saying I know the man, but if I've heard tell of him, I'm pretty sure he's into goddesses anyhow. The pretty kind you don't know nothin' about."

"And nymphs. Naked ones."

"If yer church ain't got no goddesses or nymphs you kin just give up on him and maybe try to find a better rilijin for yerselfs."

"Can you give him a message for us?" the man on the right persisted.

"Don't expect so. Ain't never seen him before. Won't probably see him again."

"Never even heard of the man."

"What kind of message?" Emeril asked. "Did he win a million dollars or somethin'?"

"No," the man on the left responded. "Not a *million* dollars. Just three hundred thousand."

The men under the trees were suddenly more alert. They looked about and then four of them pointed to their storytelling companion and said in unison, "That's him!"

* * *

Once Yeni Navarro had learned about the kindness stone event last April, she sent her staffers to talk to the television and newspaper reporters who had been on the scene for that day, and they had obtained copies of the filmed coverage, including quite a bit that had not been shown to the public. She quickly discerned that the Girl Scout leader presenting herself as the mastermind behind it all was just a silly opportunist and she further surmised that the real person responsible for a remarkable civic undertaking had been a homeless man who never appeared on camera—a man named Jasper who slept on a bench in Algonkian Park. The reporters all seemed to agree with this supposition, even though none of them had actually talked with Jasper or even met the man.

This might have been the end of the matter if she had not had dinner with a friend from the Capital City Visionary Society, a foundation that gave awards of half a million dollars to groups or (occasionally) individuals whose optimism and altruism served to uplift the public spirit and improve the social conscience of the community as a whole. This year, they were thinking of bestowing the honor and the money on the Girl Scout Council in recognition of their innovative and vivifying production and distribution of over 10,000 kindness stones throughout the metro area. Yeni told her what she knew of Jasper—and the friend was intrigued. What if the money—or a portion of it—was given to a homeless man? What a story that would make!

The staffers were put to work, gathering information that was not difficult to obtain when one possessed government credentials and resources. They quickly learned that a Jasper Donovan (local man, now off the grid) had served in Afghanistan, along with two men who were still in the area—Mickey Stoll and Darius Hill. Interviews with these two individuals confirmed Donovan's identity as the Jasper in question—and brought his life story to light.

Yes, they had served alongside Private Donovan, Darius confirmed. "Everyone called him Mellow Yellow or Hurdy Gurdy. He was a good guy, someone you could count on. Stayed out of trouble. And he loved to tell stories—tales from mythology about gods and goddesses and heroes and all. He'd rework 'em so they were about Afghanistan or, you know, relevant to a soldier's life."

After being honorably discharged, Jasper had gotten a job working as a pest control technician for Orkin and he'd married a local girl named Juliet Madison. They had a pair of twin daughters, Faith and Hope. Jasper would tell them every day that they were two of the three most important things in the world. "What's the third?" he'd ask, and they would say in unison, "Love!" But eventually the girls decided to call each other Toffee and Taffy and tried to get everybody else to call them that as well.

"He still liked telling stories from Greek mythology," Mickey continued, "and he did a couple programs at the library, relating one or another of the tales to some group or another. Don't know too much about that, but it led to him being asked to teach a class at the community college. He did that three times, I believe, and was happy and proud."

The entire family seemed to have a life that was "happy and proud," except that the mother, Julie, sometimes struggled with mental health issues. These were never fully diagnosed, but she occasionally had episodes in which she seemed out of touch, usually in the middle of the night. Jasper would miss her in the bed and find her downstairs, walking about the living room and talking incoherently out loud. Not sentences, but only words. Long streams of random words pronounced as though they were supposed to be sentences but that did not actually combine to make any kind of sense: "mind morsel or accumulation drink suburb . . ."

Because this happened at night, it was assumed she had some kind of sleep disorder, that she was walking and talking in her sleep (though she seemed awake). Jasper would coax her back to bed and tease her about it in the morning when she didn't remember a thing.

This didn't seem like anything to worry about, but over time the episodes became more frequent (once a month instead of twice a year) and Jasper thought she seemed more agitated, waving her arms about and talking louder than before: "inject! pleasure! facility! chicken! penalty! . . ."

He feared she might wake the children and frighten them. He had more trouble getting her back to bed. He also became more convinced that she *wasn't* asleep. And, though she still claimed to remember nothing when morning came, he was pretty sure that she did.

He talked to Darius and Mickey. He had told them before, when the behavior was quirky (and cute!) and something they could all laugh about. Now he sought advice and they did agree that maybe he should talk to some kind of doctor just to see. But he didn't want to make too big a deal out of it. There didn't seem to be cause for concern.

And then she lit the house on fire. Did she do it on purpose? Or just by accident? No one would ever know, but the fire burned their house to the ground along with everything Jasper owned. And the fire took the lives of his two eight-year-old girls.

"Jasper arrived at the scene," Mickey reported. "Came back from the college or the library or somewhere around 11:00 PM to find his home in flames and his wife walking about in the street, waving her hands and shouting nonsensically. He tried to run inside but the firemen restrained him, and he tried to talk to her but she didn't seem to recognize him."

After that, Jasper Donovan was never officially seen again. Literally homeless, he disappeared for a couple of years but eventually turned up living in the park; in time his friends Mickey and Darius made contact with him. They learned very quickly never to mention what had happened, not to talk about *before*, but to provide obscure measures of support in whatever ways they could.

Julie had been admitted to a mental hospital and it was impossible to determine whether the fire had been intentional or accidental. A ruling on that point could have been determinative for the insurance payout but, with Jasper missing and Julie institutionalized, the company requested the court to appoint an attorney to represent the claimant in reaching an equitable settlement. An award was granted, but the funds were quickly seized by the hospital to defray Julie's mounting medical bills.

When that money ran out, the doctors indicated that there was a need to find her husband, who might now be able to take over some of the expenses. Of course, everything was provided on a sliding scale, but they needed at least a record of his financial resources in order to continue treating her. They met with her to discuss this as tactfully as possible and to see if she might have any leads as to the man's whereabouts. She killed herself the next day, and to date, no one knew if Jasper had ever been informed of this or, for that matter, whether he had even known she was in the hospital. Since disappearing the day after the fire, he had never asked about her and neither Mickey nor Darius had ever volunteered any information.

"Sometimes, he talks about those girls in the present tense," Mickey said. "And in his mind they're still little. They'd be grown by now, but he doesn't seem to realize that."

"And he didn't attend the kids' funeral, you know," Darius added. "His own kids. Mickey and I were there. There was a memorial service with all the neighbors and folks from their school. It was a big deal in the newspaper and on the TV because it was just so sad, you know, a big deal for a day or two. You can find it if you go back, but I guess everyone's forgotten now."

"Anyhow," Mickey said, "we didn't see or hear from Jasper for over two years and we just assumed that he'd offed himself. Then Darius overheard someone on the airport shuttle talking about a homeless man telling stories in the park."

A homeless veteran! The Capital City Visionary Society could definitely go with that! And not a veteran with a criminal record or a drug problem or PTSD (well, not from overseas anyway). A veteran who had served his country and then fallen victim to tragic misfortune, lost his home and family, and still devoted his life to bringing hope and optimism to all those around him. It would all play extremely well except for one thing. Yeni Navarro told them, based on what her assistants had gathered from those interviews: Jasper Donovan would never consent to being interviewed or to being any kind of poster boy or role model for anything.

Well, then. . . an *anonymous* homeless veteran! That could play well too.

* * *

While the men who weren't Mormons were conversing with a reluctant Jasper in the picnic area a quarter mile up from the river, the collection of comrades from which he had been plucked were discussing how to spend his money.

"More benches," Samward proposed. "He could pay the park to put in some more benches, down here by the water where its coolest in summer and maybe on the other side of the hill for the winter."

"Deposit bottles," Ed volunteered. "We could always use more of them."

"Wider benches," another man offered. "These things are too narrow for some of us. I don't mean, like, Sasquatch wide, I just mean normal wide, like some of us."

"Longer and wider," a third voice said, to much acclaim.

"So that's settled then? More benches, longer and wider?" Samward asked, almost as though there had been a vote.

"I wouldn't be so quick on that," Emeril interrupted.

"Well, course *you* wouldn't. They ain't gonna put benches under the bridge and you wouldn't use them if they did."

"That's not at all what I'm saying. It's just that more benches means more bums."

"What do you mean?"

"I mean, you start putting in more benches and more folks are gonna drift this way to sleep on 'em. New folks we don't know nothin' about . . . and, well . . . there goes the neighborhood!"

"I hadn't thought of that."

"We got a good thing goin' here. I mean, we're bums, but we're *quality* bums. Not like the ones on K Street, you know. The underpass."

"And some of them got tents. People call 'em homeless and they got tents. What's a tent? Ain't that a home? They're just campers is what I say. They just doin' what rich folks do for fun."

"Yeah, but I don't know if they really want to . . ."

"Well, okay then, never mind, but they got no right to call themselves bums is what I say."

"I don't know if they do call themselves . . ."

"You want tents all over this park? I don't!"

"But the point, if you were payin' attention, was *benches*. And I don't know if people with tents would come here on account of more benches."

"Yeah but Emeril's still right. We don't want to get more benches and new benches and big, wide ones if it means we're going to get all gender-fried."

"Now you're using words you heard from Jasper and you don't even know what they mean."

"It's when new folk move in and ruin everything."

"We don't need new folks," Samward agreed. "Especially if, you know, they don't like fit in, if you know what I mean, like bring down the property values, so to speak. Ya'll know I'm not racist or nothin' but I sort of feel like Bernard here is all the *integratin'* we need, if you know what I mean. No offense, Bernard."

"No *offense?*" Bernard yelped. "What do you mean, no *offense?* And what in the holy good Lord's name do you mean by sayin' you ain't racist?"

"Well, you know, I mean, I *ain't* racist or nothin'. I just think we don't need . . . I mean we got you and that's fine but we don't need a whole *lot* of . . ."

"Whole *lot* of what?"

"You know . . ."

"Oh I know! I didn't choose to be black, and if the holy good Lord had just maybe had the courtesy to ask me about my preferences . . . well, that don't matter, because what I do know is that you all are 'bout as racist as they come. You kin all just wrap yo' asses up in one of them big red Confederation flags if you like and use your sheets to make you some white hoods."

"We don't got no sheets, Bernard."

"No flags neither."

"Well that ain't hardly . . ."

"Alright, alright, let's not start a war," Emeril intervened. "Just 'cause we're rich. We all got along when we was poor, remember? And Bernard, you know these guys don't never think through a thing before they say it."

"Well, that's the truth."

"How long have you known Samward here?"

"A piece."

"Have you ever known him to think about any fool thing afore he said it? I mean, even once?"

"Can't say that I have."

"Well then that's all that that's worth. But in any case, what do *you* think about the benches?"

"I think you probably right on that one, Emeril. We got enough as is. We get more benches and some biker bums might move in. Sam'd probably invite 'em. White supremacist biker bums, like that president's buddies."

"What president you mean?" asked a man who hadn't spoken yet. He seemed angry.

"The one what was a fool."

"That don't narrow it down. But I suspect you might be talkin' about . . ."

"Hell no!" Emeril intervened again. "Hell no! You ain't gonna bring up no politics, not now, not never."

"I didn't start it."

"Well you can end it. We ain't gonna talk about *that* stuff. And, 'sides, people that don't vote ain't got much call to . . . well, let's just give it up. I guess we don't want benches."

"How 'bout blankets then?" Samward continued. "We could get some more blankets."

"Or deposit bottles," Ed suggested, enthusiastically. "We could use more deposit bottles."

"What about sandwiches?" one of the others chimed in. "I bet you could buy a whole lot of Subway sandwiches with that many dollars. Sometimes on special they's just five dollars a piece, so 300,000 dollar. . . well, we'd need Jasper to figure it out, but I bet it'd be a few hunnerd at least."

"It would be more'n that. You might be able to buy the whole Subway."

"No, I don't want to own no restaurant. That'd be almost like gettin' a job."

"I never seen no one who owns a place do much work."

"We could just own it and not have nothin' to do with it except to come by for free sandwiches every time we want."

"And how you think it's gonna stay in business then? With us all eatin' there every day for free."

"Could we get tater chips, too? And Pepsi?"

"You're gonna bankrupt the whole place is what you're going to do."

"Maybe 'ventually, but we could make it last through the summer I bet."

"Most ridiculous thing I ever heard. It's just stupid is what it is. You all thinkin' you gonna be business men or entrapeeners or whatever they call 'em. You're a bunch of fools is what you are, and so am I, but I know it, and that's what makes you stupid."

"Take a breath, Sammer," Emeril counseled.

"Stupider than me is what I meant. I mean I know I ain't no genius but I ain't tryin' to buy no restaurant and be an entrapeener."

"Okay. We get it."

"Now what I was sayin' about blankets . . ."

"Deposit bottles," Ed interrupted. "We could use more deposit bottles."

"*What the hell you talkin' about?*" Samward exploded in exasperation. "*Deposit bottles?* You think we're just gonna buy $300,000 worth of bottles and leave 'em lyin' about for you to pick up?"

"I don't see why not."

"That's the most dimwit thing you ever said . . . I mean *ever*. And, trust me, you've said some . . ."

"We're all trying to get along," Emeril broke in. "Remember an hour ago . . . afore we had money. . . when we was friends . . . ."

"But did you hear what he said? Buy empty soda bottles so he can turn 'em in for the deposit!"

"They wouldn't have to be soda bottles," Ed explained. "Or empty."

"Oh," Samward responded, with dawning apprehension. "Oh. Yes. Now I get it. Oh, Lord! Our ship finally comes in and this drunk's gonna . . ."

"*Give it back!*" Sasquatch suddenly shouted.

"What?"

"You talkin' to the cat?"

"The money. Give it back! No good'll come of it. You can see that already."

The men stood there . . . looking at each other . . . thinking . . . he was probably right . . . but Emeril was the first to say so.

"You right, Sassy. But we gonna have to tell Jasper."

"I'll tell him."

"We all will. We'll tell him we had a meeting and . . . oh, look . . . he's coming."

Jasper was walking toward them, across the grass. They all waited, nervously, until he arrived and then Emeril spoke up.

"We got something to tell you."

"'Bout what?"

"'Bout the money."

"Ain't no money," Jasper said. "I told 'em to give it to the Mormons."

* * *

Two weeks later, Mickey Stoll and Darius Hill met with Yeni Navarro herself and with two representatives of the Capital City Visionary Society in a conference room at the US Department of Education, just south of the National Air and Space Museum. It was the first time Mickey and Darius had ever been inside a government building of this nature and, certainly, the first time they had ever met with a cabinet secretary who was an associate of the president of the United States. Previously, Secretary Navarro had sent men in suits to speak with them at their work places. Now, she had invited (summoned?) them to her office to meet with her face to face.

It was an unusual situation. The society had never issued an anonymous award before, and they had never even considered the possibility of bestowing their largesse on a reluctant recipient. But the lawyers knew how it could be done, and Mickey and Darius had come up with a plan that made it appealing. The genesis for this idea had come the Friday after Jasper's meeting with the non-Mormons, when he and Mickey had their usual lunch together.

Mickey had wondered whether the matter would come up. Indeed he was worried that maybe Jasper's strong reaction to the men in suits might threaten the fragile trust that sustained their weekly lunch ritual.

Mickey had learned early on not to talk about Jasper's "situation," not to offer help or advice, and this required mutual pretense. Mickey always picked up the bill, though Jasper promised to get it "next time." They had been doing this for eight years and Mickey was willing to do it forever. It was one of his pathetic friend's only remaining ties to what most people considered reality. If he'd done anything now to ruin it . . . *damn those men in suits! . . . he had told them Jasper wouldn't be interested* . . . if Jasper knew he had met with them . . . been a part of it . . . if he'd done something to ruin this lunch connection, he would never forgive himself.

But Jasper acted like nothing had happened. Mostly, he seemed obsessed with trying to come up with a story about a cat. Zeus had gotten a maid named Galanthis pregnant, so Hera turned the poor girl into a cat and sent her down to Hades where she became a priestess to Hecate, queen of the witches. He wondered if there was something there but, no, there wasn't. A hellcat? A *literal* hellcat?

"Maybe I should just make something up," he said. "Not completely, you know, but just *amend* one of the tales."

"Mm-hmm," Mickey assented, nodding.

"Like Circe. Instead of turning men into pigs, she could turn them into cats. And then I can make up some stuff about the cats getting into things and finally she decides men are less trouble and changes them back."

"Sounds good."

"All but one. She'd keep one because *one* cat is nice to have."

"Right."

"It's taking a lot of liberties though. Don't know if Homer could ever forgive me."

You had a dog named Homer, Mickey almost said, but didn't. The dogs . . . Homer and Virgil . . . they had been in the house.

"Well, that seems good, Jasper. I think you can do it."

And then, out of the blue, Jasper said that he wished he could take *some* of the money. Not all of it, just some. Mickey had not mentioned "the money." He had not let on that he knew anything at all about the society or the men in suits, but somehow Jasper knew that he was in this loop.

"Ask them if I can take *some* of it," he said. "Not all of it, just some and only once."

He explained what he wanted. Mickey listened and, after the lunch, reported back to the men in suits, and they carried the news to their boss.

"So now he wants *some* of the money?" Yeni Navarro responded. "Not the whole $300,000? Just part of it?"

"Yes ma'am."

"How much does he want?"

"Seventeen-fifty," the first man said.

"Seventeen hundred? Seventeen thousand?"

"No ma'am."

"Just seventeen-fifty," the second man said.

"Seventeen-fifty *what*?"

"Seventeen dollars and fifty cents."

"Out of three hundred thousand?"

"Yes ma'am."

"And what does he want this for?"

"A collar," said the first man. "For a cat."

"A collar for a cat?"

"Yes ma'am," he replied. "A pink one."

"With fake diamonds," the second man added.

"$17.50?"

"Yes ma'am."

"How about one with real diamonds? Would he go for that?"

"I don't know, ma'am. I can ask . . ."

"I'm joking."

"Yes ma'am."

"But seriously. Can we just tell him, it's all or nothing? The whole 300,000 . . . or no collar?"

"I don't know, ma'am. Maybe."

This was the gist of an idea that had grown into the occasion for the current gathering. The Capital City Visionary Society was donating $200,000 to the Girl Scout Council and $300,000 to the homeless veteran whose selfless devotion had made the production and distribution of the kindness stones possible; a press release would claim that the latter individual preferred to remain anonymous. In fact, apart from signing a single paper one time Jasper would have nothing whatsoever to do with the matter and, quite possibly, he would just think the money had been given elsewhere rather than to him.

The $300,000 would actually be given to the Donovan Foundation, a tax-exempt charitable entity with three signatories: Mickey Stoll, Darius Hill, and an attorney representing the interests of the Visionary Society. This foundation would be responsible for disbursing the funds over the next year through donations to causes and concerns that the signatories thought would meet with Jasper's approval. Mickey would take primary responsibility for running potential causes and concerns by Jasper, the ruse being that the society would donate the money to those entities *instead of* giving it to him—though legally, it would actually be given to him (that is, to his foundation) and then given *by him* (by the foundation) to causes he had authorized the trio to designate. Mickey expressed some concern over calling the receiving entity "the Donovan Foundation"—that could compromise anonymity. But then Darius proposed the foundation's motto could be "Wear Your Love Like Heaven" and that would deter anyone from associating the name with any local individual, much less a homeless man in Algonkian Park. Alright, Mickey agreed, that would work. He'd never heard of the song, but it seemed more appropriate than Mellow Yellow or Hurdy Gurdy.

As finessed by the lawyers, this arrangement allowed the society to make its gift to the individual they deemed most worthy and to benefit from whatever positive publicity the announcement of the bequest might generate. Yet it also respected Jasper's desire for (most) of the money to be given to someone else—probably not the Mormons, but someone or something that he could favor after giving the matter a bit more consideration. Mickey and Darius had two primary beneficiaries in mind. First, there was the veteran's hospital, whose attention Jasper might actually require at some point in the future. Second, there were the city's homeless shelters.

"We don't really use the shelters," Jasper said over a lunch late that month. "They're more for folks out of luck, hoping to get back on their feet. Most of us, well we just got 'issues' you know. That's different from the folks in the shelters. But sometimes when there's snow on the ground, some of the guys will go there."

It occurred to Mickey that Jasper was actually talking about being homeless. Had he ever done that before? He talked about the park and about his buddies, but he'd never actually acknowledged that he lived there. He certainly had never identified himself as a person with "issues."

"That's good though I suppose," he continued. "The folks that are just down on their luck, you know. They need the shelters. And I bet the shelters can use the money."

But then, the second week in October, they got another idea.

* * *

Christopher Columbus had fallen out of favor in the District of Columbia. Since 1999, the city had celebrated October 12 as Indigenous Peoples' Day, and schools were closed accordingly. Nevertheless, Columbus Day was still officially a federal holiday, one for which federal employees (of which the city had an unusually large number) got the day off work. Thus, Algonkian Park was filled that day with a curious mixture of adults who were supposedly observing Columbus Day and children who were supposedly observing Indigenous Peoples' Day, though neither group seemed aware of the incongruity those overlapping festivities might entail. Call it what you will, it was a day off—and the weather was fine.

Girl Scout Troop 2770 had reserved a group of picnic tables for an afternoon outing in celebration of their role in the Kindness Stone Crusade six months earlier. Jasper and friends had been invited to come and have some fried chicken and lemonade. Some of the girls in attendance were ones Jasper had met before: Terry and Shondra, and Peggy Thatcher.

As always, the girls were completely fascinated with Sasquatch, but this time it wasn't just because he was big and hairy and "looked like a Wookie." This time, he had a cat *and* he had a box full of kittens! The cat was almost as shaggy as its owner, but it was wearing a pink collar studded with fake diamonds, which Sasquatch had to show everyone. And, best of all, the collar had a round metal name tag on it, which read:

I'M

PURR-TEE

The kittens were too young to leave their mother, Sasquatch said, but girls could pick one out and reserve it for $5.00 (no more "FREE KITTENS FROM A PURTY CAT"). They'd have to come back in two weeks, but he'd be right there on October 28 and by then Purr-tee would be ready to give up her babies, provided they were destined for darling homes. And the men could all get sandwiches for Halloween (Sasquatch would be holding the money until then).

Roberta Blankenship, the troop leader, was as aghast as ever at the intermingling of her girls with these friendly but mostly unwashed citizens of the park. She doubted whether the cat had gotten any of its shots or vaccinations or whatever cats were supposed to get. She wanted to warn the girls about fleas and rabies, but most of their parents were present and seemed remarkably unconcerned. In any case, she had bigger things to worry about. One thing, at least. One very big thing to worry about: *that man* and what they were going to ask him to do. What *she* was going to ask him to do.

She had only meant to be polite. Almost two weeks ago, on October 1, the Capital City Visionary Society had presented an award of $200,000 to the Nation's Capital Girl Scout Council and an award of $300,000 to the Donovan Foundation ("Wear Your Love Like Heaven"), a charitable entity established by an individual who preferred to remain anonymous. The first award was officially received by Ms. Phyllis Booker-Hart, chief financial officer of the Girl Scout Council, and the second by a lawyer from the Visionary Society who was also a signatory for the Donovan Foundation. The ceremony was mostly for the press (to whom it was accidentally leaked that the anonymous individual who had allowed money the society had offered him to be used to establish the Donovan Foundation was actually a homeless veteran). A handful of other guests were also in attendance, and this was where Roberta Blankenship met Mickey Stoll and Darius Hill.

Roberta was full of silent opinions that evening. She thought that by all rights she should be the one receiving the award on behalf of the council, not Ms. Booker-Hart who was just an executive. She thought the dissimilarity in the two awards was unnecessary and, frankly, offensive (why not $250,000 each?). And she also thought that the one Scout from the troop she had invited to attend the ceremony was being a "pill," refusing to go on moral grounds: "You're not supposed to get money for kindness stones," Petra had said. "It ruins it."

Roberta had lots of opinions that night but she kept them all to herself and even engaged in polite conversation with the associates of the officially anonymous homeless man who were attending the ceremony. Out of courtesy, she mentioned the Columbus Day event in the park and told them that Mr. Jasper and his friends would be invited to join them. They would be celebrating the award to the council and, of course, they wouldn't say anything about what had been given to him. They would respect that.

"But it is too bad," she said. "I wish we could do *something* to honor him."

She had only said that to be polite. Any *normal* person would have known that she was just being polite.

"Oh! Well, if you want to do that . . ." Mickey responded, and she immediately regretted having spoken.

"There *is* something you can do," Darius took over. "If you want to honor him. There is something you can do that will mean a lot more to him than $300,000."

"What?"

"Ask him to tell a story."

So here they were, in the park on Columbus Day (as she would always call it, not being partial to PC fads). And now that people were on dessert, she got their attention and announced a special surprise, a real treat that she had planned for the girls. She had them all sit in a semicircle in the grass; parents and other guests remained at the tables.

There were fourteen girls today and she led them in reciting the Girl Scout Promise and the Girl Scout Law. And then she said that she wanted to recognize their good friend Mr. Jasper, who had helped find rocks for their painting activity last spring. She asked him to come over and, obviously embarrassed, he did. She said the girls wanted to tell him, Thank you, don't we, girls? And all the girls chorused their gratitude. Parents at the tables applauded.

And, then, she continued: "Now, Mr. Jasper, we hear that *you* have a very special talent. We have heard that you are a gifted storyteller. So, I know this may come as a surprise, and we didn't give you a chance to get anything ready, but I'm sure the girls would just love it if you would tell them one of your stories."

Way in back, behind all the picnic tables, Mickey and Darius were grinning. They hadn't tipped Jasper off. They thought it would be nicer to come as a surprise, and they hadn't wanted to set him up for disappointment on the chance that the woman wouldn't go through with it. But now he was in his element! And the girls were cheering and begging for a story. They could see him casting about for ideas and then he announced the story of Phaeton, the boy who drove the sun chariot of Apollo.

Uh-oh! his friends thought. We've heard that one before—and it's not really age appropriate for children. They looked at each other. What is he thinking, telling *that* story? Maybe we should have given him time to prepare.

But it was too late.

"This is a story about a boy," Jasper began. "Is that okay?"

A few groans, but general acquiescence.

"*Okay . . .*"

"Is he a cute boy?" one of the girls asked and there were giggles.

"Very cute. Extremely cute. Boy band cute—but way too old for you. He was already driving."

"My brother drives. He can drive, but only with one of my parents and I'm not allowed to ride with him."

"That seems wise, and this story may explain why. This boy had a funny name. He was called Phaeton and he had a friend named Cygnus."

"They sound like superheroes."

"Are they superheroes?"

"Can they like fly and stuff?"

"No, not superheroes. But this is all kind of magical."

"Like Harry Potter?"

"I hate Harry Potter."

"My sister is like so crazy about Harry Potter. The movies are like tens and millions of years old and that's all she wants to watch. She wants to marry Harry Potter."

"Alright," Jasper persisted. "Well, Phaeton's father had a flying car."

"Harry Potter! That's in Harry Potter."

"They copied it. They copied that from Harry Potter."

"But this car was special because it had a trailer and do you know what was in the trailer?"

Lots of hands went up. And there were multiple guesses from girls who hadn't been called upon.

"Horses?"

"Tools? Like rakes and things."

"My father has a trailer and it has a boat."

"Um, I know. A camper? With beds and a kitchen and a bathroom."

One other girl was waving her hand, so Jasper pointed to her.

"Uh . . . Girl Scout cookies?"

"Those are all good guesses. But do you know what was in this trailer? The sun!"

Now there were oohs and ahhs, with a few protests from budding literalists.

"That's not possible! The sun is too big! It's like way bigger than the whole earth."

"It's made out of fire and the trailer would burn up."

"You are very good scientists," Jasper said. "But this is a magic story, so it's just make believe. Phaeton's father had a car that pulled a trailer and in the trailer sat the sun. Every day, he would start way over there at one end of the sky and he would drive all the way across to way over *there* at the other end of the sky. And people like us, we couldn't see the car and we couldn't see the trailer because they were too far away, but we could see the sun because it's so bright."

"I can see it," one girl said, pointing at the sun. "Look, there it is."

"But look close. Can you see the car? Or the trailer?"

She squinted her eyes. "No, it's too far away."

Now lots of girls were looking, squinting at the sun.

"I can't see it."

"I think I see it."

"No you don't."

"I said I *think* I see it."

"You can't because its only make believe."

"Alright," Jasper continued. "Now you have to imagine with me: Phaeton's dad has this cool car. It is maybe the single coolest car that there has ever been. What do you think he wants to do?"

"Drive it!" they all agreed.

"Why do you think he wants to do that?"

"Because he's a boy."

"Because he's stupid."

"Because . . . he just thinks it would be fun."

"Right, right. Everybody's right. But most of all, he wants to impress his friends. He wants all his friends to see him driving the cool car. He wants all his guy friends to think, Wow, Phaeton has such a cool car. He's way cooler than me. And he wants all the girls to think, Look what a cool car he has. I want to kiss him."

"Uuuuh . . ."

Expressions of disgust.

"I wouldn't . . . I wouldn't . . ."

"Mr. Jasper?"

"Yes?"

"I wouldn't kiss a boy just because he had a cool car. I wouldn't even care what kind of car he had."

"Well, of course *you* wouldn't because you are a very smart girl. And most girls are smart like you, but boys don't always know that. Sometimes boys don't know how smart girls are and they act stupid or silly because they think that then the girls will like them. But what do you think happened when Phaeton took his Dad's car?"

"He wrecked it," someone said and then they all nodded and agreed.

"He probably wrecked it."

"That's exactly right. But do you remember what was in the back? In the trailer?"

"The sun."

"Well then, what do you think happened? What would happen if he crashed it right here and the sun fell out on the ground?"

"There'd be a big fire."

"It would burn everything up."

"So that's what this story says happened. He wrecked his car and the sun fell out in a place called a desert. Do you know what a desert is?"

"Nothing but sand. It's real hot and there's no water and nothing but sand."

"So, according to this story, the reason there is a desert is because that's where Phaeton wrecked his dad's car. The sun fell out and burned everything up. Do you think his friends were impressed?"

"No."

"Did the girls want to kiss him?"

"No!"

"What do you think happened?"

"He got grounded for . . . like, for the rest of his life."

"That's about right. He never got to drive that car again, that's for sure!"

"That's a good story."

"I liked that story."

"There wouldn't be any deserts except for boys and cars and trying to show off."

"They're always like, look at me, look at me, I'm so special, look at me."

"But there is one more little piece. He did have a good friend, remember?"

They nodded.

"Because everyone needs to have a friend. Even silly boys and show-offs need to have friends, don't you think?"

They all nodded.

"So, this boy Phaeton, he had a friend named Cygnus, and Cygnus was such a good friend that he never teased him, not even when he crashed the car and made a desert. And, then, when his time on earth was done, he was changed into a swan."

"Ohh."

"I don't just mean any swan. He was the very first swan. And so whenever anyone sees a swan they should think of Cygnus and think what it means to be a friend. What it means to be a good friend to someone who is kind of a loser and needs a good friend. And do you know what baby swans are called?"

"Cygnets," one of the girls said.

"That's right!" exclaimed Jasper, surprised but uncontrollably pleased. "That's right! Wow, you are very smart."

"I learned it in school. Baby ducks are ducklings, and baby geese are goslings, and baby swans are cygnets."

"How many of you knew that?" he asked, and almost all their hands went up.

"Everyone knows what cygnets are."

"Well, not everyone," Jasper said, "I've met some grown-ups who don't know, but I guess you all do because you're super smart Girl Scouts. Anyway, the *reason* they're called cygnets is because they're named after Cygnus, the very first swan. He got turned into a swan for being a good friend to the show-off boy who wrecked his father's car."

The story was over and the girls applauded and said they liked it. Mrs. Blankenship was both pleased and relieved. And on the outskirts of the crowd, a woman standing with Mickey and Darius said, "I think I know what you should do with the money." Then, she gave the large shaggy man five dollars and told him someone would be by in two weeks for a kitten. A black one, preferably. She had a poodle whose life needed to be more interesting.

* * *

On the Friday after Thanksgiving, Jasper went to the blue parking lot at Dulles Airport to access his winter car for the next two to three months. Darius, who drove an airport shuttle to and from the lot, always tried to let him know when there was an appropriate vehicle available: an unlocked SUV or van in long-term parking—something that he could sleep in during the cold winter nights. This year, he had scored the ultimate triumph: a red Odyssey, left for the entire winter in an ideal location, in a corner by the back wall. He had always wanted an Odyssey, maybe just for the name—and this wasn't just any Odyssey, not if Darius was right.

He arrived after the gate person left at 10:00 PM, with floor pads and seat covers to keep the car pristine. And there it was in Row 14A: a red Odyssey with a specialty license plate that read "ILIAD." It was the car he'd always said he would get some day. Had he told Darius that? Hmm. He decided not to think about it too much. He slept in the car all winter and he kept it so clean, so pristine, that the owner would never know he'd been there. It disappeared from the lot when the weather turned warm a week after Valentine's Day, but he suspected it would be back next year. Better not to think about why or how, but he suspected it would be back.

Construction on the pavilion began that next weekend. Jasper watched with special interest: a new addition to the park, funded by an anonymous donor. It was a large sheltered area, with a stage and seating for about 100 people. Jasper watched every day, waiting for the sign. It finally arrived on April 3, with large and colorful letters that read *Toffee and Taffy Pavilion.*

The next weekend the Toffee and Taffy Pavilion at Algonkian Park had a grand opening with its first weekly "Storytellers Cavalcade." Jasper was one of the four presenters. He told the story of Pegasus and Bellerophon, revised as a Disneyesque tale devoid of sex scandals and unpunished murders. He chose that particular story because the event had been advertised as a "cavalcade." He didn't bother telling the organizers that the word *cavalcade* actually means "an event with horses" (*caval* as in *cavalry*) but *he* knew that was what the word meant and he derived some private satisfaction in ensuring the event's compliance with what its name suggested it should be. His version of the Pegasus tale went over extremely well. And for the next week he promised a brand new story no one had ever heard before, one he'd made up himself about a witch who turned men into cats.

The Donovan Foundation concluded its yearlong commission six months ahead of schedule. The final accounting:

	Income	Expenditures	Total
Capital City Visionary Society	$300,000.00		300,000.00
Office Supplies (Target)		-17.50	299,982.50
Business Expense: company car		-31,790.00	268,192.50
Donation: Algonkian Park (for Pavilion)		-150,000.00	189,192.50
Donation: Coalition for the Homeless		-100,000.00	89,192.50
Donation: Veterans Affairs Medical Center		-89,192.50	0.00

The Toffee and Taffy Pavilion would be used for all sorts of programs and events but every Saturday at 10:00 AM it was reserved for a one-hour Storytellers' Cavalcade. Volunteers from all around the area could sign up to take their turn relating a tale for children and young adults. A few teachers and some amateur bards became regulars, and Jasper typically concluded the hour. He began getting requests to repeat stories told previously and eventually he had an assortment of "favorites" from which he could select the one that seemed best for the occasion.

Of course, these things change with the times. Popularity of the event waxed and waned. The park sometimes brought in professional storytellers for special events. They set up booths nearby for face painting and craft activities. There were times when the definition of "storytellers" was expanded to include musicians performing children's songs or actors presenting skits or a short play. There were years when the Storytellers Cavalcade enjoyed prestige. A first lady took a turn at reading one of her favorite children's books, and after that a number of children's authors did public presentations of their latest projects followed by book signings.

But there were also years when interest declined: the park invested less time and energy in the program; they turned it over to the public library, which sent a volunteer staff member to read aloud from predictable volumes. Sometimes only a handful of kids would show up. Jasper was always on hand, but he was no longer the headliner and some of the program directors were suspicious of him. They were also skeptical regarding the value of stories drawn from the ancient mythology of Europeans as opposed to more culturally diverse narratives from marginalized civilizations and neglected social groups. Still, Jasper could usually count on getting a slot at least once a month based on an established history with the program.

In any case, it was still called the Toffee and Taffy Pavilion, and for Jasper, that was what counted most. Come what may, it would always be the Toffee and Taffy Pavilion; it would still be called that long after he was gone, when there was no one around who knew or remembered why.

12

Noises at Night

Father McCloskey sat bolt upright in bed . . . *God!* . . . *Not again!* . . . someone was knocking on his door in the middle of the night. He glanced at his clock . . . 2:00 AM . . . the usual time . . . the *old* usual time.

Knock . . . knock . . . knock . . .

Not the door of his bedroom at the rectory. There would be nothing extraordinary about that. No. He looked to his right. Twelve feet from his bed. The door to his closet. Someone was knocking on *that* door . . . from inside the closet.

Knock . . . knock . . . knock . . .

He'd had these dreams before, but not for a very long time. He'd had them in seminary and then, as now, they had seemed more real than any other dream. There were times when he was certain he was awake. And times when he wondered if he was losing his mind. But he had worked through all that before he took his vows. Indeed the dreams were a powerful incentive, a sign from God to confirm his calling. His father confessor had helped him to realize that, when he'd had his doubts. Dreams about knocking. *Behold, I stand at the door and knock.* Revelation 3:20.

But that was more than forty years ago. He was sixty-two now and he had retired just six months ago after thirty-six years as a parish priest. He would continue to live in the rectory, hear confessions, and do some counseling, but mostly he was determined to try his hand at writing. Devotional materials, spirituality. He figured he could serve God in a manner relatively free of the hectic stress of day-to-day parish commitments.

And more sincerely: He hadn't lost his faith, but the sacramental stuff no longer swayed him. He'd come to regard it as myth and metaphor and felt a bit hypocritical when officiating a mass.

So was *that* what this was about? The knocking! Had Jesus returned to the closet of his dreams to reawaken something? Or to offer him a *new* calling?

This had not happened while he was serving at St. Ignatius. Only *before,* when he was at seminary. And now *after*, when he was retired.

He lay back down in bed and rolled over on his left side. Away from the closet. Closed his eyes.

Knock . . . knock . . . knock . . .

Dear God! he thought, trying to shut it out. And then he whispered out loud what he knew was true . . . *I'm not dreaming!* . . . I'll think I was in the morning. I'll tell myself then that I was dreaming, but right now I know that I am not. I am wide awake. And someone . . . or something . . . is knocking on that door of my closet.

* * *

Of course, he did know better in the morning. He knew that it had been his old, recurring dream, back again to haunt him in his old age.

And so it went: every night, just like before. Eventually, he had trouble concentrating during the day. He wanted to work on an Advent devotional. Texts from the Gospel of John. *But why the knocking?* Every night. *And why now?* At this point in his career?

He checked his messages. A Father Jacobson at St. Bartholomew's had called again. He had been ignoring *him*. Now he picked up his phone but, no, he really didn't want to get into that. Whatever his colleague wanted (and he thought he might know what it was) . . . he thought . . . I'm retired. I worked hard for thirty-six years. I helped a lot of people. In an era when so many brought shame upon the church, I was one of the good ones. I wasn't the best priest ever, but I did the best I could. And I dare say I was better than many. Not to be vain. But isn't that the point? *Not to be vain?* Because if I thought I was indispensable, *that* would be vanity! But I know better. I did some good and now it's time for others. Younger, brighter, more up-to-date, more in-tune *others*. It's their turn. Go knock on their doors, whoever you are.

But the dreams were back . . . *were they dreams?* . . . of course they were! . . . *but were they really?* . . . what else could they be?

* * *

John McCloskey had entered the seminary at the age of twenty-three with no sure discernment of his vocation. He wanted to devote his life to being of service to God and to other people. He believed he could give of himself; he was willing to make sacrifices, renouncing his own interests for the sake of those who might benefit from whatever he had to offer them. Or, to use his favorite metaphor, he wanted to be a valuable character in the stories of other people's lives.

Still, a seminary-trained Catholic had many options. The priesthood was the most obvious, but that demanded vows of obedience and celibacy, spiritual commitments that should only be made by those certain of their calling. Like many seminarians, John was unsure at present whether that was the way for him. Seminary itself was a time for discernment.

There was a young woman named Audrey Phillips who worked in the parish offices nearby. John thought he was in love with her and he shared that—not with *her*, of course, but with his father confessor. The latter assured him that romantic infatuation (and even sexual desire) was not incompatible with a call that demanded celibacy. Most priests experienced this, especially before their vows, and sometimes even after. Such powerful emotions might be viewed as a test, as something to be prayerfully considered, and then, if one was truly called, their vows would be more meaningful.

The seminary chapel rang with sermons on the cost of discipleship. There would, of course, be no *cost* if one renounced what one did not desire in the first place. There are people who do not crave worldly possessions: a vow of poverty would mean nothing to them. But the *rich man* to whom Jesus said, "sell your possessions and give to the poor"? That was another matter! Even so, there may be some lucky souls who care little for the softness of a woman's body or the sweetness of her whisper in the night: they may take vows of celibacy, and know nothing of the cost. The higher calling is for those who know the true blessing of *sacrificing themselves* for Christ. The higher calling involves giving up what one might desire most, renouncing what would have been dear.

But perhaps that was not for him. His confessor allowed this and told him his feelings for Audrey ought not be renounced too soon, without the prayerful consideration. There were other possibilities, other vocations: with a seminary degree, he could shun ordination and still be a chaplain or a therapist or even a professor of religion. If he could not make vows of obedience and celibacy with integrity, there would be no shame in considering one of those options.

Whenever John went to the parish offices, Audrey Phillips greeted him by name, and smiled at him, and laughed at things he said (things that were, at most, only mildly amusing). Her eyes seemed to light up when he talked to her but even then they were calm, full of what he called "tranquility." He took a work study job at the seminary that required him to visit the offices three times a week and he timed those visits so that he would arrive just before Audrey's lunch break. They shared many meals together, casual engagements that felt increasingly like "dates."

It was confusing. He could serve God in ways that would not involve renouncing her charms. But when he prayed, he said to God, "Thy will be done!" And whatever God wanted, he would do it. He just needed a sign.

And then, one night, he sat bolt upright in bed. He was in a room at the seminary eerily similar to the one he would occupy decades later at the rectory and someone was knocking on the door . . . *not* the door to the room itself . . . someone was knocking on the door of his closet . . . someone *on the other side*!

"Who's there?" he said aloud.

But there was no answer.

Just . . .

Knock . . . knock . . . knock . . .

He sat up in his bed, staring at the door and the knocking came again. The logical thing would be to get up and open the door. See who was in there (playing a trick on him, perhaps?). But he couldn't do it.

He was frightened. Cold sweat on his face and arms.

"Who's there?" he called again.

No answer.

Just . . .

Knock . . . knock . . . knock . . .

"Who is it? What do you want?"

No answer. Silence.

And in the morning, he knew it had been a dream. Otherwise, obviously, he would have gotten up and opened the door. It had been a dream, but a strange one. It had seemed so real and *even now* he could remember it so clearly. He didn't usually remember his dreams, except in the haziest fashion, and they always faded as the morning progressed, gone completely by noon unless he made a point of telling someone about them, or writing them down. He told *no one* about this one and there was no need to write it down; he remembered it vividly.

After it happened again, the very next night, he got up in the morning, determined to investigate. Even then, he waited until after breakfast, after class, after chapel, and then he went to his closet and pulled the door wide open. Something had to be banging against the door in the night.

But what?

Nothing!

He moved things about, frustrated, and then at last admitted the obvious: *nothing had been banging against the door.*

So what about the wall? Maybe something had been knocking on the other side of his wall and it just *sounded* like it was coming from the closet. But the wall was not a shared one and, no, the more he checked, the more certain, the more obvious it became that this, too, had not been the case. He called maintenance anyway and told them there might be rats or something. He was hearing noises inside his bedroom wall at night. They told him it was impossible but someone would check.

So what were the possibilities? Obviously, it *had* been a dream, though a very real one, and he felt like a fool for letting it occupy so much of his waking energy.

Three days later he wasn't so sure. Because every night . . . again and again . . . *knock* . . . *knock* . . . *knock* . . . what is it? . . . what do you want?

He didn't believe in ghosts and, though he might believe in angels and demons, he didn't believe in the kind of angels or demons who hide inside people's closets and knock on their doors at night. There had to be a psychological explanation but then the question was, What? What *was* the explanation?

So he went to his father confessor, who told him about Revelation 3:20. That didn't mean it was Jesus in the closet, not literally, but maybe those who Jesus wanted him to serve. People trapped in sin and darkness. People who needed him to open the door. To set them free. To help them get out. Isn't that what you do when someone is shut in a closet and you open the door? You help them get out, right? Is that the call of Christ on your life, John McCloskey? To help people get out of something?

The metaphor was so clear he wondered why it had not been more obvious. He understood now, what God or his own psyche was trying to tell him. He understood and he knew what to do. He had asked for a sign and a sign had been given. A sign that was not quite supernatural (since he knew it was all in his mind) but almost miraculous. I need to take my vows, he thought. I am called. It could hardly be more clear.

But first he wanted to try something, just for his own peace of mind. He wanted to find out what would happen if he opened the door.

The next night, when the knocking started, he sat bolt upright in bed.

Knock . . . knock . . . knock . . .

"I hear you," he said aloud.

He swung his legs out of the bed, put his feet on the floor, and then he rose.

It came again.

Knock . . . knock . . . knock . . .

He thought: *I am awake!*

And then he crossed over to the closet and stood there for a moment. Staring at the door. Reaching for the knob. He was sweating. He was frightened.

I am not dreaming!

I am wide awake!

And it came again, clearly on the other side of the door, right in front of his face.

Knock . . . knock . . . knock . . .

No, he thought. Not possible. It's only in my mind. There is nothing really there!

When he awoke in the morning, he didn't remember going back to bed. Had he even gotten up? Or was that just part of the dream?

I did get up, he thought. I got up and I was going to open the door, but I was afraid. I knew there was nothing there, but I was afraid.

What does that mean? Maybe I'm not supposed to see who it is that needs me. Whoever is *going to need me*. I'll find out when the time comes. It could be just one person, or it could be more than one. Who knows? It might be one or twenty-one. Thirty-one or forty-one. But they are out there, in my future. Waiting for me to help them get out. I can't see them yet. That's not allowed. But still . . .

Alright, he thought: I get the point. I asked for a sign and this is what I got: a heavy-handed metaphor. Thank you, God, though you might have been more subtle. Still, I know what I need to do.

He went that day and told his father confessor he was ready. He would take his vows. He would be a priest. And that night, sure enough, the knocking stopped.

But there was something else.

A week later, he had his first dream of Audrey. He awoke not to knocking but to orgasm, with her imagined body writhing naked beneath him. What was *that* about? he wondered, wracked with guilt but not an ounce of regret. A final temptation from Satan to dissuade me from my course?

"Yes," his father confessor said, "it could be that, but to cite Matthew 12:7, you must not condemn the guiltless—in this case, you must not condemn yourself. Such dreams are natural, not sinful, and they are common to all mortal men including priests. We call them 'sweet dreams' and some may view them as little gifts from God. Pleasant tokens of what you otherwise forego. I am not dictating now but suggesting: you may wake from such dreams with a prayer of thanksgiving. Enjoy them for what they are, only realize that you must never counsel or interact with a subject of such dreams. If she (or he) be in your parish, speak to a colleague, as I'm sure, sooner or later, some colleague will speak to you. And when that day comes, do not ask why. Do not provoke embarrassment, for some do feel an unnecessary shame. When your colleague says, 'Father, would you see this man or woman in my stead?' agree to do so without more explanation. There could be many reasons—though, in truth, there is usually only one."

"Sweet dreams?"

He nodded. "A temptation from the devil or a gift from God? There are advocates for both views, and perhaps those options are not mutually exclusive. But you must pray and decide for yourself."

* * *

He chose the more pleasant perspective and ended up giving thanks to God more frequently than he ever imagined would be the case. Once a week for many years. Then just a couple times a month, if that. But the decrease in frequency had brought no decline in intensity, and, over the years, he had done everything with Audrey in dreams that he might have done with her in reality—and, truth be told, probably a good deal more. But only with Dream Audrey, of course. The actual person—*real Audrey*—was, thankfully, not in his life. Yes, he'd kept track of her for a while but there had been no contact. She'd gone out west for a time and then returned to Boston, but it was a big city. The last he'd heard, she had joined a parish across town, far from his own. St. Bartholomew's, actually.

He smiled. Maybe he should see that persistent priest after all. Maybe he could somehow, just casually, get some new little piece of information on one of Father Jacobson's parishioners. It was tempting, but a temptation he had learned to avoid. Better not to ask, better not to know. He had not seen the woman for forty years, and did not care to see her now. How he would blush if she suddenly appeared! If he recognized her at all.

The distinction was important to him. One should not use real people for one's own gratification—not even as objects of fantasy. But he had no dreams or fantasies about a real human being named Audrey Phillips—or so he told himself. His dreams were of a made-up person he called Dream Audrey: a fantasy version of an imaginary woman loosely based on someone he had once known. He still called her Audrey in honor of the person who had inspired her: a girl with gentle, tranquil eyes; a girl who used to smile at him and laugh at unfunny jokes. But he entertained no fantasies of the real person. It was his own creation, Dream Audrey, who remitted to some degree the cost of his discipleship. And even if she didn't exist—or perhaps *because* she didn't exist—he was thankful for her.

He was also thankful that she had aged. He wasn't sure if his conscience could bear it otherwise. At sixty-two, he didn't want to picture twenty-one-year-old breasts bouncing in his hands. Twenty-one-year-old legs straddling his pelvis. So it was nice that the subject of his sweet dreams had kept pace with him. She'd morphed gradually into an attractive middle-aged woman and now she looked to be in her late fifties. Stately, not childlike. The kind of woman he probably would actually want, if he had allowed his life to go a different route.

* * *

Following his ordination, John McCloskey had, indeed, embarked on a course of opening doors for people who needed him. In his first year of ministry, there was a woman trapped in a marriage that had mutated into something like slavery. McCloskey's predecessor, an aged and very traditional priest, had quoted Scripture to this poor woman, all about turning the other cheek and submitting to her tyrannical husband and accepting violence as her portion in life, emulating the suffering of saints and martyrs. The fool! But he, John McCloskey, had helped her get out. The church forbade divorce, but he had secured an annulment which, she was delighted to hear, meant the marriage had never happened. The man was out of her life: he not only wasn't her husband; he never had been! In the eyes of God, she had been abducted, enslaved—and, now, set free, she had no more responsibility to the man who claimed to be her former husband than any former captive had to their former captor.

I did that, he thought, when he needed some assurance of his worth. I got her out! And then he thought: was it her? knocking on my door? adding her plea to God's call on my life? It must have been, he decided. In case the call of God had not been enough, she had come in the night to summon him. It had been her crying in the dark, I can't get out . . . please John McCloskey. . . *you* can open this door . . . won't you do that for me? . . . *please?*

But as it turned out, she wasn't the only one. There would be so many over the years. People trapped in sin and darkness. Adulterers who wanted to leave their lovers and save their marriages. An embezzler who just wanted to put it all back and start anew. Addicts of every type: drugs, alcohol, gambling, pornography. He couldn't save them all, but he had saved a good few.

And, then, in a manner that seemed almost too obvious he had wound up being the priest of choice for those who wanted "to come out of the closet."

The first was a young man who trusted him with his secret and asked that he facilitate the conversation with his parents. They did it in the rectory. The young man told his parents and Father McCloskey (their trusted priest!) helped them with the shock and disappointment, the trauma of shattered expectations. And then he assured them as God's representative that no one is created by God to be other than God intends. He assured them that, while the church only recognizes *marriage* as a bond between man and woman, there are *other* relationships (and always have been) and these are godly in their own fashion. God has said in Scripture, "It is not good for the man to be alone" (Genesis 2:18) and the Pope has said in Rome, "Who are we to judge?"

Word got around and he soon had a ministry. So was *that* what the dreams had been about? Twenty, and then thirty years into his ministry, he would still remember the "knocking dreams" of his youth, but he didn't think about them too much or too often. In fact, he didn't like thinking about them because they didn't fit well with the sort of consciousness that typically informed his life. He believed in science and natural explanations for things. But now and then, in the interest of honesty he would allow himself an uncomfortable acknowledgment: when I was an adolescent—out of my teens but still definitely an adolescent—I dreamed of people wanting me to help them come out of the closet (though I didn't even know what that meant) and now I am regularly meeting with people who want me to help them do exactly that.

Perhaps there could be a natural explanation (a psychological one?), but it seemed too precise. It seemed *almost* supernatural, which didn't fit with his theology or with his worldview, with his perception of how God and the universe typically function. He would have liked to discuss the dreams with a counselor or therapist (or even with a theologian) but he had not done so. He knew that anyone with the sort of credentials or competence he could respect would suspect him of inventing the dreams, of misremembering them, or at least of exaggerating the details—and he knew better! He really did have those dreams a long time ago. They were weird and disconcerting at the time and they had somehow, in some way he could not explain, forecast the progression of his life. Or, at least, of his ministry. And weren't those two things really one and the same: his *life* and his *ministry*?

* * *

He had earned his retirement—or so he thought. And now the dreams were back. What could it mean, save that a greedy God was demanding more of him? And why? There were many who could do what he could do, as well or better than he could do it. He was hardly indispensable.

He had *another* message from Father Jacobson at St. Bartholomew's across town. The priest wanted to see him to talk about a "personal matter." McCloskey didn't know Father Jacobson, but he had looked him up online: a young effeminate priest. Just looking at his picture, it didn't take much imagination to guess what he wanted to talk about. But why me? And why *now?* It's not the eighties for heaven's sake! There are resources, support groups. Call your bishop! The Church has trained advocates and counselors, people who actually know what they're doing, not just sympathetic fools like me who stumbled into being useful when no one else was willing.

He thought of Samuel in the Bible, in bed at night, hearing the call of God. Samuel replied, "Here I am! Send me!" But Samuel was young (an adolescent). Forgive me Lord, Father McCloskey thought, but when I wake to that knocking, I want to cry, "Here I am *not*! Go away! You want someone else! Samuel, maybe. Not me!"

But the dreams weren't going to stop. So, after two weeks, on a Wednesday afternoon in March, he finally admitted Father Jacobson to the rectory for an appointment. He had put him off long enough, but the young priest had proved persistent. Still, as soon as he saw him, he knew his instincts were correct. The man was *stereotypically* effeminate. If he thought he was hiding anything, he was kidding himself.

They had made the briefest introductions and sat in the parlor, McCloskey in his favorite chair and Father Jacobson on the sofa. McCloskey cut right to it.

"You're gay, aren't you?"

"Well, yes," the young father said, taken somewhat aback, "but I hardly see why that's your concern."

"Oh! Well. I beg your pardon. Is that not why you've come to see me?"

"Hardly. It concerns a parishioner. A woman whose troubles prompt me to . . . well, to share them with you in confidence."

"And seek *my* counsel? I am retired. There are others more qualified."

"I wish to speak to you."

Father McCloskey heaved a sigh of resignation. No rest for the weary apparently. Or "for the wicked." Wasn't that how the saying went? Was he being punished for something?

"Go on, then."

"This woman has been having strange dreams."

"What?" He was suddenly interested. And just a little bit afraid.

"They started many years ago, when she was young. She stands before a door and knocks . . . knocks on the door, but nobody opens it."

The room turned cold and Father McCloskey felt the dampness on his skin. Cold sweat. He was sure that if he looked in a mirror he would be white as a sheet.

"She . . . you said . . . she *had* these dreams?" he stammered.

"Forty years ago. And now she is having them again."

"Who . . . Who is this woman?"

"I think you know."

"Yes," he sighed, giving up. "Yes. I do. She told you?"

"She knows it's you on the other side of the door. But you're so afraid . . ."

"My God!" he gasped, hanging his head in his hands. "I've failed her! All these years, I knew *someone* needed my help . . . but I just thought the dreams were general. I never imagined . . . and she's right . . . I was afraid . . . but I didn't know it was *her* who needed to get out."

"Are you a fool, Father?"

"What? I hope not. Why would you ask that?"

"Why would you assume you are to be her savior—instead of the other way around?"

"I can't imagine what you mean."

"There is much I don't know, but let me tell you one thing: she has been in love with you for forty years."

"No, that's not likely. In any case, I didn't know it. And I've taken vows."

"And now you're retired. You could be released from them you know."

Laicized, is what Father Jacobson meant. McCloskey could request "removal from the clerical state." Then he would still be ordained but as a "lay priest," he would no longer be allowed to administer the sacraments or say Mass. Not that he did those things anymore anyway. Or ever wanted to do them again. Still, there was a hint of shame. In the past, priests were only laicized as punishment for some offense or scandal. But that was in the past. Today it was sometimes voluntary. It usually was, and the number one reason was freedom to marry. He knew priests who'd done this and no one spoke ill of them. But, privately, people might think . . .

"The dreams," Father McCloskey spoke aloud, interrupting his own thoughts. But then he stopped, thinking . . . *are they dreams?*

"There's more," Father Jacobson said, and hesitated, as though this part was difficult for him. "The closet dreams stopped forty years ago. Stopped until recently. But all along, she has been having other dreams . . . of you."

"Hmmh?"

"And she knows that you have been having . . ."

"Similar dreams?" Father McCloskey offered, completing the sentence for him.

"Not just similar. I think that if you were to compare dates and times . . ."

"No! That's impossible. Rubbish!"

"Dates and times . . . and *content.*"

Father McCloskey blushed against his will.

"Don't fret," his colleague assured him. "I have no details . . . just . . . she says she has appreciated these dreams, though she admits that at times she was . . . well, *surprised* may be a good word."

The paddle, Father McCloskey thought. That damn paddle.

But aloud he said, "I can't accept any of this. I don't believe it."

"Well, you don't need to believe it. I've done my part."

The man was about to leave and that didn't seem right. Something more had to be said, but what?

"I just . . . I don't mean to reject you," he said at last. "Thank you for coming. It's just that I don't know what to think."

"I offer no advice," Father Jacobson responded. "But if you will forgive the impudence of a younger man, I will tell you one more thing. Audrey Phillips is a single woman who has had a rich and fulfilling life. She doesn't need a man to complete her. She doesn't need you to rescue her or save her. She doesn't need to get *out* of anything. She certainly doesn't need you to let her out."

"Then what?"

"Has it never occurred to you? You might open the door not to let her *out* . . . but to let her *in*."

* * *

Now Father McCloskey had something to think about.

And after Father Jacobson left he did think about it. He sat and he thought. He went for a walk and thought some more. And then he went to bed.

Around 2:00 AM when the knocking started, Father John McCloskey sat bolt upright in bed . . .

Knock . . . knock . . . knock . . .

"I hear you," he said aloud.

Knock . . . knock . . . knock . . .

"Audrey?"

And then there was silence.

He swung his legs out of the bed, put his feet on the floor, and he rose.

He thought: *I am awake!*

And then he slapped his face hard to be sure. He slapped it again. I am *not* asleep. I am definitely awake.

He crossed over to the closet and stood there for a moment. Staring at the door. Reaching for the knob. He was sweating. He was frightened.

I did this forty-one years ago, he remembered. I did this. And then I went back to bed.

And it came again, clearly on the other side of the door, right in front of his face.

Knock . . . knock . . . knock . . .

And then he opened the door.

13

Later

When he was eighty-seven years old, James Haizlet had been married for forty years, but he could still remember the name of every girl with whom he had ever been in love. It was (still) a relatively short list: Cheryl Lee Vaughn from the third grade; Diana Wooten, starting in fifth; Dana (aka Sparkles), whose last name he technically knew but never used; Sandy Huebner from Missoula, Montana where he went to college; Janet Madison from Bozeman where he got his masters in wildlife biology; Patricia Kiefer, an archaeological researcher whose heart he had pursued throughout the 1980s; and *finally* . . . Kimana. And no more.

So now James was being treated to a celebration of his fortieth wedding anniversary. He had been retired from his longtime job as a Yellowstone Park Ranger for two decades and neither he nor his beloved Kimana (Number Seven—Favorite and Final) felt that they were sufficiently spry to take a cruise or anything of that sort. Instead, Kimana's sons Daniel and Matthew were doing all the work for an at-home family cookout with a few surprises.

The boys' presence was something of a treat because they had moved on with their lives in ways that kept them from visiting the old homestead often, much less at the same time. Dan Booker had ended up in Oklahoma where he had bonded amicably with his biological father and stepmother. This meant immersion in a conservative Protestant stream of culture and tradition that the Haizlets regarded as philosophical devolution: a recessive withdrawal from the enlightened milieu in which they had taken such delightful pains to raise him. Kimana had retained a civil relationship with her first husband when the children were small but she had always thought William a Neanderthal and she regarded his second wife as a hopeless naif though, to be kind, she was no doubt good at teaching children before they were old enough to think. She might be just the sort of woman to meet William's uncomplicated needs. They were "good folks" of course, and good for each other, but the more Dan talked like them and thought like them, the harder it was for James and Kimana to hide their disappointment. They would never realize this was one reason they didn't see a lot of him.

The situation with Matthew was completely different. James and Kimana could not be more pleased with him or proud of him, but his position as director of Indian affairs for Montana kept him busy and away much of the time. He spent the year traveling between Helena and DC and despite or perhaps because of the professional ambitions that had brought such success, it had taken him a while to find personal closure. But five years ago, at the age of thirty-eight, Matthew had charmed and married a twenty-three-year-old "Indian princess" he met in DC, a lovely Shawnee woman. He called her "his Pet." She didn't seem to mind and had given him a son they called Kai (Navajo for "willow tree"). James and Kimana saw far less of their grandson (or his endearing mother) than they would have wished, but now, the anniversary celebration had become an excuse to gather everyone for a full week. Kai had predictably become the center of attention and he also seemed to be having the time of his life.

The "homestead" was in the little town of Pray, Montana, just thirty miles from Yellowstone and three miles north of Chico Hot Springs. James had lived there for sixty years, returning to Florida just once a year to see his parents, usually for Christmas, and one time in 1987 for the funeral of his "science fair friend," Todd Meiner. It was a suicide: Todd had lived alone and hung himself after being diagnosed with HIV. There was a lot of talk, James's mother said, and it would be nice for the Meiner family if the church could be full. It wasn't. James flew back just to add one more person to the occupancy, but there wasn't anyone he knew in attendance. He had hoped to maybe see Diana but, no, not a single person from his high school was there. No one with whom Todd used to smoke cigarettes, cussing and complaining in the school parking lot. Certainly not Ben Stewart, with whom there had been a pretty serious falling out.

In any case, Pray, Montana was now James's home and he had become something of a local icon: he was the only resident who knew how to walk among the elk that frequently gathered in the village square. Pray was an unusual locale in that, although the community had a zip code and a post office, the entire five acres on which it was situated was privately owned. Until 2012, the owner had been Barbara Walker, a photographer who was, by default, the mayor. Population was around 700, though the picturesque setting would have prompted an exponential increase if geography allowed it.

The lead-up to the Haizlets' anniversary celebration had been fairly low key: a week of family bonding time fueled by extravagant attempts at spoiling Kai and somewhat desperate hopes for re-establishing Dan's place in the family milieu. But then, when the day itself arrived, there was a big surprise that the boys had arranged for their mom and stepdad. They had flown James's old friend Audrey and her husband in from Massachusetts. James had often spoken of Audrey as the closest "woman friend" he had ever had and Kimana had always wanted to meet her. After all, James credited Audrey with awakening "the spiritual tendencies and enthusiasms" in his soul that would eventually lead him to Kimana, who he claimed was his religious savior as well as his lover and mate. Kimana, too, gave Audrey the credit for bringing the two of them together.

James had met Audrey through Barbara Walker, the photographer mayor who owned his hometown. Audrey was also a photographer and she had first come to Pray when taking pictures of gas station attendants. An extended relationship with James had led her to stay in the area and, so, to take up another project: documenting Yellowstone's "hellish beauty." James had been in love six times and was certain Audrey would be Number Seven but for some very strange and inexplicable reason that did not happen. She lived with him for five years and was his domestic and sexual partner, almost a wife, but he did not fall in love with her and that was and would remain a baffling enigma. Of course, she didn't *want* him to fall in love with her but that had never mattered before. He had often bragged that "unrequited love" was what he did best.

He had asked her about it once. Why wasn't he in love with her?

"I don't want you to be in love with me," she said.

"That's never mattered before. I mean, no one has ever *wanted* me to be in love with them. I just fall in love with them anyway."

"Not this time. My heart is sequestered. It belongs to someone or something else and that's all you need to know."

"But it's never mattered before."

"I have powers."

That was what she said. She said she had powers. She allowed that a better word would be "gifts" but she called them "powers" for his sake because it was closer to something he could understand. He still didn't know what it meant. Spiritual powers? The power to control hearts—not only hers but his and maybe someone or something else's? He asked her if she'd ever been struck by lightning and she quoted Tinkerbell to him. Then they had sex and he forgot about love for a while.

Quoting Tinkerbell was something she'd do now and then. James had never read *Peter Pan* so he didn't know what Tinkerbell had said. "You silly ass!" was what she said, several times. It was pretty much the only thing she said in the original story, though not in the Disney version.

Audrey Phillips was Catholic but nevertheless the most spiritual person James had ever known. She was a charismatic Catholic, which meant she spoke in tongues and believed in faith healing and the power of prayer. Sometimes he heard her praying in tongues in the closet, out loud and with some enthusiasm. The first time he thought it was some Indian language, but she said it was a language of angels. And she said that in the Bible, Jesus told people to pray in closets and that she had found them to be spiritual enclaves. "A lot of spiritual things happen in closets," she told him. "You wouldn't believe it—the things that can happen in closets, where Jesus said to pray."

She also had visions and, if he understood correctly, other people had visions of her. These visions happened when she was asleep.

"So . . . dreams?" he asked.

She said he didn't understand, and couldn't. He agreed on both counts. He did appreciate that she didn't try to push her religion on him or try to convert him or anything like that. But one time he told her he was "spiritual but not religious" and she called bullshit on that.

"SBNR is better than RBNS," she said, "but it's not like the two are mutually exclusive."

He had thought they were.

"I get that you're not religious," she said. "Obviously. But what in the world makes you think you're spiritual?"

"I fall in love a lot."

She quoted Tinkerbell. And she said that in her experience a lot of people who say they're "spiritual but not religious" are neither, but don't have the humility or self-awareness to admit it. Not all, but a lot—including him, for example. They've lost (or they never had) whatever spirituality religion can bring but they are afraid or embarrassed or ashamed to admit that they haven't found it anywhere else.

"God hates me," he told her.

"Well, maybe some god does. What if there is more than one?"

"Was that in your Catechism?"

"No. Old Testament."

This was a surprise because he was pretty sure that Jews believed in only one God, but the last thing in the world he wanted to do was argue theology.

Still, Audrey diagnosed his love problem as a spiritual problem. He said it wasn't a problem; it was a gift: the gift of staying in love, of never falling out of love with anyone, ever. She said well, okay, in Catechism, she *had* learned that "love never ends," but she didn't think that was what it meant. And, in any case, it was a problem that he only wanted romantic relationships, not spiritual ones.

"So you think I should embark on some great spiritual quest?" he asked sarcastically. "Church? Crystals? Pyramids? Try to find a god who doesn't hate me?"

"Goddess," she said seriously. "For you, love is worship, and that's okay. It's not that for everyone but it is for you and that's okay. But it's a spiritual need and so far you haven't found any woman spiritual enough to know that. For you, unrequited love is unreceived worship, like when God accepted Jacob's offerings but not those of Esau. How do you think Esau felt when God wouldn't let him worship?"

"Like God hated him."

"Well, yeah. And my guess is he wasn't too keen on religion after that."

James was stunned that she knew the Jacob and Esau thing. And that he was Esau . . . Eeh-saw . . . Hee Haw . . . the guy named for a donkey. Lots of Jacobs in the world, but he had always been a Hee Haw. How did she know that?

Then she told him about Kurt Vonnegut and Bokononism, the religion of the irreligious, offering a glimmer of spirituality for the unspiritual. Jesus was a Bokononist when he blessed unspiritual people, the "poor in spirit," the SBNR fakers who weren't S or R either one.

James asked if maybe the solution to his love problem was to find a goddess and fall in love with her. She said real goddesses would probably be too vain but a priestess might work. He could unwittingly worship a god or goddess or "the universe" or whatever *through her* and she would delight in his lavish adoration knowing that while he thought she was the object she was only a conduit—but also realizing as his spiritual superior that she should condescend to his limited understanding and grant him the fantasy.

He decided to be a Bokononist and began trying to pray, mostly by singing ditties or lines from pop songs that seemed appropriate. That didn't work very well, but he also began reading everything he could find that was kind of spiritual: Kahil Gibran, Deepak Chopra, Paulo Coelho, Scott Peck, Mitch Albom, and Erick Fromm. Just not the Bible, which was what Audrey actually recommended most (along with some almost-but-not-really Catholic woman named Basilea Schlink). Still, he knew two Bible verses and decided that was enough and he also figured that all the guys he *was* reading had read the Bible and they would let him know when it said something worthwhile. He could get the good stuff without boring begats and whatnot. In any case, he ended up reading Fromm's *Art of Loving* six times and couldn't believe he had lived so long without it. The best book ever written. And, then, two years after Audrey moved back to Boston, he called to ask her if she was a prophet.

"No," she replied. "Not one of my gifts . . . powers, you would say . . . it's the top one, actually, but not for simple folk like me."

"Well," he said. "I'm in love with a priestess."

"Anglican?"

"Shoshone."

He hadn't actually been looking for a priestess. He had thought what Audrey said was metaphorical. But now he was in love with Kimana, a Shoshone priestess of Wakonda (basically, the spirit of the earth and of nature). For him, she *was* Wakonda (though she told him she wasn't) and he knew that lavishly loving her was the closest he would ever get to loving a god who didn't hate him. And he had told her that, sort of. He had told her he was so thankful she was who she was and not just one more pretty angel who someone had sent down to break his heart. "Isn't that from a song?" she asked. "Well kind of," he replied. "But I changed the words just enough so I don't have to get permission."

Romantic love, he told Audrey, was now a spiritual experience. And sex was a sacrament.

A year later, he had asked if, as a wedding present, she would use her powers to seal his heart—not to make him fall out of love with any of the prior six (oh no! not that! not ever!)—but to keep him from ever falling in love with anyone else, anyone new, ever again. He wanted Number Seven to be final. She said she could pray for that to happen and he said he was sure that would do it. And it did.

* * *

When Audrey and her lover and mate arrived at the Bozeman airport, it was Matthew Booker who picked them up and brought them to the house in Pray. And it was Matthew's young wife who admitted them.

"This is my Pet," he told them with evident pride. "And, Pet, this is the famous Audrey Used-to-be-Phillips and her husband John. The McCloskeys."

"Are you also his wife?" Audrey asked the pretty person who took her hand.

She nodded, grinning.

"He likes to call me that," she said with a suppressed giggle that intimated how much she liked for him to call her that. And after some more profuse greetings and courteous introductions, Matthew's Pet retreated into the kitchen.

Matthew led the McCloskeys into a living room with which Audrey was quite familiar. The furniture had changed in the last forty years but the three large bookcases were basically the same. Their shelves were filled with bones, geodes, and fossils, many of them trilobites. Audrey and John sat, as directed, in an overstuffed sofa behind a large coffee table on which a worn copy of *Hellish Beauty* vied for attention with copies of *National Geographic* and apparently unread mail. Then Matthew explained that James and Kimana were out in the backyard but no one should go out there yet because some big ritual of surprise was being prepared. "Maybe you can just wait here for now," he continued, explaining that he had to leave them and get out there or he would be missed and they would know something was up. "Plus, Dan can't cook for shit but he thinks he can so he'll make a total mess of things."

The McCloskeys had been married for fifteen years now. John, of course, had realized after a period of disorientation that the "closet dreams" had been nothing more than that—nothing magical or supernatural—just dreams. Audrey had had similar dreams over the years, but not the *same* dreams at the *same* time. She might think so but he had often noted that charismatics could convince themselves of anything. Most likely, Father Jacobson was a charismatic like her and he had probably encouraged her in the fantasy. Well, no harm had been done. And that night when he dreamed he opened the door—that had been a breakthrough, a psychological, emotional, spiritual (why not?) breakthrough for him that had changed his life and given him a new calling: loving her and being loved by her. At present, there were only two things that God asked of him: to love Audrey and to be loved by Audrey. No more, no less. And now, at last, he was going to meet the man who wrote his favorite song; Audrey had taught him the tune, and he sang "Lucky Mud" in the shower every morning. He was going to tell that guy, that . . . Ranger Jim!

But for the moment the McCloskeys were cooling their heels on the Haizlet's living room sofa, listening to all sorts of noises emerging from the kitchen: dishes and bowls and pans were rattling and clanging, getting utilized in various fashions, and a young mother was talking over the din to a child in a voice that waffled between strained patience and mounting exasperation. Then the voice (clearly that of Matthew's Pet) addressed them from around the corner.

"Matt and Dan are still grilling," it said. "They'll come get you when they're ready. Are you alright with lamb?"

The couple looked at each other.

"Sheepeaters," Audrey whispered to her husband and they both grinned.

"Sure, that sounds great," John responded loudly, answering for them both.

"It's more tender than beef," the kitchen voice shouted. "Popular here in Montana."

"Is there anything we can do?" Audrey asked, hoping she could be heard.

"Well . . . why don't you let Kai entertain you? That would help."

"Sure."

"Kai," the kitchen mother called, summoning her son from some place to which he had scurried. "Can you come in here?"

They heard some scuffling as the boy apparently emerged from somewhere.

"What were you doing under the table?"

"I was going to get Feabag."

"Okay. Well, why don't you get Fleabag, and show him to our guests?"

"Okay!"

There was more scuffling, sounds of a child crawling around on the floor in what was possibly a dining room. Audrey wondered if she should go in and crawl around with him but she resisted, and momentarily the boy appeared, a bit tousled and staggering through the doorway with a large gray cat pinned to his torso in a tight embrace of both arms. The animal appeared to be almost as long as Kai was tall, especially with its legs splayed out as they were, stretching for earth and sky.

"This is Feabag!" he announced and plopped the animal down on the floor in front of their sofa. He pinned the cat to the rug, holding it there with both hands and the press of his full body weight. "He doesn't like strangers."

"Hmm . . . I guess not," John observed.

"Is Fleabag your kitty?" Audrey asked, smiling at the name.

"Yes. He doesn't like strangers."

"That's okay."

Kai relaxed his grip a bit then and, as if to prove the boy's assertion, Fleabag dashed out from under him and back through the doorway into the other room.

"*Feabag!*" Kai yelled, and, scrambling to his feet ran noisily after the fugitive. Now the guests heard more scuffling and crawling, probably under the table, as the boy sought to recapture his prisoner.

"Feabag!" he yelled, or rather, scolded in an exasperated tone.

"Kai," Audrey called, wondering again if she should go to him. "Kai, that's okay."

"He likes to get under things."

"That's okay. Why don't you just come in here and tell us about Fleabag?"

"I got his *leg!*"

"That's okay, Kai. Just let him hide for now, okay?"

A moment later, Kai appeared, catless and defeated.

"He's under the hutch."

"Alright. We got to see him. You can tell us about him."

"Do you want to hear a joke?"

"Yes!"

He stood in front of them and put his hands behind his back as though reciting.

Jack and Jill went up the hill,
Each one had a quarter.
Jill came down with fifty cents,
Do you think they went for water?

The couple looked at each other and smiled.

"That's a good joke," Audrey said. "Did your father teach you that?"

"Yes."

"Do you know why it's funny?"

"She took his money!" he exploded and giggled profusely.

"That's right. Do you have any other pets?"

"I can't go in the basement."

"No? Why not?"

"There's an alligator."

"You have an alligator in your basement?"

"Yes."

"Is it a little one?" Audrey asked, indicating a length of about eight inches with her open hands.

"No." Kai shook his head from side to side, then stretched his arms out as wide as they would go. "It's big."

"You have a big alligator in your basement?"

He nodded his head.

"Her name is Amy."

"So, does she just crawl around down in the basement?" Audrey asked.

"No," Kai giggled, as if this were *too* silly. "In the pool."

"The pool? There's a pool for Amy."

"And a wall."

"Down in the basement," Audrey said, putting all this together. "There is a wall, like of bricks?"

Kai nodded.

"And on the other side of the bricks, there's a pool with an alligator?"

"And sand."

"Of course. Sand and water on the other side of a wall."

"You cannot swim in the pool," Kai announced in an authoritative voice that no doubt echoed something he had been told.

"No," Audrey agreed. "No, of course not."

"She will bite," Kai said.

"Okay. Well, this is interesting. Do you have other pets?"

"Yes."

"Which ones?"

"You cannot pet the alligator."

"No, because she bites."

"She will bite."

"That's right."

"And you cannot put Feabag in the pool."

"No. I would think not. That's a good rule."

A voice came from the kitchen: "Alright, I think we're ready. Thanks for keeping him occupied."

"It's been great."

"We're going to eat out back, but you can gather in here and then Dan or Matt is going to announce you or something . . . I don't know."

The guests followed Kai through the doorway into the adjoining room. There was a table and a hutch, but the room was dominated by an enormous 500-gallon aquarium that Audrey remembered.

"Wow!" her husband exclaimed. "That's a big turtle!"

"It's Flagg the Fourth," Audrey told him.

"Are you sure? Forty years ago."

"Right. Probably Flagg the Sixth. Or Seventh. They live a long time."

"It's a monster turtle!" Kai exclaimed with happy excitement. "It eats fish!"

"Does it?"

"Once it ate a turtle."

"It *ate* it?"

"It ate its leg." This was more than anyone needed to know but as the couple moved on into the dining room, Kai continued exuberantly, "It's a *monster* turtle. Like a *dinosaur*."

* * *

Seven years later, Kai and his mother spent the summer with Matthew in Washington, DC. James had passed away a year and a half ago and his body had been returned to the fortunate mud from which it had emerged. Kimana moved back onto the reservation where she was now regarded as "elderly," which is to say "supremely esteemed and remarkably respected." With all those transitions, Kai had spent the previous summer with his Methodist grandparents in Oklahoma and with Uncle Dan, who was now a deacon in the Methodist church. He had returned with a new appreciation for Bible stories, which he claimed were almost as good as comic books. "The Bible is full of superheroes," he told his parents. Why hadn't anyone ever told him that?

But this summer he was in DC and Matthew wanted him to take advantage of everything the unique city had to offer. They explored all the memorials around the mall: Lincoln, Jefferson, FDR, Vietnam Veterans, and so forth. So much history—and Matthew tried, with some success, to get him interested in the stories of these "superheroes," the men and women (but mostly men) honored with magnificent works of art and architecture. Of course, they also toured the Capitol and the White House and climbed to the top of the Washington Monument. They spent a couple of days at the National Air and Space Museum and made three separate visits to the Museum of Natural History. And it worked: Kai was impressed, if not awed, by the rockets and missiles and fossils and dioramas. Most important to his parents, Matthew took his son to the National Museum of the American Indian once a week where he could learn firsthand about his ancestors (Shoshone and Shawnee) and their "cousins" (all the tribes that now realized their common interests outweighed historical differences). And then in August, just before returning to Helena, his mother took him to one of the area's minor attractions: a pavilion in Algonkian Park that had celebrated its twenty-fifth anniversary of inauguration the previous April. Perhaps Matthew was a little disappointed when his son decided the latter was the highlight of a summer filled with adventure.

Kai Booker was twelve years old and one week after Labor Day he turned in the following assignment for his seventh-grade English class:

> This is my 200 word esay on what I did in the summer. We went to Washington DC where my mother used to live and met a famous person at the Toffee and Taffy Pabilon. I also saw buildings and dinosaurs, just the bones, but this is what I want to tell. We got to this Pabilon in a park and the famous person was a old man named Jabber who told stories. Also there was a giant like in the Bible who had never cut his hair and it was all white like Santa Claus but more. He had a funny name that I don't remember and a cat named Purdy the Fifth and the number was part of the name like with turtles. Jabber told us the story of Akiles who was like Superman except the foot. After the story Jabber showed me a rock with a picture of a bug on it. He said my mother gave it to him when she was my age and she was more famous than him and the best artist he ever knew. I know she is a artist because she draws things but I never knew she was famous once.

www.ingramcontent.com/pod-product-compliance
Lightning Source LLC
LaVergne TN
LVHW100523110826
845146LV00002B/757

* 9 7 9 8 3 8 5 2 4 5 9 3 2 *